BALGA BOY

JACKSON

A NOVEL
BY MUDROOROO

2017

ETT IMPRINT
Exile Bay

First published by ETT Imprint, Exile Bay 2017

ETT IMPRINT
PO Box R1906
Royal Exchange NSW 1225
Australia

Copyright Mudrooroo 2017

ISBN 978-1-925706-05-5 (Paper)
ISBN 978-1-925706-04-8 (ebook)

Cover: Revel Cooper's Untitled
(South West Landscape Design
on Guitar)

Design by Hanna Gotlieb

CONTENTS

*In Remembrance of all my family
and those good friends I knew and loved. Most of them
are in the realm of ghosts now. Live on in this book.*

BOOK ONE

BALGA BOY BLUES

Western Australia is unique in having, well, a unique tree Xanthor-rhoea, the Black Boy. It is a grass tree with a thin black trunk and a spiky headpiece. It puts up a long shoot or shoots which flower and then die leaving shells like the barbs of spears. From a distance these grass trees look like a group of warriors laden with spears on the warpath. Indeed legend has it that they were a marauding tribe transformed into trees by a maban or shaman. These trees were found all over the bottom part of Western Australia until the white settlers grubbed them out to cultivate wheat. They also grubbed out most of the native people, except for a few who were left to work the land for their new masters; but that is another story. This is only about one of them, a boy born long ago in 1938 who was named Balga or Black Boy. He had an Aboriginal mother and an African-American father who bequeathed to him the spiky mop of hair which gave him his name. So it is said. Now read on.

CONTENTS

ONE

GROWING PAINS

Balga and Kylie Jackson were two skinny long-legged brown kids appearing here, there and everywhere as they tried to make the country town of Shiloh into their patch of turf. That day they stood in the middle of the black strip of the Perth-Narrogin road that raced away from them in both directions. Their bare feet felt the rough pebbles beneath as their toes overlapped the macadam to spread in the soft dust of the road edge. They stared to the right where Narrogin was, but imagined nothing about that town. The road itself was simply the south eastern boundary of their territory. They sprang about and skipped along the turnoff that eventually became the main street. On their left was the street that led to the hospital where their mum had been put once when she had taken sick. That day stayed in their minds, because she had been very restless and went to the outdoor lavatory a number of times. In the early afternoon she took to her big bed then in the late afternoon told them to run to the hospital to tell them she was very sick and to send the ambulance. It came and took her away. Being alone didn't alarm Kylie or Balga except the night was a bit scary. Next day they went to see her and found their mum in the tent next to the hospital which was for the native people. Fortunately she was only there for a day and came back to look after them. She didn't say much about her sickness and of course being kids they didn't ask her.

The two children didn't like school at all and often wagged it not caring if anyone knew or not. They even ran right past the school buildings, located on both sides of the street, throwing their freedom in the face of any that saw them. On the right was the pre-primary school which had been okay for Balga except for a run-in with the teachers; but when they had crossed the street to enter first class, they had been placed right at the back with some other native kids. The teacher never asked them any questions and hardly glanced their way, so they wagged school whenever they felt like it. No one seemed to care if they attended or not except for the school Inspector. If they stayed away for too many days he arrived to protest to their mother. The white man entered their place with a frown on his face, stared around at their poverty, then rattled out a warning about how they should not play truant and their mum should ensure that they did not as it was against the law and children had to attend school. After delivering this rapidly like a babbling brook he all but ran out of the kitchen door. 'Truant-ruant,' their mum muttered after him. She had once flung a mug of tea after his disappearing back; but after his visit she always got them to go to school for a few days at least.

Just along from the school buildings, again on the left was a hotel with a forbidding front of green and white tiles. Next to it was the Town Hall which also served as a picture theatre on Friday nights. After that the street opened up into what might have been a town square; but wasn't. The open area served as the parking lot for the railway station and for the farmers that came to provision up at the main store: The Farmers' Cooperative. The two children never entered that store or the station even to stare at the stationary trains. They avoided it again on that day. They turned right to go along the tracks to the big low sprawling wheat sheds. These were rarely closed up tight unless chock-a-block with wheat. The two children enjoyed climbing up the piles of grain and sliding down. Once they managed to get one of the kids to wag school and go there with them. He whined about missing school and they didn't have as much fun as they would have had without him. Worse, he must have told his parents, for Balga was called before the headmaster and given six of the best on the hand from a cane that really stung. The punishment didn't make him regret his action. It did make him sneaky however.

Kylie and Balga walked balancing on the railway tracks away from the town. The twin lines veered towards the stockyards that marked the end of Forrest Street, their street which was named after the Western Australian hero, John Forrest. After an auction or sale of sheep or cattle they collected the descriptive cards which were left tacked on the gate of each pen. It was there also that they met shy native kids who lived in the bush. These, a few boys and girls at first approached them warily, before they found out that Kylie and Balga were not snotty like white kids. Their mum however warned them about playing with these kids saying it could bring the welfare down on them. They didn't listen to her. They felt happy with them and learnt a few things about the bush such as how to find and when to pick "native" chewing gum from the Banksia trees, "native" toffee from the white gums and the time of the year when "native" carrots could be pulled from the earth. Not only did they learn to recognize the spiky tops, but when they turned brown that meant that the vegetable was ripe. Of course, there was also the centre of black boys (grass trees) that you could chew on, but then everyone knew that.

They weren't there that day and the two kids thought of going into the bush beyond the stockyards and looking for bush orchids. It was spring and Everlastings and Kangaroo Paws grew just about everywhere, but the orchids took some finding. They stared up at the sun and seeing that it was near midday decided to go home to see what they could get to eat.

Just about opposite to the stockyards was the big paddock that was the town's aerodrome on which an occasional Tiger Moth fluttered down to send them racing there to stare open-mouthed. This was seldom and at the beginning of the rains, or was it at the end, they went mushrooming there. Along from it was their mum's bloke, Mr. Winter's property. This was a weather board house with a verandah next to the road and behind it was a galvanized hut in which a big old man, Paddy lived, just waiting to "kick pick the bucket" as their mum put it. The old bloke was kind to them and always said 'Hello.'

Mr. Winter was a wood cutter and in the paddock beside his house were logs of wood piled next to his saw which revolved so fast that they were scared of it, though he used it so deftly that the only hurt they saw him receive was when a stick sprang up his nose bringing forth great gushes of rich red blood as well as a lot of cursing. The saw was powered by an old truck motor still attached to the chassis which served as the foundation of the saw bench. As they watched, the motor smoked, coughed once or twice, and stopped. Mr. Winter lifted his head and took off his wide brimmed hat to wipe his red face and huge white mustache with one gnarled hand as he muttered something that they couldn't decipher from their distance. He noticed the two kids and waved a hand in what could have been a greeting or a sign to leave him be. They stood there neither going away nor going to him. They watched as he turned to check the nosebag of his old chestnut horse swishing its tail near the cart which was different from the others they had seen. The front dipped down towards the shafts whereas the others had a low back and a high front. Balga stared at this vehicle then at the owner bending over the truck motor. It was then that Kylie hit him on the arm ran off. He followed slowly.

Just after Mr. Winter's place Kylie stopped at the beginning of the twin lines of Eucalyptus trees which were beheaded by the council every year so that they had thick trunks and rounded tops just like trees in picture books. Balga didn't go to his sister. Instead he wandered off the road to check the empty space opposite and just down from Mr. Winter's place. This was the Town Aboriginal Reserve. Few natives ever camped there. They preferred the bush just beyond the aerodrome. Still, maybe someone might have camped there overnight and left empty soft drink bottles behind or perhaps there might even be a family with some kids of their own age. It was gilgie season (fresh water crabs) and they all could go and collect themselves a feed. They were so easy to catch. The crabs lived in old tin cans or under sheets of tin close to the bank, but their mum didn't like her kids lighting a fire to boil then up when they had a tin full so if there were kids there they could use their fire. Their mum had been very upset when they had set a patch of bush afire. She had to promise the town constable that they would never be allowed to have matches again.

No one was on the reserve and when Kylie joined her brother they picked some Kangaroo Paws as well as some honey-coloured Wattle before running on to the big old dilapidated two storey building that had once been a hotel. Some time ago when the Second World War was on an army detachment had been based there. Their house was just a bit up on the opposite of the street and they watched the army men playing with a couple of big anti aircraft guns, they had brought with them and set up. They appeared to be loading wooden shells, but from hindsight these were most likely copper, the colour similar to the wood of red gums had misled the children. By the time the soldiers left they had   trashed the building so that it looked a job for the wreckers. The upper storey was a complete mess. On leaving, the soldiers stored a few things in the cellar which merely had a wooden cover pulled over the entrance. Kylie and Balga shifted this and slipped down into the dark interior. They found nothing of interest for their childish greed, though it whetted their appetite for more such adventures. They visited the cellar a few times to get used to the darkness. No jinak or ghost there, but still it was a bit scary. On a last visit Kylie found an army trumpet from which they couldn't get a note. It was useless even as a toy and it moved around their place as it was picked up, blown through and flung away in disgust.

Beyond the building and opposite to their home lay a flat piece of ground stretching to the river. This had lodged in their memory for ever when one year it had flooded. The water came right up to the road and they had a lake to paddle in for a week or so before the river subsided. Next to their home was an empty paddock with a big dead tree in the centre. This was their core territory and in the far corner near the road

Balga made a play ground. He built an entire miniature village made from mud and pieces of bark and twigs for doors, roofs and verandah posts. Often he stayed there for hours playing happily. He glanced over it now marking out future changes before catching up with Kylie as she crossed the cement gutter that came from somewhere in the town to go under the road and into the area beyond. There it just stopped. They had thought that it might reach the river. Going through the tunnel under the road was fun and often they crawled along from their side of the road to the other and then back again.

Now as they got through the fence into the area about their house, Balga saw his mum sitting on the back door steps. She looked a small fragile figure, separate and distinct, and lonely. Their mum had no friends except for Mr. Winter in the town. The boy felt his eyes water as he came towards her. Balga remembered how in the paddock he had been digging in the dirt and suddenly jerked out his hand to find that the skin had been slit open by a jagged piece of glass bottle. He had stared at the blue flesh beneath. It didn't hurt at all as he ran to his mum who took one look at it and went into the tin shed behind the dilapidated shop. She returned with a lot of cobwebs which she placed over the wound. The blood stopped gushing forth and soon the wound was a scar which would remain with him all his life to remind him of his mother. Balga looked at the half moon scar on his right hand as he raised it to gesture at the lavatory. He left Kylie to run to where it stood surrounded by bamboos. It lurked, too far from the house to use at night, so that if he needed to pee he did it just outside the back door and from the back steps too. No way could he make himself go to that dunny so distant in a back corner with who knows what looking out at him from that rustling patch of bamboo. A man came to exchange dunny pans every week, taking the used one out through the small door which Balga had opened once to spy on his sister having a shit.

A path made by their feet in the grass went from the outhouse to the back door of the house. It became a patch at the doorway of the tin shed with a brick floor which perhaps because of the cobwebs and spiders was never used for anything except an occasional shit, just as they used under the back part of the house, or rather "building" which was raised above the ground. Once it had been a shop or business with two front rooms made of brick onto which a backroom of weather board had been tacked. The two brick rooms were as dark as sin, for the two large front windows had been covered with sheets of galvanised iron that kept out all the light. The front door was always locked. It was about a metre above the street level and without any steps.

The dark front room was where the two kids slept as best as they could. There were only two pieces of furniture the iron frame of a bed and a cot. But they had a few blankets in which to snuggle and were quite content. The cot was too small for either of them so they shared the bed. A doorway opened naturally into the second room which was their mum's. This was furnished with a big double bed, a dressing table and a wardrobe. Once a salesman had made the mistake of selling these on the never-never to their mum who after the down payment never paid a shilling more. In fact, it was merely by chance, the receipt of the child endowment, that she had had the down payment. No one came to reclaim the furniture and so it remained with them. This room also on a wall had their only two pictures. Illustrations of a bearded man and a woman both with exposed hearts and pinned next to each other. These had appeared mysteriously in the mail one day and must have come from their sisters in St. Joseph's. They arrived with broken frames as they had not been packed properly and their mum tacked them onto the wall. Every now and again they stared at these strange pictures, but their mum never told them who or what they were. She considered herself Catholic enough to put up the pictures and that was enough. Religion wasn't an important part of her life, but then what was?

Their mum's room door opened into the weatherboard part of the building. This was the kitchen and where they spent most of their time when in the house. Now just as at other times in they rushed hungrily -- to find their mum cutting thick slices of bread from a loaf bought directly from the bakery cart that very morning. The man stopped to turn near their place every morning and if they had the money, they bought themselves a loaf of still warm bread. Their mum dropped the slices into a frying pan sizzling with hot fat. It sat on top of the big old wood stove that was never completely dead. Mr. Winter sometimes dropped off a load of wood; but they were often short of matches so the stove was kept alight to have a flame handy for the candles or the lantern they might need at night, though usually mum thought the stove was light enough.,

Stoked up and with the front grate left open it did shed enough light through the door into her room where some evenings they spent on the big bed or crouched before their pride and joy a big Kreusler wireless set. This brought them the world when they could afford the dry cell batteries or get the wet cell battery charged up. At times the family cheerfully went without meat to get those big cardboard batteries or begged the man at the power house to charge the wet battery on tick, which he often did. He knew that they would be back, though once he was so nasty to keep their battery until he was paid some of the money they owed. They loved that radio for its company. It brought them the eerie laughter of The Shadow and the deadpan voice explaining his special ability: "Once in the Orient, Lamont Cranston learnt a strange and mysterious secret, the ability to cloud men's minds so that they could not see him." Tales from the Crypt; the Australian Smoky Dawson, and the Lone Ranger with his "Hi Ho Silver" They loved all these shows.

Now they sat around the big table that shared the kitchen with the stove and an old sideboard gobbling down the bread. It was delicious. Mum drank black tea from a mug, sipping and munching in turn. She paused to pour her kids a couple of cups of water from the only tap in the house. It hung over the table. As she plonked the cups down she said: "Seein' you kids ain't at school today say we go for a walk talk and see your little brother. Poor little tyke, like all alone out there and who knows if we don't he might come and visit us at night right!"

They felt chilled at her words. They had never or couldn't remember ever seeing this phantom brother and the mere thought of him gave them the willies. They could imagine their so-called brother as a jinak thing that went bump bump in the night, then creep, creeping into their room. The mere mention of him brought back to Balga a recurring dream he had of some dark thing bending over him. Nervously he finished off his bread and thought about running out and away while his mum was dressing in her room. He was getting to his feet when her voice came out to hold him back. 'You kids stay sit right tight there.'

A minute or two went by and she came out in a dress that was clean but as crumpled as the one she had had on. She wore a pair of shoes and her hair was in a tidy bun. She left her kids as they were shoeless and with greasy faces. She shooed them out of the kitchen and closed the door behind her. It had no key. They walked to the nice metal gate that she had found the money to buy. This was to put a barrier between her and the road as Aboriginal folk kept coming in to use the tap beside the kitchen door. She had put it up herself, but not very well. There was a gap between it and the fence post. It never could be closed to keep anything out. Once even a pretty terrier cross dog had trotted in to give them its company for a week before it disappeared. Perhaps it wanted more food than they could give it or the owner had found it and taken it away without telling them. Whatever, it had come, stayed and then disappeared. Such was life!

Now their mum pulled the gate shut. They watched it swing back half open as always. They turned left to cross the short track that had led to what had been a blacksmith's shed. The German bloke that ran it had been taken away when the war began. Now it was just a dirty old shed filled with spiders and cobwebs. The kids fussed about a tree, checking to see if the gum was ready to chew. It wasn't. They ran and caught up with their mother at the side of Priors' Hardware Store. It had on Forrest Street a large yard closed with two big open mesh metal frame gates through which they squeezed without any trouble to wander about among the stacks of petrol drums. It was at Priors that a paved footpath began. As their mum crossed over to the other side of the street, Balga and Kylie peered in the big window of the store. They had never been inside, not even when their mum had bought the gate.

Now their mum stopped on the corner at the small park dedicated to the soldiers of the First World War. Her kids didn't run to join her, but crossed the main street to Gillespie's General Store. They hadn't a penny to spend on a lolly and just stared in the windows a moment before going down the side to the grating of a cellar. Their eyes wandered over it. The bars looked loose enough for them to pull up. They might have tried except their mum hollered for them to come to her. They didn't instead they crossed over to the Freemason's Hotel from which on Fridays and Saturday evenings male voices floated down to their house so that sometimes they braved the gathering darkness to see what was happening, but the windows were too high for them to peer through and the doors were closed too.

They caught up with Mum at the fire station. During the War the town fathers had established a place to collect aluminum bits and pieces to aid the war effort. Their mum had taken down an old pot and exchanged it for a better one. Still, that didn't stop them from feeling pleased that they had done their bit to keep the Japs away from Shiloh. The woman with her two kids went past the court house and the police station. She walked onto the bridge across the Avon River. The kids stopped in the middle to hang over the railing to peer down towards the deepest part of the river which never ever dried up even in the severest drought. They were very wary when they wandered along the banks of that pool for the native kids had told them that in it lived a big snake that might drag them into the depths if it was disturbed. It was like the ogre that lived under the bridge as in one of the stories in their class reader. Now they looked to see if they could catch a glimpse of that big old snake but only saw an old black fellow who sometimes came to their house for a drink of water. Once he had even brought their mum a kangaroo tail which she had hung in a sugar bag for a week before making a long lasting soup out of it. They watched him stop at a tree and pull out a gidjee and flex it. They too had come across it in their rambles. The spear was made from a piece of thick fencing wire with a point and barb at one end and a loop with a bit of string tied to it at the other. He carried it off and Balga wondered if he was going fishing, though he had never known anyone to fish in that river except for gilgies. Still, Mr. Winter had long bamboo fishing poles that were brittle with age, so once upon a time people had.

'What's that old bloke doin'', their mum asked from the far bank.

'Fishin'?' Balga suggested.

'Fishin'' smishin,' she scoffed and left it at that.

Just beyond the bridge to the left was the gravel road leading to the cemetery. Their mum hesitated and they scuffled their feet in the dust waiting for her to lead them in. The two kids didn't relish going to that dead man's field, and perhaps their mother didn't either, for she stared up the road towards the Catholic convent and the church.

'That little bloke wasn't baptized,' she said more to herself than to us. 'You fellas haven't been either. Maybe it's time,' and with that she set off along the road. Balga and Kylie raced ahead then came back to her. They didn't know where they were headed. Beyond the convent and church was nothing much, except at an adventurous distance a huge strip of an airfield which had been built during the War and as far as they knew had never known the wheels of a plane. Once, they had gone there with Mr. Winter in his cart. The two kids had stood there on that long, broad, barren strip in the middle of the bush feeling bewildered. It was something alien. They couldn't understand that flattening of the bush to lay a road in the middle of nowhere and going nowhere. Now when they thought about it they considered it one place that they didn't want to go to; but their mother had a different goal in mind. She stopped at the church and entered it. Reluctantly they followed her inside. They huddled about their mum frightened at the strangeness of sight and smell.

'Yes,' a grave voice asked, and they darted a glance up into a white face with eyes that were looking past them at the poor box.

Their mother saw the direction of his gaze and her voice turned hostile as well as demanding: 'We come for baptizin',' she exclaimed.

'Baptism,' the voice stated and blue eyes, neither friendly nor unfriendly examined the two children.

'Yeah,' their mum said.

'Yes,' the man repeated.

'Yeah, pair, more 'n' anything wrong with that,' she said, lowering her voice instead of raising it.

This made the children aware that the bloke was important, like a policeman though he didn't have on a uniform. They got up enough nerve to stare at him with wide brown eyes. He was very white as if he never went outside into the sun, was wearing a funny white collar about his neck and his clothing was as black as his skin was white. But whatever strangeness he was, his face didn't seem all that forbidding. It held a puzzled look as if he was trying to understand how this small dark woman, their mum, with two wild looking kids wanted at that very moment to have them baptized,

Balga and Kylie had no idea what "baptism" meant and became apprehensive. The sun sent bright rays of light through the door and beckoned them with its freedom. Just one threat of pain and they would have bolted out and run right to that length of tar and cement which was some distance even for them.

They would need Christian names...' the strange man began.

They got 'em, Balga, the boy and Kylie the girl.

'They must be good Christian names,' the priest said sternly. He shrugged spreading his hands and examining his fingernails. There was no dirt at all under any of them. He went to a wash basin that he called a font which was to one side of the church in its own little room. He removed a cover and checked the water. Balga and Kylie peered over the edge. There wasn't that much water in that funny dish thing.

'The boy, make him Thomas after his dad and the girl, well, Mary will do fine for her.'

'And God parents …' the white man clad in black began. He stopped to consider the matter. 'Wait here and I'll find someone. It's really only a formality after all.'

He left and while he was absent, Balga and Kylie checked out the strange interior and its furnishings. There wasn't anything that could disappear into their pockets, but the pictures on the walls were interesting. They wandered along right to the front, before being stopped by a little fence that separated a small area from the rest of the space. Inside was a high table covered with a white lacy cloth on which two candles fluttered on either side of a small box also covered with a white cloth embroidered with gold letters. To one side hanging from a chain was a lamp with a red light. That place enticed them and they were about to get over the fence when their mother yelled: 'Ey, you two.' They ran back to her just as the man came in with a big white girl in a dark blue uniform. She was a school girl from the convent who darted a glance at them but didn't smile.

'Of course, you're Catholics,' the priest asked.

'Would we be comin' plumin' in 'ere if'usuns weren't,' their mother said getting upset about the whole business which she herself had begun.

The priest nodded and checked the kids over again. Dirty bare feet made him decide on a hard stool on which the children could stand with their grimy dials bent over the water. Kylie went first and emerged without a tear. Balga followed bravely heard the muttering of strange words and then the splash of water on his cheeks. He grinned in relief. Nothing had happened to him. Next, the priest wrote in a big book. Mum sighed as she scrawled her signature on it and that was that.

'Now you got two little Catholics,' she said good-naturedly to the priest.

'Well, I hope that we'll see you in church this Sunday,' he began, but their mum was already out of the door.

Now she turned back towards the town and anxious to avoid the cemetery, the kids ran ahead hoping that she would follow. No such luck.

'Ey, you two, get back 'ere,' shouted their mum from the turn-off.

Meekly they trotted back and dragged their feet to the cemetery gates. Their mum was already beyond them. She gestured at them angrily. Reluctantly, they came to where she was staring down at a small mound of earth marked at its foot by a round piece of metal with the number 13. They let their eyes fall and found an interest. The jam jar with a few flowers from their last visit was still there, though the flowers had long drooped into death. This made them sad and to escape their feelings they stared about at the nearby graves for fresh flowers to decorate their little pile of earth. Balga saw a nice vase with fresh flowers on a nearby grave. He went over and brought it back..

'That's nice,' his mother commented.

This set them off. They raced about the cemetery grabbing flowers and bringing them back to strew over the mound. 'No more,' their mother finally said in a whisper, 'that's more than enough.' And she turned and went slowly away. Her children looked behind. The sun was sinking and shadows were stretching out long fingers ready to grab them. Suddenly frightened they ran to catch up with her.

TWO

TAKE AWAYS

In 1947, it was openly stated by the Native Affairs of Western Australia that children of a so-called mixed ancestry combined the worst traits of both the so-called races. Genetically, it was declared that children like Balga and his sister, Kylie, were mongrels inclined towards criminal activities. They indeed running freely about the town without supervision were merely tilling the ground for their criminal proclivities to grow. They did. Balga and Kylie became little thieves. Balga's first offence to which he readily confessed was stealing a reader from the school and in his second week too.

Balga was fascinated by the idea that sounds could be written when he was introduced to the alphabet and that symbols could be added together to make words. He wanted to learn this method. As he had no reader the teacher lent him a book for the class and left him to ponder it. He easily followed what she was saying. He decided that it was no big deal once he got the hang of how cat and mat might be formed and then with the addition of other words become: The cat sat on the mat. This excited him and Balga knew that if he had his own reader at home, he could learn very quickly. Not having any money to buy a book, he decided to take one not during class as the teacher made sure to collect them, but on a weekend when the school was empty. Balga even left unlatched a window so he could get into the classroom.

On Sunday the school building was completely deserted. Balga pushed a rubbish bin under the window. He stood on this. The window was still unlatched. He put his fingers under the sash, and made space enough through which to slither. The class room was still and dusty. It had a moldy smell about it that for ever after he associated with schools. Some readers were on a bookshelf. He took one and left. It was then Balga found he couldn't quite close the window. There was a gap of a few centimetres at the bottom. He left it, but put the rubbish bin back where it had been. Balga ran home with his prize. He and his sister spent the rest of Sunday making words at each other. It was great fun.

On Monday the teacher at first noticed the window and then the missing reader. Immediately she knew the culprit. She asked and Balga confessed. He was sent home to fetch the book and then led to the Principal's office.

This man in a grey suit and with grey hair and steely eyes to go with it looked the child up and down, before asking: 'You did take the reader?'

'Yep.'

'Yes. And you know that it is thievery?'

'Mmm...'

'Well, don't you?!'

'I took it 'cause I wanted to learn to read.'

'And thieves are punished?'

'Mmm...'

'Well they are, aren't they? Yes, no, well, they are as I am about to demonstrate.'

The white man had a thin stick on his desk. He picked it up, got to his feet and swished it a few times to get the feel of it and perhaps to scare the dark kid. He succeeded.

'Hold out your hand. Not like that, palm upwards. Level! Right!'

Before Balga could jerk his hand away the first blow fell. Five more followed. He received "six of the best." The rushes of pain sent him into a state of shock so that he couldn't even cry. He found himself out of the office, out of the school yard and down the street before the hurt hit with a sudden gush of tears. Balga stared at his bruised and reddened palm, Yelping like a wounded puppy dog and with tears streaming down his face he ran home to his mum. She cried along with him before smearing some eucalyptus oil on his palm to soothe the smarting.

'Well'un you steal, you get caught and you get hit,' she told him grimly. 'Yep, you took book and wit'out askin' so it's stealin'. Teacher maybe would've giben you an old one, if'n' you 'ad asked her. You 'ave to go to school so t'ey 'ave to gibe you books, for sure, maybe.'

'Not 'er,' Balga yelped, 'not 'er, she nebber eben talks to us. She don't eben see us, let 'lone teach us. No one will give me a book. If I want one, I 'ave to take it. I 'ate t'at school!'

'Maybe, maybe, saybe, but you got to go and go you must. Kylie still at school, ain't she?'

'Yep, she didn't steal no book, I did it all by meself,' Balga said proudly.

'An' got caught! Welfare'll be down on us like a bus, if you go on like t'is or t'at. Promise me t'at you won't weary me so much, son. Don't take t'ings wit'out askin'.'

'I promise,' Balga said and meant it as his palm was still smarting.

His promise lasted until Friday came and he needed a little cash.

The films screened in the town hall on Friday night were only sixpence for kids. This was big money for Balga and Kylie, but not unobtainable. The return deposit on soft drink bottles was a penny and so if they found a dozen they had enough for a picture show. They collected a few when the natives came into town and left empty bottles behind in the bush; but these were never enough except after a month of collecting. So the two kids cast their eyes about and discovered the source.

This source was the aerated waters factory or rather its yard which was filled with crates of empty bottles. Balga, or rather his sister had noticed this when they had gone to the power house to pick up their recharged battery. On one early Sunday morning, their time for thievery, they slithered under the gate and checked out the crates. Some of them contained cashable bottles and from then on that yard became their piggy bank. When they wanted to go to the pictures they went, at times even just before the show, and grabbed enough bottles for their tickets. The shops they took them too never challenged them. They only took enough for their sixpences. They were never too greedy.

They enjoyed the films, usually westerns, sitting right at the front of the hall where the Aboriginal people had to sit. This they liked because they thought these the best seats in the hall. They would have liked their mum to come along and share their pleasure, but she never did, muttering something about the front rows being too hard on her eyes, though they knew she had eyes on her like a crow and could spot a lost two bob piece on the ground from metres away.

The widow's pension wasn't very much and when the money gave out they had to live on bread and dripping at the most and damper at the least. Often their bellies rumbled as they roamed about the town. Hunger made them mark the few fruit trees from which they could get a feed when they were in season. These were mulberry and fig trees that no one seemed to own, or at least the children thought so, having no concept of private property. Indeed anything they found was theirs to take. They ran about the town, early and late, and one Sunday balancing their way along the railway line in the direction of the station, they reached the road and stopped. At the door of the Farmers' Coop sat a large box. They ambled over to it, stopped, looked down and saw a treasure. The box was filled with groceries. The whole box was too heavy for them to carry away. They snatched up a bag of fruit including bananas which they had rarely tasted and scooted away to share their loot with their mum. Thus they continued their thievery. Farmers left their orders to be filled and if they were stayed until closing time in the pubs, the Coop left the groceries outside the door for the farmers to pick up on their way home. At times they forgot them and they were got at by the two hungry kids.

Eventually and as with the soft drink bottles, Balga and Kylie were ready to explore when they found the bars over the grating of the Gillespie's store cellar loose. So one Sunday morning, not too early as both were scared of the dark they got up from the iron frame of their bed, crept past their mum snoring in her big bed and ran off though not without trying to shut the gate. It closed for a second then half opened behind them.

Outside all was quiet and serene and as it was just getting into winter somewhat nippy. Not a soul was about or rather they couldn't see anyone as they ran up the slope, across the main street and to the cellar grating. The bars went across the rectangle opening rather than lengthways. Balga tugged at one as did Kylie. They came out leaving a space enough for them to squeeze through and down onto a ledge which had a narrow window. This was unlocked and swung open. Again a short jump down onto the floor of the cellar. It was gloomy, but not scary as the outside light fol-lowed them inside. They made out a big round yellow cheese from which a wedge had been cut. There were boxes, but they were too hard to pry open. They saw stairs. They went up them to stand in awe in the main body of the store. Not a single person was there to watch them. Balga went to the main counter and got a bar of chocolate. He shared this with his sister as they wandered about, staring and not daring to touch anything. Finally, Balga saw a dress that might fit his mum. He grabbed it and then they filled a paper bag with a few things such as tins of corn beef and baked beans, added a handful of sweets and suddenly frightened at the silence and emptiness and their own audacity rushed down into the cellar and out into the street. Quickly they put the bars back then lugging their bag they trotted home to show Mum what they had found in the bush where the natives camped. She readily believed this. Perhaps the reverse was too awful to contemplate..

'Loose 'eads lose t'eir legs if'n't growin' on t'em. Good, could, 'ave one of those tins of baked beans for breakfast. Maybe I should try on t'at dress, nicely pressed ain't it? Neber knowed t'em to leave such t'ings behind, sorry for t'em, but we got 'em now.'

Their mum put on the dress and she did look nice in it, though she had a pot belly that pushed out and as it was a button down job, she couldn't do up the middle buttons. She then put up her hair in a bun and looked as tidy as if she was going out shopping. Suddenly she shuddered and the dress fell from her. 'Wish'n I 'ad a fren' to give 'im to; but no matter, me belly goes out an' in. Maybe I'll get t'inner,' and she put it in the wardrobe where it waited as she might say as a sin to be found.

Next Sunday they went to Gillespies' and found a new grating. No way could they get through. Disappointed, they wandered to check the Coop for forgotten groceries (there weren't any) and reached home empty handed; but not empty minded. The breaking in of Gillespie's had whetted their appetite for further adventures. It wasn't so much the things that drew Balga and his sister, but the entering into a forbidden space and claiming it for a little while at least. Their wanderings almost always took them past Priors' Hardware Store and they had played in the back yard amongst the petrol and oil drums many a time, now they saw it as a place to get into.

They squirmed through the gate to enter the yard and went to the back of the building. Balga saw a small wired in area at one end of a verandah from which a window gave access to the store proper. The wired enclosure had a door which was closed only by a bolt. Balga and his sister entered the enclosure which had only a few empty drums in it. Balga stared at the window, went closer and brought his eyes close to the sash. There was a lock, but it had a lever like catch that might be pushed out. The problem was how to get something against it to exert pressure. Well, he would ponder the problem later and they went to play among the petrol drums.

The following Sunday, they returned with a long thin bolt they had picked up in Mr. Winter's place. Kylie stared at the lever of the lock showing through the window pane and placed the end of the bolt against the glass. Balga picked up a piece of metal from the floor and gave the top of the bolt a sharp tap. It went through the glass without even cracking the pane. Kylie pulled out the bolt. Balga took it from her and pushed it in again. The end rested against the lever. He pushed at the bolt managing to manipulate it so that it followed the lever around to release the catch. Now, it was a simple matter to use the piece of metal to edge the sash up a little so that Balga could get his fingers in and under. It came up slowly and then the interior was there, dark and gloomy just waiting for them to enter and claim.

There was a drum under the window and they used that to get height enough to slip through. This store was different from Gillespie's homeliness, being a big open space with tins, tools and farm implements stacked here and there. Every object seemed hard and metallic. They wandered about looking at things and even went to the window to stare out at the empty street. They looked at each other disappointed at the emptiness of their adventure then Balga tiptoed for some reason into the office which was behind the counter at the Forrest Street side. Inside was a desk with papers on it, a filing cabinet and a small safe. Maybe there was money in one of the desk drawers, but they didn't check. Light was streaming in from the outside and through the window they could see a few people moving along the main street. If they could see them, that most likely meant that they could be seen and so they scarpered.

They hadn't found anything they wanted; but maybe next Sunday they could search for something. No, for next time when they checked they found the door of the wired enclosure was padlocked and inside they could see that the pane in the window had been replaced. This put an end to Priors' and they wondered about another target for their predations; but there was not to be. On Monday, a day they spent at school, they arrived home to find the town policeman in the kitchen talking to their mother.. He sat at the table and in front of him was the frock they had stolen.

When the two kids entered, the cop didn't even glance at them, but their mother stared at them with tears in her eyes.

'Ah, the little thieves,' he said occupying himself with taking out a note book from his left chest uniform pocket. He also had a pencil which he thrust into his mouth as he pawed through his notebook to the appropriate page. He glanced at it, and then began to speak in a flat tone of voice: 'Now,' he said, 'you shall give me all the details of what you have been up to. Don't mention the reader, I know about that and the school has taken action. Now, speak up.'

Strangely, he didn't scare the two kids and Balga rattled away, only hesitating every now and again to let his sister put a word in.. 'Well, that seems to be enough to lock both of you up,' the cop grunted shutting his notebook. 'I'll be back to get your Mum to sign a statement. She's responsible for you two at least for the time being. Don't go bush!'

'T'ey, t'em won't be take aways, stay with me, t'ey will won't t'ey?' their mother questioned her voice and body suddenly beginning to shake.

'Not my part of the job; but better for them, if you ask me! They ain't got much of a chance here. I can't have 'em robbin' and lootin' the town either,' he said still in the same monotonous tone of voice. Balga and Kylie stared at their mum trembling so much that she seemed about to shake her false teeth out 'The little one, tyke, right had nuttin to do with it,' she managed to get out, 'Nine year old boy, 'e can't do a t'ing can 'e, no!'.

'Both of them were in it. Well, we'll see and a good day to you,' and strangely he saluted just like an army man before marching out. The two kids were struck by this gesture and actually followed him to the gate. They watched him close it and watched it come half open. They went through and played in the bush. Balga even found the dry fallen body of a Black Boy and they carried it back to their mom who they found still sobbing.

The policeman came back the next day and even bought the kids a bag of lollies. He had their mum sign the statement and then gave her a blue form, the summons that required her to bring her two kids, Balga and Kylie to the court house at Monday at ten o'clock.

'You make sure that they don't go shopping over the weekend,' the constable said with that monotonous tone of his that somehow made the kids grin. 'You ain't got a clock either, I've bought you one, bring it with you when you come. Ten O'clock you understand. And keep that clock wound up. I'll show you how.'

'Know 'bout clocks,' their mother declared, staring at the thing on the table as if she had seen it for the first time in her life. 'Yeah, know 'bout clocks,' she repeated.

The constable marched out and the kids followed him and as before ran off into the bush to play. They had little understanding about what was happening. In fact, they had little sense that they had done wrong.

On Monday they got going and shutting the gate behind them, they saw that it remained closed this time. 'Firs' time t'at 'appen,' their mother exclaimed and went back and opened it then closed it. 'Got better' she muttered. She stared at the clock. 'Come on you kids we b't late. She shook the clock. 'No, it stopped and on ten too. Oh well.'

They were late and the constable was waiting for them. He said: 'Just about goin' out to round you up. Thought that maybe you had gone bush. Anyway, the magistrate's having tea. Wait here and I'll just tell him that you're here.'

The atmosphere was such, sort of stern and bleak that Balga and Kylie began to snivel. Somehow it seemed the thing to do and it wasn't long before their mum joined them.

The constable arrived and gestured the sniveling trio through a door. There was no escape. They looked behind them, but the blue uniform was behind them. Too close and it pushed them into a big room with a raised platform at one end with a high desk on it, but this was not where they stopped. The policeman pushed on the reluctant trio into a side room where three men in suits were drinking tea. They stared up at the three and the gray haired bloke in the centre stated: 'So these are our little villains and the mother too. Well, it's a simple enough case and I have your report with all the details in it. The only thing to decide is where to send them. What are they quadroons or something, more than a touch of the tar brush and we may take that into account. What religion are you,' he asked the woman.

She stared at the constable waiting for him to answer for her. 'He would like to know if you are Catholics,' he explained, having noticed Jesus and Mother Mary on the wall of the woman's room next to the wardrobe where the stolen dress had been found.

'We'uns Catholics, sir, yer 'onour,' she said agreeing with the policeman.

'Ah, well, that can settle the institution. Both your children are declared to be wards of the state until they turn eighteen, or other circumstances warrant an extension, though I don't think that will be necessary as you obvious live in a house and where they are going they will be well and truly civilized, I mean educated. The girl will go to a Roman Catholic home for girls to be decided later and naturally the boy to one for lads. The people in Perth will have the details by the time you get there. Nothing else on the agenda is there, so we'll end the proceedings for the day. Good day to you, Constable.'

Stunned and ignorant, though aware that something awful had happened, the two kids clung to their mother. She was ushered out by the policeman. He took them back to the Station for her to sign the necessary papers. When this was done, he took the two kids to see the station cells. There were half a dozen cells about an exercise yard enclosed like a giant bird cage. 'Shiloh's a pretty peaceful town,' he declared, 'so the gaol's usually empty. Now don't get alarmed you don't have to stay here. It's for the big boys and girls, not you two,' he declared with a strange laugh. Balga and Kylie stared at him them at each other. Something had happened and what it was they couldn't work out.

'Okay,' the constable said, 'go home and enjoy the time you got left together. I'll get in touch with you in a few days when the traveling arrangements are finalized.

On Thursday they were on the train to Perth with the big constable who was wearing civvies. He handed the kids a lolly each then dozed off.

They were confined to a single compartment. At York, the constable woke up and stopped their mum just as she was about to open the door. The kids stared out and sulked. They wanted to be out and away. The station and the town beyond reminded them of Shiloh. The train lingered and Balga pointed out the station sign and spelt it, Y, O, R, K and then said the word. This was no big deal for him. He was already reading books and had brought his little library along in the old case Mum had given him for his few possessions. Now the steam engine huffed and puffed out what was now an adventure for him at least. He enjoyed the train and was even looking forward to Perth, a big town that was called a city.

The train continued along and the countryside became hilly and wonders of wonders it actually passed through a hole in the earth. Day turned into night, then into day again. There had been such a thing in Balga's books and now he had experienced it. What else lay ahead of him?

The policeman dozed on and so did their mother. Balga opened his suitcase and took out a big tattered book he had picked up somewhere or other. There was a picture of a train going towards tall buildings. They were on it. He fell asleep as the train reached Midland Junction and headed for Perth.

THREE

THE MONSTER BASH

Once upon a time, many years ago in 1947, a nine year old boy was taken away from his mummy and after that wrenched from his sister with whom he had spent all of his life. Well, that boy was Balga and on an awful day in late April, he entered the city of Perth a large town with tall buildings he had never seen before. It was a place, a maze in which he might become lost and isolated just by entering it. On that long ago Thursday afternoon he left the train at the busy station to cling tightly to his mother and sister until the constable ordered them to follow him. He led them to the Police Headquarters which was close by. There other blue uniformed men consulting papers. They continued clinging together then Balga was wrenched away. His mother and sister were left behind as he was carried to a police car.

Balga was dumb and numb. A feeling of dread held him paralysed. For some reason he thought of the great snake that lived in the Avon River. It glared at him. He thought of the Black Boy trees and one was toppled over. He felt like crying; he felt like wailing, he felt like running to his mother or sister. But he was alone and huddled there all alone.

The policeman, the driver wasn't all that unkind. He was simply doing his job. He drove swiftly through the city streets. It didn't take long. He began driving across a long bridge which he said aloud to himself or to the boy was "the causeway". Beyond the "causeway" the road passed into more familiar country, the almost empty bush. Only a few houses and this cheered Balga up just a little. The driver called this "Victoria Park". The car drove along and reached a stretch of road edged by the gloomiest trees Balga had ever seen. These were rows of pine trees planted so closely together that he knew the word for it: forest -- and who knew what evil witches or ogres or jinak dwelt within. He knew the tale of Hansel and Gretel which usually made him hungry. Now it brought the tears streaming from his eyes. He yearned for the familiar scattered growths of his eucalyptus trees and the tall protective Balga warriors, the grass trees from which he had been named.

No longer numb he felt his heart sink down into his one and only pair of boots which he once had worn with pride. He touched them to feel something familiar. He moved closer to the old cardboard suitcase tied with string into which Mum had packed or rather flung his few belongings: three shirts, two pairs of short pants and his library of six books. His favourite one was A Boy's Own Adventure Book. It came into his mind that he was on or beginning his own adventure and he felt terrible. He was so alone. He sobbed.

The pine tree rows suddenly became confined behind a low brick wall that seemed to go on for miles. Balga had been in the car for so long that he even began to enjoy the ride buoyed up with the hope that it was taking him back to his home in Shiloh. He felt that he was having one of those dreams in which he had been abandoned and would soon come awake to find his sister snuggled beside him. The vehicle slowed as the low brick wall curved into an imposing entrance. The car turned and wheeled up a long and well maintained driveway towards an imposing double-storied sandstone building. It pulled up in front of it.

'Your home for the next eight or so years,' the policeman driver said cheerily, 'Clontarf Boys' Town and don't worry,' he added, as he noticed

Balga's tear drenched cheeks, 'it's not all that bad. You get used to it. We don't get that many calls to round up runaways, so it must be okay.'

Balga stared out at the terrifyingly strange. Automatically his head began to sink down below the level of the car's window. He tried to hide there. The d oor s uddenly o pened t o f urther s trangeness. A b ig white man clad in a long black dress with his pants' bottoms showing beneath appeared there. Balga shut his eyes in terror. It was no use. He felt a giant hand fasten on his head. He was lifted out even though he desperately clung to his suit case. He had been captured by an ogre. He shrunk to the ground beside the black clad monster. This lifted him to his feet as the car, his only hope began moving. Balga tried to run after it. He yelped like a mongrel puppy dog as that heavy hand with its great fingers settled again on his head.

The giant rumbled: 'Well, well, welcome to St. Joseph's,' and then with Balga's suitcase in one hand and the top of his head in the other, the boy was half carried through double doors into the building.

The giant turned right with the sniveling child who knew he really at the top of the bean stalk and in the giant's lair. A large and long room better furnished than any he had ever glanced into before and as clean, as his mum would have said, as a new pin without sin. Everything shone gleaming with polish and Balga couldn't help gasping as his eyes widened at an entire wall lined with books. He couldn't believe that so many books could exist in the one place. His eyes clung to them; but then the hand turned his head to line up his eyes at a big armchair in which sat a really old monster. His long white face was a mass of wrinkles radiating from a pair of faded blue eyes and a caved in mouth. His hands of the same dead white colour poked forth from the sleeves of the black gown that completely covered his skeletal body. Some sort of round hat sat on top of his skull. Balga quaked before the apparition as the giant holding him up said: 'Brother Crowley, the Principal and Superior of your new home.'

'Please see that he's settled in, Brother O'Doherty,' the old ogre whispered. The trap of his mouth emitted a sigh as his faded blue eyes stared at Balga. Bony white fingers tapped on the arm of the chair. The air quivered. 'What's your name, boy?' His voice sounded like the rustling of leaves or of the bark hanging from a gum tree rasping against the trunk as a breeze stirred it.

Balga was too frightened to reply. He was lost in the deep dark forest with nary a gum tree in sight and that giant still held his head in one huge hand that now tightened.

'Answer Brother Crowley,' rumbled the voice above him.

The only reply Balga could manage was a gulp in his sobbing.

'No matter he'll settle him in,' the apparition sighed as he settled back into his chair with a rattle of bones.

Brother O'Doherty marched him away and out of another door into a space with strange low green trees growing about it. His hand fell from the boy's head. He spoke down at Balga telling him that he must reply when spoken to and each and every brother, as the adults in black skirts were called, must be replied to with a, "sir". With this, to give an example he called over a "sir" who he addressed as Brother Connelly. Balga shot up a glance at him. His tear filled eyes took in a watery vision of a man with short brown hair and steel framed spectacles that glinted some dangerous sign at him. 'Settle this skinny chap in, brother,' O'Doherty ordered Connolly and stamped off.

'Come on Skinny,' the brother said stressing "skinny" so that as a name it would stick with Balga for the next eight or so years he would spend in that place, 'pick up your suitcase and follow me. Say "yes "sir". What cat got your tongue,' and he gave the sniveling boy a tap with the stiff strap he carried in one hand. It wasn't a hard blow still it made Balga huddle further into his self.

This didn't suit the adult, he wanted his "sir," and gave Balga hard whacks on his behind as he intoned. 'You say "Yes sir. Thank you, sir" now say it.'

Balga managed a stuttering, 'Y-y-yess, s-s-sir?' He was frightened out of his wits and knew he had reason to be.

'Ah, a little strapping loosens the stiffest of tongues. Fine, fine now let's store away that suitcase. You won't need anything from it. You will receive everything from us, thanks to the goodness of Our Mother, The Apostolic and Holy Roman Catholic Church. Yes, you belong to us now!'

A whack elicited a sodden 'yes sir'.

Brother Connolly hitched up his gown and hurried away. Balga ran after him dragging his suitcase. He went at a diagonal across a large square of concrete. 'The quadrangle,' the black clad adult flung over his shoulder as he reached the end of the wing of the main building. He strode right to go to the second door along another building. The brother unlocked the door with a jangle of keys and flung open the door. Balga reached him and they went into a store room stacked with other cases. The man took the case and flung it onto a pile. It instantly blended in and Balga lost sight of his possession.

The brother gestured him outside, locked the door and took him to the first door which was unlocked. A large room filled with four rows of wooden lockers taller than he was. He stood there sniveling as Connolly said, 'Now your locker and your number; but first I suppose you should have a shower and get into some decent clothes. You look pretty shabby and grimy to me. What do you say?'

'Y-y-yess, s-s-sir,' Balga pushed out through his snivels.

The adult rushed the boy in the opposite direction, across the quadrangle and past the right wing of the main building to another building which housed the laundry and clothes room. An ordinary bloke there, a big boy passed over to him a towel, woolen shorts, a shirt, a pullover and lastly a pair of sandals which were only to be worn on Sundays or special days. 'Winter wear,' he smiled at him. 'Now give me those things you have on. They'll make good polishing rags, I suppose.'

Balga had to strip down right there and then and then and there lost his pride and joy, his boots. As he took them off, his sniveling turned into sobs. They were his last possessions to go. He never saw them again.

'Stop that nonsense,' the monster Connolly ordered him, giving the boy a hard whack on his bare behind that started him yowling. 'Wrap that towel about you, pick up your clothing and come after me, you skinny black thing!'

Balga was rushed away from the laundry and into the right wing of the main building. He gaped at further strangeness. He had never seen a bathroom. Now he was confronted by lines of showers and wash basins. 'Get in that one,' the brother ordered making his point with his strap. Balga did so and stood there not knowing what to expect. Connolly reached in and turned on a tap. Cold water gushed down and he yelped; the brother turned another knob and hot water flooded down. He yelped again. The man turned off the water. 'Pick up that soap, that thing there stupid and give yourself a good rubdown. Sweet Jesus where have you been all your life. In the bush? The boys they send us these days. You're dark too. They should've sent you to New Norcia, that's for coloureds. Now wash off some of that blackness.' The man turned on the water. 'Now dry yourself, that's what the towel is for.'

And so Balga was introduced to showering. Everything was new and terrifying. He stood there naked and shivering, but not from the cold. The brother told him to dress and to stop his sniveling.

'Now to the locker room Skinny,' the adult ordered.

Back across the quadrangle to the end of the other wing and the building there and into the room with the four rows of numbered lockers, they went. The brother strode down a row, expecting the child to follow.

'Reds, Blues, Yellows and Greens. You'll be Green 22 and don't forget your number or your locker either. Come here you. Quickly! Stop that sniveling, Green 22. Put your towel in your locker and tomorrow we'll get you a full set of clothing. Go on do it!'

Balga managed to do so under the brother's glare. He had to close his locker and then they were on the move again. A siren rang. It was time for tea. The boy was taken to what the brother called the refectory. 'After this we'll finish off with you,' the man all but snarled.

Balga could well believe it. "Tuck it; tuck it,' he thought while saying, Yes, sir; thank you, sir'

And so the black boy, Balga, found himself in a place he had never known could exist. He hated it and didn't settle down. He sobbed for the first week then as his tears dried up, he decided he wanted to go home. Everyone, the other kids and even the brothers addressed him as 'Skinny'. He used to say that his name was Balga, but then the brothers said that it was no Christian name. He retorted that nor was Skinny and received a blow from one of the straps that all the adults carried hung over the tops of their sashes or pushed through it. Do or say one wrong thing and out it came and down it came. They put Balga to work washing the dishes after the meals. He dropped a plate and out came the strap. He had to wash dishes in scalding water. He sought to make it bearable by adding cold water and out came the strap. 'Tuck it' tuck it,' he thought. He had stopped crying as his anger grew. He wanted out.

Once the nine year old boy had made up his mind on escape, his festering anger set him to carry it out. The very night of the very day of his decision, he lay in his dormitory bed waiting for the silence of deep sleep to descend on the kids. Eventually from the snores and occasional cries as well as restless twistings, he decided that the time was ripe. There were toilets at the end of the dormitory. He got up and went there as if for a piss. Except for the lighted toilet the whole of Boys' Town was dark; but there was a full moon which would light his way. Balga went back to bed, pulled on his clothes and headed for the stairs. Down he snuck.

Outside not a soul in sight, not a light glowing and keeping to the shadows he made his way around to the locker room building. The door was unlocked. The moonlight was streaming through the large windows. He could see to go to his locker for his sandals. What else to take for the journey? From another locker he took an ex-army water bottle. He needed a blanket; but he wasn't brave enough to return to the dorm for one. He decided that his towel would do.

He left the locker room turning away from the quadrangle and past the door of the room where they had put his case. He tried the door, but it was locked. He sat on the steps and put on his sandals even though the soles of his feet were tough; but he had to cross a paddock and there might be prickles there or even snakes. Balga ran through the field and into the scary rows of pines filled with darkness. With his heart in his mouth he raced through and jumped the low wall to crouch at the roadside. It took him a minute to get his breath and bearings. On his way to Perth the train had come through hills and so he turned in the direction of the Darling Escarpment. As he trotted towards it, a mark on it turned into a giant black face that watched him keenly. It wasn't scary. He hoped it was guiding him home.

At last he was free. Not a single vehicle came along the road The big face smiled at him. He skipped through a silver world vacant of the hateful white men in their black robes and their heavy straps. But, no, yes in the distance coming towards him were the twin headlamps of car. He jumped to one side of the road to hide. Shadows fled away from him as he crouched beside the low stone wall. He shut his eyes. The vehicle came to a halt. He heard doors being flung open. He heard feet coming towards him. A large hand came down on his head. He jerked like a rabbit well and truly caught.

'Well, well, what do we have here, the skinny sniveler, eh,' Brother O'Doherty, the white monster exclaimed sarcastically.

The adult lifted the boy up by his head. Dangling from his handBalga was carried to the car. His eyes sprang open. It was the green Ford Zephyr of Boys' Town. Two brothers sat in the front seat and another was in the back. He was flung into the back against him. Brother O'Doherty heaved himself in after the boy. Balga squeezed into a shivering, quivering ball of despair. His attempt had failed..

'So where was our little wanderer off to, eh,' O'Doherty asked as the car jerked as the gears were changed roughly.

How could Balga answer him? He had lost his voice and was sense-less with dread. What would they do with him? He wanted to sob, but couldn't. Unable to escape physically, he was building a wall around his heart. He felt nothing as the car turned through the gateway and wheeled towards his prison. What was to be was to be and he gave up the struggle and much of the right to think and feel as a free human being.

The vehicle lifted as Brother O'Doherty got his bulk out. Balga crept after him and followed into the big room with the ancient monster still sitting in the chair exactly as it had been a week ago. The faded blue eyes in that wrinkled white face radiated nothing. It muttered something, stopped, cleared its throat and murmured in a soft voice: 'My boy, we are not here for our benefit, but for yours. God put us on this earth to ease the lot of such as you. I have helped many and I am sure that after tonight we shall have none of this seeking to evade our ministrations…' Balga didn't understand a word; but no answer was expected, not even a "Yes sir".

The old man now spoke to O'Doherty in a voice as normal as the rasping of dry leaves: "I take it he was running away and not just out on a midnight stroll?'

'He was. No need to ask him. His guilt is there in his very posture. You were running away from us, weren't you, Skinny,' he growled asking the boy and thus contradicting his words.

Skinny said: 'Yes, sir.'

'Oh, it's "Yes sir" just like that, is it now?'

'Brazen, already,' Brother Crowley, the old man murmured. 'He must be shown the error of his ways. He must be made a good boy!'

Balga watched as the old monster elevated itself from its chair and then bent to feel for something along one side of the chair. It found what it was looking for pulling forth a leather strap as ancient and as withered as its hand.

The old man winced as he tapped it on his left palm. 'Ah, yes these things must be done,' he said to himself and then to the boy; 'Bend over. Hold onto the arm of the chair. Ah, that's good. I must do this you know.'

Six blows fell weakly onto Balga's rump. The old man did not have the force to hurt him physically only spiritually. He bent there and let what happened happen. And then it was over.

'There, that hurts me more than it hurts you,' the old man said breathing heavily. 'Now what might you say to the kind brothers that are looking after you?'

Balga knew what they wanted and spoke it. 'Yes, sir, thank you, sir. I am sorry, sir, I won't, won't –'

'Won't what?' O'Doherty snapped.

'Won't do it again, sir! Be a good little boy,' Balga said attempting a sob, but managed only a gulp.

'The correct and proper attitude,' Brother Crowley whispered. 'Now off with you to bed. It's too late for little sleepy heads to be up. A good long sleep makes for good boys.'

Balga thoroughly tamed went alone back to his bed, put on his pajamas and lay there with wide open eyes staring into the darkness. The events of the last week were too much for one skinny brown lad to endure; but he had done so and, well, what happened would happen whether he willed it or not, then it wasn't happening to a kid called Balga but to one called Skinny. A tough kid that could handle anything and any place, and he went to sleep.

FOUR

A FRIEND FOUND

Next morning, Skinny leapt out of bed and didn't forget to say: 'Good morning, Sir.'

'See that you put those things back in your locker,' the brother grumbled. He walked off down the rows of beds looking to find any sluggards. The sound of whacks followed by yelps revealed that he had. Time to rise and shine with a shiver or two as it was getting into winter and the weather soon would plague the boys as much as the brothers did.

But in Skinny's second week, winter was still out of range and feeling and thus out of his head. He had other things to occupy his mind. One was how to make his bed.

'Ey, you'll get the strap for that,' a voice piped up after he had just pulled up the blankets..

Skinny started then looked up and at the strange face of a kid about his own age standing at the bed next to his. He held his stare for the kid didn't look white or even coloured for that matter. His face was covered by large brown patches but there was white skin between them. Still whatever sort of freckled freak he was didn't matter to Skinny. He needed a friend. He grinned at the boy, but before answering darted his eyes about. He knew that to speak often brought punishment down on you; but Brother Connelly was at the far end of the dormitory and so he whispered back: 'Don't know how, just week in t'is place.'

'Yeah, but you 'ave to get the 'ang of it they won't excuse you now;' the freckled kid whispered back. 'Let me give you a 'and, naw both of them,' and he grinned down at the two brown and red paws that might have belonged to a wallaby.

But they were capable hands and attacked Skinny's bed furiously to quickly reduce it to a neat white rectangle. Yes and with time to spare as the monster was some beds away from them, stopping at every third or fourth one to toss his strap down to see if it bounced. When it didn't, he bounced it off the owner of the bed. He barely glanced at theirs and now with the inspection over, they raced to the next item in the morning routine.

'Come on, quick or we won't get a basin, and to be late is to be whacked,' the kid, who was sticking to him a bit like gum, shouted, though in a furious whisper that didn't draw attention. Skinny grabbed up the bundle of the escapade of the night before and raced out after him, along the verandah and following his example slid down the concrete banister of the stairway leading to the ground floor and the huge bathroom. He pushed his way to a basin. Both kids splashed cold water over their face and hands, before rushing out again and along to the far end of the building to the locker room. Skinny dashed in to put the things he had taken for his trip into his locker. His chum came after him. 'Fling 'em in, tidy 'em up later. Now come on.'

Out again and along to the front corner of the main building where the chapel stood with one tower looking like a finger accusing the sky of sinful thoughts. Their steps slowed at the doorway and they entered decorously. After a week, sad as it had been, Skinny had learnt to genuflect though he had no idea what it meant. They entered a pew neither too far from the front nor too close to the back ones where the brothers lurked ready to spot any lack of piety. The priest preceded by two boys dressed in red skirts with a lacy shirt over them appeared from the side (the sacristy) to genuflect in front of the altar before beginning what was called a mass.

Skinny watched and followed the movements the other kids made. He kneeled, stood, sat and made the sign of the cross, but when the majority of the kids went to the front to kneel down there, he didn't follow as the freckled kid shook his head. The priest with one of the altar boys carrying a small silver tray came to stand before each boy briefly. The altar boy put the tray under the kid's chin and the priest placed something in his mouth which he took from a big metal cup. Skinny couldn't even guess what it meant or what it was. After the boys gulped what had been put in their mouths, they returned to their places and knelt with their heads lowered. A short time after this event the altar boys led the priest out and in a short time Skinny followed the kids out.

Time for chores! 'See you hat breakfast,' his new chum whispered as he dashed off.

Skinny went slowly to his job which was cleaning his dormitory. First, the floor was carefully swept and then cloths were rubbed over it to make sure that it gleamed. If he noticed the slightest scrape or scratch he grabbed a tin of polish applied it lavishly and then furiously rubbed it until the mark was gone. Once a week he was told they had to polish the whole floor, clean the windows and dust what was to be dusted mainly the bed frames and window sills. These were all that might collect dust, for the dormitory was bare, sterile and gleaming. After the work was done, Skinny and the other boys held their breaths as their work was inspected by a brother. A speck of dust could mean a strap across the body or if they were lucky on their hand.

Eight o'clock was breakfast. There was a clock tower in the quadrangle but Skinny had to learn to tell the time. This didn't matter as he just followed the other kids. He was starving, but had to wait for the siren to sound. The freckled faced kid came to stand next to him. He was a mine of information as well and able to talk without moving his lips. He whispered that Clontarf had been taken over by the R.A.A.F. during the war and one of the things they had left behind was the siren system. As the sound was fading in front of the refectory the kids lined up in their colours, Reds, Greens, Blues and Yellows according to their numbers.

The "colours" took turns week by week to file in first and this time it was the Reds and after the Greens. The kids queued around to the right of the tables where raised shutters showed the kitchens. The cooks stood ladling out porridge. After his plate had been filled, Skinny went to his place at a table. He stood there until everyone in the other two teams had received their food. Then and then only did the brother in charge intoned grace. Skinny didn't know the prayer, but moved his lips. He then sat down and stared at the plate of congealed glumk in front of him. All that goo had to be forced down. He knew that by now. Just as he knew that if breakfast was awful the mid day meal was just as bad. His mum hadn't been the best of cooks, but much better than the men that cooked the stuff he had to eat here or be punished

Skinny ate everything and drank his milk. The ordeal over, he looked up and about him. He was allowed to do this, though no talking. There just a few seats away sat the freckled kid now his chum. He grinned at him, just as the command came to stand. Skinny leapt to his feet to thank God or something and then when "Green" was called filed out to dump his plate, cup and utensils at the dish washing place, where the unfortunate boys selected from the Red Team to do the job were already filling their basins with hot water just below boiling point into which they would soon be sticking their hands.

Skinny hurried away and a load lifted from him as he cleared the refectory. Now the kids were free for about a quarter of an hour. He could use to go to the toilet or simply horse around until the siren sounded to assemble for classes.

'So Skinny, you're not 'ere for an 'oliday are ya,' said the freckled kid, who now introduced himself as Tommy Cooper, the whole name to be used, as they hung about the quadrangle waiting for the siren to sound to imprison them in the class room.

'Sure ain't, Tommy Cooper,' Skinny replied, 'and now t'at I'm all but settled in just call me Skinny, t'ough's Balga's me real name. 'You're on 'olidays yerself, are ya?'

'Mum, and maybe Dad, well they gave me me 'ols when I was a mite of two months,' the irrepressible Tommy said without a trace of the sadness and despair that still haunted Balga though the new persona of Skinny was taking over. He even grinned as Tommy went on: 'Naw, two years I was and put in that Castledare place that's for babies. When I got to six, well about then, they shifted me 'ere, and now I'm a real Clonny kid,' he finished with such an obvious pride that Balga suddenly shivered as if a future belief had walked over his mind.

Suddenly the name "Castledare" bought up a memory. Hadn't Mum once mentioned that that was where his big brother, Frank had been sent? And if he had been, maybe he too had been transferred when he had reached six or so to Clontarf. The very idea that he might have a big brother near thrilled him. His eyes began flickering around looking for him. Maybe he was one of the kids mucking about in the quad. He would recognise him by his dark skin. Skinny stared at the one black kid that he could see; but instantly knew that wasn't him.

'Had a bradda, Frank, 'e was 'posed to be in that Castledare. You hever met him, seen him?' he asked Tommy, hoping that he had.

'Not that big Abo,' Tommy Cooper exclaimed, looking at Skinny strangely. 'I seen him, but t'at's all. He was is a big kid, a working boy, almost grown up an' right in with the brothers. I t'ink e's still there to this day...' He broke off staring at Balga.

'T'at doesn't sound a bit like him, he ain't no Abo,' Skinny replied.

'I ain't an Abo either. He must have left long before you even got there,' Balga said, sadly feeling the happiness of having a big brother to look after him fall like a useless tear. He perked up. It wasn't as if he was a real brother after all as he had never met him. Anyway Balga Jackson was no more. He was Skinny Jackson and that was that.'

The siren moaned. They lined up to go to their classes. Skinny was glad to find Tommy was in the second grade with him. They marched in and sat at their desks. Brother Connolly was their teacher. He prowled the aisles between desks, looking down at their work for mistakes.

The kids kept their heads down ignoring or feeling the thud sounding or hitting, but no cries. Except for answering questions, reciting poems and the multiple tables, classes were held in dead silence; from the boys that is, for often Connolly marked his blows with detailed corrections of where the boy had gone wrong and dictated to him the correct answer or piece of writing which he then had to learn by heart by the morrow.

Skinny was clever. He had no trouble with the subjects and breezed through them, so that he was only given an occasional blow or few to keep him on his toes. He did however have one worrisome problem: the pronunciation of 'th'. Sometimes when he answered a question, Brother Connolly mocked this as did some of the other kids. Tommy Cooper who only dropped his 'aitches' as an affectation sought to relieve his mate of the problem. He failed as did the brothers who tried to beat the correct pronunciation into him. He tried to hide the impediment by sliding over it with three sounds, z, d, t which definitely weren't "th".

Classes went smoothly to the tune of a leather strap with a fifteen minute break at ten o'clock and then more school work up to mid day when who should walk in with a swagger and a swish of his strap, but Brother O'Doherty, nicknamed Dicky as Tommy Cooper whispered. He was there to give them religious instruction, a trial by ordeal if ever there was one. Before in that first tearful week the man that had labeled him as a skinny little sniveler drove the tears away forever. He didn't even jump when Dicky immediately grabbed him by the head to lift him out of his seat as he said: 'My God, your hair's like a wire brush. You must be one of those little heathens you skinny hairbrush; but soon I'll make you into a good Catholic or my name isn't Patrick Lawrence O'Doherty. .. Now what is this?'

'Sir, it is a book.'

'Of course, idiot, but what sort of book?'

'The Catechism, sir,' suddenly spoke up Tommy Cooper.

'Who asked you, yes, it is a catechism which you'll learn by heart and now Cooper seeing you spoke out of turn, how does it start?'

'Who made the world? God made the world.'

'Now you skinny hairbrush, repeat it!'

Skinny's mind was a blank. 'Sir,' he stuttered, 'it b-b-begins with the words "T'e Catechism"'.

The hand lifted him bodily into the air and he was placed rump up over his desk. He received six of the very best from that huge thick strap. It sent him into shock. He almost fainted. He would have fallen; but the kind brother picked him up and placed him on his bruised behind at his desk.

'Now,' he said, 'I want the answer. This sacred book begins with the question: "Who made the world?"'

'God made t'e world,' Skinny replied.

'Good the strap aids the memory, doesn't it? By the time I finish with you, you'll have the entire book down pat under that hairbrush. You will, won't you?'

'Yes sir.'

And by God it was true. The entire contents of that book went into his head; but this was not all for Balga may have been baptized, but he was only nominally a Catholic and ahead of him as Skinny stood his first confession and first communion. A half dozen other boys also were beginners and to these and to Skinny, Dicky volunteered to give his undivided attention with a special homework class just before prayers. These were the first things that were beaten into him so that he could intone along with the rest of them.

'I believe in God the Father all mighty and in Jesus Christ his only son, Our Lord, who was crucified, dead and buried and on the third day he rose from the tomb ...and so it went on the Apostles Creed which all good Catholics were compelled to believe. After this came the rosary of the Blessed Virgin Mary, the prayers of which were recited with the aid of rosary beads which only the brothers possessed; but which Skinny soon knew all about. The beads of the rosary were arranged in five decades (sets of 10), each decade separated from the next by a larger bead with the two ends joined by a small string holding a crucifix, two large beads and three small beads. First came the Lord's Prayer, bang, followed by fifteen Hail Marys and finally, bang, Glory be to the Father, the Son and the Holy Ghost, and thank you sirs for all that you have given us, amen.

These prayers were the beginning incantations for Skinny the little heathen hairbrush. They would, as Dicky continually reiterated, open the gate into the mysteries of the Holy Roman Catholic Church. These incantations had to be mastered word by word, all to the tune of the great strap of Brother O'Doherty beating out the rhythm to Skinny's steps leading on to his first confession in which he would confess those sins that had already piled up on him, a skinny kid just going on ten. Dicky knew exactly what some of these were. He had read Balga Jackson's report and knew that he was a little thief. It was his duty to belt this out of him as well as any other inclinations to further evil. Dicky did his work well. He taught Skinny that when he made his first confession even though the priest might be a withered specimen of a man with thick glasses, short legs and a long body he was a representative of God himself able to forgive sin as long as the sinner was sincere in asking for forgiveness. This sincerity was encased in an act of contrition which he recited at prayers every evening just in case he died in the night or the devil came to tempted him in his dreams to some imagined sin.

Yes, the good brother declaimed, the hands of Satan were always reaching out to kids like Skinny and without sincere sorrow for all the evils he had committed those hands would grasp him and fling him down into the infernal pit to be eternally tortured. Skinny was horrified by this revelation. Thank God and his son, Jesus that they had given to Their Holy Mother the Church the sacrament of confession and contrition to keep such skinny hairbrushes in a state of grace and able to enter into the wonderful mystery of the Catholic communion, the consubstantiation of bread and wine into the actual body and blood of Christ. When he heard this and partway understood it, he couldn't accept the idea of eating somebody's flesh and drinking his blood without throwing up. Dicky emphasized the necessity of a faith that must grow and be nurtured so that he could accept with joy this act of cannibalism. The good brother even declared that good Catholics couldn't get enough of this flesh and blood which they had to eat at least once a year or be guilty of a mortal sin.. Oh My God, Skinny, the ten year old boy prayed, please, please give me the necessary faith to eat your Son's body and drink his precious blood and not throw up.

Skinny's school subjects were easier to accept in comparison to the religious mysteries and the absolute necessity to believe, which so often perplexed him that he suffered from brain fag. Worse, he knew that because he lacked faith hell was gaping to receive him. To escape the emotional turmoil, he too often (a venial sin) stared with longing out of the class room windows which gave a view of the wide, playing fields on which brain work gave way to the physical joy of running, jumping and kicking a ball around.

The kids escaped from mental work at 3-30 p.m. As soon as the siren wailed they raced out of their classroom and down the path towards the gateway and through onto the playing fields that stretched from East to West along the bull rush lined banks of the wide Swan river smiling blue under the sun of winter or summer and marked with a line of posts showing the boat channel. These, Skinny learnt, were a monument to other prisoners, the British convicts that had been sent into Western Australia to develop the colony.

Much of the kids' free time was occupied by work and organized sports. The brothers hated the idea of unorganized time and thus had their charges play games over which they arbitrated as umpires. In fact Dicky and another brother, Basher Dole loved to umpire the kids and urge them on to greater efforts in projects they initiated. Dicky replaced the ancient Crowley who vanished like a ghost, and after prayers they were informed that Brother O'Doherty was now their principal. Under his direction work increased and on Saturdays while some of the kids toiled building a new grotto for the Blessed Virgin Mary, the remainder were out in the back paddocks grubbing or burning out stumps. Skinny once perhaps to escape his mental turmoil worked with such enthusiasm that he was noticed by the working brother in charge. As a reward he was allowed to drive the tractor back to the buildings. That night in chapel his enthusiasm for work was mentioned, though not his name. Still, he felt proud.

The grounds had been excavated out of the banks of the Swan River. The buildings sat on a height above them and a steep incline had been walled up with sandstone blocks to make cliffs. Only a single pathway lead down into the grounds from the buildings, though beyond both ends the walls gave way to the original incline. At the eastern end, forming a natural boundary was a small creek that flowed from a patch of swamp down into the Swan. At one place its banks had been eroded into a small beach below the general lay of the land and when Skinny could steal a few precious minutes he went to play in the sand and construct little buildings as he had in Shiloh. Up from the swamp was an orchard of orange and loquat trees and after that the cliff began. Here there was an old grotto and high up a weathered stature of the Virgin Mary stared blindly out. Below her at ground level was an artificial cave. The grotto formed a curve beside the first sports ground on which Dicky had a work team planting kooch grass which was heavily watered until the sand disappeared under the rapacious grass that grew even as the kids planted.

This ground was below regulation size for Australian Rules football and was used by teams (the so-called Seconds) made up of younger kids. Skinny flung himself into the sport but for some reason was left in the Seconds until he was twelve. The western boundary of this ground was made by a line of big old pine trees, one in particular which Skinny loved to climb. Right up at the very top, he hung there precariously, swaying in the breeze and feeling far from all petty strife and the captured life below him. Eventually Brother O'Doherty had a long thick rope attached three quarters up the tree and now Skinny and other kids could swing out high into the sky and back again. It gave him a wonderful feeling of freedom, hanging right at the end, then the rush back. He actually made up a song about being in a tree that the other kids took up in an act of defiance. A group of kids perched rocking up and down on the boughs of a dead tree at the side of the main ground following him as he sang:

Mummy, daddy take me way
From this awful place so drear
No more eating stew like glue
No more eating bread like poo.

Beyond the main oval lay the Western ground smaller than even the eastern and thus also only used by the Seconds. Skinny's last few games as a little kid had been played on it. By then he was quite a big boy, though skinny of course, and thundered from one end of the ground to the other winning matches through sheer size until Basher Doyle sent him to the Firsts where he specialized as full forward lurking at one end to dash at and catch the ball and send it through the goalposts. He was very good at keeping position, seldom moving above the centre of the ground beyond the cricket pitches which he came to feel was his natural boundary.

The games after school filled only an hour and at 4.30 the siren whined for the beginning of the late afternoon or early evening chores. Clontarf was more than a boys' town or less if you prefer. It was a settlement or a village semi-self sufficient. There was a piggery with pigs that had to be fed; there was a dairy with cows to be milked; ducks and chickens to be fed; horses to be curried; plants and trees to be watered. The duffers at schooling became working boys for their last few years and they did most of the chores; but not all and so Skinny found himself carrying canvas buckets of water to water the twin rows of roses on the sides of the carriage way. Later among other chores he fed pigs or chickens and even milked the cows. This mostly was done by machines and it was a simple matter of putting the cups on; but after this the last drops of milk had to be stripped out. Skinny failed to master this and by the time more efficient machines came along that completed the milking he was being readied to leave Clontarf. The pigs were fed a concoction of molasses and wheat cust which was obtained from the wheat silos in Fremantle. Every so often, a group of boys would be selected to go in the truck to shovel this up. It was a product of wheat grains rubbing together and had little commercial value, though the pigs seemed to thrive on it.

The boys had to finish their chores before 5-30 because then it was showers and unless Skinny had been detailed for special work that necessitated his being late, he had to be ready with a towel wrapped about his waist The brother in charge turned the showers on without overly caring whether the water was too hot or too cold. The kids had to get wet as the showers were turned off after a minute. Then they had to soap themselves for a minute before the showers were turned on for them to wash away the suds. All the kids could pass through the spray in about a half an hour. If was a Saturday, Skinny collected newly washed clothes from the laundry and tea was put off by an half an hour to 6-30 pm which meant that prayers had to be adjusted to a later time.

The food for tea wasn't that bad. A couple of slices of bread and jam and a cup of milk to enjoy and Skinny never left a crumb or a drop. Saying grace usually took longer than for him to wolf his food down. Tea was over by twenty minutes and this left the kids ten minutes to play before doing an hour's homework. This was followed by prayers and by eight o'clock the kids were in bed.

FIVE

THE CHILD MIGRANTS

It was in 1952 on one hot summer afternoon that was just waiting for the Fremantle Doctor (the sea breeze) to arrive when the kids bounded out of their classrooms ready to enjoy the fresh air and relative coolness of the playground and stopped in amazement. The quadrangle was filled with a mass of very strange kids who huddled there like a flock of sheep waiting mutely for the chopper. The inmates stared at the new mob of kids. There must have been about fifty or sixty of them and definitely not Aussies. Rude colonials, tall, rangy and almost as brown as the wide land they inhabited, the inmates pushed among the strangers marveling at everything about them.

Just about all of them were very short compared to the Australians and they were very, very white. Skinny hadn't seen such white kids before and he even rubbed a boy's skin to see if the white would come off. It didn't. Then there was their clothing totally unfit for a Western Australian summer. Each and every one of them was wearing heavy shoes, thick woolen knee socks and equally thick coats and pants. Skinny and the other inmates wandered amongst them, sometimes asking a question and receiving back a reply in funny English. Skinny stopped in front of a taller and bigger boy. 'Ey, you, where you comin' from?' 'Liverpool,' was the reply. 'Where's t'at,' Skinny asked. 'Great Britain.' 'You Protestant?' was the next question 'Of course not,' was the answer 'Why did you come all the way 'ere, if you ain't,' Skinny demanded. ''Cause we are Catholic and Brother Conlon, that one over there came and told us that we were going on a long voyage to a sunny land. So we were put on this ship --' 'You liked t'at ship, plenty to eat? Did you get seasick?' Skinny asked having seen that in a Bud Abbot and Lou Costello picture.' 'Not on my life, it was smooth sailing all the way and the food was better than we had at home.' 'Oh wus it,' Skinny replied, mocking his accent. 'An' from your belly I bet that you got your share. What's yer name anyway?' 'Leahy!' 'And yer Christian name is Beefy huh?' The boy opened his mouth to reply; but Dicky had stopped talking to Brother Conlon who now clapped his hands and shouted:

'This is Brother O'Doherty, the principal of Clontarf Boys' Town and these are Brothers Doyle and Connolly. You know that you must address them as "sir" whenever they talk to you and they expect an answer. Now as it is so hot and you all must be sweltering in those heavy suits, get undressed.'

The boys were slow to react to this direct order and to make them obey Brother Doyle slapped his palm with his strap and shouted: 'Undress!'

The inmates stood among them as they took off their clothes. "Beefy" was beefy or perhaps "Piggy" Skinny thought, for he reminded him of one with his yellow eyes and bristly straw coloured hair. He had a bit of muscle under his fat and bluey-white skin, but most of the others were puny. They really looked like they needed a good feed, but Skinny knew they wouldn't be getting that there. He watched as Basher came among the new kids flicking the slower kids with his strap. 'Right, now follow me and we'll give you each a shower.' They trotted off after him and Skinny and the other inmates took the opportunity to check out their clothing. Thieving might be against one of the Ten Commandments, but Skinny could always confess couldn't he; but there was precious little to steal. Beefy only had a biscuit wrapped up in a handkerchief. Skinny couldn't believe they had nothing. He turned out empty pockets and even ripped at the lining of a coat to see if anything was concealed there. Nothing; but between the lining and the outer fabric he saw a layer of rough hessian sacking and wondered what it was for.

Now Dicky appeared and ordered half a dozen kids to gather up the clothing and the others to get to the playground. Skinny was one of the chosen and with a pile of clothing in his arms he entered the room where long ago Balga had deposited his case. He dumped the clothes and poked among the cases. There was one that once might have been his. He opened it and saw a few old books and odd pieces of clothing. Skinny didn't recognize anything and shut the case with the sudden feeling that he had lost something for ever. He realized that he was a bit like the English kids who were being stripped of all that was familiar. They would be feeling as strange as he had felt, strangers in a strange land and among monsters only too ready to give them a welcome into Clontarf (and Australia). Suddenly Skinny felt sorry for them, but pushed down the feeling as he left the room. Beefy's biscuit tasted moldy and he spat it out.

With the arrival of the migrant kids the numbers of boys had doubled into almost two hundred. Skinny and other kids were crowded into the left wing with the bed wetters on the balcony alongside it. This wasn't as quiet as his old one and was under the charge of a Brother Boulten who used to get the bed wetters up in the middle of the night to pee. Even this didn't work for many of them and these he flogged for being sinners that were content to lie in their own water in spite of everything he did. In this dormitory Skinny made friends with Laurie Fields who slept in the bed next to him. He wasn't liked by the other kids, but Skinny didn't let this worry him. Brother Boulten had made him his pet and Laurie used to clean his room out as his morning chore. Skinny one morning came back to the dormitory to get a polisher and Laurie took him into Boulten's room. He began his work by stripping the bed and giggled as he showed his friend a small stain. Skinny didn't understand the joke. He didn't know what a nocturnal emission was and just thought that the good brother had almost peed in his bed and thus might be a bed wetter himself. When he told Laurie this, the boy shrugged and smiled in a superior way. Skinny shrugged in turn and stared about the brother's room. It was as bare as a dormitory. The man had little in the way of personal possessions.

Skinny's friendship with Laurie ended when Tommy Cooper told him not to have anything to do with a brother's pet. 'Who cares,' Skinny protested. 'He's in the bed next to me an' our faces are usually only t'is far apart.'

'Well, 'e may be in 'is bed now, but watch out or 'e'll be in yours soon,' Tommy Cooper said darkly.

'Naw, not enough room,' Skinny replied not understanding.

Tommy Cooper merely rolled his eyes at these words. When Skinny thought it over later, he knew there was something there that he didn't get, but he avoided Laurie after that.

The English boys' arrival caused a stir that upset Clontarf's routine. With the doubling in numbers there weren't enough brothers to supervise and the boys got to spent a lot of time out of classes down on the playground enjoying themselves in the disorganized fashion that O'Doherty so disliked. One working brother kept an eye on them as they played as they wished. The banks of the Swan were mostly covered with bulrushes, but next to a jetty that had been allowed to lapse into a dilapidated state under the R.A.A.F. was a small sandy beach, though a few yards into the water it became mud. Still it was nice to splash about in the tepid water and stare across the river at the other side wondering what magic might be there, even though apart from a house it seemed pretty much like their side. Well, what matter, they could always dream about lollipop trees for example.

Then one free afternoon, Skinny decided to see those lollipop trees. Boys over the years and months had made canoes out of single sheets of galvanised iron and hid them in the bulrushes. He poked around and found one, though it didn't look very river worthy. Skinny caulked the nail holes with mud, got into it and using two pieces of board for hand paddles set off. Slish-slosh, the canoe rocked from side to side as he paddled. It was nice being out on the wide river and he was enjoying the serenity of it all, when the canoe rapidly began filling with water as the mud dissolved. Skinny was more than halfway across as the canoe began sinking. He couldn't swim and surely must drown. Unable to do a thing about it he muttered an act of contrition as he waited for death. Scenes of his past life flashed before his eyes and Mum and his sister, Kylie, appeared before his eyes. The canoe sunk and he stood up. The river was extremely shallow.

Feeling a bit of a fool, Skinny upended the canoe, righted it, caulked the holes again, got in without capsizing and paddled to the row of convict posts. There he plugged the holes again and skimmed across the narrow channel to the bank. He saw the house, but no lollipop trees. 'Well, I didn't expect any,' Skinny muttered to himself as he got into the canoe and paddled back with only two stops for caulking. At least he had had an adventure and from then on knew that when you were dying or thought you were dying your life flashed before your eyes exactly as they had said in some picture or other.

When Skinny returned to the playground the other boys had already been called up to the buildings. He rushed after them, expecting the worst; but all the kids were milling about the quadrangle. As he joined them, Brother O'Doherty came out of his office, frowned at the disorder and organized the boys into two teams to play a rough and tumble game based on Red Rover, but starting with all of one side in the middle. He called this game "Poms and Aussies" and divided the kids that way although the Aussies were much bigger and stronger than the English kids. With Dicky looking on, the Aussie boys got into the game flinging the Poms onto the concrete to win over and over again. They played for an hour or so until it was time for showers and then tea. After that they were all ordered to gather in the quadrangle where Dicky had Doyle read out a list of boys who were to be transferred to Bindoon the next day to relieve the overcrowding.

Half of the English kids were on the list and only six or so Australians, mainly working boys that were fifteen or sixteen and almost men. Skinny hadn't been selected which was a cause for the great big grin that flashed over his dial.

He heard the name "Leahy" called and looked about the quadrangle to find the kid. He wasn't the Beefy of a few days ago either, for he was bright red and his face was peeling in patches. 'No more the white pig,' Skinny thought and made his way over to him.

'Ey, what happened to ya,' Skinny flung the question at him and stepped on his toes, even though he was much bigger and older. Skinny had taking lessons from Tommy Cooper on how to be obnoxious. 'What t'e sun got hold of you? At least ya kept yer shirt on and yer back should be all right.'

In answer to this, Beefy pulled up his shirt and Skinny saw that the cloth hadn't prevented him from being burnt. In fact he had a fine mesh pattern all over his skin. 'Perhaps you should be called "Ruddy" or "Bloody",' Skinny grinned at him, trying a joke in the Tommy Cooper style.

'I hope that you get to England one time and you freeze your bloody balls off, you brass monkey,' Beefy whispered fiercely. He too had quickly learnt not to draw the attention of the brothers down on him. Even a tap on his burnt skin would be agony and wisely he held Skinny's hand away as he listened to him say: 'Ya know ya goin' to be a pioneer an' build up the empire or Australia or somet'ing. You going to t'at Bindoon bush camp where t'e bloke t'at built up t'is place has begun t'e same t'ing again. I suppose t'at when he began t'is place it was virgin bush too. Anyway ya look strong enough to tote t'ose loads and build t'ose walls.'

'Yeah, yeah,' Beefy replied, refusing to be put off. 'It's not like that at all. Brother Conlon told us that it is really nice and we'll get to learn how to farm. He said that there's plenty of vacant land about and when we learn enough we can have our own farm.'

'Farm, warn ya scum,' broke in Tommy Cooper playing on words just as Skinny's dear Mum had done. 'Ya listen to them brothers, but keep it in that fat 'ead of yers that they are all liars. They tell you one thing you better believe the opposite, 'cause ya goin to get it.'

'But they're brothers,' Beefy protested.

'Yep and that means they got a dispensation from the Pope to lie.'

'Ah, Tommy Cooper,' Skinny in turn protested. He didn't want to believe they were evil. They might hit him too much, but then often he deserved it.

Skinny found himself reassuring Beefy that Bindoon was a decent place which the boy believed until he reached there and found it terrible, got pneumonia and had to be returned to Clontarf for medical treatment in Perth. He never forgave Skinny for lying to him and it was one of the first things he brought up when he came back to Clontarf. Indeed he went on and on about it and Skinny might have decked him except he was too weak from his pneumonia so he just kicked him in the leg and raced away.

SIX

GETTING AN EDUCATION

In 1950 Skinny entered the fifth grade class and found himself being taught by a new brother who had come to Clontarf at the beginning of the year bringing along with him some radical ideas on education. These were not to bash everything into the kids as they might learn just as well with a little kindness. Of course, he had a strap, a regulation one and used it on occasion as it was impossible for a brother not to. By then Skinny was so used to the other brothers and their constant beltings that for a brother not to use a strap constantly was a sign of weakness. Brother Walsh found this out when Skinny's marks fell away as he loafed in his classes. Skinny even failed composition, one of his strong subjects. This made him angry and he accepted the punishment when Brother Walsh finally administered a few weak whacks. It made him buck up. He hated to fail a test and even told Brother Walsh that he would never ever fail another one. The brother smiled, though not sarcastically at this, and said that he shouldn't make promises that he couldn't keep. 'But I can keep t'is one,' Skinny retorted, to which he received the reply: 'I believe you can.'

Towards the end of O'Doherty's term as principal when he would be replaced by Basher Doyle, Skinny was in class one day doing the easiest of punishments as set by Brother Walsh, five hundred lines on not talking in class, when Basher came in and began a conversation with Brother Walsh or rather it was the other way round. Naturally he listened as it was the way kids gained information on what was happening. Both could see that he was in the room, but ignored the boy in the usual manner as if he was just an empty desk without ears to hear or a brain to think.

'Brother Doyle,' Walsh began, 'the constant thrashings of these children, the English ones especially, well, it's not helping their studies at all. Most of them don't seem to have a brain in their heads. It's just a waste of effort trying to make them good at their schooling.'

'Lazy blighters, but corporal punishment does have a worthy history. It keeps the helots in place. Relax the strap and there goes the discipline.'

'Brother Doyle what do you mean by "helots"?' Brother Walsh asked.

'Perhaps the term was ill-chosen. I really want them to be, well most of them good Catholic laymen. When they arrive here these, well, they are rubbish and unfit to be anything. Our strong discipline helps to mould them into strong Catholic soldiers in Christ. We must never forget that they are the future of our church. Hopefully, the best of them will become Christian Brothers and fill our order and govern our institutions. Think of that when you are teaching them.'

'But the majority won't join our order and they will have to eventually settle down and marry –'

'And produce little Catholics - good!'

'Yes, but most of them haven't the foggiest idea about women. They haven't spoken to a girl in their lives.'

'A good thing too if you ask me! They are better off without knowing about such things; but I take your point that they will marry and thus am thinking when I take over from, well, from Dicky, to arrange dances with the girls of St. Josephs in Subiaco. Still, I am only thinking of it. It might spoil them, for we are like Spartans bringing up male children free from the influences of women. They'll be stronger for it and as for our beating some sense into them, they will be harder all the more for it. Our founder Edwin Rice, may he soon achieve sainthood, said: "We are not in the business of producing weakness, but strength, and hopefully our boys will reflect the same attitudes as the martyrs of the early church.'"

'Perhaps, and returning to your example of Sparta, a pagan state in Ancient Greece, that was thousands of years ago. I don't know how the Child Welfare Department might react to this example. They are only too ready to interfere in our affairs as it is.'

'Oh, they are happy to receive the occasional report, so forget them,' Brother Doyle rejoined, 'and if you think the Spartans pagan, then surely you can't quibble about St. Augustine. He as a boy in school endured punishments that were never as lenient as ours often are. And did that affect him for the worse or the better? In his Confessions he tells us that not only did he deserve them, but they were essential for his betterment. It was through them that he obtained strength to devote himself to his studies and eventually become a Doctor of the Church. With his example before us, no wonder we feel it our duty to thrash these boys into shape. It is for their good just as it was for the good of Saintly Augustine. So when you must belt one of the little blighters think of what you might be producing.'

'But Saint Augustus was never a duffer.'

'Perhaps, but we can always get a second opinion, for what do I spy here but the Skinny Sniveler. Hey Skinny Sniveler, stand up! Ah, see how quickly he obeys. Now tell us if the punishments you have received have affected you for the better or worse, eh? Now speak up, don't snivel and don't grovel. Speak the truth, boy.'

'Sir,' Skinny began and suddenly became angry at how these men were treating him. He snapped. 'I don't snivel anymore!'

'Why, Sniveler?'

'Because my mother said t'at it was unmanly, Sir?'

'And why did she say that?'

'Well, a friend, Mr. Winter lost his son in t'e war and when he learnt t'at he began crying and Mum, she said t'at it was terrible to see a grown man cry. So I don't cry anymore, even t'ough I'm still a kid.'

'Well, well, well and do you think six of the best is good for you or not?'

'Perhaps or perhaps not, sir, I'm just hit and have to put up wit' it.'

'Oh a doubting Thomas, eh, and perhaps I should test you now to see if you have become a Spartan and really stopped being the little sniveler you used to be. You're not a St. Augustine, are you?'

'I don't know sir, but t'en I suppose I might be one of t'ose helots, you mentioned.'

'Oh eavesdropping, were you, well, we'll just have to make you learn to block your ears when brothers are engaging in conversation. Now bend over, right over that desk!'

Obediently Skinny lay across the desk. Doyle landed a hard six on his bum. He refused even to flinch. When it was over stood up and faced his tormentor, though his behind was aching.

Basher Doyle turned from the boy smiling in triumph as he declared: 'There this skinny lad was a sniveler before we knocked some strength into him. Look at him, not a tear. He'll be a worthy soldier of Christ. Now, tell me can you say the same about your approach?'

'No, not exactly, but --' Brother Walsh began uncertainly.

'Well, there is no argument,' Doyle declared and left swishing his strap in his hand.

Brother Walsh stared at Skinny who was rubbing his behind.

The boy said: 'Sir, I have finished my lines.'

The Brother replied: 'I don't know-- - but Brother Doyle has a point. You are like a piece of iron which can be beaten, heated and annealed to become a fine piece of metal suitable for the blade of a sword – the sword of St Michael.'

'Maybe, maybe sir, but I don't feel like a piece of metal and even less t'at I'm becoming a sword blade. I hurt too much. I know t'at I deserve a whack or two to keep me on my toes, but some of the ot'ers, don't. '

'No, never doubt it. Don't be a Doubting Thomas feel that you are becoming worthy to serve our Holy Mother the Church.'

'Sir, I don't know if a strapping can do t'at or do I t'ink I am such a Doubting Thomas. Why, I don't even know what t'at means.'

'Well, your Christian name is Thomas and I assume that you were named after the apostle who doubted the divinity of Jesus, the son of God, hence the term.'

Skinny knew that he had been named after his father, but he let it pass as he replied: 'Sir, I am not in doubt about anyt'ing, but merely saying t'at beating a dead horse to make it gallop is a waste of time.'

'Perhaps, perhaps, but sometimes it does help, helps to save a soul from hell, so it is more a matter of the will of God rather than our personal proclivities. Ask yourself: "What use are weak souls in this world?" Pain gives strength and turns one towards God. It is wonderful and truly an act of grace if punishment is seen as a necessary method for our purification and when that is accomplished we become attuned to the will of God.'

'What is t'is will of God,' Skinny asked him though he doubted six of the best as a method to approach God.

'God works in mischievous ways, I mean mysterious ways,' Brother Walsh corrected himself. 'St. Augustine as Brother Doyle said was beaten much more than you have been. He could have rebelled against this, but he accepted it as the will of God working through his school masters to render him a fit instrument to serve his Holy Mother the Church. He learnt obedience and submission to the will of God. God began to work through him and he became a doctor of the Church. Read his Autobiography. See how the will of God manifests and how His purpose is made known. Why, who knows, He may be working right here now and asking you to completely accept and become His instrument. Have you ever thought of becoming a Brother? No, that it not the right way to put it. It is not a matter of thinking; but of opening up to God and receiving a vocation, a call from Him. Without it, it is impossible to accept the vows of poverty, chastity and obedience and serve God through helping others, for as you have learnt from your catechism, "faith without works is dead."'

Skinny muttered "amen", then excused himself and ran down to the playground seeking to outrun his disturbed mind. It was too late to participate in the games and so he went to stand on the wrecked jetty and stare out over the turgid stream as he contemplated what the brother had said. He came to wonder at "a vocation". They even spoke about it in church. How exactly would he know if he received such a call? Did he even want to! He thought on. There were as many types of vocation as there were orders in the holy church. There were for example monks, but what did he know about them? A priest; but that seemed far beyond his abilities though he knew very little about what being a priest meant. Clontarf had a chaplain; but the man had nothing to do with the kids. He served mass, heard confession and stayed in his house behind the church. Skinny had watched him pacing up and down reading his breviary, but the word that summed him up was "unapproachable". Why he never even had boys to clean his house. Of course he had contact with other priests when the Society of Jesus came to conduct retreats; but even then he had never talked to one face to face. They were mysterious men, spoken to through a veil, agents of God on earth who could and would do no wrong.

Skinny had never pondered or thought about these things before and blamed Brother Walsh for putting ideas into his head. He stared out over the water and pictured himself in a black gown and swishing a strap. The image caused him to jump off the jetty and run for a mile around the ground seeking to get the silly image out of his head; but the idea of a "vocation" sat there to plague him. He found himself praying to God for this mysterious thing, this absolute determination that would solve the direction of his life forever more.

That night he lay in bed on his right side and whispered to God: 'Dear God, My Lord and Savior, give me the gift of a vocation that I might serve you.' He waited for the reply and waited. He fell asleep and came awake without even the memory of a dream to enlighten me. He made his bed morosely.

Tommy Cooper had managed to get shifted next to Skinny and now he whispered: 'What you been ridin' - a nightmare?'

'Nuttin, nuttin,' Skinny replied then made a silent prayer to God asking for an instant response, but there was only emptiness within his head where there should have been a warm, loving feeling. In desperation, he decided that he needed to read St. Augustine, for surely, the saint had not only received a sign from God, but would have seen him as clearly as he could see that bloody Brother Boulten coming towards him.

'You not speakin'', Tommy Cooper asked.

'I'm listening for t'at inner voice,' Skinny replied.

'You, what?' his chum asked incredulously.

'Just jokin',' Skinny yelped as Boulten slammed his strap across his shoulders.

Well, that put paid to any silly ideas until Brother Walsh remembering their conversation from the day before gave Skinny a book after class. He even let him stay there to read it. Brother Walsh wasn't one for sports and didn't care if Skinny missed them or not.

Skinny was amazed to find that St Augustine had been a black man perhaps the same colour as he was and this caused him to thumb through the volume until he found the section on St. Augustine being punished. Yes, he had been beaten and 'yes' he had put it down to the will of God. Skinny read on trying to grasp the saint's image of God. It was too vague, to faint, to void. St. Augustine addressed endless prayers to Him, received no voice in return, but only certain signs such as a child murmuring, "read this". St. Augustine even had been a Doubting Thomas and what put his doubts to rest didn't seem very spectacular or real. Anyone if even he might find the will of God then Skinny should because he was a bigger sinner than the saint. As a child St. Augustine had merely stolen fruit from a tree, whereas Skinny-- but no matter, for if God had heard St. Augustine surely he would not only hear but listen to him. Skinny was the greater sinner and thus more in need of redemption.

Ready to hear His voice, Skinny began ducking into the church for a quick prayer and a short wait. Doyle found him there once an' chased him out. Few brothers, with the exception of Brother Walsh, were religious in the sense of wanting to see God, though all of them must have received a vocation. Skinny asked Brother Walsh how his had come about or rather how God had passed on the decision for him to become a brother. He said that it was a sudden conviction.

'Nuttin like God speaking or you seeing him,' Skinny asked.

Brother Walsh laughed at this before replying: 'Only great saints are given a glimpse of God. It is a privilege that I did not aspire to even then, for the face of the Lord is said to be terrible to behold. It is better if you want to feel the presence of divinity to pray to Our Lady, for the Blessed Virgin is much easier to approach. Children in particular are favoured by her. We have the example of the children of Fatima as proof of this.'

Skinny nodded at his words and decided to follow them though he wanted to go directly to the boss himself. Praying to the Virgin Mary was easy. There was the grotto just off the quadrangle and next to the first playground the older dilapidated one with the weathered image of Her standing above an artificial cavern in which Skinny could pray in peace and wait in quietness for that magic voice to sound. Only it didn't!

Desperately, he prayed: 'Dear Lady Blessed Virgin Mary, Mother of God please heed my voice. Give me a sign that you are listening to me, just a sign. This will do for starters, but what I really want is to know whether I have a vocation or not?'

No reply! He kept on and every night tried to say an entire rosary before he fell asleep. He seldom succeeded but his ardor increased to such an extent that he convinced himself that it was only a matter of time before She replied. Indeed one night as he was lying in bed saying the rosary Skinny fell asleep into a dream in which he saw the statue of the Virgin Mary, the one down next to the playing field. It was immaculately white, but as he stared into its eyes maggots began falling from them down her cheeks and onto his face as he stood below her. The dream was strong enough to jerk him awake. He lay there trying to decide if it was a sign or not. If it was it had been so dirty that what it must mean is that he should purify himself.

Skinny remembered how Dicky had a favourite would be saint, Blessed Matt Talbot, a simple working man from Belfast who practiced intense devotion to God and indulged in extreme penances such as wearing a hair shirt. He had made them pray to God to make this man a saint, but it appeared that God had not answered the prayers as yet. In order to be sure about this, Skinny went to Brother O'Doherty to ask him if their prayers had been answered. Dicky was most annoyed at his question. He found it impertinent and grabbed his ear as Skinny's head had grown too big for his hand to hold.

'See here, you skinny hairbrush, God works in mysterious ways and at his own pace. If you wish for the Blessed Matt Talbot to achieve sainthood, pray from your heart and not from your lips. Blessed Matt Talbot was a man that indulged in the most extreme of penances and here is a taste of what he suffered in order to purify himself and reach heaven.'

Dicky gave Skinny a couple of whacks from his long strap to send him on his way. The boy had wanted to ask the brother about hair shirts and tormenting the body to find God. Not even Brother Walsh seemed to think it a good idea when Skinny broached the idea. He went to his favourite spot, the grotto cave to say a few prayers to the Blessed Virgin Mary. After receiving no reply he climbed above the grotto to the orchard. The oranges were ripening and he filled his shirt with the biggest and juiciest ones. Loaded down he walked to the quadrangle where he expected the wrath of God to descend on him. He smiled, perhaps a saintly smile, as Brother Mitchell, a working brother came towards him. Skinny didn't know much about him, but he was sure to be punished.

'What have you got there?' the man asked as he stopped next to Skinny. 'Ah, oranges! Give me a half dozen and don't get caught with the rest unless you have been ordered to pick them.'

Strange were the ways of the brothers as strange as the ways of God, The Virgin Mary and the subject of vocations. Yes, indeed, Skinny thought as the kids descended on him and fought over the succulent fruit.

SEVEN

THE DANCE

Brother Doyle had been planning his stint as principal for some time and when he took over in the last months of 1953 his first action was to increase the classes up to lower secondary school beginning in 1954. The favoured dozen, which included Skinny and his chum Tommy Cooper, were expected to pass with distinctions helped with liberal applications of the strap. He taught the class himself making a special class room in the main building from a room which had been used for storage.

The R.A.A.F. had left behind them a lot of stuff such as old, but new uniforms, one bundle of a funny coffee colour made for the use of prisoners of war. Apart from other stuff such as tins of rations, there were a few slouch hats one of which Skinny appropriated as none of the brothers seemed interested in making an inventory of what was being moved out. He loved Western pictures with his main heroes being Randolph Scott and Gary Cooper. Apart from their ability to fight and being faster on the draw than the outlaws they killed, he liked the way they fashioned and wore their hats. These had to have a plaited leather band and a thong chin strap which could be pulled up over the front to give it the shape of a tight vee.

Creating this model took some knowledge and skill. The hat had to be soaked first and then the felt rolled constantly as it dried to make it hold the desired shape. Skinny had always envied the few boys that had such hats and now that he had one he worked diligently to get it proper. When finally he had it right, he put it on and looking in the mirror he imagined he saw Billy the Kid. Now he wore it most of the time without the brothers objecting or asking where he had stolen it from. He was a big boy now and given a degree of freedom. He strode about and even got into a couple of fights just so he could fling himself about the yard or wherever it was just as Randolph Scott or Gary Cooper might do in their movies. Once one of the brothers came across him fighting, but instead of stopping them stood and watched. Skinny was fighting a Maltese boy because he looked like a Mexican. He cuffed him a couple of times then round housed him down. Skinny smiled at the brother and helped the Maltese up. 'Just playing at cowboys and Mexicans,' he told the brother who nodded and walked off. Yes, strange were the ways of the brothers.

Brother Doyle had made over the store room because his office was next to it with an adjoining door through which he could keep his students under observation. He would sit in his office doing the paperwork that the position of principal required and every now and again he would rush in to prowl about the desks, staring over the kids' shoulders in the hopes of detecting an error. If he stayed behind one of them long enough, he usually did, for his presence brought on what he was looking for.

For Skinny apart from the hat most of that last year in Clontarf was a torment. It was as if the devil was playing dice with him and he was losing every throw. It was then that he began to hate the very idea of the devil. He was evil and Skinny had been driven to reject evil by the likes of his teacher, Brother Doyle who was more like a playmate of Ole Nick than Skinny could ever be. Brother Doyle who now in spite of his many duties that teaching as well as being the administrator of a large and flourishing institution entailed decided to add more weight on his and his students' shoulders by making them learn ball room dancing. Yes, he was ready to put on dances with the girls of St. Joseph's Girls' Home.

A foreign woman volunteered to teach them and she came every Thursday to form them into couples and march them around the floor of the hall while chanting one, two, three; one two, three. She attempted to teach them the two step, the modern waltz, the foxtrot, the Gay Gordons, the progressive barn dance, etc. etc, each one of which the boys hated as much as the very idea of dancing with girls. It was too scary to contemplate. The boys for a long time had had no contact with females, except for nuns. They hadn't any idea on how to introduce ourselves and keep a conversation going. Still, there was no avoiding their fate, for what Brother Doyle wanted for his charges they got. Indeed he came every Thursday during the dance sessions to observe their progress. If he saw none, after the woman had gone, he belted them to get their minds to urge their bodies into one two three, one two three etc. etc. which continued on for the first quarter of the year and in April, he decided that their first dance would be in the month of May, the first of May to celebrate the beginning of Mary's month. It would be held at St. Joseph's.

The day, it was a Friday, dawned bright, but it was the evening that they dreaded. At four the selected boys were herded to the showers and at 4.30 they were shining their shoes and practicing walking in their new long pants. Skinny would have loved wearing his cowboy hat, but didn't dare, though he did put it on to strut in front of Tommy Cooper, who drawled: "Dude." In answer Skinny did a parody of a Gabby Hayes square dance. Five o'clock it was off to the ref. for their tea. At about half past five, just as it was getting dark and the first mosquitoes were buzzing about their ears, the lads scrambled onto the back of the big green International truck to be taken to Subiaco for their ordeal. Skinny couldn't understand why he found it such a trial. Indeed it was the first time that he was about to see all of his three sisters although he wasn't sure if they were still there. The only one he knew was Kylie and that had been so long ago that he couldn't remember her face.

The truck reached the Girls' Home just after six o'clock. The lads hopped off the back of the truck and under Brother Connolly's direction formed up and with a nun leading the way they marched into a hall which had been decorated with coloured paper cutouts. It looked tatty rather than cheery; but then perhaps this was because of their mood. They marched to one side of the hall and slumped into the chairs arranged along the wall. Skinny sat there stiffly hardly moving but darting glances up and around every now and then to see if the girls were coming. He even began to hum with the band playing a medley of tunes some if which he liked. They swung into a sort of march the signal for the girls to enter.

They trooped in self consciously, flashed looks at where the boys were then went to sit on the chairs along the opposite wall. Skinny examined them seeking for his sisters. They might be those brown skinned ones. Well, he could get to talk to them when the dancing started. He hoped the first one might be a waltz as you stayed with one girl and moved quietly.. He looked to see if Brother Connolly was arranging things, but he was nowhere in sight.

At last the Brother appeared. He went over to the band leader who announced: 'Take your places for the modern waltz.'

Brother Connolly stood at his side as the band began. He waited for the floor to fill with happy couples. The floor remained bare. Balga was on his feet, but no other boy or girl was. Connolly motioned for the music to stop and conferred with the band leader who then announced: 'Take your places for the progressive barn dance.' Balga actually moved forward and then came to a halt. He was alone, that is Brother Connolly ordered the rest of the lads to stand and marched them over to the girls. He put each one in front of a seated girl. 'Now ask your young lady for the pleasure of this dance,' he instructed them. They obeyed the girls stood, and the dance began. Skinny was happy because he had selected a brown skinned girl he hoped was Kylie.

'Lo, Kyl,' he grinned at ease with her. 'Care to trot or rot?'

'Why not, besides we've been told to enjoy ourselves. They teach you the progressive barn dance?'

Skinny nodded and they were the first out onto the floor. The music began and Skinny's feet followed the simple rhythm and he skipped about. He swirled her to Tommy Cooper and took hold of another girl. The next dance was a foxtrot and he clutched his sister all the way through. The evening went more or less like their dancing practice, though the best thing was when the music stopped for refreshments, a glass of some orange liquid and a cake. It was then that Skinny got the time to talk to Kylie to find out that his other sisters had already left. She told him she herself was leaving in a week or two to begin training as a nurse and she would be going to a country town called "Southern Cross".

'T'ey sending you t'ere 'cause you from t'e country and it'll be like home,' Skinny attempted to kid her as he might have done in the long ago past.

'Oh yeah, yeah, I know only Shilo and St. Josephs. Just those two places so a country town will be better for me, and I'll be staying in the nurses hostel so it'll be just like here.'

'Oh,' Skinny replied not knowing what else to say. The long separation had made them virtual strangers. There was this crevasse between them that he didn't know how to jump or bridge. At least Kylie made an attempt. She grinned, suddenly looking like her brother as she touched his cheek and exclaimed 'See those marks on your cheeks?'

'No,' Skinny replied, feeling female fingers stroking his cheek. He actually flushed as he enjoyed it.

'Well, they're scars from the scratches you got from me. We used to fight like cat and dog.'

'We didn't.'

'We did.'

'Did we?'

Skinny wanted to remember, but couldn't. This was the first time that a girl had touched him and he remembered nothing from their mutual past except the final farewell. They were strangers and soon they were dancing their blues away to what else but "Learning the Blues" which he thought should be renamed "Balga Boy Blues". He smiled at his lost sister, walked a few dances with some other girls that he didn't want to touch and the dance came to an end at 9-20 pm. The girls left to the same marching tune on which they had entered. The lads were collected by Brother Connolly and taken to the truck. As they wheeled through the city streets and hit the road out to Clontarf Skinny thanked the darkness for hiding his wet eyes. Kylie, the sister he had seen after a half dozen years and how instead of rushing into each other's arms, they had stood apart with the only intimacy being her fingers on his cheek. Yes, he certainly had learnt the blues. Along the years he had lost any sense of family and he doubted that he could ever regain it. Yes, Kylie was lost to him and all that existed was Clontarf and so Balga found the blues.

The tables are empty/ The dance floor deserted/ You play the same love song/ It's the tenth time you've heard it/ That's one of the clues/ You've had your first lesson in Learning the blues

EIGHT

THE SOLDIER OF CHRIST

Brother Doyle announced in the chapel one evening that confirmation was a sacrament instituted by Jesus Christ which conferred the gifts of the Holy Ghost (grace, strength, and courage) upon the recipients so that they could then be enrolled as soldiers in the one Holy Apostolic Church. He said that The Archbishop of Perth was an extremely busy man, but had kindly offered to lay his hands on and anoint with holy oil all those from the 5 and 6th grades, the Junior Certificate scholars and the working lads. 'Such a great and sacred event,' he continued, 'has never been held in this chapel before and of course we shall prepare a fitting reception for His Eminence, the Archbishop of Perth. We shall begin rehearsals this Sunday and continue until we are feet and hands perfect. I don't want any of you to disgrace me and I know that under my supervision, you won't. So now say a short prayer for the success of this great and holy event.' It was then that Skinny winked at Tommy Cooper who grinned back, though without turning his head, for most of the other brothers were sitting at the back having gathered to hear the good news.

The boys were not entirely unprepared to give the archbishop a fitting welcome. In Brother O'Doherty's time a cadet unit had been formed. Its main purpose was to give the older boys military training so that they could oppose Godless communism when the confrontation arrived as not only the brothers but the Australian government seemed to believe was imminent. Skinny as an older boy naturally was told to join the cadet unit. In their khaki uniforms and berets they practiced marching, close order drilling, how to manage the heavy 303 Lee Enfield rifles, shoulder arms, present and port arms, and how to clean and to strip the Bren light machine gun as well as learning the theory on how to set booby traps and throw grenades. They learnt all this one afternoon a week when a regular army soldier came to instruct them.

Brother Doyle slotted the cadet unit into the spectacular he was intent on making out of the Archbishop's visit and his lads becoming soldiers of Christ. He wanted to and would use them as an honour guard as they found out next Sunday afternoon when before engaging in the first of their rehearsals he had them nuggeting their boots, blancoing their webbing and garters and brassoing their brass bits. When they had finished this, he lined them up for inspection, but without their 303s which he felt were unnecessary as they would get in the way of his general inspection. Where officers had their wands, he had his strap which unconsciously in parody of such sticks, he tucked under his arm as he strode along the line. His troops quaked in their heavy army boots as he stopped in front of each cadet and if he found something not to his liking whack went the strap on the offending article. Every cadet received a whack or two or three and Doyle must have been exhausted by the time he had finished and was about to dismiss his troop when one of the brothers reminded him that the whole school had turned out for the rehearsal, so warning the cadets that next time he expected perfection, he ordered them to form into two columns and march to the front of the main building. There they waited in formation and then at his order they stepped out smartly between the civilian kids who lined both sides of the roadway. They reached the big entrance gates and halted at the command. The brothers' Ford Zephyr car, the one that had picked Skinny up a few years ago now, waited there.

Brother Doyle consulted with his brothers for some minutes and then he commanded the cadet unit to side step and let the car drive through their ranks. It was then that he remembered that they should have carried their rifles to present arms. 'Next time, will do and I want those rifles polished and gleaming,' he snapped. With the maneuver accomplished, he ordered the cadets to reform and follow behind the vehicle. They stepped out and he ordered them to halt. He had decided that it might look better if the cadets marched in front of the Zephyr. Doyle tried this to his dissatisfaction and then had the cadets come behind the car again. Still not content, he had them march on both sides of the vehicle and finally in front of it again. This he decided would do for now and dismissed them until next Sunday. The lads rushed to the cadet room to fling off their uniforms and run to the playground to play.

All were happy for the school holidays still had a few days to go and there wasn't much work to do. At least the kids thought so until that night after prayers, Basher announced he had decided that they should go in batches to spend a day working on the main building at Bindoon. Brother Keaney, the Principal there wanted it to be finished by the end of the holidays. He had called on him to help him to achieve his goal and by Christ he would do so. The first lot would go at six next morning. He read out a list and on it was Beefy.

Skinny remembered how much he hated Bindoon and wandered how he would take being forced to go back there even for one day. Skinny was also on the list but looked forward to the trip as Bindoon was about 60 miles in the country and thus they would be stopping along the way. Also Brother Keaney was the principal there and he wanted to see him. From what Dicky and Basher had said about him, he was the real life person that Spencer Tracey had played in the famous film, "Boys Town". This was shown at regular intervals in Clontarf and the boys believed that in America there existed places like Clontarf which were run by kind and gentle men, just as there were churches that had parish priests like the one in the film "The Bells of St. Mary's" as played by Bing Crosby. The next morning the group assembled where the truck was parked. Beefy was in revolt. He declared that he wouldn't go to that "horrid place."

'Well, how you goin' to get out of it,' Skinny sneered. 'Run off into t'e bushes or what?'

'This,' he replied and fell down upon the ground as if in a faint.

'What's wrong with him,' Connolly asked, rushing up and prodding the kid with his boot.

'Don't know, sir, he had the shakes and then collapsed just like t'is. We have to get him to the infirmary.'

'Well, get him there, but be quick about it. We're late already.'

They carried Beefy to the infirmary and left him in charge of the hastily summoned nun, who stared at him as if she too was in shock.

'Don't worry, Sister, he usually comes around in awhile. It's called Bindoonitis,' Skinny told her before racing back to the truck and jumping to go and do his bit for the glory of Brother Keaney.

The rehearsals for confirmation continued as did instructions in what the boys were expected to do and feel. The great occasion after the receiving of the archbishop was to include a high mass for which Skinny was chosen to be one of the six altar boys that held long candle sticks. This was a great privilege for the Archbishop himself would celebrate this mass before doing the confirming. But this was not the only thing Skinny had to do. Basher selected him to carry the ecumenical flag out in front of the cadet squad. The school didn't have one of those leather pouches in which the end of the flag pole was placed and when Tommy Cooper saw his chum strutting his stuff, he asked: 'Why does yer stomach go right in when that flag pole presses against it?'

''Cause it's pressing on a hollow that can never be filled wit' t'e grub we eat in t'is place.'

'Yeah, yeah,' he grinned, 'you just fasting till confirmation day.'

'I am too, 'cause fasting is good for t'e soul and I need some inspiration to pick me confirmation name. I can't take anot'er Tommy as I'm t'at already an' don't want to double up like a silly nong.'

'Well, why not Cassius? Basher quoted Shakespeare directly at ya yesterday. "Yon Cassius 'as a mean and 'ungry look; such men are dangerous, give 'round me fat men that sleep all nights."'

'Well, t'ere's only t'at Beefy who can be called fat and he, from what t'ey say, does a lot of bed hopping. Anyway I need a good Saint's name.'

Tommy wasn't very helpful and Skinny had to think it out himself. He wanted one that meant something, for example Francis which was his lost brother's name and if he took it he might feel better. Skinny was still hurting from meeting with his big brother. The man Frank who worked in Castledare had come to Clontarf on some errand or other and when Skinny saw the brown skinned chap talking to Brother Connolly he instantly knew that it was his brother. He rushed up to him almost laughing in delight. He was giggling like a loon when the man stared at him and Skinny saw that the eyes were similar to his. 'I'm your little brudda,' he blurted out. 'We never met before, but I know yer Frank. You look a bit like me an' I suppose t'at when I grow up we'll really look like bruddas.'

'Yeah, I s'pose we might,' the man said without a trace of warmth in his voice.

'We will; we will,' Skinny reiterated, refusing to be put off.

'Maybe, maybe, anyway nice meetin' up with you, next time when we come across each other we'll have a bit of a yarn, but now, I gotta get movin'. See you,' he said and hurried off.

'Who was that bloke, not that Abo from Castledare,' Tommy Cooper asked, coming up to him. ''E would've become a brother, but 'adn't what it takes,' he added.

'Oh he's a nice enough bloke,' Skinny replied wiping his eyes. He couldn't understand. He knew that when he had met a brother he had never ever seen, he had been leaping with joy, but now after meeting him, he felt like crying.. 'Oh hell, let's go and kick t'at ball around,' he shouted angrily at Tommy Cooper. He raced him to the centre of the field. A chum was better than a brother any day, he thought even though he knew it wasn't.

That was Skinny's first and only meeting with his elder brother. He didn't know what to make of him. Still, he was the only brother Skinny had and he thought that if he took Francis as his confirmation name, next time they met things might be different. There were quite a few saints with the name of Francis. Two of them were prominent: St Francis of Assisi and St. Francis Xavier, the missionary. Skinny felt attracted to the latter because he was a Jesuit a member of the same order that ran their retreats. In them they were often given missionary magazines such as The Far East to read in the hopes that they would find them edifying. In one of these magazines he had read the sentence: their skins may be black, but their souls can be made white. These words depressed him for a while, but he went to confession and made his soul white and this cheered him. He remembered this now and it decided him on St. Francis Xavier. This saint had brought so many people to Christ that when he died his right arm remained free of corruption.

Having confessed any and all his sins of commission and omission and having selected Francis as his confirmation name Skinny began enjoying the rehearsals. He even felt privileged to be serving in the high mass and in his state of elation he sailed through his lessons without a single mistake. Brother Doyle must have wondered what had happened to him. He might even have put it down to the coming sacrament, which was to be given on the third Saturday in August as the Archbishop had that day free. This redoubled Skinny's happiness as it was the day before his sixteenth birthday.

At last the day dawned and the lads weren't given breakfast as all of them had to take communion later on and thus had to fast. With the rest of the cadets, Skinny went and dressed in his khaki uniform making sure that everything was spick and span and shining bright. He put on his beret at the correct regulation angle, picked up his freshly polished rifle and went out into the quadrangle where Connolly deputizing for the over-busy Doyle checked the platoon over. Satisfied, he marched them to the front of the building and down to the side of the gates where they stood at ease waiting for the Archbishop's car. The rest of the boys in their Sunday best stretched out on both sides of the carriage way.

Brother Doyle had been anxious to make an impression so they were early or perhaps the archbishop was late. The time dragged and discipline fell. The cadets whispered to each other how hungry they were and how they hoped that the late dinner feast would fill their bellies. Skinny almost drooled over imaginary heaped plates of cakes and chicken legs.

'You'll see, you'll see,' whispered Tommy Cooper, 'lots and lots of tucker.'

'Cakes and chook with roasted spuds,' Skinny mouthed, just as a black car swerved into their driveway and stopped. The cadet platoon sprang up and formed ranks. With Skinny at the head, they marched around the car and stopped in front of it. Skinny felt the butt of the flag pole sticking into his empty belly so that he almost puked. A big kid all of seventeen in charge of the platoon ordered them to present arms, then shoulder arms. The cadets formed a column on both sides of the car and with Skinny right in front of the vehicle marched up the driveway and about the roundabout to halt in front of the building. They presented arms and Skinny dipped the flag as the old purple-gowned figure pulled himself out of the car. A group of brothers came to him. Now their part over the cadets rushed off to put on their school uniforms.

Skinny had to speed up his rushing to reach the sacristy in time to put on his red gown and white surplice. The two main altar boys wore black gowns. The archbishop entered and dressed quickly aided by the chaplain. Now the boys lit their candles and escorted him out into the chapel, genuflected in front of the altar and knelt just in front of the communion railing as the Archbishop began celebrating mass. Naturally Clontarf had a choir and they sang the responses from the back of the chapel so the altar boys with the long candles could relax and feel their hunger. The mass dragged on more than the normal low one, but eventually they received the Lord on their tongues. He didn't fill their bellies and then the confirmation ceremony began.

Skinny had thought that being pure in an absolute state of grace and officiating at the high mass celebrated by the Archbishop himself would result in a doubling of his elation; but instead the pain in kneeling on a polished wooden floor made him fidgety. He endured his pain as he watched the old man, all dolled up in his fancy robes and mitre, come to anoint him with the holy oil. At his touch he waited for a flash of lighting to mark the event or that once awaited vocation event to strike him. Neither lighting nor conviction and disappointed he let the rest of the ceremony roll over him watching with disinterested eyes as the Archbishop on rickety legs ascended the pulpit to give them an intimate talk rather than a sermon in which he stressed that now as they had truly entered the church they were never to turn apostate and forsake their holy mother. He hesitated letting that sink in and then added that even if they did She would always be there waiting to receive the prodigal son back and as always when these religious men entered into this theme, he brought in the example of Voltaire who after he had turned totally against not only the church, but God himself begged forgiveness when he lay dying.

And so it went on and Skinny's stomach growled as he wondered if their dinner would be early as well it might seeing that the brothers and the Archbishop were fasting too. Of course he wouldn't eat with them, but some of the brothers would share their holy feast and they too must be dreaming of the goodies. Skinny sighed and smiled when at last the Archbishop finished his little talk and the choir broke into a joyous hymn of thanksgiving. Decorously the altar boys slowly left the chancel, but once in the sacristy they and Skinny ripped off their gowns, flung them on hangers and charged off to see if dinner was ready. It wasn't and the lads had to wait an hour before queuing up for chicken and roast spuds. This was not all. At the tables which had been reserved for the new Soldiers of Christ there were plates of cakes and bottles of soda pop which were not to be touched until they finished their main meal. The chicken was tasty, but the spuds were hard as rocks. Skinny tossed them under the table. Today was such an important day that he wouldn't be punished for such a slight thing. With his plate empty, the bones had followed the potatoes, he got stuck into the cakes and soda pop. The cakes were a bit stale and the pop warm, but no matter. Wolfing them down, Skinny could even imagine and believe that he and his companions really had had an experience that would affect them all their lives.

'It was great, wasn't it,' Skinny said to Tommy Cooper using his normal voice as it was a feast and a day of rejoicing.

'Yeah, 'appyiness to ya too, that bit of cake 'ad a fly in it, ya know. Anyway only 'ope that Basher treats us as good Catholics from now on. We all sons of one mother now, ya know.'

Whatever hopes the boys might have entertained that they had entered a different and more mature part of their lives was quickly dispelled by Basher and the other brothers who treated them just as roughly and sardonically as they always had. The big event of their confirmation quickly fell into the past as it was replaced by another event that meant much more to the brothers than to the kids. One evening after prayers a somber Doyle bobbed his balding grey head that was shaped like a soccer ball and Skinny saw that he was growing old as in a husky voice he informed them that the great Brother Keaney had passed away He said that they would say a rosary for the repose of his soul and tomorrow there would be a special requiem mass for him. With sad eyes he stared around at the boys to see what effect the death of this man had had on them. Their faces remained resolutely blank as he began the rosary. None of the boys cared about the death of the old bloke except those that had transferred from Bindoon to Clontarf and if Beefy was an example they were glad to see the last of him. Skinny had glanced his way when Doyle told them and caught the grin that flashed over his dial before he could clamp down his lips and blank his face.

The brothers took their charges to Bindoon so that all might pay their last respects to the Orphans' Friend. Skinny stared down at the waxen face of the old man. He lay there in state all black in his gown; all white in his collar, his hands, his hair and his face. Skinny wondered if he should say a prayer. Tommy Cooper was in front of him and behind was Beefy. Skinny heard him hawking deep within his throat and looked behind just as he let go a big greenie that splattered across the face of the corpse. He whispered fiercely: 'I know that you rot in hell you old coot!' Skinny was appalled and pushed Tommy Cooper aside so that he could get away from what he considered a sacrilege.

They left the big main building completed with so much of their sweat and found a spot under a tree. Skinny sat down and shook. He really expected that God would intervene to strike Beefy down for desecrating the body of a bloke that some of the brothers especially Doyle and O'Doherty expected to be made into a saint and within their very lifetimes at that; but nothing happened. Beefy sat down with them and wasn't even called to account. The incident passed away and the Clontarf boys re-embarked on their truck .Skinny never visited Bindoon again. Also this was Beefy's last act, for a couple of weeks later he went off to a job in the town of Wagin none the worse for his sacrilege.

Skinny's last full year in Clontarf was almost over. The end of November came and he sat for the Junior Examination. Some of his courses such as wood and metal working were judged by project; but the rest were test papers of which a certain number of questions had to be answered. When the examination was over, the papers were sealed in envelopes and sent to the examination board. He had no problem with any of the questions and sailed though. Skinny knew that he had topped the class because Brother Doyle after the examination went through the papers question by question, checking to see if each boy had got them right. After working each question out, he asked them if they had answered it correctly or not. The boys replied if they had or had not as the case might be. As Skinny had done everything correctly, he said yes to those questions he had answered and thus escaped the punishment meted out to his classmates. The strap came down hard on them for each wrong answer. It was then that Skinny decided that he hated the short pudgy Irishman with the vicious temper and snarly face. Before he had respected as well as feared him now he began to despise him. Indeed, Skinny wondered how he might get back at him.

He doted on this and was thinking about it one Saturday film night. It was an old gangster film, Public Enemy and as usual heavily edited to remove any trace of love such as a kiss or any naked part of a. woman's body. The brothers liked this film because it depicted a Catholic boy, played by Jimmy Cagney, who went from rags to riches by snarling his way up killing anyone that stood in his way, before he ended by being shot by the police. It was a simple enough story, but Skinny had glimpsed in the film a method to get into a locked room. He decided to try it on the door of Basher's office.

One afternoon when everyone was down on the playground he snuck into the deserted classroom and went to the connecting door. Skinny smiled as he saw that the lock was an old one and that the key was in it. He slid a big sheet of paper under the door angling it so that a lot of it was under the lock. He pushed a pen against the end of the key and exerted pressure. It moved and fell onto the paper. He carefully pulled the sheet out and the key came with it. How easy it had been and he thanked the film makers as he unlocked the door and entered the forbidden space.

He sat in Basher's chair smiling and opened the desk drawers staring at papers and money, and then got up to go to a big cabinet. He opened a shallow drawer and saw a large wrist watch. The last time he had seen it had been on Basher's wrist. He picked it up, watched the second hand traverse the dial then put it back and closed the drawer. Now Skinny pushed the key back into the lock, but there was no way he could lock the door and thus leave no evidence of his intrusion. The only thing he could do was to leave the door unlocked hoping that Basher would think that he had forgotten to lock it. He did this and left. There were no repercussions Skinny had found that entering into Basher's office had given him a bigger thrill than raiding the orchard. He waited for another opportunity to break into the forbidden space.

With the Junior Examination out of the way Basher Doyle at last congratulated them all for passing. He said that his class were a cut above most of the other boys that left school after the sixth grade and because of this, they would get better jobs and become clerks or Public Servants. He further stated that when they had settled in it was and would be their duty to not only remain Catholics, but take an active interest in church affairs and what better way to do this than to join laymen's associations such as the Knights of the Southern Cross. Skinny might stifle a yawn as he went on and on; but he was frightened about leaving Clontarf. Why he didn't even know what he wanted to be? A cowboy was out of the question and, well, he stopped thinking, he knew that something would be found for him. This last thought comforted him. He wasn't used to making up his mind on anything. The brothers had done it all for him and he hoped that they would continue to do so until the very end and perhaps outside some else would take over.

NINE

CAST(E) ADRIFT

Skinny or rather Balga had reached the end of his schooling and had to enter the wide world. The prospect terrified him. He didn't know how he could handle living alone and making his way. Clontarf had become his home. He needed to be surrounded by walls with someone in command. The brothers knew what was best for him and when they ordered he obeyed. In exchange for a little work he was fed and even got special food on feast days. The idea of a vocation still hung in his mind; but it had to be real and not counterfeit. Perhaps while he waited for it to come he could continue his schooling. The Christian Brothers' Aquinas College was almost next door just a walk through the back paddocks and with his results he should be able to study on. With this in mind Skinny went to the good Brother Walsh who was ever ready to listen to boys and give advice. He was kind and considerate and listened to Skinny with a frown on his fair face. He advised him to see Brother Doyle..

'Yes, he'll agree,' Brother Walsh declared. 'It will reflect well on our academic standards which Brother Doyle is intent on elevating to the highest levels. Yes, see him as soon as possible as the school year will start in a few weeks.'

Talking to Basher was more than Skinny was capable of. How could he talk to that man from whom he had never received a kind word and indeed had never engaged in any sort of meaningful conversation? He spoke and commanded; Skinny listened and obeyed. To see if he might find courage he decided to break into Basher's office once again, sit in his chair and wait for inspiration; but when he went to the door there was no key in the lock. He was turning away in disappointment when the door opened and there stood Basher wearing glasses that glinted malignity at him.

'What are you doing here,' he demanded.

'I-I-I just came here to see you 'bout my future, what I should do,' Skinny blurted. Well, he had done it and now waited to see if the man might take up the burning issue of his future. He would or he wouldn't – whatever!

'What you should do? What, you thinking things over? Well, don't! You'll soon be in a job in an office and for that you'll have us to thank. Don't think, just don't let me down. Be a good Catholic and have faith. Remember God has given you a Guardian Angel who will aid you if you keep from sin. Now seeing that you are loafing about, I'll put you on milking duties, up early morning at four to get the cows in and again the same thing in the afternoon. That should keep you busy enough, though if I catch you hanging about here again we'll see what else we can give you to keep you occupied. So get going and don't come back in here again. It is no longer your class room.'

So much for Walsh's advice and so much for even thinking to approach Basher! Him and his guardian angels! When did his angel ever get in touch with him and when did he or it or whatever stop them from belting him? Thus thought Skinny.

A few days after he had seen Doyle he was dawdling over a job when a boy pelted past him. He raced after him, drew level and panted: 'Hey, what's t'e hurry.'

The boy stopped, took a couple of deep breaths and expelled the last in a gush of words: 'The truck, on the road through the pine plantations.

It tipped over. Kids are lying everywhere hurt. Get help!' And he was off again running so fast that he seemed to skim the ground.

Skinny looked after him then ran off in the direction the kid had come from. He sped around into the turnoff leading through the pines. He felt that he must've have done the next mile in four minutes, for it seemed that he was quicker than the pommy racer Roger Bannister. He stopped at the scene of desolation and isolation. The big International truck had run off the road, hit the sand and tipped onto its side. It didn't look much of an accident, but it had carried a load of logs and when the truck tipped these had rolled over and onto the dozen or so boys that had been perched on them. Many had been squashed while a lucky few sat stunned in shock. The brother that had been driving was in the same state. Other brothers and boys arrived and they set about freeing the poor kids. They heaved and shifted logs to show crushed bodies and limbs. Most of the really hurt boys were luckily unconscious, but the few that weren't moaned and some yelped like puppy dogs. It was so pitiful that Skinny began to feel shaky. Now an ambulance raced up followed by the Ford Zephyr from which Basher Doyle jumped out to take charge. Skinny helped to get the worst cases into the ambulance. It raced off and another two came to be loaded up. Blood was pooled about and over the logs. He helped get the truck back onto the road and reload the logs.

This awful accident made Skinny wary of being in Clontarf. He decided to make a good impression in his next interview this one for a mechanic and not for an office worker. His nerve failed when he reached the garage. Instead of going in directly and asking for the boss, he hung around like a black shadow. It was only after an hour that he summoned up the courage to go and ask for the boss. The man came out wearing greasy overalls and wiping his oily hands on a rag. He examined the youth with oily light blue eyes then asked him what he wanted. 'A j-j-job,' Skinny stuttered. The man looked him up and down then said: 'I don't think you'd be suitable for it. You don't look the hard working type.'

Balga shrugged and retorted: 'I can work along with the best of them.'

He turned to go and the bloke stared after him and said: 'Hey, wait, you can start on Monday on the dot at nine, okay.'

'But,' he began.

'No buts, Brother Doyle can see to the details.'

Balga felt a rush of joy. The great big world flowed about him – and he grinned, things happened to him just as they always happened and all that he had to do was give them a nudge. It was the way of, the way of life. He leapt into the air as if to catch a football and ran off along the street. He felt free at last!

BOOK TWO

*BALGA'S BODGIE
TOWN BLUES*

CONTENTS

TEN

FREEDOM, OH FREEDOM

Balga gunned the FJ Holden along the river road. He suddenly flung on the handbrake. The light sedan twisted almost about a corner, but not quite. It shuddered and went skidding across the esplanade to come to a halt at the ferry crossing to North Perth. Balga scrubbed one thin brown hand through his short bristly hair. The engine had stalled. He pressed the starter. The engine caught and he eased the car back onto the road and swiftly changing gears charged up towards the city. He swung around a corner and into a car repair garage. He stopped and got out. It was still early in the morning, about seven, but he saw that the workshop was open. The boss was there. The man came out at a run.

'What the heck, we have to fix 'em, not wreck 'em. Look at the dirt on it. How many times have I told you to take it easy if you have to drive 'em. You haven't even got a license. Keep off the roads.'

'Well, t'ere was a sort of knock in t'e transmission and I had to check it out,' Balga said screwing up his eyes and looking down at his hands.

'Well, clean it down, boy. Mr. Wills is coming for his vehicle at nine. Don't do it again, No license, no drive,' the man commanded and went back into the workshop.

'Yes, boss,' Balga called to his back then got onto cleaning the car. He was beginning to dislike his job; though it did give him the sense of security which he felt he needed as much as the five pounds a week it paid.

The lad had been tossed out of his orphanage home of Clontarf just a few months ago. He had felt like some sort of refugee and had hardly any time to say goodbye to his mates. Well, boy, was he glad to be out of that place. Now he had the freedom to do what he wanted; but what did he want? Surely not working from 8:30 am to 5:30 day after day with only Sunday off! What could he do on that day when everything was shut up? He wanted to explore the city; he wanted to find some mates; he ached for some sort of life he could enjoy. Balga really needed a new place to stay. He hated his present accommodation; the people that owned it and the bloke he shared his room with. As he dried the sedan, the lad thought of the first day out when he had come to the house and knocked on the door. A foreign-looking woman, black-haired and dark-eyed like a Maltese, came to the door to stare suspiciously at him: 'What you want!' she demanded.

'I was sent here by the Catholic Welfare,' he had replied not liking the woman at all. Nervously, his hand had lifted to scrub at his wire hair.

'Ah, yes, already they pay your first week, after that you pay me two pound ten, you understand and on dot, like they say.'

His hand fell away as he nodded. There was no need for a smile or even a scowl for that matter.

'You come on in now,' and she stepped away from the door.

He walked down a short passageway and was at the back kitchen before she called.

'You come on back here now.'

He did and she was holding a door open to a front room. Balga saw two beds and a wardrobe, a small table and nothing else.

'You share with 'nother boy,' she informed him.

He continued to stare in silence then followed the woman to the back of the house to the bathroom opposite the kitchen in which he would eat his meals: breakfast at 7-30 am, dinner at 6-30pm and on Sunday lunch at 12-30. A routine just like Clontarf's and he nodded hoping that the food would be a bit better. The woman left him in his room where he sat for awhile before wandering out into the passage way. As he opened the front door the woman appeared to hold out a key. Balga noticed she passed him the key in such a way that their hands didn't touch. Outside, he walked to the end of the street. He stood there and looked both ways. There was a milk bar along a bit. He went towards it. Next to it was a news agent shop. Balga opened the door and heard a bell tinkle. A man came from the back of the shop to stare at him. The boy ignored him turning to a rack of books with yellow backs and covers featuring women in various states of undress and shock. He picked a book by Carter Brown, another by Larry Kent featuring a private detective named Larry Kent and lastly something called "The Saint Strikes Back" by Leslie Charteris. They cost him only 7/6 so he still had over four out of the five pounds they had given him to start his life. He counted his change to find it two bob short. He looked at the bloke, who opened his till and snapped the coin down on the counter. Balga stared at it for a full minute before picking it up. He shrugged and ran his hand through his bristly hair; shrugged again and returned to the house and the room which was half his. He lay on one of the beds and opened the Carter Brown. It featured a wise cracking detective and he lapped up his adventure as well as the descriptions of molls as women were called. He enjoyed the world he found there. The story was easy to read. Balga finished it in an hour or two then went through it again picking out and learning some of the wisecracks to use when and if the opportunity arose. He even got off the bed to begin practicing them in the mirror on the wardrobe door, but his dark face spotted with acne made him hesitate until he hit on the right way to say a wisecrack. You had to scowl, or grin lopsidedly while letting the words ooze slowly out. 'Well, well, well, do me again, man oh man,' he whispered his hand coming up and opening slowly then clenching into a fist. Yeah that was the way; but how to get to using it and where?

Balga opened the wardrobe to find space for his few clothes. They were enough for a while. He checked the other bloke's clothes. He saw a shirt that he admired and loathed at the same time. This was a western shirt of the Roy Rogers and Gene Autry style. It was of a shining blue silk-like material with a green fringe. Balga stared at it and suddenly put it on. He stared at myself in the mirror and shuddered. He was about to take it off, when the door opened and a very dark Aborigine entered.

'Hello,' Balga said sticking out his hand, 't'ey used to call me Skinny and I suppose t'at t'at'll have to do for t'e time being.'

To this the bloke replied "Jack Mirritj" or some such name.

Being in the wrong, Balga pulled off the shirt and replaced it in the wardrobe. 'Just trying it on; you know tying one on, ha-ha,' he said attempting a wise crack.

Jack didn't reply and so Balga picked up another of his books and stretching out on the bed began reading. It kept him busy until tea. The woman called it dinner. It consisted of a couple of chops, mashed potatoes and boiled carrots which he devoured with relish. 'Things indeed were getting better already,' he thought, feeling sorry that he had gotten off on the wrong foot with Jack and wandering how he might make things right. He glanced at the bloke morosely eating next to him. He spoke to him. The youth chomped away like a chump ignoring what he was saying. Balga had to admit his words had no listening value at all. 'To talk you need to walk the walk, he said then smiled finding that good. 'How'd yuh like t'at, man,' he said to Jack who replied out of the corner of his mouth: 'You walk, the walk, you talk the talk, so shut up while I eat t'e eats.'

'Hey t'at's how you do it,' Balga grinned. 'My mind may be private, but my mout' isn't.'

Good, he was getting into the language of that pulp fiction. Why, he was even settling into feeling like a wise-cracking Private Eye rather than the scrawny pimply adolescent he might see in the mirror. Pudding was plunked in front of his grin. It was some sort of sticky concoction which he shoveled in and gulped down. With a wave of his arm at Jack and a flashing grin he left for his room, strode in flicked up his towel and shuffled to the bathroom where he washed up using some scraps of soap he found. He peed, buttoned up and strode back to his room, flung down the towel then himself on the bed and picked up his third book, "The Saint Strikes Back". It looked good and had a skinny sticklike man figure with a halo on the cover. He fell into the story. Wisecracking was okay in its place, but being a suave, cool-talking gentleman was what he might aspire to be when he got older. Whatever and then The Saint was a Pommy and he didn't go for them all that much.

Still, the yarn was too good to eat in one sitting. After the first few chapters he rested to fall asleep. He dreamt that he was a different kid, indeed a bloke only to awake to find that he was the same old Skinny, but one with a whole weekend to fill before he began his job. Balga lay there for too long a while and got up to find that breakfast was over. He shrugged at the news. He needed at least a clock and decided to go to the city and see if he could buy one. Buses ran along the road at the end of the street. There was a stop outside the news agent. He sat on a bench and waited and waited. No bus! Finally he went into the shop to enquire. The bloke remembered him from yesterday and scowled before smiling. He relished telling the dark kid that as it was Saturday the buses ran only every two hours. 'If I was you,' he said, 'I would walk down this road until it hits the river. There's a quay there and ferries come and go pretty regularly as it's a weekend and parents take their kids to the zoo.' Balga nodded and bought another Saint Adventure Story before setting out.

'I have to learn the streets and how to get about,' Balga thought. He reached a high fence which he guessed from the sounds of animals coming from behind was the zoo. When at Clontarf Boys' Town he had come there three times in three different years with a mob of kids. On impulse he continued along the wall until he reached the gate. He bought a ticket, it was only half a crown, and went inside. Balga wandered about feeling as lonely as a private eye on a stakeout. He examined a chimpanzee lonely as a crook in a prison cell. It gave him the willys. He almost ran out of the place. 'Rock me on the waters,' he sang softly as he reached the ferry.

The city beckoned him with life. He grinned as he got off the boat. He strolled up towards the city centre, hit St. George's Terrace and went up Barrack Street. 'What am I going to do; what am I going to do,' drummed in his head.

The lad turned into the botanic gardens and stopped in front of a big old blackboy tree growing all alone. 'Well, how are you going, mate,' he said. The grass tree had had its top cut back flat and his hand went to his own spiky hair. 'I think, I'll get a haircut just like yours,' he said to the tree and walked on towards Hay Street.

Saturday afternoon. All the shops were shut. What to do? Balga continued walking along Barrack Street and came to the Liberty Theatre which was featuring a gangster film called The Big Sleep. He stared at the stills pasted up. It was black and white and old; but looked okay. It was. Balga was introduced to the writer Raymond Chandler and his private eye, Phillip Marlowe played by a bloke named Humphrey Bogart who was not at all flash, but had a lip on him. Wisecracks sounded from the screen. Balga was hooked. He strutted out, his finger pinching at his ear lobe in the Bogart style.

He got home in time for dinner and then Sunday the landlady awoke the lads for mass. Balga went along as he was too sleepy from reading most of the night to protest. He dozed during mass.

'Hey, Jack, I see t'at you are a Cat'olick.' he said after church still seeking to make amends for trying on the bloke's shirt.

'Yeah, I'm from Beagle Bay up Broome way. It's a mission run by the Benedictine monks.'

'Oh, did t'ey make ya sweep a lot' Balga exclaimed, attempting a wisecrack and then asked seriously, 'and do t'ey carry straps like t'ose Christmas Bruders?'

'Of course not,' the Aboriginal youth exclaimed. He quickened his steps so that he walked in front of Balga.

ELEVEN

MAKING UP HIS FACE

It was about eleven o'clock in the morning, mid October, with the sun not shining and a look of hard wet rain in the clearness of the foothills. I was wearing my powder-blue suit, with dark blue shirt, tie and display handkerchief, black brogues, black wool socks with dark blue clocks on them. I was neat, clean, shaved, and sober, and I didn't care who knew it. (Raymond Chandler)

'You better pull your socks up, mate. You can do the job alright, but you ain't one for taking orders are you?'

'I do my best,' Balga retorted, his fingers tugging at his eye lobe and leaving a smudge of oil. That's what he hated about the job. The oil on his hands, in his hair, sometimes on his face and the scrubbing it took to get it off, though the smell remained.

'Yeah, I do my job,' the youth repeated then added. 'Mind if I take my lunch break now.'

'Okay, back in half an hour.'

'Yeah, boss.'

One good thing about Perth was that it was small. Of course if the boss had been out, Balga would have borrowed a car, but with him there scowling it was no go. Balga scrubbed the oil off his fingers then slipped out of his greasy overalls and raced away from the boss and his whining.

He had little time or money for lunch. His books ate up his ready cash and he was buying some clothes to get away from the orphanage institutional look. He wanted to deck himself out like Phillip Marlowe. Yep and how did one become a Private Eye?

The dark youth Balga came along the western end of Hay Street munching on a bread roll. Hunger had caught up with him. He had been this way before, and further up was Subiaco and St. Joseph' Home for Girls where his sisters had been placed and who knows where they were now. Balga stopped. His eye caught and clung to a group of terrace houses. In a window, there was a sign: "room for rent". Pinching his right eye lobe, he stared at it, made up his mind and let his legs walk to the door and his forefinger press the door bell. A heavily built dark-eyed and dark-haired woman opened the door and asked him what I wanted. 'I've come about the room,' he said. 'One pound ten a week,' she replied. 'Nice, quite roomy and the linen's changed once a week' She ushered him up the stairs and the room was big. Balga wanted it, but waited to find out what else she might say, one of the tricks he had picked up from the orphanage 'There's a share kitchen below where you can do your cooking. Gas meter takes coins and it's the same with the bathroom if you want to have hot water.' She showed him the bathroom and he stared at the gas meter and the hot water geyser. 'Pennies?' he asked. 'Pennies, sixpences, shillings and two bob pieces,' she told him. 'You can work out how much water you need, otherwise the next one that uses it will get the benefit of your coin. You are working,' she asked, eying the youth suspiciously. 'Yeah, and gosh I'm late, I'll get back to you, off and away now,' he exclaimed and flashed off. He wanted that room.

There was no long goodbye and at lunchtime, next day, lugging his suitcase Balga made his way to the rooming house. He paid a week's rent to the woman who called herself Mrs. Simpson. She was chatty and as a wouldbe private eye Balga listened and learnt. She told him that she looked after the place for an old dear and hoped that he was the quiet type. Balga showed her his books then went to his room. She came with a front door key and one for the room. Balga flashed a happy grin. He had found his own place.

That evening he lay on his bed in his new room smiling letting the traffic sounds of Hay Street wash over him as he read words of Chandler. The writer spoke directly to him. In everything that can be called art there is a quality of redemption. It may be pure tragedy, if it is high tragedy, and it may be pity and irony, and it may be the raucous laughter of the strong man. But down these mean streets a man must go who is not himself mean, who is neither tarnished nor afraid. The detective in this kind of story must be such a man. He is the hero, he is everything. He must be a complete man and a common man and yet an unusual man. He must be, to use a rather weathered phrase, a man of honor, by instinct, by inevitability, without thought of it, and certainly without saying it.

'Wow,' Balga thought shutting the book on these words. His belly was growling at him. He got up deciding to go out to get some tucker. He went downstairs and a smell of cooking drew him into the kitchen. Mrs. Simpson stirred a pot from which came a delicious smell. 'You've just moved in and surely you can't have bought anything as yet. Eat with us. Mrs. Freeman won't mind. The old dear loves company. Precious little she gets of it.'

The old biddy was as gray and white as that Brother Crowley in Clontarf had been. There was one difference. She was kind whereas the man hadn't been. 'Too busy tending his burial plot,' Balga thought as he spooned down the stew.

He was in luck Mrs. Simpson decided to teach him cooking fussing over him as well as her pots and pans. She declared: 'You're a bachelor and have to fend for yourself until you find some young lady to look after you.' Balga listened but never cooked a thing. He mightn't have found a young lady to take care of him, but a middle-aged woman who fed him in exchange for keeping the old dear company sometimes. This wasn't a chore in itself. He just sat with her and let her babble on while he thought of the latest detective story he had read.

One day at work Balga glanced at a paper on the desk of his boss. He saw an advertisement for the annual Clontarf concert with a special bus to take people there. Instantly he decided to go and take a gander at his old home. That night he asked Mrs. Freeman if she would like to go with him.

Both women found this idea delightful and when the evening came, it was a Friday night, Mrs. Simpson bustled about the old dear. She got her looking nice as only an old lady with property can be. Then to top it off, she poured her a large glass of sherry to keep her warm for the evening, though it was warm enough.

Balga felt important squiring an old granny to what he felt was his home. He made a show of introducing her to Brother Walsh. The brother smiled politely before asking if they had paid. He said 'of course,' though he hadn't. This after all was his home. Balga settled Mrs. Freeman into a chair. He made sure she was comfortable and then went off backstage. All the bustle and preparation went on around him. He was out of it. Just an old boy! Nevermore would he be part of a Clontarf concert. Sadly, he remembered the old days when he had an act to perform. Now ... and he went back to the old dear and sat next to her just a spectator. A part of his life was over and he could have cried.

TWELVE

THE BODGIE

Bodgies And Widgies Stage
Their First Jazz "Jamboree"
By A STAFF CORRESPONDENT
T'HE Sydney Town Hall last night was the scene of the largest gathering of
"bodgies" and "widgies" yet assembled in Sydney.
(Bodgies are youths who wear long hair and American-style clothes. Widgies are
their female associates. They are devotees of jazz music.)
The occasion was a jazz concert billed as "The Bodgie and Widgie Jambo-
ree," and was the first function of the newly formed Bodgie and Widgie Associa-
tion of Australia.
A fairly large proportion of the audience of 2,000 appeared to consist of authen-
tic bodgies and widgies, wearing the distinctive clothing of the cult.
Many of the males were in long, loosely cut coats, without lapels, and trousers
tight at the ankles. Large numbers of the girls wore blouses, some of them off-the-
shoulder, and tightly fitting skirts.
A number of the young people present, however, were in non-bodgie or unwidgie
garments, while some seemed to be borderline cases.
A few parents were there with bodgie or widgie sons and daughters.
The programme consisted mainly of dance music. There was loud applause when
a singer named Edwin Duff, a popular figure among the cult members, embraced
the microphone stand in amorous attitudes while he sang.

*Behind the orchestra was an object draped in black, carrying a
placard "The Thing."*
*In charge of the proceedings was Mr W McColl, who runs a recorded music
session for a radio station and is the director of the Bodgie and Widgie Association of
Australia Between items he reminded the audience that entry forms for the association could be obtained in the foyer.*

Balga checked the date of the old Sydney Newspaper. It was from
1951 and now it was 1955 and not much was happening in his life at all.
He had tried to look like Phillip Marlowe but the clothes he felt weren't
all that stylish, not like this"Bodgie" clothing at all. But where could he
get such stuff?

He had been reading the paper in the city library. This was one of the
few places opened on a Sunday. He left to prowl the deserted city, went
through and up to King's Park where there was a bit of life. White faces
cast suspicious glances at him. He took refuge in the wild part and stood
confronting his plant mate, a tall old Black Boy. He smiled and thought at
him: 'My life, you know, is continuing on a track t'rough the Great Sandy
Desert and I ain't got no particular place to reach. T'ere's a desert wind
ablowing and I'm edging into edging into manhood without friends and a
social life except talking to the two old women where I kip. T'ey give me
tucker, but I need somet'ing else Well, work fills my week days, but I hate
t'at boss and one day, I know, I'll just get up and leave. Maybe I need the
country, get out with you lot and let the sun bake me dry. No feeling, no
feelings at all.' He brightened up feeling better for the chat and suddenly
knew his life was about to change. He saluted the Black Boy. 'You Balga,'
he said, 'you ain't no black boy, you a big warrior so send me some, well,
some action.'

Back into the empty city streets. He moved putting one foot carefully
in front of him and then he saw him, his first bodgie and he was with not
one but two Widgies.

Balga took a long gander at the young bloke, not caring if he knew it or not. Yes, this was a real Bodgie.

There was the American style draped coat. A long lime green sports coat with heavily padded shoulders over a black shirt with a white horizontally black striped narrow tie. The single button coat was finger tip length and undone so that Balga could see the trousers pleated at the top and decorated by a white leather belt threaded through tunnel loops. A long chain was fastened to the right front tunnel belt loop and descended in a glittering arc before entering the slanted hip pocket. His examination took about five minutes. The bloke had stopped. Now he twisted his lips and snarled. Balga had had his share of fights in the orphanage and wasn't scared.. The kid was a head shorter and a bit fat. He had meat on his bones and that meant he would be a bit slow. So Balga stared boldly into his round and pink face and then suddenly winked and grinned while his brown eyes locked with to the blue eyes. He waited daring him to make his move. This kid with his long blonde hair slick with oil and styled so that a curl hung over the middle of his forehead couldn't take him.

'Well, well,' Balga exclaimed cheekily, 'I remember you from somewhere. You Phillip Morris?'

'Ain't a cigarette?' the kid retorted. He undid his wrist watch, handed it to one of the two girls and then took off his sports coat. He carefully folded it over the arm of the second widgie..

He cracked his knuckles. He might have been fattish and white and clad all in black, but he was very self possessed. . Balga wanted to know him, not fight him; but he had to play the show through. He boldly stared at the widgies. Perth didn't have such molls as these? They were like the sexy girls not of Raymond Chandler, but Carter Brown. He liked them. He wanted them. Their hostile blank faces cast him off, but he wanted them. Their bloke was waiting for him to make his move; but the dolls held him spell bound. Both had short hair, the smaller and cuter one dark and the other ash blonde. They had smeared their mouths with vivid red lipstick and rouged their cheeks with some pink stuff. The small one wore a mid calf length tight skirt and a long sweater while the blond was wearing what he knew from his reading to be pedal pushers, that is quite tight trousers that ended mid calf. These were pink and went with a soft pink sweater that reached mid thigh. Both wore slipper type shoes and short socks, and both were gorgeous.

'Don't ya t'ink t'at it's a bit too warm for t'ose sweaters,' Balga drawled in his best Private Eye voice at the widgies then snarled his next words at the bloke: 'Same for yer coat too. No wonder ya took it off. Last time I saw t'at sort of gear, it was on kids from England. You lot must be pommies too.'

'Ever hear of Melbourne,' the bloke snarled back.

'Nah, only Sydney…'

'I'm from there and I have a hundred and eight that'll back me up.'

'What'd ya mean?' Balga asked, mystified at his number. Well, whatever, he wasn't going to back down. He began enjoying the confrontation. He could do him. Hadn't he almost made it to the Western Australian School Boy Boxing Championships?

'You heard of the Saints?' the bloke said and Balga knew that he wasn't ready to scrap. The prelims were over and now he wanted to gas and skite.

'Heard about the Saint?! Fancy dresser, fancy talker and you know he carries something like this,' Balga retorted and flashed the stiletto blade he had stuck in his sock a direct copy from his hero.

'It takes more than a shiv to scare me,' the bodgie sneered

'Not trying to, just showing you t'at I'm like t'at Saint bloke. He has one of t'ese in his sock too. T'at t'e fellow you talking about, ain't you?'

'You know this,' the bloke retorted, pushing up the sleeve of shirt to show a tattoo. Balga flashed on it and saw the sticklike figure he knew from Leslie Charteris.

'Too right I know t'at,' he retorted. 'You t'ink I'm dumb or somet'ing.'

'Well, maybe, for sure you ain't a saint. You look and dress real square. Are you being inconspicuous, like hiding out from the cops? You're no cool cat, for no cool cat dresses like that. My God, man, I can't fight a yokel like you,' he sneered, 'I've got standards to maintain.'

'T'ere aren't no corners on me,' Balga replied tartly and invented an identity for himself. 'T'ere sure ain't. Ya know my fad'er was a Yank and his brad'er a famous blues singer, you know: Robert Johnson from New Orleans.'

'Never heard of him,' snapped the bloke, but obviously impressed.

'He plays rock'n'roll,' Balga shot back, though he had only read about the music and as far as he knew had never heard it.

What he had asserted must have been impressive. It bridged the gap between them. The bloke introduced himself as Eddy Grant and said the girls were his sisters going by the names of Audrey and Leslie. 'You know Leslie Caron and Audrey Hepburn,' Eddy said with a wink.

Balga walked along with them as Eddy told him that he was he was a progressive dresser and not a Bodgie as "bodgie" was slang for a wrong one and he considered himself a right one. 'You know,' he said, 'when I saw you I knew you were one of us inspite of those awful threads you're wearing and that haircut. With hair like that you need a bit of style to make it, it "hep".

Balga modeling his clothes on Phillip Marlowe, felt anger at the bloke's remarks, but let it go to say: 'Can't help t'at when I ain't got t'e dough just yet and as for t'e haircut, t'ey gave it to me. I'll get it fixed soon.'

'Yeah,' the Progressive Dresser replied, 'dough's always a problem. Must be a bugger to live in this town. Gee, it's so small I bet that the cops get to call you by your first name in no time at all.'

'Yeah,' the blonde girl, Leslie, agreed coming into the conversation. 'I want to get back East. Sydney, Melbourne – anywhere but here.'

'No peeping, chick, be a cool doll, eh' Eddie drawled. 'The dough's coming in and soon we'll be out, so keep your britches down until we've made a roll.'

'I'm outa here, Eddie, soon, soon, soon,' the dark-haired, Audrey threatened.

Balga thought they didn't look like brother and sisters but then what did he know about family matters? He nodded as Eddie evaded any arguments by turning his attention his way. He said: 'We have this hangout: the Royale milk bar. It's allowed to stay open on Sundays to sell milk. The cat that owns it – maybe is old, but don't let that fool you. He's really hep and knows his sounds. A Ted from London!'

'A Ted,' Balga had to ask.

'What they call a Teddy boy, though he's a bloke. A little bit like us' but they look back to the Edwardian period to get their style. They wear coats with velvet collars and ain't real gone progressive dressers like us.'

'Yeah, 'Balga replied completely out of his depth.

They took a right and went from Hay to Murray then turned into Wellington Street going along it towards the hospital until just past an army disposal store they reached the only shop open: The Royale, the one and only Bodgie hangout in Perth as Balga soon found out. He followed after Eddie and his sisters and winced as he was hit by a loud music he had never heard before. His introduction to rock'n'roll. He would never forget it. The one and only: 'One two three o'clock rock; four five six o'clock rock. We're going to rock around the clock tonight. We're going to rock rock rock until the broad daylight.' The rhythm took over his feet as he glided into the joint each foot hitting a beat. He was getting into something at long last.

THIRTEEN

THE AMERICANS

Monday back at work and after work Balga kept The Royale in his mind. Mrs. Freeman had piles of Pix and Australasian Posts and he went through them looking for information on these Bodgies and their music. The woman talked on, but he ignored her as he flipped through picture after picture until he came to some of black American singers wearing what the Bodgies wore and what he wanted to. He could picture himself dressed in the drape suits and as for rock'n'roll music – the square writers called it an ugly jungle music infecting America. A negro music catering to the animal passions of the young, and there was a photograph of two white youngsters jiving to the beat. Balga smiled and the next evening went to one of the newsreel theatres that showed the latest shorts and lo and behold there was the black guy called Little Richard pounding away at a piano for a few precious seconds. Balga didn't have a radio, but he wandered into a shop and emerged with one. He listened to the music and was disappointed. Old sounds sung by the likes of Vera Lynne and Theresa Brewer as well as Buddy Williams, Burl Ives and Nat King Cole. Only once his ears pricked up as a group called The Coasters sang a song with a wailing sax.

Balga kept away from the Royale for a few days as he felt he had to be right for the place. After all he was as a Black man with an American father and an uncle who was a blues musician. He thought through his new identity. In Clontarf, Sporting Life was a favoured magazine among both brothers and boys. It featured mainly men and he had avidly followed the life and fights of Joe Louis, the heavyweight champion of the world. Now he felt he was one of them; but first how to get the threads? He had the right coloured skin and even the hair, but it was cut all wrong and as for his Phillip Marlowe clothes, my God, they belonged to old men. They weren't what was that word "hep".

Balga saw a shop in Barrack Street, between Hay and Murray. He stopped entranced by the clobber in the window. The clothes were gone, real gone as one of Fast Eddie's expressions had it. They were what he needed to make an impression in The Royale and he had his week's pay in his pocket. He went inside and a young bloke looking a bit like the movie star Tony Curtis took him in then looked away as if he didn't exist. An older man came out of a back room. He trotted over to Balga. 'What can I do you for,' he said with a Pommy sense of humour.

'How much are t'ose shoes,' Balga asked, pointing at a pair of brown suede shoes.

'You wouldn't want to know, you just wouldn't,' the bloke replied getting his goat. Now he hated both of them.

'Well, try me,' he snarled curling his lip..

'Twenty pounds!'

'Okay,' Balga said with a shrug, 'and t'ose pants, t'at drape coat, and t'at t'in tie?'

'Trousers, ten pounds ten; drape sports coat a cool thirty five and as for that tie just five. I can let you have the lot for two fifty.'

'Can't you count,' Balga snarled. 'I'll think about it and see if I can get 'em for less.'

'You can't,' the Pommy smiled and the young man grinned.

Balga was depressed: but he wanted those clothes. He needed them; but on his lousy pay he could hardly afford the tie.

He walked on, crossed over the railway tracks into William Street. His lunch time was almost over, but what the heck. He came to a barber shop and there were illustrations of the Bodge cut in the window and he went in to be confronted by an Italian man who sat him in a chair, pushed his hand through his hair and then asked him what he wanted done with the broom.

"Dunno, but something to go with the times.'

'Can give you a flat top, flatten the sides so they look long and, well, what else can I do?' he finished with a shrug.

'Well, do it,' Balga snarled, curling his lip. 'And make it as fine as wine.'

'Yeah, as rough as Grappa,' the barber rejoined and set to work.

Balga emerged from his ministrations to find that he indeed had a haircut that might have come from an American movie. He stared at his new self in the mirror. Now he knew he had to have those clothes. He just had to!

When he arrived back at the garage, his boss stared at him and told him to be back on time from then on or be docked a day's pay. The man left. Balga stared after him. He went to the cash drawer and opened it. He counted the money. There was enough, but the boss would know instantly that cash was missing. What to do? It was then that a bloke came in for his car. It had had a new radiator installed and he paid enough for Balga to get his threads. The customer didn't even wait for a receipt and that sealed the matter. The boy could say that the man hadn't paid and his boss would believe it for a week at least.

Shops closed at five so he had to wait until his next lunch break to get the cloth. The older bloke beckoned him in mockingly. 'And what might I not do you for this time,' the man said breaking into his mind.

Balga, curled his lip and snarled, 'So you remember me?'

'Yeah, how could I forget those awful clothes,' the young bloke with the perfect Tony Curtis hairstyle broke in.

'And today I'm here for the lot,' Balga grinned, staring him down.

Money brought a respect of a kind. The older man hung about while the young bloke carried the clothes to him.

This time Balga avoided the green threads, deciding on blue. He stared at the rack of shoes. 'T'ose blue suede shoes?'

'Like in the song,' the old bloke said gesturing the young guy to bring them,

"Now what sort of jacket do I need?"

'That powder blue sports jacket. Long drape and the material, soft like a baby's bum.'

The old man held it up. 'Look at that drape. Try it on, it'll give you shoulders.'

It did give him a shape. Wide shoulders tapering down to a narrow waist and hips. It was mostly coat but Balga knew he looked swell. He admired himself in the full length mirror beside the counter and then said: 'T'at'll be fine. Now for the pants, trousers, eh?'

'Ah, slacks, dark blue of course. Look at these, tunnel belt loops, pleats, loose at the crutch, but flowing down to the cuffs. Ten inches! Any smaller than that and you would have to cut off your feet to get them on; but then you couldn't wear those cool blue suedes, could you?'

'No, I couldn't,' Balga said with a smile, enjoying being served. He let the old bloke stack up a line of accessories: clocked bobby socks, a thin leather belt, a couple of narrow ties and even underwear.'

That took care of all his cash; but the feeling was worth it. He rushed home with the big bag, dumped it and rushed back to work. His boss had checked the cash drawer. He told him off for letting the bloke have the radiator. The words went in one ear and out the other. Balga hung in there until the day was over. He rushed back to his room to try on his new clobber.

He posed in front of the wardrobe mirror. He practiced walking up and down or rather bouncing up and down. His suede shoes had thick crepe soles so that he bounced from step to step rather than walked. It was a great feeling. Balga bounced out of his room, down the stairs and along the street noticing how the squares were eying him. He liked that.

The lad learnt how to glide silently along so that at times he came up behind a man or woman. Suddenly the person became aware of his presence and darted a quick frightened look over his or her shoulder before speeding up or slowing down to get away from him. Now he began feeling like a "Bodgie" and the knife in his sock added to his edge. As if he belonged he swung into The Royale, nodded at Ted the Ted and went immediately to the booth where Audrey and Leslie were sitting bent over spiders listlessly sucking up the melted ice cream in the soda. They looked down in the dumps.

He plonked his self down across from them and tried: 'Dig me you two.'

Both looked at him with serious sad eyes and his joy evaporated. 'What's up?' he asked.

'It's Eddy,' Audrey replied, 'the bloody cops picked him up on Sunday.

'Why? What did he do?'

'Bloody nothing, that's what?'

'Nat'ing?'

'Yeah,' Leslie said, 'they booked him for being without visible means of support; but they.

know that we support him and we certainly aren't invisible.'

'No too visible,' Audrey put in, 'that's why they got him. Couldn't get him for anything else, you know.'

'Yeah, they use that vagrancy thing when they aren't sure that something else will stick.'

'Or if they don't use that, they have the consorting act to get whoever they want to. Square dicks are like that. Keep you always under their thumb and if you get out from under they use their fist to hammer you down.'

'How long will he get,' Balga asked.

'Well, three months at the least; six months at the most. It's this town, they don't like people like us,' she replied.

'T'ey pretty square,' Balga added using one of his new words. 'So what happens now to you two, he queried.

'He'll go before the beak tomorrow,' Audrey said, 'and be sentenced. He'll plead guilty, what else can he do? '

'Yeah, yeah and a double yeah,' Leslie added. 'Shitty town, shitty deal, now we are stuck here...'

'And the beak is sure to say, you can bet on it that we'll hear him say,' Audrey mocked: "There's no reason for a young man like you to be without a job. I advise you to get one after you are released and to help you make up your mind I am giving you six months.'"

'Yeah, squares are great with the preaching,' Leslie snarled and then gave a sudden hard suck at her spider. It sent the liquid gurgling down her throat.

'If you are going there tomorrow, want me to go along?'

'You're just a kid. They mightn't even let you in.'

'What'll you do wit'out Fast Eddy?' Balga asked.

'He's Steady Eddy now, man. No fast moves left except hold onto our cash. You not looking for a job, man,' Audrey replied.

Both laughed.

'Well, they know us now too. We'll leave this burg as quick as we can scram,' Leslie sneered. 'Every corner opens out into a square with a d waiting to pounce on you.'

'A "d"?' he queried.

'A dick, a detective! Yeah, Steady Eddy has this scene to do. We don't. His being outa commission means we can get outa here. How many outas does that make,' Audrey kidded again with a smile that Balga really dug. She was a real gone doll all right, as a Private Eye might say in one of his stories..

'Does t'at mean that you won't be coming here again,' he asked.

'Oh we'll hang here until we go,' she replied. 'We're Widgies after all and this is the only joint a chick can go in this burg without having to evade the hard word. Squares, they think they can get it for nothing, not bloody likely.'

Balga asked them what they were drinking and then went to the counter to get a couple of refills for them. Ted the Ted who had been winking at him for some time, now scowled for some reason. He lifted the corner of his mouth in a sort of George Raft expression to say: 'Yesterday this square came in and man was he all corners. Now today this cat glides in as if he was born on the street and he's wearing threads that only the worst can afford. I got a song for you, man,' he added as he began to make up the drinks, left them and went to the juke box, the god, he called it.

> *It's easy to be good;*
> *Hard to be bad;*
> *Stay outa trouble*
> *And you will see*
> *How happy you can be.*
> *So I'm glad*
> *I'm not a juvenile delinquent.*

FOURTEEN

THE BURGLAR

Balga was out on the prowl like, as a black cat, just gliding across the tracks to find what he might locate. Reading pulp fiction did give him ideas! He came to the corner of Lake Street and turned right into North-bridge. He reached James Street and went along it towards William. He stopped in front of a large store with heavy and ornate furniture in the window and a foreign language sign. He remembered that many Italians lived in that suburb and there were shops such as this one for them – and maybe for him? He went down a lane going along the side of the building and turned down another which ran behind the store.

The furniture store yard had a high wire fence which Balga clambered over using a drum abandoned in the alley. He jumped down into the yard. It was lit by a single bulb above the heavily barred back door of the shop. He knew he couldn't get though that in a month of Sundays. Then he noticed the shadow of an indentation in the building and went to it. On one side was a small window with glass louvers and without bars or other obstructions. 'How dumb can you be,' he whispered.

Balga touched a louver and slid it up and out. The others were just as easy. He clutched the window sill, heaved himself up and wriggled through. He was in a dunny. The lavatory door was unlocked. He went through into the store proper. Light came streaming through the large street window, but the furniture gave enough cover for him to reach the counter. He squatted behind it and worked the till. The cash drawer sprang open. He felt around and found only two five pound notes and some coins. He pocketed them scowling down, and saw a drawer in the counter. It was unlocked and – a cloth bag. The real thing! He had hit the jackpot. It was filled with notes, a couple of hundred pounds at that. With a huge grin splitting his dial, Balga got out of that place. He needed to get under cover.

The lad was far from home, but close to Roe Street where the pros were. He wouldn't be noticed as there was always a crowd of blokes there on Saturday night. Balga had never been down that street before, but felt powerful with the money weighing his jacket pocket. Yes, there were the blokes hanging out in front of the low cottages which were the brothels. The front windows were open and illuminated. He glanced in at the women sitting waiting for customers.

He stopped at one of the cribs and gave a start. He knew the girl. It was Audrey. She was a pro; but so what, now she was just as the molls were in the stories he dug. He watched the doll yawn. She had on a lacy dressing gown and sat so that it showed a lot of leg. Nice slim ones too. Well, he was more than a kid now, a Bodgie! With barely a qualm he bounced right in through the door at the side. She didn't even glance at him as she said: 'A fiver for a short time, okay?'

'Sure,' Balga replied then said: 'Lo Audrey, how you digging t'ings?'

She jumped, still didn't look at him and snarled: 'Do I know you?'

'You sure do. Once I was green, but now I'm just blue. Remember I actually picked a fight with Fast Eddy. I mean Steady Eddy. Hey, hey, don't think twice, it's alright. Is Leslie the sexy blonde next door?'

'Yeah, with a blonde wig. You're the kid with the American dad. You prowling about for something. No action here for a kid your age.'

'What do ya mean, I've got the dough.'

'You better scat. I can't service a kid. This ain't a kindergarten. Just what is your age anyway?'

'I'm seventeen on Wednesday.'

'Old age, eh Daddio? I've forgotten that year,' Audrey sneered, but finished with a smile which was a relief for Balga. He had been ready to get out of there as the doll didn't seem to dig him in spite of his flash clothes and his absolutely flat top hair cut.

'Come on back then and it'll be cool,' she said actually smiling.

'Oh, no matter, I'm not here for t'at. I just saw you and dropped in to say "Hi doll".'

'I've heard that one before,' she yawned though she left the snarl cut of her voice. 'You know I have to charge by the time and not what happens. You'll be surprised –'

'Yeah, so here's a fiver for your time. Nice seeing you. How's Eddy?'

'Steady as it comes. On ice, man, so he's real cool. Hey, keep your fiver, I was only half kidding and it's a slow night. What's your name anyway?'

Balga had to think a bit, then said: 'Just call me Bodgie!'

'Okay Bodgie and you just call me Widgie. We're two of a kind, like bread and butter.'

'Y-y-you must b-be b-b-buttering me up,' Balga stuttered.

'Maybe, but well I can be a Widgie to your Bodgie, for sure you're some sort of cat not one of those squares gawking at me from the street. Anyway, yeah, be cool eh, give it time, huh?"

'I'm just a black cat on the prowl,' Bodgie said with a grin.

'Maybe a wild cat,' she said with a giggle.

'Yep and wild for'- Balga began. He was going to end with "you", but was too shy and just tapered off like one of those songs that just fade away. Now he really was embarrassed as well as concerned that the police might find him there and: "Well, now kiddio I'm off to prowl, eh?"

'Yeah, Daddio, though you should be kiddio not me. Go catch some rats, cat.'

'Meow. Dig you,' and he was away.

Dig you later,' she called after him.

Some of the blokes hanging about at front glanced his way and guffawed. Well let them, he knew one, no two molls and they didn't. Poor squares! Balga bounced away on his crepe soles. Life was going his way, oh yeah, he was rocking and rolling.

FIFTEEN

THE SON

Late Sunday morning found Balga restless. He went down Wellington Street, came to The Royale, to find it closed. He went on past the hospital and wandered to East Perth and a large park. Aborigines often came there and Balga sometimes sat with them for company, though not since he had become a "yank" He walked into the park and gave a start. A small, dark, dowdy woman with grey hair was huddled on a park bench. He stared long and hard at the sad lonely figure. Was that his Mum sitting on a park bench? So long ago, nine years, yes, it was! Balga rushed over 'Mum, mum, mum it is you! I'm your son, Balga.'

'Well, 'pon my word, give me a hug son. Been too many years. I'm smilin' and cryin' appy as a lark. Your 'air it's as flat as, well, as the palm of me 'and.'

'It's a flat top, like with it,' Balga drawled, feeling ill at ease and withdrawing into his self just a bit. He allowed himself to be hugged and even caressed. It had been so long and now he was all but grown, well into his teens at least. He was what did they call it? A teenager!

'Mum, mum, we gotta work somet'ing out,' he said. 'You staying in the city long?' he almost cried.

'They got me outa me 'ome, 'ad to leave just like that. The old bloke let me camp on his verandah for a time. Side one shut in so it was fine, rain and cold was kept out as well as flies and mossies. He wouldn't gib me old Paddy's place. He went just after you was took away. Then the son came, snotty bloke waiting for the property. Pain - couldn't stay, pension came and so to Perth. Country no good for me sort at all sport. Just chucked me out as if I was a bag of rotten spuds.'

'Bastards,' Balga exclaimed. So you living around here,' he asked feeling strange at having found his Mum and unable to decide what to do about it.

'Yeah, 'ostel place. It's fine though not so dandy. Close to the park so I can come and park meself here. Other oldies come. I gab with them for a bit of company.'

'Well, let's go so I can see it. Meant to come to Shilo, but just out of Clontarf these last months. So that old place of ours is no more. Bastards, you lived in there for years. Maybe later, yeah, we can be a family again, nice. You know one day I'll fix t'em t'ose t'at tossed you out.'

He couldn't believe that he was with his mum again. It had been so long. He went with her across the park to Hill Street where there was a row of decaying cottages. Mum had a back room in the middle one. She let herself in and they went down a passageway to the very back room which seemed to have been tacked on. The door was pretty flimsy and there was a mark at the bottom as if it had once been kicked in. Inside, there was a double bed, a table and a couple of chairs, a big old wardrobe and a meat safe that held all the food she had. He looked inside and there was only half a loaf of bread, tea, sugar and a tin of Sunshine milk powder.

"Where do ya cook?' he asked.

'Opposite possey you go and see gas too if I have pennies. Don't now, but pension day Friday. I'll have a little cash after the rent for the gas.'

'I'll come back in a few minutes,' Balga exclaimed. 'Got to go for a while. You just set tight. Just a mo and I'll be back.'

'Yeah, what's it been, five six years, no seven eight years and a few minutes. Go, be back soon, or never ever,' she added with a resigned shrug.

Balga was annoyed that his mum was so down; but then life hadn't treated her with respect. As he hurried away he checked his pockets and found that he had about a pound in change. He found a milk bar open near the hospital and bought a loaf of bread, a tin of jam, butter, a pint of milk and got the change back in pennies. It was Sunday and so there was no buying meat. He took the stuff back to Mum and gave her two bob's worth of penny coins. She made him a cup of tea and he had to drink it alone as she had only one chipped cup. 'I'll see what I can bring next time,' he promised her. 'I've got a job and can let ya have a bit now and again. I'll keep my eye out for a place too. You know, I've been lonely living by myself.'

'Don't know what happened to the others, yer sisters,' his mum said with a sort of sob in her voice. 'Guess they don't care, forgotten their old mum.'

'Kylie isn't in Pert'. She's becoming a nurse and doing her training in Sout'ern Cross,' Balga told her. 'As for t'e ot'ers, haven't seen even one of t'em, wouldn't recognise t'em if I did. You know t'ose homes do somet'ing to you and you don't – I don't know.'

'Patricia, Betty, Joan, you never knew them; you never knew 'em, did you? If your dad hadn't died….'

'I met Frank, he was still in t'at Castledare, now's 'es somewhere in t'e city, I guess.'

And so they talked until the sadness lay about Balga like a fog and he had to get out of there for a bit of brightness at the Royale which must be open by now.

SIXTEEN

THE TRIAL

He missed work on Monday to make the trial scene with the two dolls. He met them at an eating place in Northbridge. They ate sausages, eggs and potato chips. The girls looked a bit tired from their night work, but the food and then coffee perked them up. They began commiserating on poor Eddy and his coming gaol term. It was about eleven when they walked along James Street to Beaufort. Balga felt a little shook up as this was where he had busted into that furniture shop, but what the heck? No one could ever pin that on me. He tightened up again as he realized that he had his knife in his sock. 'Don't'ey search you before they let you in t'at trial room,' he nervously asked the girls.

'No,' replied Audrey.

'But they look at boys dressed like you and file your face in their memories,' Leslie declared mockingly.

'Yeah, you shoulda dressed square, like we have,' Audrey added.

Balga took a good look. They were dressed demurely in mid calf skirts and high necked blouses. They had even scrubbed off their makeup. They could be taken as ordinary girls square as barnyard chickens. Balga didn't like that. He wanted the flash of molls as in his pulp fiction. Still, it was best for court if you didn't want to stand out like you were going to a dance.

When they entered the courtroom Eddie's trial was just getting under way. They crept to seats. Not a sound came from Balga and he knew why his crepes were called brothel creepers as Audrey had told him with a giggle. He found the court room a strange weird scene. Even the Christian Brothers were more modern than the funny old chap in a red robe and a long grey wig seated on high above men in black gowns and short wigs bent over a long table scribbling furiously. Fast now Steady Eddie, the modern progressive dresser clad in a dark draped suit and white shirt with only a red tie for relief stood to one side in his own little box. His face was strained. Balga looked at him and saw Jimmy Cagney. A bewigged bloke got up and read out his crime to wit being without visible means of support. 'How do you plead?' the judge asked. 'Guilty,' Eddie replied. 'Six months with hard labour,' the judge snapped and it was over as quickly as that. Eddie turned and vanished. They left. The girls said that as they were his sisters they would be allowed to see him in the holding cells. Balga nodded and said that he would be at The Royale on Wednesday afternoon. 'Yeah, it's your birthday, so I'll be there too,' smiled a wan Audrey. They went one way and he another.

SEVENTEEN

SEVENTEEN AND GOT THAT SWING

There were sign posts marking the road to hell, but Balga or as he called himself now, Bodgie ignored them. He had missed work for two days now; but with money in his kick what cared he. Perhaps tomorrow he might turn up and explain to his boss that he had been very sick or that his Mum had turned up out of the blue. Whichever; but today was Wednesday, his birthday and he needed to celebrate the event. He felt on top of the world and even went to the Cathedral to say "hello" to God, though he was almost certain the blighter didn't exist. This seemed true as the big bloke didn't return his greetings or even wish him a "Happy Birthday".

He put a ten shilling note in the poor box then bounced along the street as rain began to fall like tears from a huge face in the sky. He hated having the drops spotting his threads so he ducked into a shop to wait for the shower to stop. The woman behind the counter stared at him as if he was the devil himself. Balga merely grinned at her and to show her that he had cash ordered a big cake and a large bottle of pop to take to his mother. He wanted to celebrate his birthday with her. It had been so long since he had done so that he couldn't remember if it had ever happened.

"Such a dump," he thought as he entered the hostel and went down and into his Mum's desolate room. He found her really down in the blues.

She slumped there a little dowdy figure, sad as hard times, neither moving nor acknowledging her son placing the bottle of soda and the cake on the table. She didn't even wish him a happy birthday. This depressed him into wondering if she even remembered the day when she had birthed him.

'Hey, Mum, I'm seventeen today so we have something to celebrate,' Balga said trying to raise her spirits as well as his own. 'I know, let's go and get some tucker, chops and sausages and later you can cook me up a big birthday dinner, eh?'

His Mum brightened up at this and they fled the room to Charlie Carters' Supermarket where he spurged on whatever she fancied. Tea, sugar, milk, steak, sausages, bread, butter – she wished it and he got it. He saw and he bought only one thing for himself a big screw driver that he might find a use for. The groceries were packed in a cardboard carton and he carried it back to that dreary house and into that dingy room where his mother suffered all alone; but not today because it was his birthday and a time for celebration.

Balga put the carton on the table and his Mum started unpacking it. The lad knocked the cap off the bottle of soft drink and poured out drinks in the new glasses he had bought for her. They sat at the table and his mother talked about her last days in Shiloh.

And as she talked an idea came to him and he asked if Priors had changed much.

'Priors owned me home,' she moaned. 'I think a son took over or something like that and scat he said and I scatted. Been there ages, years and all that and rent not much and I as quiet as can be, but one day the man comes and he says they want the land and out I go out.'

'Mum,' he interrupted her, 'So it was t'em t'at hardware place, t'ey still have it?'

'Yep and they owned me place. I stayed on paid the rent mostly always on time too. Years and years and now only a heap of bricks. They only wanted to be rid, get me out and then they broke the house so I couldn't creep back and camp there. Yeah, them Priors did that.'

'And they didn't do anything with the paddock?'

'No, na, nothing, not a thing, you go and see. House a heap of bricks; the paddock still empty. Just a heap of bricks.'

Balga urged cake on his mum to cheer her up. They ate cake and drank pop then she said that she needed to rest and went to the bed. He replied that he would go and meet some friends and return later. She was already asleep and so he rushed out and to The Royale. He needed some cheering up as his Mum had turned his day sour. It was quiet. Only a couple of kids were hanging there. No Audrey. He turned to Ted the Ted for company standing at the counter, ordering a vanilla spider then telling him that today was his birthday and he was all of seventeen.

'Ah, yes, the magical number seventeen,' Ted began in his gregarious Pommy fashion. 'No one sings about eighteen or sixteen, well, Chuck Berry does, but no matter, an exception proves my point, but seventeen, everyone has a shot at it. She was just seventeen and beyond compare, and before too long I fell in love with her etc, and so on. Now just for you, in celebration of reaching this magical number I shall play a song and I'll give you one guess at what it's called. Well?'

'Seventeen?'

'Right on and now dig it.'

Ted the Ted was trying his best, but Balga wasn't in the mood for his banter and when the man went to the god, he drifted off to a booth. The platter began grating and the song sounded.

> Seventeen and got that hit
> To get my kicks at seventeen.
> Yeah, seventeen graduated and got that bit
> Juke box baby at seventeen...

Well, it went something like that and Balga sang it as that while thinking of Audrey and what was keeping her. After ten minutes she still hadn't arrived. Keeping away from Ted the Ted and his garrulous mouth he got into a few words with a Chinese kid from Broome who was more Aussie than Chinese though his nickname was Chinkee. He mentioned that he had roomed with a bloke from Beagle Bay mission and he didn't get on that well with him.

'That was most likely 'cause he was not used to ya. If you had stayed there after a month or two you most likely would have been the best of pals,' Chinkee replied.

'What matter he was square,' and Balga snarled at the thought of the awful shirt he had tried on and been caught in it.

'Well, they dig cowboys and hillbilly up there just as we dig rock'n'roll down here,' Chinkee retorted.

'But not Indians or Chinese for that matter,' Balga said and moved the chatter into his dream of going east. Balga had only been to the milk bar a couple of times; but had picked up the dream along with his new hair cut and bodgie threads. It was natural that the talk drifted onto money and Balga remembered the idea that had come to him when his Mum had been gabbing. He knew where to get some. In his old home town; and he could take revenge on the bloke that had done Mum out of her home.

Balga shouted Chinkee a soda and hunkered down with him in a booth. He stared at Balga as he launched into a spiel: 'Listen, man, I know you ain't fixed with cash and I ain't loaded eit'er. You know, I've been just talking to my Mum. She's just come from this town called Shiloh. She used to live next to a hardware store called Priors. It's on the main street, but on a corner so that we won't have to park right out in the open. Well, she got to talking and you know in their office is t'is safe, small, easy to move. It's a hardware store too so we can get what we need to open it A sweet, easy job with hardly a risk at all, 'cause these towns only have one cop and he's usually tucked up in bed with his wife early on in t'e night. You wanta get in on t'is wit' me. '

'I dunno, I don't want to drive half the night to some bush town and then we got to get back. Sounds risky to me!'

'Man, it's only a couple of hours from Perth and it won't take t'at long to open the safe. We'll be having breakfast back here in t'e morning.'

'But opening that can?'

'A hardware store will have all that we need.'

'I know how to use an oxy torch.'

'So t'ere, knew you were t'e bloke for t'e job.'

'Need the dough, ya know.'

'Yeah, you got a doll back home. With dough in your kick she'll do you right.'

'Yeah I got a chick.'

"T'e right time is t'e now time. We go okay?'

'You mean you wanna do it tonight?'

'Yeah, why not; but my frail's just come in. Keep everyt'ing quiet and we'll get toget'er here, later, after ten. Yep!'

'Yep.'

And so it had been decided and Balga moved into a pulp fiction story forgetting that the crims in them never came out on top.

EIGHTEEN

DOING THE THING

Audrey and Leslie entered wearing identical outfits of off the shoulder white blouses and dark skirts stretched over a stiffened petticoat so that it stood out from their slim legs. They had on white bobby socks and ballet slippers and looked old and sophisticated with lavish makeup. This was how Balga wanted to see them and he did. They slid into his booth in a swishing of petticoats and took up the whole of one side of the booth. They smiled and said that they had gotten over the now Steady Eddie as out of sight was out of mind. Balga went to get them a couple of spiders and when he came back they wished him a happy birthday and made a joke out of his age adding "man" after every remark they made. Balga laughed along with them at last enjoying his birthday. Still, he hated being a kid. Yeah, seventeen and never been kissed and all that. Yeah, he was just a juke box baby at seventeen.

Ted the Ted came to them with free sodas before the song had finished. Balga grimaced as it begun again. Ted nasalized: 'There is a spectre haunting the fifties and what is this but the juvenile delinquent. I admit I was one before there was any such thing; but today I feel, indeed I expect that the name has been coined to fit our bodgie mate here who is not only that in dress, but in name, though why he wants to be known as "Bodgie" is out of my understanding.'

'And this from a bloke who calls himself, or wants to be known as Ted the Ted. Jesus, it sure takes one to know one.' Leslie retorted, stretching out her hand into which Ted dropped a couple of tabs.

'Anyway,' Audrey laughed, 'he calls himself Bodgie to fit in with my Widgie. So from now on, I'm not Audrey, but Widgie. So dig that.' And she too held out her hand for tabs.

Balga or as he now called himself Bodgie too held out his hand. A half dozen purple hearts dropped into it. 'Ah, you give me your heart,' Bodgie said his mood lightening. 'I'm goin' to be a big bad man at seventeen and scare all t'e squares as I go on the prowl. Yeah, but not just yet, I have ot'er things to do,' the lad said trying to suppress the tremor in his voice. 'Now let me pass on my heart to you,' and he pressed two tabs into Audrey's palm. Her fingers closed on them and she tickled his palm in return.

Bodgie washed the purple hearts down with a swig of soda and then got up and up. He swaggered over to worship their god, the rainbow hued juke box. He fed coins into him and his first selection hit the air: Halley's Crazy man Crazy. Bodgie felt the music, the beat and as he turned from the juke he saw Chinkee and Leslie bopping. He smiled at Audrey and Widgee came to Bodgie. They jived. She taught him and from somewhere he remembered a move and held her hand and leant right back. His head almost touched the floor and he came up still moving his feet to the beat. Man, he knew that he was a natural.

They were sweaty when they returned to their booth. Ted came with cold sodas which must have been laced with his magic pills as Bodgie felt he was flying as soon as he downed his drink. Then he felt tuckered out. He sat slumped down and sort of drifted away, though somehow he had shifted to sit beside Audrey. Bodgie felt half buried in her voluminous perfumed skirt. He came to to find that the girls were stirring ready to hit the road..

'Can I tag along,' he asked.

'Sure why not, it's not even dark yet, man.'

NINETEEN

THE LOVER

It was a great day and seventeen was a great age to be too, Balga (no Bodgie) thought. Why, he was almost a man. Yeah, a man, he felt as he strutted along with the two dolls conscious that the squares on the street were eyeing him - envying him for the clothes he wore and the two chicks that looked as tough as he felt.

Yeah, tough chickees that did the night trade on Roe Street. He was in one of his pulp novels. Yeah, this was the life to live he knew. They turned into that infamous street where Leslie left them while he continued on to Audrey's crib which they entered with a giggle. She started to put on her working gear, a simple shift saying that the hoop skirt was okay for standing up, but not for lying down. 'This is better,' she said, twirling around so that her scanties showed. The girl went out the back. She came back with a soda and more pills which they gulped down.

Audrey kept the front of her crib closed. She sat on the bed with him. He began talking telling her how he had just been out of Clontarf orphanage for a few months and was just feeling his way.

'Just feeling?' the moll asked, somehow making it sound dirty.

'Yeah,' he replied as he awkwardly took her hand. 'In Clontarf it was all boys. We never talked to or touched a girl, never held a hand ever!'

'Uhuh, maybe it was for the better. 'They say fresh meat is much better than stale.'

'Yeah,' Bodgie agreed wondering what she meant. He felt as shy as hell and wanted to scarper. He told her that he had to go soon.

'Come on, man,' she retorted, 'be my Bodgie to your Widgie, and help out. Hang until eleven and do Steady Eddie's duties. He looked after us and we need another bloke now. Anyway, it's your birthday so have a real gone time with me.'

Saying this she stretched out on the bed and Bodgie stared down at her. He was feeling a little dizzy. 'What were those pills?' he asked her.

'A bit more than Ted's and you can jive all night on them. Wish we had a radio here, or something for music, but it's not allowed.'

Now Bodgie's mind was off on another wonder. What would he do if a customer came?

'Man, you are a bit slow,' the girl told him flashing her legs at him..

"Oh that,' she pouted when he told her what he had been thinking. There's a back room where you sit and keep an eye on things; but not tonight. This is a quiet night and I'll keep the place closed. Leslie can handle the trade while I handle you,' she said with a laugh and then grabbed Bodgie's hand and pulled him down next to her. 'Now for that birthday present,' she whispered then mock ordered. 'Take off your trousers and take it like a man.'

Bodgie was used to obeying orders and began to do so. He didn't even feel embarrassed as he knelt to take off his blue suedes and then his pants. As he carefully folded his trousers and looked around for somewhere to put his jacket, he caught her pushing up her dress. She reached out and pulled him on top of her. She shook her hips, reached out to free his dick of his underpants, did something similar to herself and guided him inside her. Bodgie got up on his elbows as she bucked a few times to get him moving. He began and continued finding it so natural that he even thought of a song to go with his rhythm: "The Stroll". Nice and slow and come on baby make it last. Stroll, don't run; walk not talk and slow to the rhythm that beat him into an intoxication.. Bodgie began singing softly then stopped with a gasp. There was nothing that he thought or felt. He closed his eyes on the void and began moving slowly. Just strolling, just strolling. Turning over and strolling some more into a realm that held all meaning. Oh yeah, man, oh yeah, man! His body began to rise to a crescendo in spite of itself. 'I love to stroll,' he moaned. 'Let it all come out, baby, give me all of it' Audrey whispered and thrust a few times with her hips. As Balga spunked deep within her he knew that he indeed was a juke box baby at Seventeen.

'Wonderland,' he murmured.

'Fresh meat is always the best meat,' she said, and got up to fix herself.

Bodgie lay there in the afterglow feeling fine and wondering why his teachers, The Christian Brothers had condemned what he had just done as one of the worst of all mortal sins. 'I'll never understand them,' he whispered to himself, as Audrey came back from the back.

'Hey,' he exclaimed in surprise, 'I pronounced them as them. Now - then as then, thee as thee. Wonderful,' and he explained to her about his speech impediment and how he had tried and tried to be rid of it and now it had gone of itself.

'Oh that,' she retorted, 'I thought it was part of your American accent. I found it cute.'

"I can always keep it up,' Bodgie replied, but when he tried he found he had lost it. His speech impediment had gone and never came back. At times he had wished the same might happen to his skin colour, but alas he was stuck with that for life. 'A part of my American self,' he said more to himself than to her.

'What is?' Audrey asked.

'My skin colour.'

'Oh, I supposed all the people in New Orleans were coloured, just like Fats Domino and your dad.'

'Sure, sure, he said feeling that he was caught in a lie that he would have to live with; but then it was better than being a native, an Abo. He couldn't even begin to think of what Audrey's reaction might be if he confessed that to her. Yeah, you never could tell how people would take it. Best to keep it hidden until you knew what the cat or chick you dug really thought of such a thing.

These thoughts were upsetting his mind. He remembered the job he had planned and needed to cut out. 'Hey, time for me to prowl,' he whispered to the girl beside him who seemed to be dozing or in some wonderland of her own.

'Why?' she muttered, opening her eyes and bringing herself back to their scene.

'Cause I got this little job to do. We'll groove again tomorrow, won't we? Make it a date and I want you to tell me all about yourself and where you grew up. You're a city doll in my country flic, Next time, we meet we'll get a car and try that dance place, the Snake Pit. The only place in town you can jive to the bop.'

'Whatever,' she replied with a yawn. 'Sure, sure, if you gotta go, you gotta go,' she added sitting up and watching him pull on his trousers. 'Tunnel loops,' she commented then added: 'Before you go give me some skin. I'm widgie to your bodgie even more now.'

'Skin?' Bodgie queried.

'Yeah, but not this,' she said flashing a white thigh to show a tattooed stick figure with a halo, 'our very own hand shake. You're one of us now and when you go East you give them the sign. There's lots of Saints in Melbourne.'

'Huh,' Balga grunted. Being with Audrey wasn't just being with any girl. She knew things that he didn't and could open doors for him in that mythical east. 'Let's go strolling, strolling, take my hand, baby and lead me to that wonderland,' he sang.

'Uhuh,' she said, 'so stick out your hand and I'll show you.'

He did so.

'Nice long fingers, you should take up the guitar,' she commented.

'Yeah, but they are the reason why I have a powder puff punch,' and he told her about his short lived boxing experience, to which she retorted: 'You were lucky. Boxing is a mug's game.'

How could she know that, he thought, but let it go as she showed him the bodgie hand shake. There was a simple version that could be extended into a complicated one if you really wanted to get into greeting someone or testing them. The simple one was merely the brushing of palms after the shake, but the second version employed all five fingers. You went from finger to finger twisting your hands and finally brushed the palms. Balga practiced on Audrey enjoying caressing her palm and fingers as he did so. Her palm was crisp and cool. 'Your skin is fine like wine,' he muttered, still self conscious about using such compliments.

'You a bodgie now', she said.

'Yeah Bodgie to your Widgie,' Bodgie replied softly.

'Yeah I'm widgie to your bodgie,' she whispered back.

TWENTY

GOING HOME

'The sooner we do it, the sooner you're on yer way home. Just remember that it's a cinch.' Bodgie said as he walked along the street sizing up cars.

'You know how to make one of these start without a key?' Chinkee asked him.

'Sure do, work in a garage, don't I," he replied, 'Holdens are easy, even if the doors are locked. No mucking about with a coat hanger or bent piece of wire, you just get on the back, I on the front and you on the back. We bounce up and down and the doors spring open. As for starting the engine, a two bob bit or a strip of silver paper across the ignition wires will get it turning over.'

'Yeah, yeah,' Chinee said, 'you're a pro, ain't you Bodgie?'

'Sure am now, just seventeen and got my kicks tonight, huh?'

'Yeah fine, nothing will go wrong. Will it?'

'Nothing can. Mum lives in this dump. Smelly isn't it? '

Mum had cooked up an enormous amount of grub and they got stuck into it. They hardly said a word until they had finished. They sat back over steaming cups of tea then Bodgie said: "Time, let's get the show on the road.'

'Tonight?'

'Yeah, midnight, we'll be back by morning.'

Bodgie's Mum looked from Chinkee to her son, then back again and said" 'You boys, take it easy-peasy. Sleep, stretch out on the floor. Tomorrow is another day light. Night time is dark, hard to see yer way, you know.'

'Mum,' Bodgie said, 'we're just going out to a dance hall. It stays open to two, only place in town to do so. Time for your bed now. We don't want to keep you up all night.'

'Be good, sonny, don't let your mother get down in the dumps aga.n.'

'I won't, I won't, but we gotta go.'

Bodgie's load lightened when he left that dismal room. Tomorrow, he must find a nicer place for her before he left for the East.'

They moved up to Murray Street and went along looking for a suitable car. They came to a Salvation Citadel and there was a Holden parked a bit down from it. Feeling lucky, Bodgie tried the door and it swung open. The street was deserted. He got into the vehicle. Chinkee came after him. He got the engine started and they were on their way

After an hour the town of York came up and Bodgie turned onto the Narrogin Road that would take them to Shiloh. The darkness tensed about them and closed about their headlamps. The motor throbbed and rattled as if it needed the differential seen to, but beyond it was a silence that was not marred by any manmade sound. They passed neither vehicle nor man. At intervals and usually away from the road lights showed, but that was all. They seemed to be passing through a land in which everything and everyone had died. Chinkee began getting the willies and wanted to get back to the city lights, but Bodgie clung to the steering wheel determined to reach his goal.

The Shiloh turnoff was marked with a sign. Bodgie slowed and went down it. The town was silent and abstract in the night. Few lights showed. Their head lamps reached out the whole length of the main street. They went down it and turned off at Forrest Street. His Mum had been right. Where her house had been was a heap of bricks though the front gate now rusting away still hung on its hinges half open. He parked the Holden under the tree that he remembered from his childhood. They sat there letting their eyes get used to the darkness. It was then that the moon came out to give them enough light to show them the way. Bodgie looked in the glove box and his luck held. There was a torch there.

'Well, let's go and get at that safe. We go through that yard there to reach the back of the store.'

They got out and Chinkee slammed his door. The sound resounded and he said: 'It sure is quiet.'

'Yeah,' he replied, 'everyone is asleep except for us cats on the prowl.'

The yard was still filled with petrol and oil drums. The gates were loose and held in the middle by a big padlock. The lads jumped over them. Bodgie flicked on the torch. He directed it towards the building, keeping it low so that the beam would not betray them. They reached the back of the store. Bodgie saw that there had been some changes. The window he was aiming to force was now enclosed in sort of cage of mesh wiring. The door to this was padlocked, but he pushed the screwdriver he had remembered to bring between door and hasp. He jerked. The screws came out. The whole thing fell with a clang onto a rusted ploughshare. It was then that Chinkee put a hand on his arm. He was about to shake it off angrily, when he glanced up and saw the beam of a torch crossing the front store windows. It turned and passed over the Forrest Street office window. Someone, the town cop of course, was coming to check their car. The damn head lamps had given them away.

Bodgie wanted to stay there, but Chinkee anxious to keep his transport out of the town was already moving towards the gates. The idiot stumbled against a drum. Bodgie watched. The torch was at the car, examining the inside. It turned and caught Chinkee astride one of the gates.

'Hey, stay there and identify yourself,' a gruff voice commanded.

Chinkee leaped off the gate. He made it to the car and into the waiting arms of whoever it was, surely the town cop. Yes, Bodgie heard the clink of handcuffs as he made it over the fence. He ran off away from the town dashing silently past the police station on his brothel creepers. A window was lit up.

TWENTY ONE

GOTTA KEEP ON MOVING

Bodgie crossed over the river. He went on along a dirt road until he found himself in the town cemetery. Headstones stood up like rotten teeth. A little scared, the lad started along a path between rows that would take him to the far side. Somewhere his little brother was buried there, but in an unmarked grave so that he could never find it. Bodgie cursed himself for being an idiot. He had really stuffed up the bust. Why hadn't he thought of the headlights going far out to advertise that a car had entered town. The beams most likely had gone right through the cop's bedroom window and out he came to investigate and cop Chinkee. He sat on a grave stone just before the back or side fence almost crying in frustration. In front of him was a small mound overgrown with weeds. A vase held dead flowers. It scared him.

Gotta keep on moving sang in his head as he got up almost running. Just beyond the fence the lad got onto a bush track. This meandered along and down across the bottom of the dry riverbed. Dawn came to spray light across the bush.. There wasn't much to be seen only trees and bushes and the Balga grass trees after which he had been named. Now he had thrust them aside and renamed himself Bodgie, wrong'un. He felt guilty about this and he looked away from the dark trunks and the spiky tops that would have been his hair if he hadn't had it flattened. Now he really felt afraid and lost on the track snaking through a whole forest of the blackboys. Too many eyes were staring at him. Dead tired! He was about to slump down and rest when the bush thinned. The track came out onto the highway some distance from Shiloh. In front of him was the railway line, a small tin shed beside it and between track and road a cleared patch of ground on which grew the largest blackboy he had ever seen. It had multiple arms thrusting up holding many spears and a huge crop of hair grayish green. Beside it was a dome of a dwelling, an Aboriginal gunya or whatever it was called. A rounded dome shaped structure about the height of a tall man, made of leaves and bark with a small entrance at which sat a dark old bloke. Bodgie stared at the man who stared right back.

'Good morning,' Bodgie said, 'just been out walking and got a bit lost.'

The Aboriginal man examined the lad and then nodded.

Bodgie reverting to Balga said:' You a Noongar? I'm from Shiloh, well, at least originally, but I've been in Perth, do you know Ben Bowyang? He throws boomerangs in Wellington Square sometimes. You know, I found me Mum, just like that, sitting there in that park…'

'Ben Benbow,' the Aboriginal man corrected. 'Yeah, know him, but do you?'

'Not exactly, just watched him throwing a boomerang and listened, heard his name mentioned.

'I'm Ben Benbow, you know, a Noongar?'

'Yeah, what else could you be, you're black aren't you.'

'And what about you, mate, with that flat head? A goanna? Shouldn't it be like that and he nodded at the ancient grass tree.

'Naw, my father was an American.'

'Well, mine was English, but that doesn't make me a Pommy.'

'If you're Ben Benbow how come you way out here?'

'Same as you, just visiting.'

'And what about your shelter? Did you make that, a gunyah, isn't it?'

'Yeah, I made it, an igloo.'

'But isn't that made of ice?'

'You ever see any ice in West Aussie?'

Bodgie was feeling too tired to keep his side of the banter going. He just wanted to lie down and die. Ben Benbow could see that the lad was on his last legs. He told him to take the weight off his legs. In front of him was a small fire to the side of which a black billycan stood. He turned and fumbled through the entrance of his shelter. The man brought out two enamel mugs. Balga slumped beside the fire. The Noongar poured tea and passed the lad a mug of the thick black liquid. Gratefully Bodgie sipped at it.

'Well, your father was a Yank, but what about your ma,' Ben Benbow asked the boy.

'She was from near Williams,' Bodgie replied, not giving anything away.

'I know an old mother from there, related to the Colbungs. Maybe her?'

'Well, she's in the city now. They tore down her house in Shiloh. Nowhere else to go.'

'Yeah, Shiloh does that to us.'

Bodgie finished the tea, chucked the dregs into the fire and stared at the smoke. He could feel the Balga close to him, too close. Suddenly his tiredness left. There was the sound of a vehicle coming from the direction of the town. It sounded like a truck. He decided to try for a lift to get out of the mess he was in. 'Thanks for the tea, I got to get moving.'

'Yeah, I know, enjoy the ride. Don't worry, the driver'll stop. He's a mate of mine.'

'See you,' Balga said getting up and going to the side of the road to stick up his arm.

The truck filled with milk urns stopped. He hopped into the cab and waved a hand at Ben Benbow and the ancient grass tree. He had escaped, but was on the run just like in some of the stories he had read and enjoyed. Now it was for real.Gotta keep on moving.

The truck took the lad as far as Bassandean. From there he got a bus to the city and walked to his Mum's swaying with tiredness. He reached Wellington Square, crossed the park and got to her place. He knocked and she opened the door. He staggered in and collapsed onto the bed.

TWENTY TWO

CATCH A FALLING BOY

Seventeen began playing when Bodgie crept into the milkbar feeling like James Cagney on the lam. Ted the Ted complimented him on the suit he had just picked out to get his spirits up. It had taken most of his remaining cash, but what the heck. Ted said that it could be improved by a velveteen collar. 'Steady Teddy,' Bodgie exclaimed, 'these are rolled lapels, the gonest, so dig it as you might a ten pound note.' In answer the man slung him a soda and then put on Seventeen again. Bodgie shrugged then jumped as he felt hands on his back. 'Give me some skin, man,' murmured a sweet voice, almost low and as husky as most heroines were described as speaking in pulp fiction stories. No, it wasn't. It was more like the voice of Frankie Lymon singing: 'I'm not a juvenile delinquent.' Still he wasn't about to complain as they passed skin. They went to to sit together in a booth just sipping soda.

Audrey was wearing the new fashion of dungarees and a man's white shirt. With her short hair she looked a regular tom boy, but after last night he knew that she was all dungaree doll. Now she swayed to the juke box, swinging her hips just for Bodgie. He watched her wink at Ted the Ted. The coin dropped into the slot and Ready Teddy screamed out courtesy of Little Richard. The girl crooked her finger at Bodgie. He got up and grabbed her. They began a slow jive to the fast music. He went over the steps and moves she had taught him. See You Later, Alligator swinging in short riffs came on to urge him on faster. He leant right back so that his head just touched the floor then sprang up to twirl his doll around in the beginning of a series that would end with the song, except the music stopped suddenly. The lad and lass stopped and turned to complain. They saw two squares one tall and thin, the other short and fat standing beside the juke box. Mean versions of Bud Abbot and Lou Costello in their pin striped suits.

'D.'s,' Audrey whispered.

'You know, Lou,' the tall thin detective said to the short fat one. 'I think there's a city ordinance against dancing in milk bars.'

'Well, well, there may be, but kids need their exercise, don't they, Al,' Lou replied.

'Yeah,' Al replied, 'or else they get up to all sorts of mischief.'

"I say they do. Now take this one here, the one dancing with the Roe Street moll. He's wearing a suit that would take all my monthly salary just to layby.'

'And yet this kid is wearing it as if he had the money to buy it.'

They went on like two pulp fiction police detectives, except they were real and worse, they were after him. He knew it.

Bud (Al) crooked a bony finger at Bodgie. Sullenly, the lad went to him. Any hope he might have had vanished as the detective said. 'We want a little talk with you at the station.'

'Yeah,' Lou added, 'it's a slow afternoon and we want your company.'

Bodgie had to play a tough guy role though he felt like crying. He quivered a smile at Audrey and croaked: 'Bye bye love.' To which she replied: 'Bye bye happiness.' He managed a: 'Catch ya later, Gator' and she responded with 'After a while, Croc.' A last glance over his shoulder as they took him out to their car showed her staring after him with shining eyes. Ted put on I'm Not A Juvenile Delinquent. It didn't cheer him up. No way at all!

At the station after a punch to the stomach he was ready to confess to anything. They typed up a statement and thrust it at him to sign. He read it over and saw that he had confessed to a dozen busts.

'A good job well finished,' Al stated.

'Yeah,' Lou informed him, 'thanks for your co-operation.'

They watched as the kid picked up the pen to sign away his freedom.

TWENTY THREE

BODGIE'S VERY OWN TRIAL

And so it began. They took away his threads and gave him some nondescript rags that rendered him, well, nondescript. Then they locked him in a cage so that he felt just like that chimp he had seen in the zoo. His knife had made him dangerous and dangerous animals had to be caged.

He was left alone except for feeding. Next morning a square, a nondescript bod approached the front of his cage. Bodgie stared at the high forehead where the mousy hair had receded. It was combed in strands across his dome. He took in the man's crumpled gray suit and the soft shoes that made no acknowledgement to fashion but only to practicality. The square had a file in his hand and was accompanied by one of the keepers in charge of the juvenile reception home. He unlocked the door, let the square pass through and then locked it behind him. Bodgie rubbed his hand over his crew cut and twisted his mouth as the bloke nervously smiled at him. He poked out a limp mitt which Bodge found to be also clammy. He dropped the thing. The bloke introduced himself as Mr. Ian Robinson, an officer of the Juvenile court. He had come to help him prepare for his trial.

'You should get probation,' he said in a voice which was flat and expressionless as his face, though his hands weren't. He spread them every now and again when he wished to make an important point, as he did after the world probation now. 'Be contrite,' he advised Bodgie. 'The juvenile court is set up to consider your well being and your future prospects. Yes, we are, I am here to help you. You must not see us, me as being on the opposite sides,' (he moved his lips in a thin smile) 'of, of a great divide. No we, I want to help you to straighten out and become a worthy member of society.'

'Yes,' the boy agreed, and so it went on while he stared through the bars and imaged himself back with Audrey hugging her tightly as they listened to, oh no, Bye Bye Love. He had become a juvenile delinquent and must have his day in court.

Bodgie had to put on his own clothing. It was amazing what a change of clothing did to his mind. When he put on his own threads and gave his hair a brisk brushing he became strong enough to take on the world. He felt like a hero as he bounced into the court room on his thick crepe rubber soles that made him inches taller than anyone else. He was dismayed to find that he had no audience except the court officials. Audrey wasn't there or even his Mum. Mr. Robinson came up to him and said that he couldn't find her and that only family members were allowed to be present.

'Now,' he said, 'be polite to the magistrate, call him sir and no lip understand. It's up to you to make a good impression. I'll be sitting next to you and keeping you in line, trust me.'

'Yes, sir,' Bodgie said with a twist of his upper lip.

'No lip,' he repeated and he led the boy to a table where they sat down-- and stood as the Juvenile magistrate trotted in. Bodgie saw that he was almost a dwarf. When he took his chair he was sure that he had a couple of cushions to raise him up a bit. Mr. Robinson gave his charge a dig in the ribs to prepare him. Bodgie glared and settled into his day.

In front of the magistrate were the books from his room and the knife from his sock. The magistrate stared at the knife and then sifted through his pulp fiction before opening his case book. He called Mr. Robinson to present the details of the juvenile offender. Robbo, as the lad thought of him, passed the magistrate the file and then detailed what he was charged with. He declared that the youth might seem incorrigible, but he was not unintelligent so that under close supervision he might come to his senses and turn over a new leaf. Bodgie watched as the magistrate moving his lips went through his file.

'Yes Mr. Robinson, but an untypical juvenile offender, I should question this boy. That is him, I assume?'

The magistrate got Bodgie's goat. Forgetting all of Robinson's advice he got to his feet twisting his upper lip. 'Don't I have to swear or somethin? You know like on the bible, like in the pictures,' he snarled.

'Well,' the magistrate began.

But Bodgie hadn't finished: 'You know that I don't believe in God so how can I swear on the bible when I don't believe in it or him?'

'So you don't believe in your creator?' the magistrate asked with a stern face.

'No, I don't!'

'I take it that you believe in the truth?'

'How can I when I don't believe in God? All truth comes from God and if he does not exist then how can there be truth?'

'Enough of this, this sophistry if we have to I shall decipher the truth from your words. As justice is based on cold facts it doesn't matter if you believe in God or truth, or whatever. Now pay attention. You committed a number of criminal offences?'

'I didn't, the D's said I did,' Bodgie exclaimed.

'But you signed this statement, did you not?

'Yes, but they told me to.'

'They told you to. They made it all up, did they?'

'No, I mean yes.'

'And you didn't commit even one of these offences?'

'No, yes....'

'Why, you had a good job, didn't you?'

'No, yes...'

'And you stole the money.'

'No sir, I put it back.'

'Those clothes you wear, they are expensive?'

'A bit, not all that much.'

'And,' he said, looking down at the file, 'you wanted to dress well, to impress those hoodlum friends of yours that frequent that milk bar in Wellington Street. Isn't that correct?

'Well, sir, we like looking neat.'

'And what is a square?' the magistrate asked..

'Oh ordinary people, those that don't dig the rock, like Robbo here, or dress progressively.'

'Oh decent people that must be protected from the likes of you! Now look at this pile of, well, of literary trash. I take it that you read this stuff in your spare time?'

'Yes sir.'

'And the knife,' the magistrate asked, and then essayed a joke, 'what's that for cutting your steak or simply skinning a kangaroo?'

Bodgie only glowered. Things weren't going his way, but Robinson had assured him he would get probation.

'Incorrigible,' the magistrate stated summing up the lad. He ordered the juvenile offender to sit down. Bodgie did so.

'I'll recess the court for ten minutes while I discuss this case with you,' he said to Mr. Robinson.

Bodgie waited and softly sang to his self: Seventeen, seventeen, graduated and got that twist. Juke box baby ain't no square at seventeen. He had showed them; but oh, God why did he feel like dying and getting away from it all?

The court reconvened.. The magistrate cleared his throat and looked grave as he stated: 'Mr. Robinson, you as the officer, appointed by this court to help juvenile offenders agree with me that this is a difficult case and that the youth shows absolutely no remorse at what he has done. In fact he is given to carrying a. concealed weapon and thus is a danger to society. It is my sad duty to sentence this youth to a term of twelve months in Fremantle Prison where hopefully he will take stock of himself and learn to separate right from wrong.'

TWENTY FOUR

BODGIE BOY BLUES

I got the blues, the goddamn bodgie blues;
They said you're a juvie delink just a freak
So they put me in the clink without a drink
Do 12 months without your widgie girl
The sky so blue too true my mind a sad bye bye
For you my sweet sweet dear I've got the blues,
The goddamn Bodgie blues oh me, oh my.

The night was long and his fears too real to bring on sleep. The morning came at last. Bodgie was taken to police headquarters. He was placed in the holding cell. About ten o'clock the cops marched the prisoners out to the Black Maria, a big black van with wired in windows. An old bloke brushed against him as he got in. Bodgie played the tough nut and snapped: 'Ey, don't step on me blue suede shoes!' Faded blue eyes regarded him with disdain: 'Fuck you! You'll get there soon enough.' Bodgie quaked at the violence of his words. Clontarf Boys'Town had rendered him pure in words at least and he never blasphemed or used profanity. Now he found himself amongst men who did so casually. What else to do, but glare at the old lag. Too gone to be a threat anyway, he thought to himself.

The Black Marie rattled out onto the road. Bodgie peered through the wired windows for some glimpses of the city. He saw Audrey standing on a corner with a hand upraised. It gave him the blues, the goddam blues. The v an g ot o nto t he S tirling H ighway g oing t o F reemantle w here h e would be living the next year. How to escape? No way! The vehicle rattled along. The highway receded under its wheels. Bodgie entered a state of depression. He called it the valley of despond: a sinking in his stomach leading to a feeling of nausea; a smarting around his eyes, and a wish in his heart to be dead. Bodgie boy blues for sure!

His mood as gray as the walls stretching out on both sides of the van as it stalled in front of double wooden gates. They opened and the motor kicked over to take it through to stop in front of double gates of iron. These opened and the van rolled through to stop at a low building. Behind rose a tall long building with small barred windows: the cell blocks. The back door was flung open. Bodgie scrambled down with the others. Most of the prisoners huddled in a group. A few looked about and even smiled as if they were home. Bodgie assumed they were the old lags. They lifted his spirits a bit. If they could relax it couldn't be all that bad. 'Hey bud back home are you,' he even essayed a remark at an old grizzled crim who looked like he had been in more times that out. Bodgie knew from the slight grin on his dial that for sure he was glad to be back.

'No talking, you,' snarled a dark uniformed warder, ex-army as his ribbon strip showed.

'Damn screw,' a man muttered.

'No talking!' shouted the screw. 'Line up you sorry lot. Now march '

They trundled into the Receiving Centre. They were ordered to strip completely and utterly. No big deal! Bodgie had done the same in Clontarf. He even tried to ask the screw who was superintending the convicts packing away his stuff, if he could keep his books. A glare silenced him. They were tossed on top of his clothes. Bereft of everything and stark naked, the men were marched to the showers. Bodgie had to scrub himself with a rough soap. It smelt awful and made him smell just as bad. A big screw with his peaked cap pushed to the back of his head inspected the men and made sure that they used the soap. 'Lice and nits and stuff is what we don't want,' 'he rumbled, then added what perhaps was a joke. 'They antagonize the bed bugs so that they bite harder. All right you lot get out and get into your new suits. Welcome to the Savoy, you wish it, this ain't it.'

Bodgie sank to the floor of the Valley of Despond. The cloth the pants and coat were made from felt like hessian. The striped shirt without a collar was rough cotton. The undershirt flannel like only old men wore. Rough woolen socks and shoes that resembled girl's shoes in that they had a strap instead of laces. The tailoring of the clothes was as awful as the fit. The pants were short by inches and the coat hung on his adolescent frame. He protested to the con that passed them over to me. He was told that he might swop them with someone or else wait until next week when a new lot was issued. 'You're a kid, but cop a tobacco ration and exchange that for good clobber,' he was advised.

A column of grey they marched across an open stretch of ground with flower beds. These were tendered by groups of Aborigines. The big screw with the hat on the back of his head led them to wooden double doors set within the gray sandstone wall. He had an enormous ring of keys and with a great rattling he selected one and opened a padlock, selected another and opened a lock in the doors. They swung open. He marched them through into a long dim tunnel. They had to wait while the screw locked the doors behind them. Bodgie's eyes adjusted to the dimness. What he had taken to be a long tunnel was in fact a narrow building lined with four tiers of black doors. Just above his head was a wire mesh stretching from opposite landing to opposite landing. Now the big screw delivered them and a file over to another ex-army type. With pale blue eyes he thumbed through the file and found a list which he fingered as he read out a number of names. These were to be accommodated in that section, the main division. Now the big screw retrieved the file and ordered the rest of the prisoners to turn right. He marched them to another door, unlocked it, passed them through and relocked it. Another screw met them and a selection of prisoners was dropped off in Division Two.. Six including Bodgie remained.

These were marched on and through another door into the First Division where the new offenders and/or juveniles were to be settled.

The screw in charge of First Division was a short neat little man with a neat little moustache. Scowling at them he said that he was Major Collins. He ordered them to line up for haircuts. Bodgie went into a cell where a con ran electric clippers over his head until he was all but bald. He could have cried when he saw his head with the tight twists of hair sticking up. The con laughed and he had to control himself. Major Collins ordered them to follow him up the staircase that led to the three landings. At one or another the screw opened a cell and ordered a man in. On the second landing with a great clashing of keys he opened a black iron door. He gestured Bodgie in, slammed the door and locked it.

The lad collapsed on the bed. Alone he felt his tears come and flow down his cheeks. The first time he had done so since he was nine. Strangely this made him feel better. He pulled himself together. He stared at the small narrow barred and thick glassed window. This could only be opened a few inches at the top. When he stood on his bed he could peer through and beyond the gray prison walls and the yellow sentry box in which an armed screw yawned to the boundless ocean. A ship was anchored where the water met the sky. Nothing else except for the bored screw, the yellow box, part of the sandstone wall and some of the ground before the angle became too narrow.

Bodgie got down off the bed. He tiptoed to the metal door white-washed as were the walls. In the door was a peephole. He put his eye to it. Blankness, it was covered. He stared at the table and the stool. On the table sat an enamel mug and a plate. He looked about. In a corner was a red lidded bucket which was empty. It smelt of shit and disinfectant. Next to it was an open bucket filled with water. Nothing else! He stripped the bed and stared at the stained mattress. Nothing under it! The blankets were neither clean nor dirty. Bodgie remade the bed and stretched out thinking of his widgie, Audrey. He drifted away into sleep. He jumped up at the rattling of a key in the lock. The door was flung open with a crash. A con stood there. A half loaf of bread was thrust into his hands. He had to get the mug to get it filled with tea. The evening meal and he was hungry.

'Where do I piss?' he asked the convict as he poured the tea. The man nodded at the red lidded bucket in the corner.

The screw slammed and locked the door. Bodgie took his bread and tea to the small table. Next to it was a stool and he sat on it. It was screwed to the floor as was the table. He sat there and tasted the tea. It was sweet and milky. He broke up his bread and dipped pieces in the liquid. As he ate there came the sound of many feet coming up the stairs and rumblings along the landings. These eventually stopped. Only a single pair of feet walked along. There was a tinkling sound which Bodgie thought must be the con dishing out tea. After this came the sound of heavy boots, rattling of keys, slamming of doors and the clunk of big bolts hitting home. There then fell a silence punctuated with various snufflings, coughs and creakings. The whole building breathed and echoed with the suffering of locked up men.

TWENTY FIVE

THE CONVICT

Next morning, the youth followed the rest of the convicts. They went down the stairs and out into a yard to empty their buckets and wash them out. Bodgie stood in line yawning and waiting. He stopped in mid yawn as he sensed someone close behind him. A hand touched him on the shoulder and fake gruff voice intoned: 'Well, well, well, who do we have here? Audrey said that you had been picked up by the demons. What did you do? Don't tell me. It must've have been something awful for you to get the jug and not probation at seventeen. Well, welcome to the big house, man. Real gone, though not so hep, eh?'

'Hey, hey', Bodgie exclaimed turning and grinning. It was Fast no Steady Eddy and greeting him as an equal rather than a Johnny come lately. He reached the trough, quickly washed out his bucket, copying what the others had done and scooping up a bit of phenyl, then got out of the line and with that wide big grin still on his dial yodeled: 'Hey man, give me some skin?'

Steady Eddy gave him the short version saying that there wasn't much time for Mrs. Palmer and her five sisters. 'No matter man, no big or small deal about this, you're a Saint now and I'll stand with you,' he told Bodgie and proceed to fill him in. 'You can work this place. Suckers suffer and do it hard while hepcats like us learn the ropes and which ones to pull. Still, no time now for gassing, the screw is looking our way. Get to the school and we'll meet there. Hansen the school master is one of those blokes who believe in reforming us, you know making us over into squares, that means he's a softy. 'You're a juvee and his heart'll be bleeding for you,' Eddy told him in a rush of words as the screw was already shouting for them to shut up and get to their cells.

As they rushed the gate, Bodgie couldn't be cool and blurted out: 'Gee, it's great to see you, Eddy!'

The screw standing at the gate pushed him and grated: 'One more word outa you and you're on report.'

Bodgie snarled and got back to his cell to wait in the doorway to receive his loaf of bread and mug of tea. Behind the cons dishing out the refreshments came the trim little Major screw accompanied by a bigger one who slammed the door behind the boy and wrenched the key around so that it grated as if someone was grinding his teeth. Bodgie drank his tea and ate half the bread and then just lay on the bed thinking about his good luck in having Eddy in the same division. He dozed off.

The door was flung back. He came out and followed the rest of the men down to the ground floor. They lined up except the group of new chums who just huddled together and waited until the screws turned their attention to them. It was the big screw again that ordered the men to line up to go to the main division where they would be assigned workshops. Bodgie joined them, but was called out. The major gestured towards a half dozen men –no, lads who waited on one side as the men marched out. He joined them and oh boy was it his lucky day. First Steady Eddy and now there was the flash of a familiar grin followed by a familiar voice. It was his mate from the orphanage, Tommy Cooper. There was no mistaking that freckled face and lopsided grin.

'Was looking for you all over Perth,' he said. They must've got you as soon as you left Clonny. Is that why I couldn't find you? Don't call me Skinny anymore, the name's Bodgie.' He stuck out his hand for a square handshake. Boy was he glad to see him. He clutched his hand for a full minute before dropping it.

'I've been in a few months,' Tommy replied. 'I got nine months for nothing.'

'Yeah and I got a year for not believing in God.'

'Say you don't say t'at and t'ere anymore. What happened, you meet the right teacher or somethin'?'

'No, just a living doll! How about you, not dropping your aitches anymore?'

'Grew out of it.'

While they gassed, Bodgie was flinging glances at the other five kids. 'Hey,' he yelled, making his move, 'they call me "Bodgie" and you all can call me that. Who are you lot anyway?'

His attempt at friendliness was received with scowls.

'Yeah,' a brown skinned kid retorted, 'I can see by the shoulders. All coat,' and he sniggered.

'That's Kevin Holliway and next to him his brother, Keith,' Tommy informed him. The other Abo is something Yarram. Then we have Dennis the Menace a little perve who loves telling you all about his smelly escapades and lastly Phil the Double Dealer who stole my loaf of bread the first day I was in. He still owes me one, don't you Double Dealer,' he called out.'

'You'll never get it for I'm on the way out this week,' sniggered Phil.

'You better pass it over or else you're going to be thumped. We'll both go up on a charge and you'll be getting a little something extra to add on.'

'Eh, you little blighters are you going to pass wind all morning. Get to work or you're all on report' grumbled the screw coming out of his office, though the blame didn't lie with the kids. He had been swilling down a mug of tea and had forgotten to unlock the door next to his office where the cleaning things were stored. They got out mops and buckets. The screw unlocked the yard door so they could fill the buckets with water. The juvees were assigned two to a landing. The ground floor was left for all of them to do when upstairs had been finished, though Phil as the odd lad out began cleaning there. Bodgie managed to be coupled with Tommy who told him that they had to drag out the work as the ground floor was afternoon work

'You better watch out for the Abo kids, mate,' Tommy advised him. 'The older ones have a special yard to themselves and get to work out doors gardening; but the juvees stay with us. They are sort of in between and when they reach eighteen they have the choice to either join everybody or go off to their yard. And you better watch out for that Yarram kid! He's a Tiger snake bad tempered and quick to strike. I think he's doing it hard. I heard that he got a girl pregnant and when she was having a miscarriage he stole a car to get her to a hospital. Well, he may be saved her life, but they put him in here for it. Just goes to show, you don't sow what you reap; but reap what others have sown.'

For sure,' Bodgie agreed.

'Come on, enough yacking for a while. Let's get cleaning up. No sweat though, the major doesn't get out of his office that much, never gets off the ground floor so we're free of him. He doesn't care as long as the work is done and there isn't any dirt or stuff laying about. The Chief Warder hates the screws as much as he does the cons.Watch out for him! Don't get on his bad side, or he'll have you on report and into solitary before you can say, "yes, sir".'

They set to work. There was very little dirt on the landing boards. They didn't need sweeping only swabbing. Tommy (he had dropped the insistence on having Cooper tagged on) told Bodgie that every Monday the screw had them scrubbing the boards until they were almost white. 'I think they were originally Jarrah red,' Tommy said, 'but with all the rubbing, well, over the years us poor buggers have got them as white as mothers' milk.'

They took opposite sides of the landing mopping from the walls where the division ended at a doubled locked and ironed barred door. Bodgie used to such work in Clontarf did it without any fuss and bother. When a bucket of water was dirty he went down to disturb the little Major who flung open the gate to the yard, glared at him as he emptied and refilled the bucket, then yelled at him to get a move on as he cleaned the mop. Bodgie could feel his hard stare on his back as he hurried past. The little bastard scared him. He raced up the stairs and out of his glare.

'Gee,' he exclaimed to Tommy, 'that little screw is a nasty little---'

'Prick,' finished his mate who just as in Clontarf in his first days was checking over his work to see that it would pass inspection.

'Yeah, that's what he is,' Bodgie exclaimed. 'Hey, I want to get into the school. Do I have to ask him if I can go and see the school master?'

'Aw,' replied Tommy, 'he'll let you go. No skin off his nose. The school room is just off the first landing so he doesn't have to put himself out or phone up for an escort for you.'

'Will it be easy to get in?' Bodgie asked.

'Why not, if you want to, though I don't 'cause I haven't got all that time to go, what with my remission. School room is three days a week, today, Wednesday and Thursday so you can go and see the master this afternoon and hang out there for a couple of hours until it closes. There's lots of dull books and you can thumb through them.'

'How do you know all this,' Bodgie asked his mate although knowing that he had always been a bit of a wheeler and dealer, a type that Bodgie liked his mates to be. Just like Steady Eddie who could put him straight on just about everything whether he knew it or not.

''Cause I too thought about doing a course at first. I checked it out; but there was a bloke hanging about there that began bothering me. Christ, he was a nasty piece of work and he was the last bloke I wanted for a mate.'

'Is he still there now,' Bodgie asked.

'Naw, he was such a vicious prick that they had to put him in segregation.'

Segregation,' Bodgie queried.

'Yeah, they have these petas, that's cells with their own exercise yards for blokes like him.'

'Oh,' Bodgie replied only half understanding what he meant. He was an innocent just months out of Clontarf and just a day in boob as Tommy called prison. It would take months before he knew as much as his mate did.

Morning work ended at ten thirty. They were locked up in the juvenile yard which was just to the right inside the second division doors. It was a narrow space with an open shed in the middle and two open toilets at the ends where the exercise yard ended with a wall which was scalable up to an open stretch of ground extending to the outside wall.

Tommy Cooper saw his mate staring there and said: 'A bloke tried to escape and was climbing the wall when the screw took a shot and took off his balls. He had orders to shoot low and he did. I don't know if it's true or not as I heard it from an old con that might have been having a kid on. He also told me about the last hanging when the Chief Warder had to swing on the legs of the bloke to break his neck as the drop wasn't far enough. That bastard would do that too.'

'My God, but don't they have one of those gallows you see in the pictures?' Bodgie asked with a shudder.

Before he could answer Kevin Holliway came up to him, stared and then said: 'You ain't no white fella. You one of us, or what?'

'My dad was an American,' Bodgie told him.

'Yeah,' he said examining his face. 'Your nose ain't a Noongar nose.'

This seemed to satisfy him, but not Bodgie. He stared at the boy's nose and it was flat as was that of his brother, but Yarram had a nose which was similar to his own. He pointed this out to Kev, who merely shrugged and said that it didn't matter to him at all.

They had an hour or less to kill and Dennis the Menace was latching onto Bodgie to regale him with an account of his perverse acts when Kev began picking at the back wall. Parts of the sandstone blocks crumbled into fragments. He collected a pile of these and started flinging them at the other kids scattered about the yard. They dodged them or stung by a hit picked a piece up and flung it back. A hard game similar to brandy which they had played in Clontarf with soft tennis balls! Not rocks that hurt and bruised when they hit. The boys dodged and ducked. A rattling at the gate made them put an end to it. Dinnertime was on hand. The screw flung open the gate and the juvees walked to the First Division door which he opened and locked behind them. They lined up to receive a dixie straight from the kitchen and piping hot as they were first in line. Carrying their dinner they went to their peta door and had to wait while the rest of the blokes from the division yard were served. Finally the little Major with another screw in attendance went around locking the prisoners in. By that time their food was cold.

The round aluminium dixie was in two sections. The bottom part held a soup which by this time had lumps of fat floating around on top. Bodgie gulped it down. It was awful, like Clontarf grub, but he was hungry. The second section under the lid was the main meal, meat and a couple of veggies. Stone cold! The meat had congealed gravy on it. All he had to eat his tucker with was a spoon. He used his fingers. With the grub done, he was stuck for something to do. The next work time was one o'clock whenever that was. There was no way of telling the time, though when the wind was off the sea the striking of the Fremantle town hall clock reached the prison. Last night he had heard it as a lonely sound; but now nothing. He slept.

TWENTY SIX

JUST A NUMBER

Major Collins glared at them then went into his office to drink the mug of tea he was carrying. Bodgie waited awhile and finally grabbing hold of his courage with both hands and ignoring the whispers not to disturb the screw went to the office to ask him about school. The division door bell rang. Major Collins left his office and marched to unlock the door. A brown-suited, gray-haired man was delivered over to him. 'That's Mr. Hansen the schoolmaster, now's your chance. Ask the screw that you want to talk to him about school. He won't be able to refuse in front of him,' Tommy whispered coming up close to him. Bodgie stuttered out his request. The screw glared at him, looked at the school master and told the lad to accompany them. The school room door was set in the side wall of the first landing. The screw unlocked the door. Mr. Hansen switched on the lights. Major Collins left, without locking the door behind him. The schoolmaster went to his desk and began to fiddle with his papers. 'It's a mess,' he told the juvenile. 'A new lot of lessons just came back uncorrected. Now what can I do for you?'

'I really want to study,' Bodgie replied putting eagerness in his voice. 'I did the junior certificate and passed, now I think I should build on that, maybe take an English course. I want to get on, not end up here time after time.'

'How long are you in for?'

'Twelve months, but with remission, it's nine.'

'Well, that should be long enough for you to complete a course. Do you think you're up to it?'

'Yes, sir,' Bodgie said knowing that he was ready for anything to get into school.

'Well, just look over this list of correspondence courses and see if one takes your fancy. I have to put some sort of mark on these before the rest of the students come in.'

He bent his head. Bodgie stared down at the grey head. 'English expression,' he exclaimed.

'Good, good, fill in this form, don't bother me now.'

Bodgie stared at the form. It began with his prison number. He had been ordered to remember it. It was his identity and would remain with him forever. Now what was it? He wrinkled his brow, ran his hand over his cropped skull and watched his fingers write: 74254. He knew that it was that one just as he knew his Clontarf identity had been Green 22. Bodgie finished the form and gave it to the school master just as there was a stamping from the landing and about 20 men came in. He saw that he was the only juvee. Then Steady Eddy gave a thumb's up sign to him. Instantly the lad asked if he could stick around the school room and look over the books. Mr. Hansen nodded too busy returning lessons to give his attention to the request. Bodgie grabbed a book from a shelf. He and Eddy went to sit at the end of a table as far from the teacher as they could get.

'Eh, man, give me some skin,' Steady Eddy said settling himself down beside him.

They had time to do their elaborate hand greeting. While doing it Bodgie noticed that Eddy still had the remnants of his hair style. Only the sides and back had been clipped. As for his clothing this had a close relationship in shape to bodgie threads.

'Even in boob you're cool,' Bodgie said admiringly. 'How come you manage to keep the style? Just look at what I'm wearing. Man, it's the living end. Rags, man, rags!'

'Because I work in the tailoring shop and I don't smoke and that leaves me an ounce to trade with. Get your bacca ration and you'll become as smooth as me. Yeah, you have to learn how a place works. Don't know how and you get lost and go down like a lot of these blokes do.'

'So I'll learn how to handle this place,' Bodgie replied unsure of his ability.

'Of course you will man,' Eddy said reassuring him. 'You're a Saint and Saints know how to get the best of things. Just go along, man, just go along with me. You'll have better clobber in a few days. I'll take your measurements man and, hey, Bodgie in Stir, eh? Get your baccy ration and I'll handle it for you. You'll get what you need, I'll see to that. Mates, eh and Saints forever.'

Again they did the special handshake. Bodgie relaxed and felt that he was back in Clontarf and, well, if he had survived that so-called Boys' Town, he could hang on in FreO.'

'Boob can be hard and tough,' Eddy went on. 'I've got a six months gap now in my life and I could be mad as hell if I wanted to waste my time and try to hit out. Man you can't win. You try to be a hard man and they pounce on you. You have to be cool. Just hang in there, find something to occupy your time. Yeah, you know I have this technical drawing course.'

'A technical drawing course,' Bodgie exclaimed. He had done the subject for his Junior Certificate and naturally passed, but had found it too finicky.

'Yeah,' Eddy told him, 'well, there's these square assignments you have to do or else they throw you out of the course, and then there's this.' And with that, he began opening a portfolio. It was filled with loose sheets of drawing paper. 'If you take a correspondence course they give you an extra hour at night and turn off the lights at nine. So you can use up your time in better ways than playing with yourself.'

'Oh,' Bodgie replied.

Eddy placed a sheet of paper in front of him. He looked down at it, puzzled and finally identified a detailed drawing of part of a pistol.

'It's a Luger pistol, a P.38 to be exact and the 9mm.version,' Eddy explained. 'The Luger is a beautiful weapon made by the Germans and accurate up to one thousand yards with a stock attached. It is a multi-purpose weapon and can be turned into a machine gun with the addition of a stock and a snare drum magazine attached beneath the hand grip. I was lucky to find a detailed set of pictures and drawings in one of the old books here. This is the pistol grip and the bullet feed in the grip. I'm working on the snare drum attachment now.

Bodgie stared down. 'What's that,' he pointed at a design.

'The breech! See those two claws? They are gripping the flange of a shell in the process of ejecting it.'

'Yeah, the breech,' Bodgie repeated. He wasn't interested at all.

Eddy was and went on happily explaining his drawing. 'Yes, a toggle-joint breech with the spent round being gas ejected. You know the P.38 has three stage recoil. The barrel recoils into the breech and the breech into the hand grip so that there isn't much of a kick when firing a round or even the whole magazine. It is an automatic after all. That mechanism there flips out the spent round and then receives a new cartridge from the eight-round, removable box magazine in the grip.'

Bodgie listened on. He considered himself smart and liked smart cats. Now Steady Eddy had flashed into Fast Eddy (he went by both names as if he couldn't make up his mind to be cool or hot). Bodgie couldn't help having a dig at him: 'Have you actually seen this pistol gun,' he asked.

'Of course, man, of course and I dug it for real,' Eddy retorted. 'When you get to Melbourne and I know that you're not going to hang around this square burg forever, you go, to the museum there. It's a great place for picking up dolls. That's why I went there at first that is until I saw what a fine collection of weapons they have Man so much more interesting and far better looking than any of the sheilas I picked up there.'

'Melbourne, yeah, sure I'll get there,' Bodgie replied then changed the subject. 'And talking of chicks, so Leslie and Audrey visited you?'

'Yeah on the very day you arrived and carrying a piece about you from the newspaper. You shouldn't have got on the wrong side of the beak.'

'What could I do? He had it in for me and those Ds they loaded all their unsolved breakins on me.'

'You should have conned him, tried some tears or something. You missed your chance there.'

'I'm a Bodgie, I don't do the tear thing, I do the tear thing,' Bodgie snapped and then his curiosity came up and he had to ask 'What chance?'

'A heaven send opportunity,' Eddy replied with a grin, 'I being indisposed for six months (with remission four at the least) and Audrey digging you as Bodgie to her Widgie you could have moved into my old place.'

'You mean in Roe Street?' Bodgie asked somewhat mystified.

'Into the profession, pal. With me gone they needed a bludger, a pimp to look after their interests. A good job, though you have to be firm with the chicks. Give them the stick when they need it. Do that and you'll find them working twice as hard to fill your pockets with loot. Yeah, great job and it would have taken you to Melbourne. Sadly, but too late now so all you got is your holiday in here to enjoy.'

'Yeah, they were getting ready to go back to Melbourne.'

'Not now, Bud, not now. That Ted the Ted at The Royale put them on to a Pommy mate. He's talked them into going to Singapore. There are commies in Malaya and they have lots of soldiers there to fight them, so good money can be made by a couple of molls.

'Well, well well,' Bodgie grinned, pleased as punch at being thought capable of taking Eddy's place. He was getting into the big time.

'Ted the Ted is a bit pissed off at you, though' Eddy went on. 'The cops have been in and out of his place since your arrest and that piece in the newspaper. That magistrate stirred things up and that's one of the reasons why Audrey and Leslie are leaving. They don't want the demons to check them out too closely. They're on the wrong side of eighteen.'

'They aren't!' Bodgie exclaimed

'They are. They use their big sisters' I.D.s and no one's the wiser. With the makeup they smear on their dials they could be thirty, couldn't they?'

'No, they are two fine Dungaree Dolls,' Bodgie exclaimed heatedly because he couldn't even imagine doing it with an old woman.

It was then that the Warder came to get them out of the school room. Eddy was locked in the First Division yard and Bodgie in the juvenile one where the kids resumed their game of throwing rocks at one another.

TWENTY SEVEN

BODGIE IN STIR

Bodgie in Stir was such a fine title that it put a little swagger into his walk. He felt that he was doing his time easy as pie. Most afternoons he gossiped with Eddy and at work with Tommy. His course materials had not arrived as yet and when they did he would have something to do at night. Now all he had going was staring at the book the library bloke delivered to his door. This time it was The Leaves of Autumn by Christopher Wells. He thumbed through the pages. The novel as it proved to be was boring about a tedious English family. It was worse than nothing. Bodgie lay back and dreamt himself into a tough story in which he was a crim battling his way through the dark streets of a city. Next day at work he asked Tommy if there were any good books in the library and how to get them. His mate recommended. Poor Man's Oranges by Ruth Parkes as it was a good read and with sex. When he asked Eddy, he said that Escape from Devil's Island was okay because it was about prison life, but he couldn't think of any other as he had no time for reading. Bodgie put a note in his returning book for one or the other and eventually they came just as he commenced his course. He found Practical English easy enough and time consuming which suited him. Eddy was always there with suggestions and he told him how to make a kerosene lamp from a small bottle and a piece of rag. This could be used under the blankets so that the screw on sentry duty could not see any light through the window or the screw on night duty in the division when he peered through the peep hole.

Bodgie also found out that the prison had a radio system of a sorts and he could apply for a head piece from the Major. Spare ones were kept in his office.

Eddy explained this and then told him: 'Don't expect to hear any of our music. Many of the blokes in here date from the war and Swing's their thing. You know Harry James, Benny Goodman and that lot. You don't? Well, now's your chance to hear what they were listening to years ago. Drum boogie by Gene Krupa isn't exactly Rock a'beating Boogie by Halley. It hasn't got a backbeat that you can't lose. There's even a request programme, but don't listen to that if you don't like hillbilly. A Deck of Cards is worth a laugh, but Guitar Boogie, by Guitar Boogie Smith is close to rock. First time I heard it was when I got in here. The guitarist is an Aussie too.'

Bodgie got his earphone and his music. He knew hillbilly from, well, it was a favourite West Aussie sound, but it was the first time that he had actually listened to the big swing bands. Woody Herman and his Woodcutter's Ball raced along. Glen Miller and his String of Pearls bored him, but In the Mood kept him smiling. Filling his days and a lot of his nights with study and sometimes wireless listening made the time pass not rapidly but at a satisfactory pace. In no time at all Eddy's release date drew near and when he thought about his mate leaving, he felt himself descending into the Valley of Despond. It was only a week away and he spent as much time as he could yarning with Eddy in the school room examining the latest drawing of his favourite weapon while he questioned him about the fabulous east..

In the division things were still pretty relaxed under the Major and Eddy even wagged school once. The major opened his cell for him to get something or other and went away. Bodgie and his mate sat there gassing until Eddy decided that before he left he wanted to give him something to remember him by.

'I'll tattoo a Saint on your arm,' he said.

'Do it, yes, and every time I look at it I'll remember you,' Bodgie exclaimed.

The tattoo was done with three needles wound together by cotton thread and the ink was soot. It hurt, but not so much. Soon it was done and Bogie was a marked man. The tattoo was an amateurish prison job with the halo looking like a boulder about to hit the head of the stick figure; but it held meaning like an initiation. A few days later, Kev. Holliday, who had love and hate tattooed on his knuckles, saw it and decided to add a scroll beneath the feet. Bodgie told him to put B.W.A. in it. "What does that mean,' the Noongar asked, 'Blacks of Western Australia?'

'For sure, Bud, for sure,' Bodgie said grinning. What it meant was Bodgies and Widgies Association like in the newspaper article he had read long ago when he had been young and green.

TWENTY EIGHT

REBEL WITHOUT A CAUSE

And then Eddy was gone and Bodgie was so down in the dumps that he picked a fight with his juvee mate, Tommy. He gave him a bloody nose. They made it up quickly, but Tommy seemed a bit uneasy in his presence. 'The Bodgie Blues.' explained Balga, but his mate didn't even know what a blues was and there was nothing in the music on the radio to enlighten him so he let it go. He was bored; he was sad; he was in the Valley of Despond; he needed action!

He had it when he flung a fragment of wall at Yarram and got him in the thigh. The Noongar started hopping and then turned into a whirlwind of fists battering against and through Bodgie's defense. He fancied himself with his fists, but in no time at all he was down and decided to stay down. He was no match for Yarram.

'That'll teach you, you Bodgie bastard,' the Noongar said and it was over.

Three days after the fight, Major Collins came out of his office with a pile of papers and his favourite tea mug. He looked about giving his charges a last glare as the bell sounded at the division door. The screw fumbled at the lock. Without a word of farewell he strode on and out to sentry duty. The new warder came in and locked the door. They soon learnt his name. Mr. Cousins a gray-haired square head with faded blue eyes and a set expression on his mug which showed the rigidity of his character and nature. In a short time he made the juvees remember with almost affection the major's glare and his mugs of tea.

'What are you boys standing around for? It is a work period and if your duties aren't finished on time, I'll put all of you on report. Now get on with!'

Keith Holliway pointed out that the cell holding their mops and buckets hadn't been unlocked. Cousins regarded Keith with no expression at all. He opened the door and stood next to it to see that they only took out what was required.

While the juvees worked, the new screw prowled from landing to landing. Whenever they heard his steps on their landing they instantly began mopping furiously and when he left they slowed. He appeared not to notice. It didn't worry him either that he had to go down to unlock the yard gate when one of them wanted water. In fact the screw followed the juvee out to the taps to make sure that he didn't waste time or water. He then marched whichever one it was back into the division, ordered him to wait, then locked the gate and followed the kid up to where he worked. Cousins had them all nervous. They began glancing over their shoulders. They began imagining that he was creeping up to spy on them. He had got to them on his very first morning on his very first day. Cousins even kept an eye on them when they went into their yard. No skylarking allowed. How glad they were when the mid day meal time came. They thought they could escape his surveillance. No! Bodgie heard the screw's restless steps echoing from landing to landing, and to his very door. An eye appeared at the peephole. Bodgie tried to ignore it. He breathed in relief as it disappeared.

The screw's constant supervision made them fnish their mopping before the mid day meal. He found other work for the juvees to do. At the afternoon work period after the men had gone, Mr. Cousins lined them up. He handed each a piece of emery paper. He explained what he wanted them to do by example. The landings had metal railings or rather the frame including the top was of metal and between top and bottom there was three strands of wire. These he was not interested in. It was the top railing unpainted and rusty which had drawn his attention. He showed them how to abrade the rust off. Bodgie was thankful to escape to the school room. The screw stood at the door and watched the students doing their work. They bent their heads and not a single voice broke through their industry.

When school was over Balga came out to find the juvees still at work. Cousins locked the school room door. He escorted the students down to the ground floor, sent the men through to their workshops then turned to Bodgie. 'Come,' he said.

He took the juvee to his office and handed him a tube of Brasso polish and a rag. 'Get to work,' he grated.

Bodgie stared at the tube with its red top and at the rag.

'You blacks are missing a lot of yer brain. I'll show you this, once,' the screw snarled.

Bodgie had to polish the scraped railing. Only a quarter had been done and by the time he had finished that another part was there for him to do. At that point the men returned to the division. Cousins locked them in their yard and then called the kids down. He took the tube of Brasso from Bodgie and the emery paper from the others. He then lined the juvees up and put them in their own yard, though there was only about half an hour before general lockup time. The Major had kept them for that short time in the First division yard; but not Mr. Cousins. No, and so the kids were locked in their yard and almost instantly, it seemed to them, taken out and escorted to their cells.

Next morning, the juvees dragged out the general cleaning as much as they could in spite of the screw's constant surveillance. They made it last until the mid day meal. After this, it was school for Bodgie and when he got out he found the other kids as hard at work as they had been yesterday afternoon. This time the emery papering was over and they were using pieces of rag soaked with Brasso to polish the silvery metal. He joined Tommy who smeared on the Brasso paste. Bodgie came after him rubbing it off and leaving the metal a dull gleaming gray. Not a speck of rust showed. After they finished the job Cousins told them that it was now part of their morning chores to keep it polished and free of rust. He inspected the railing and everything else they did minutely each and every day.

They still had spare time and the screw found more work for them to do. The double width of floor boards extending beneath the railings had once been polished and had not been done for donkey's years. These now were to be polished. It wasn't as arduous a job as the railings had been. In fact it was no big deal as both Tommy and Bodgie had done the same thing in Clontarf. They soon had their landing edge gleaming as brightly as the chapel floor in Clontarf. Mr. Cousins was impressed. He said so, but his face remained blank. As he left the two juvees looked at each another and wondered what was next in store for them.. Whatever it was, Bodgie would have to do all of it too as Christmas was approaching and the school room was shut until January.

One day the big screw O'Shea came into the division. Mr. Cousins began muttering to him. The juvees looked at each other and wondered. They didn't have long to wonder. The two wardens came up to the landing and shouted Bodgie to them. They were outside his cell. The door was open. The lad looked on as they gave his pet a thorough going over. They found nothing, but ripped off the wall the double spread of Elvis Presley which he had bartered from the library con who had access to magazines. After doing his cell, they called Tommy Cooper and with both of them in tow they methodically went from cell to cell. They found little to con-fiscate except the illustrations many of the cons had pasted on their walls. These they had the kids carry behind them until they finished searching all of the cells on that landing. The spoil was dumped before the office and the two screws went up to the third landing and got the boys there to accompany them as they did the same thing. After this it was the turn of the first landing.

When the men returned from work and went to their cells you can imagine the uproar that sounded when they found their walls bare and anything they might have kept hidden confiscated. If Cousins had been alone he might have had trouble, but he had the big and tough O'Shea beside him and things proceeded as usual except for the mutterings that came from the men locked in. Everyone was pissed off, but what could prisoners do?

Next afternoon, Cousins had found something worse for the juvees to do. The ground floor was paved with flag stones and these were covered with years of grime which was also caked in the cracks between the blocks. It was such a difficult job of cleaning that other screws had ignored it, but not Cousins. He handed the lads each a piece of pumice stone and a tin of caustic soda. He lined them up at the end of the division and ordered them down on their hands and knees. The flag stones had to be rubbed clean of the grime and then finished off with the caustic soda. It took about an hour if not longer to clean a stone and after the caustic soda was used revealed to be a warm honey colour. Cousins examined the result his face remaining expressionless as usual, but he must have been pleased with it. He had the kids continue on, closely inspecting the cleaning to make sure that each stone gleamed.

Cousins continued to work the juvees hard. Perhaps he wanted the division spick and span for the New Year. This may have been true for he never let up and even had them doing over those places which had been soiled before Christmas. He pointed out each spot and had a kid scraping away. Finally, they had had enough. One afternoon when he was in his office, though he might appear anytime, the juvees came together. They had decided to rebel. Joined as if by mental telepathy the group went up to the second landing and Bodgie pulled out from a crack a duplicate key made from wire. This had been a going away present from Eddy, but he had never used it. The key worked. He opened the cells of the juvees so that they could get their bread. They selected an unoccupied cell in the middle of the second landing. Bodgie opened the door, the others went inside. He stayed outside to hide the key. There was no way the door could be locked from the inside, so he quickly got them to get another bed from the next cell. He hid his key again and joined them.

They ripped up the table, put it against the door then jammed the beds behind it. Keith Holliway tested the firmness of their barricade. The door didn't budge. The juvees grinned at each other. They settled in to endure a siege. Not a sound, then footsteps began moving down below.

Tommy whispered that it must be Cousins. They nodded and Dennis retorted: 'Who else? We all in here, aren't we?'

'What's he up too,' Kev spoke a thought as there was silence again.

It took a while for the screw to find them. He ascended the stairs and began checking the cells. They listened to his feet stopping at each one.

'He's checking them through the peep hole,' Bodgie said.

They listened and waited. Kev pulled out a pack of tobacco and papers. He began rolling cigarettes passing them out in an act of solidarity. Even though Bodgie didn't smoke he lit up with the rest. They puffed away. It took the entire cigarette before a faded blue eye appeared at the peephole.

'Okay, you've had your fun, get out here, now,' the screw commanded.

'Don't say nothing,' Keith whispered.

'Out!' the screw shouted.

Not a word from the juvees.

Cousins double locked the door and left.

'Now we're in for it,' Bodgie whispered. For some reason they were all whispering.

'We were anyway,' Tommy said in a normal voice.

They began eating their bread.

'This'll be all that we'll get in solitary,' Kev said smugly.

'Isn't it one week on bread and water and one week on normal food,' corrected the know-all Tommy.

'You'll find out,' Kev retorted.

'How long do you think we'll get?' Dennis asked.

The kids stared at each other. They hadn't considered what the consequences of their action might be. Now they did and it began to scare them. It meant the loss of days from their remission and time in solitary. They were sure to get the maximum, twenty eight days!

'No worry, we can handle it,' Bodgie said not noticing the quaver in his voice.

They nodded, knowing that even if they couldn't they would have to.

Nothing was happening and one of the kids, the cheeky Dennis got up to look out of the window. The men had been left in the yards. He was seen and a cheer arose. Now every minute or so one juvee or another showed themselves at the window. It pushed the apprehension away, but it kept coming back. The waiting was hard on the nerves

Bodgie began a dialogue in his mind:
'Why are we doing this?
'Because Cousins went too far.'
'Yes and he pissed us off.'
'So we locked ourselves in a cell in a prison, was that bright?
'What else could we do?'.
'Nothing.'
'So we imprison ourselves?'
'What else can we do?'
'And now we are waiting for them. We cannot escape.
'They are coming to bash the door down.'
'We could open it and save them the trouble?'
'We can't?'
'Why not?'
'Because Cousins doublelocked the bloody thing.'
'Jesus, we are in for it, Jesus we are in for it.'

And as he was beginning to panic and lose it completely, there were loud steps outside. A crashing smash and the door came off its hinges. The bed was pushed away and the big O'Shea stood there holding a sledge hammer. It was over. The juvees shambled out and were hustled away to solitary confinement.

TWENTY NINE

THE LONELY BOY

Twenty eight days in solitary confinement. They called it mutiny. Most of their remission was gone too. They told them that they were lucky that further time wasn't added to their sentences. Bodgie was sorry for Tommy. He had been only a few days from freedom. They had been really, really stupid and now were paying for it, Bodgie thought as he prowled about his 7 foot by 4 foot cell empty of everything all the daylong except for a bible they gave him to read. He held it as he paced up and down, up and down. He tossed it up and down as he paced up and down. He sat under the window, feeling the hard cold concrete floor under his behind. He got up and paced up and down. He sat down. He got up and paced up and down.

He opened the bible and began to read. "In the beginning God created the heavens and the earth. And the earth was waste and empty, and darkness was on the face of the deep, and the Spirit of God was hovering over the face of the waters...."

Towards evening, the light had weakened a screw came to unlock both the outer and inner doors that sealed Bodgie away from everyone and everything. He got a mattress and blanket from between them. The screw filled his mug with water and he was alone again. Bodgie didn't even try to tap on the walls. What was the use and what was there to say? The window had been reduced to an air vent by having a metal plate pierced with holes bolted over it through which the light came to form a rectangle of light circles on the floor. Now it was night, dark, complete and utter like before the beginning of the world. Then a little light finally filtered in. The gray of dawn! Keys rattled and doors sprung open. He had to take his mattress and place them between the doors. In return he was given a small loaf of bread and a mug of water. The light strengthened. Keys rattled at the door. It was flung open. Bodgie was taken out to walk up and down in a narrow enclosed yard. He didn't even see the watching screw. He walked up and down, up and down that narrow passageway with the closed and barred doors. He was absolutely alone in the universe.

"Behold, I cry out of wrong and am not heard; I cry aloud, but there is no judgement. He has hedged up my way that I cannot pass, and he hath set darkness on my paths. He has stripped me of my glory, and has taken the crown from my head; he breaketh me down on every side, and I am gone; and my hope has been torn up as a tree …"

Bodgie shut the bible and thought about Samson losing his hair. He couldn't find that passage. He slumped in the middle of his cell. The tears came. He was utterly and completely forsaken just as Job had been in the bible. The screw arrived. He ordered; Bodgie obeyed; he went away and the boy was alone completely and utterly alone. He slumped in the middle of the cell and let the days happen. The screw came; he ordered; he did, and after awhile the man went away and the boy slumped down again either on a mattress or not. What did it matter? He had been a real mug. Yes and this was what happened to mugs.

"And ye, seek not what you shall eat or what ye shall drink, and be not in anxiety; for all these things do the nations seek after, and your Father knows that you have need of these things; but seek his kingdom and all these things shall be added to you."

So what, it made no sense to an idiot like him.

Yes, Bodgie decided his life was a mug's game. He knew he was clever and so he had to change, better himself. For sure, he didn't want to end up like some of the old convicts out one day and in the next. Hopeless, hopeless, hopeless; but how to escape into a better future? How to when he would be out in the streets of Perth again without much money, no job and known to the cops as a crim? Oh God and he drifted down into his Valley of Despond and heard the Bodgie Blues begin with a hard beat that drove him towards the end of his solitary time filled only with the words of the Bible which he had read from Genesis to Revelations. Now he began softly singing all the songs he had ever known and when he couldn't remember all the words, he made them up. Thus he endured the rest of his days in solitude singing the blues.

THIRTY

SALVATION

Out of solitary Bodgie kept away from doing any stupid things. No matter how many flagstones he had to scrub and scrape he would do it without a murmur. Alone in his cell, sad that he had lost all of his remission days he calculated and recalculated his release date. It would fall on his eighteenth birthday when he would pass from being a juvenile into adulthood. His childhood was just about over and he had to think seriously about what would happen to him outside. His Mum had nothing but the blues and Steady Eddy changed into Fast Eddy had gone as had the two girls. What to do; what to do, and he began a comparative English course. It kept him occupied and he even scribbled songs more hillbilly than rock'n'roll; but that was how he felt.

Tommy flashed a last grin out of his freckled dial as he was led out for release. They had promised to meet outside but had not named a place or a time. If it happened it happened. Now Bodgie was without a close friend. Kev and Keith Holliway although they put out that they were brothers but were really cousins hit eighteen together. They opted for the native yard. Yarram hung about for only a few more days before he was released. Only Dennis and Bodgie were left. No other juveniles were sentenced to prison. Mr. Cousins was ordered to put the two in the

First Division yard filled with first timers. They were no longer alone. Bodgie even began playing hand tennis and became good at it.

Then one day, a fortnight before his birthday and release he was marched to the administrative section and placed in a room before a group of people including a fair haired and light complexioned energetic woman in her late thirties. She immediately introduced herself as Mrs Doreen Trainer. She even thrust a hand towards him. Bodgie didn't know what to make of it. He went on guard. A man indicated a seat and he sat. The woman asked him how his studies were going. He replied, 'Fine,' and left it at that. A man who looked like a parson of some protestant sect enquired if he was intending to continue studying when released. Bodgie hadn't given it a thought, but said, 'yes.' He wasn't giving anything away. They or one of them asked him if he was an Aboriginal. He replied that his father had been an American. They left it at that going on to tell him that they were a welfare group formed to help young men in need. They were interviewing him to see what they might do for him. The parson asked Bodgie what plans he had after his release. Bodgie couldn't reply. He hadn't any idea about what to do. Doreen Trainer spoke for him. She said that it was the most natural thing in the world that young men in his position didn't know what to do with their lives. Bodgie listened and said not a word. He had thought about what to do on release; but it depressed him so much he fell into the Valley of Despond. He remembered the trouble he had adjusting to the outside after he had been thrust out from Clontarf. Would it be the same again? His heart quaked. He didn't want to spend most of his time that is time after time, sentence after sentence in prison; but how to avoid that. How to?

His release day was only a few days ahead. He had heard nothing further from the welfare group then he was escorted to meet them again. He still didn't know what he was going to do. Check on his Mum, he sup-posed. Bodgie was more communicative this time because he was more desperate. He needed help, but who were these people? He asked them if they were a religious group. They were and they weren't. They had come together as Christians, though undenominational, Mrs Doreen Trainer informed him, to aid and help, to proffer a helping hand to young Aboriginal men who were in danger of losing their way.

'But my father was an American,' Bodgie protested.

'Of course,' Mrs. Trainer replied with a smile, 'but he is no longer here and we are extending a helping hand. Do you wish to take it?'

'Yes,' he declared, knowing he really had to.

The group began discussing his future as if he wasn't in the room. They called up two opinions. The first was to send him North to become a stockman, which appealed to him because he had once wanted to become a cowboy. The second was to send him to the Eastern States where he could continue his studies. He leaped at this because he could find Fast Eddy and join the Saints. They also favoured this latter option. He listened as they worked out his future. They were in contact with the Aboriginal Advancement League in Melbourne, Victoria and with them had formed a policy to send youngsters in trouble in Perth there so that they might get away from any bad influences and begin afresh.

With his future settled, they looked at Bodgie and asked if he would like to leave Perth for Melbourne?

'Yes, yes,' Bodgie said unable to stop a wide grin forming over his lips. 'Thank you, thank you, I want to go,' he said happily.

BOOK THREE

BALGA IN THE BIG SMOKE

CONTENTS

THIRTY ONE

HOME SICK BLUES

Got the blues in my head;
got the blues in my heart;
got the blues in my belly,
legs and feet wobbling just like jelly,
'Cause I'm leaving my state (state of mind)
So I've got the homesick blues
The bloody homesick blues. (oh yeah)

Balga couldn't help feeling the blues, even though he didn't know quite why? Western Australia had never been kind to him and here he was escaping from the state. He should have been elated. He had made it and was on the way east away from all the heartache and pain. He should have been grinning from ear to ear, but here he was down in the dumps and feeling glum.

He slumped down on the seat in the train compartment not noticing anything. He was getting onto nineteen, but felt tears in his eyes. He wondered how he would handle the long trip to Melbourne over a thousand miles away from home. A map of Australia was on the wall with a line right across the bottom. There he was on that train pulling him away from all he knew.

Yeah first of all to Midland Junction then straight east. Man, he wanted to cry; he wanted to, and just then he was raised from the dumps by a voice.

'What's wrong with you, bud? Homesick already and we haven't even left the bloody station. Mind if I kip here?' and the bloke was sitting in the seat window across from him and grinning at him from a broad brown face.

'Yer sitting, ain't you,' Balga replied not wanting to show how happy he was to see another face as dark as his own.

'Going to be okay after all, ain't it bud,' See you got yer long coat on. They gave it to you, huh? Hangs on you a bit, Skinny.'

'Me name's Balga, not Skinny. And they tell me you need a coat like this in that Melbourne,' he replied shrugging off the coat and tossing it on the seat. 'Shitty weather. It's right on the south coast and the wind comes howling up from the bloody Antarctica. Yeah, bloody cold,' he repeated looking across at the brown face and a body that was similar to his own and wearing a similar silly long coat.

'Yep, they told me that too. It gets pretty chilly in Melbourne an' I would catch me death if I didn't have this coat on. Bud, it's a heavy burden on me shoulders, I can tell ya' he answered, shrugging off the coat and flinging it on top of Balga's.

They both regarded the pile silently and Balga said: 'Yep, pretty cold and they may be right and they may be wrong too, 'cause a bloke told me that it may get cold in winter, but in summer it's the same as here and gets so hot, so hot to melt yer liquorice stick.'

'Ah,, everyone's good at the stories, but not at the jokes,' the bloke laconically answered.

'Maybe, 'cause no one ever told me a Melbourne joke, just that it's not a bad place to be in for us. Well we'll find that out sooner or later and if we really need these things in November,' Balga said gesturing at the coats, then recognition hit him; 'Hey, you're Revel Cooper, aren't you? You were in Freeo. You're the bloke that does all those paintings. How come you're going east, monaitch, coppers after ya??

'Putting me bod on the line, bud, yep just putting me body on the line and getting away from all the trouble and strife even though I ain't got a wife. Naw, just got a couple that I see when I'm out,' and he gave a loud laugh before going on. 'These Watjelas wanted me to go to Melbourne to attend an art school an' I finally decided to say 'yep' to them. Anyways, I know you from the Grove. You came there with an, what's his name, Charlie Perkins. Ya looked more like one of us then, now ya look, well…,' and he shrugged his shoulders.

'Yeah I like a nice bit of clobber: black shirt, black jeans with pink around the pockets, black suede desert boots. Swinging, man! Ready to go on the prowl like a cat that avoids the trouble. That Grove was something wasn't it. A feuding and a fighting, like the bloody Hatfields and McCoys. Good place to get out of. It was just after there that I went to FreO prison to have a nice long rest for a year and now I'm here after that long spell of doing almost nothing.'

'Yeah, and now we're both here, Bud.'

'Yeah, listen to that lonesome whistle blow.'

'We're going away from home.'

'A thousand miles from home, but, hey, hey, new scene and all that. The east, man, Melbourne! I'm starting to get a good feeling about that city because it's a bit free and easy and they give you a chance to get ahead.'

'And not send you off to the clink for just having a drink, eh,' then he went on switching from what he had just said. 'Nothin' can beat yer own ground. I'm a Sandgroper born and darkened by the hot sun. I ain't got no time for the cold even here, so if it's too chilly I'm off back home.'

'Nor do I, but what's the point in hanging about Perth? It's only a matter of time before you run outa dough. You do a job and the demons pick you up and you're inside again. That ain't my style at all. No way, I want to tread a different road, one less rocky.'

'Arh, what's a few weeks in boob,' Revel said with a grimace that reminded Balga of pain, but also sort of put him down for being weak. 'Ya meet lots of yer cousins in there. It's as good a place as any at least for us Noongars. You get some tucker and a place to kip.'

'Yeah, I suppose it's not all that bad for a lot of blackfellas. I guess you can work at your art there. I had this mate and he did a lot of that, technical drawing stuff that he didn't have time to do outside,' Balga replied with a shrug that sort of belied his words. Fast Eddy might've done some drawing there, but he hated being inside just as much as Balga had. He could never just accept it as just another place to stay as Revel apparently did. Balga didn't dig being locked up and unable to prowl at all; but then Revel wasn't a crim, just someone the cops picked up to pad their arrest lists. He guessed that his offences would be only drunk and disorderly and petty stuff like that. Nothing big time at all, Balga thought, not knowing then that the Noongar had done the biggest thing of all. He had killed a man and they had put him away on a manslaughter charge for four years and in four years you could get used to any place. Yeah, so jail was a second home to him, and Balga decided that after such a long time freedom would become nothing at all. Perhaps, not even a word worth knowing the meaning of.

'Yep, it's not that bad,' Revel went on, 'they always give me a cell with good lightin'. Even the super there has a couple of my sketches on his office wall. It's okay, bud, believe me, it is,' he said seriously as if trying to convince himself.

Balga was about to say, yeah, but it's not my cup of tea when the train gave a shudder and then a lurch that rattled their bones and sent Revel sprawling into the seat next to him. 'Hear that mournful whistle blow. Last chance to escape,' Balga grinned thinking of the adventure beginning. The train pulled out of Midland Junction and headed east, ever east to where his dreams were. Right at the end of the line, yeah right at the end of the line hard against the southern coast.

'So' Balga spoke, 'I know that they're sending you away for the same reasons as they are me, that is, as my teachers often said, to avoid the occasion of sin and bad companions. I was in Clontarf for a donkey's age, then out for just on six months and then they slammed me into clink on my seventeenth birthday. My God, I've had enough of that. I want to be free, as free as the bird on a tree.'

Revel looked at him quizzically and Balga saw that he didn't have a Noongar nose. It was what you might call an aquiline one and with his longish hair combed straight back and sort of this way and that he looked a bit like Elvis Presley and thus not at all your average black fellow. He watched him scratch that white man's nose as he screwed up his face in thought before speaking out what he was thinking: 'They put me in that Carrolup Native Settlement. That was for Noongar kids and there well, I made some sort of mark. You need that if you want to survive. They gave some of us Noongar kids training in drawing and they discovered my talent and gave me a specialised art training. We became what they called the Children of Carrolup. Our work just after the war in the late 1940s was exhibited in Perth and overseas in bloody India of all places. This English woman Florence Rutter even had our paintings exhibited in New Zealand and in Europe and the sketches appeared in Mary Durack's book Child Artists of the Australian Bush, yeah that's what they called us, though really we were just kids of Sister Kate's Home for Coloured Children.'

'Gee, you're famous,' Balga couldn't help exclaiming, 'I'm just a no body in black jeans with pink pockets and a black shirt with white buttons. I have to do something, be something or I'll be too old before I know it.'

'Ah, you'll find something to do, maybe singing or something like that. Maybe even try sketching. They say we got the, the ability, the natural talent for that. Ya know when I was eleven I studied under Mr. Noel White. He got me started and now it brings in a crust as well as a wet yer whistle more than some times. Yep, I even sell some of me paintin's and sketches; but that woman painter Elizabeth Durack said that I needed more trainin' and put me in touch with a welfare lot, or rather I was in Freo and they came to see me and said that I should get away and concentrate on me art. So here I am travelling east.'

'Yeah, same thing, I met that Mary Durack, but who is this Elizabeth?'

'Her sister, an artist that was helping that Noel White bloke train us. She even got me to illustrate a book of Mary Durack's. It was about our Yagan, the hero of the Bibbulman tribe that they wiped out at Pinjarra. There's even a tree that drips his blood so red and I sketched it with him kind of lurking inside, as if he was part of that tree and his spirit had gone into it.'

'Good for you,' Balga said and stared out of the window where the lights of the houses fell behind and the welcome dark coolness of the bush closed in on the speeding train. Now they were well and truly on their way and there was no backing out. The train didn't stop until Kalgoorlie, the mining town rough and ready to pick on you if you were different from the miners there. He got up and stared in a wall mirror to check to see that he looked just like everyone else, except for the clothes, the brown skin of course and the nappy hair all spiked up and really all he looked like was Balga Jackson and as different as hell.

Revel eyed Balga and he didn't like the stare and snapped. "Ain't you looked at yourself in a mirror, better check yourself out, those Kalgoorlie blokes don't like anyone that ain't like them.'

'Yep, but we not there for long. Anyway what are ya some sort of poof ogling yerself in that glass?'

'Do I look like a poof,' Balga snapped back, his Bodgie nastiness coming out.

'Well, ya don't look exactly like an ordinary bloke what with those black clothes and that spiky hair,' Revel exclaimed screwing up his face.

'I ain't a poof, never, Balga snarled. 'Naw I'm a Bodgie, but if you don't believe me let me tell you the time when I met one of them from where we're going and we got on real fine. No shellacking at all.'

Balga stopped to collect his thoughts. In truth, the incident he was recalling hadn't happened to him, but to a fellow juvenile delinquent they called Dennis the Menace, a bloke that loved yarning about his sordid adventures real or imaginary. Well, what the heck, he thought deciding to make his story his own and began: 'You know I was out one night just checking out the streets and maybe find an easy shop to bust into. Well, I'm up near King's Park and remember there's a kiosk there selling drinks and things. I decided to look it over and am going towards it when this bloke comes up to me. Not a big chap, just a little bloke with a snout on him as if he loved sniffing up foul smells. Naw, not like that, he just sorta looked like a rat and was a bit nervous. I listened to him and the upshot was he wanted me to go into the bushes with him. He didn't say what for, but well, you know what for. I suppose he was frightened of the cops that patrolled the place sometimes and didn't want to be disturbed. "I'm a bit short of change," I tell him and he gives me a ten bob note just like that. This gets me thinking that he must have more and I begin to follow him towards a dark patch of scrub. It was then that I stopped, gave a laugh and ran off. Well, I ask you -- is that the way a poof would've have acted? Naw, he would have done what the bloke wanted and got his enjoyment as well as the rest of his wad.'

Revel stared at him strangely and then looked out of the window. Balga realized that he must have startled him with the story and to tell the truth it had startled him too. He hadn't realized how boob had coarsened him. He was no longer the innocent Clontarf boy; but an ex-con that knew the ways of the world from learning about them in the best college possible: prison! But this, he suddenly decided with a frown, was a bit like Revel accepting boob as just another place, but the difference was that he saw it as a school from which he had graduated and need never return. No way could it become a home away from home.

He dozed off morosely and awoke to stare out of the window and saw the Southern Cross station move across the windows and be left behind. It saddened him because that was where his sister Kylie, was supposed to be working as a nurse. Now feeling worse than sad, he pulled over his coat and hid under it. The night fled and he woke up with gummy eyes to find out that they stopped at the dreaded Kalgoorlie where they had to change trains. They got off and loitered on what was signposted as the longest station platform in the world. It certainly was long and as deserted as a prison division after all the cons had been locked up. They were there for a half hour enough time to go into the dining room and have a cup of tea and baked beans on toast sitting in a far corner so that no one would notice them, then it was out and onto and into an empty compartment where a conductor checked their tickets. They settled back just as the engine gave a mournful sad groan that echoed all along the mile or so of platform. This was answered by a guard's shrill whistle. Outside began the flatness of desert that would last for miles on miles, hundreds of miles in fact in a tedious flatness that made Balga pull out one of his Saint stories and settle into a ripping yarn set in a big city like Melbourne.

When he finished a couple of chapters Balga glanced across at Revel where he sat near the window busily sketching. He stared out and saw nothing much to get a pencil moving, only a flat plain scattered with clumps of small Mallee trees. Still there was a sort of feeling of infinity about it and Balga supposed that Revel as an artist was trying to capture that free feeling of space. To check this out, he went and sat next to him, looked down at his pad and was surprised to find that he was ignoring what was outside to draw and colour in what was exactly the landscape around Beverley, black boys (grass trees) standing well like warriors holding a clutch of spears and several tall trees hanging down their branches as if they were limp from the heat of the day. This was almost as Balga remembered it except for a few kangaroos hopping along. He hadn't seen a kangaroo in the bush his first being in the Perth zoo where they just lay about not doing much.

'Eh,' Balga exclaimed, 'look outside, not a black boy in sight and there's only those clumps of little scrub-like trees so how come you sketching our landscape?'

He grabbed the sketch book from the bloke and looked through it ignoring the artist's angry look. There were pages of roughly the same drawing repeated with a few variations such as kangaroos hopping across a landscape or one just sitting and watching Revel sketch him into the landscape at sunset, dusk or night with the scene all blackened but he supposed lit by the moon to reveal the hard silhouettes done in charcoal.

'Ah, yes,' Balga exclaimed, 'please, man, you must give me one of these so that I can remember my home bush from when I was a little kid. You know my name's Balga, black boy and I need one of those sketches you did, well, of me ancestors. Give me one and I'll treasure it forever.'

'Yeah, man, I'll give you one, I give lots away. I do 'em and pass 'em on. Maybe, I'll even do a new one for you. Spiky hair, eh-' and he took the sketch book back and set to drawing.

Balga left him to it and went back to his book, finished it and then stared out at the nothingness of the Nullabor plain until it began filling out with a special clump of grass, a bent over lonely tree, why even a wallaby bouncing through the nothingness. He stared and the landscape was filled with details just like one of Revel's drawings.

'Deserts aren't exactly deserted,' Balga said aloud. He had picked up the habit of talking to his self in his prison cell and had not as yet managed to break the habit. The lad felt Revel's eyes on him and looked up. For a long instant they stared into each other's eyes and then the artist nodded.

'Huh,' Balga exclaimed and turned to the desert and picked out details again. An hour or so passed and he was beginning to feel hungry, but he didn't know how to get any food. They hadn't seen anyone, including the conductor since Kalgoorlie.

'You finished that sketch yet,' Balga said to disturb Revel.

'Yep, take a look,' and he ripped out the page and passed it over.

'Hey, man, you captured me. Yeah and you made me into a bloody black boy tree. I love it, yeah and it's mine?'

'Yeah, Bud, all yours so you won't miss West Aussie or forget your name.'

'Man, you sure have got talent,' Balga exclaimed staring at the sketch in which he stood petrified into a grass tree. 'Real good,' he repeated and got up and carefully put it in the big old suitcase they had given him along with the coat which he now put in too.

'Man,' he exclaimed, 'I'm hungry how do we get some tucker?'

'There's some sort of dining place, I think, but it sells grog and so I don't think we can go in and eat there. We'll just have to hold on until – I don't know, until we get to where we're going,' Revel replied.

It was just then that a conductor or attendant or whatever they had on this fancy train poked his head into their apartment and regarded them from his white face and blue eyes.

'You missed dinner,' he stated.

'Yeah, bud, but I think we're a little too brown for that place.'

The bloke examined them again and nodded: 'Don't worry I'll get you some sandwiches and stuff. Give you special cabin service.'

'Yeah, bud, we're special.'

'It's a favour so keep your lip buttoned,' the conductor or whatever cautioned Revel.

And so they got their tucker, a real meal of meat and potatoes as well as cups of tea and ate and drank as the train pushed them ever east and into another night.

They awoke in South Australia. It wasn't very different from Western Australia, except for the lack of black boy trees, but the desert was past and now they had trees and when they steamed into Port Augusta they saw water. Both wandered about the platform not seeing much and welcomed the whistle to order them back on aboard. They were only hours from Adelaide and the country turned into farms and orchards. They were back in the white civilization. The houses grouped together and the train thrust into the noise of the city. A long hour at the station and then they were off on the run towards Melbourne rushing through the night.

It was about nine or so o'clock in the morning when they crossed the border into Victoria and stopped at Serviceton to hesitate before the run to the big smoke. Revel looked out and suddenly sparked up and said 'Hey Bud, ya know in Victoria we're allowed to drink. How about comin' to the bar an' havin' a cold one.'

'Yeah, why not,' the lad said sparking up. He couldn't imagine how it felt to legally go into a bar. In Perth he had braved it a few times for a bottle of soft drink and never lingered in such alien territory. He wasn't sure if he came under the Act or not, but any barman had the right to refuse him a drink or even entry if he thought him a black fellow. The only way he could legally drink was by getting a citizenship paper saying more or less that he was assimilated and living the white fellow way. Well he was, but being as good as a white fellow was something they didn't exactly allow you to be. 'Let's go,' he jumped to his feet and got off the train. Balga saw a bar sign and went into the wet canteen. Revel came after him. Both hesitated then followed him to the bar. They didn't even rate a raised eyebrow. The barman merely said: 'Well, what will it be, gentleman?'

'Give us a couple of beers,' Revel replied.

'Schooners or pots?'

'Two schooners will do.'

'We have Vic. Bitter on tap. You're from the West and I suppose are used to Swan or Emu, but Vic has the taste whereas the others have the gas,' he essayed the joke as he filled two glasses which Balga guessed were schooners.

Revel paid for the drinks and they leant an elbow on the bar and stared across at the waiting train. Balga took a gulp of the beer and it was bitter and cold; but otherwise the taste, well to essay a joke, hit the spot.

'A legal first for me,' Revel exclaimed raising his glass: 'Here's to Melbourne.'

Balga raised his glass in turn and said, 'May it bring good cheer?' and drained it.

'In yer eye,' Revel retorted following suit.

'Time for another,' Balga said and this time paid for the drinks.

'Vic Bitter, not a bad drop,' Revel said with a relaxed smile. 'I'm going to like this state where they call me "gentleman" while in the West well, I'm a bloody "boong".'

As if on cue came the call: "Drink up Gents; your trains about to depart. Happy journey and get your beauty sleep until you meet the Southern Queen of the East, Melbourne City."

'Maybe we should get a bottle of wine,' Revel suggested.

'Maybe we shouldn't,' Balga replied, 'we haven't been eating all that much and we …'

But Revel had already ordered a bottle of port wine.

'This'll put us to sleep,' he said as they went into their compart-ment where he instantly opened the bottle and they passed it back and forth and yarned much of the day away and slept the night to awaken with sour mouths.

After going to the W.C. and rinsing out their mouths and flinging water over their faces, they sat and stared at the damp looking country. Soon it began to be covered with rows and rows of houses, more than they had ever seen in their lives. 'My God,' Balga couldn't help exclaiming, 'this is it, isn't it!'

'It is, Bud, it is,' Revel replied, 'and it's big,' he added with awe.

'And it looks cold,' Balga couldn't help adding.

Protected from the outside by the walls of their compartment and the speed of the train, big eyed the two West Australians stared feeling the gray scene fill them with, well, with a grayness that had them longing for their sunny home. Not only was the sky gray, but so were the houses, the roads and the cars and buses and, what was that a street car, huge in comparison to Perth trams, rolling past and then a suburban train flashed by a dull red streak.

'You'll have fun capturing all this with your pencil,' Balga said to Revel.

'Yeah, Bud an' not a kangaroo in sight,' he replied with a grin. He appeared to be coping better than the boy. He ventured a grin at his mate who muttered,' and there won't even be any grass trees either

THIRTY TWO

RAILWAY PLATFORM BLUES

Travelling, travelling 'cross the plains, bud,
Now the rain is pissing down (pissing down)
Yeah, and I've got those sorry old railway platform blues.
Thought I would meet you, kiss you or shake your hand
Thought I would meet you, kiss you, shake your hand
Smile into your face and dream awhile in glee (grin)
Oh ain't it lonely, oh so lonely no one here to greet me
I've got those sad old railway platform blues today
The sad old railway platform blues all day today
No one to meet me, no one to greet me,
Smoke in my eyes hiding the tears,
Yeah, hiding the tears, oh ain't it lonely,
Oh so bloody lonely, so lonely, awful lonely.
I've got the sad old railway platform blues, oh yeah,
I've got the sad old railway platform blues, (yeah, sadness).

The train pulled into a sooty station. Balga read Spencer Street and guessed it was the end of their journey.

'Well, this is it,' he said to Revel. 'Do you think we'll need our overcoats?'

'Yep, Bud, for we ain't got a sweater between us and theres a little nip in the air.'

'I've got a sports coat, but it's in the suit case. Anyway it wouldn't go with these black shirt and jeans.'

'Hey, Bud, we gotta stick together in this town. It ain't our country,' Revel said almost in a whisper as he pulled on his long coat.

Balga followed suit. The thing hung on him like a shroud. He was feeling down in the dumps again and he knew Revel was too, Balga glanced at this fellow Noongar suddenly wishing it was his mate, Fast Eddy who knew his way around this burg. But only Revel was here and he was even hesitating about getting out onto the platform. Well, what the heck Fast Eddy most likely was home in St. Kilda and he would look him up when he had settled in and had some new clothes to sport so that he wouldn't appear a complete square just in from the West.

Balga pushed past Revel and got out onto the platform with the suitcase. They stood there not knowing what to do in the rush and crush of people. What to do, and just as they were thinking this a small dark intense man with a shock of white hair rushed up and thrust out a hand.

'Doug Nicolls, Pastor Doug, the field officer of the Aboriginal Advancement League. Welcome to Melbourne. How was the sunny West? Sunny I expect it was as it wouldn't be called that if it wasn't. Too many "its", eh? Like your coats, there's a bit of a cold breeze blowing. Got your cases there too, I see. Come on, we'll catch a tram to the office. You got them rattlers in Perth too, haven't you?'

Pastor Doug hurried them out of the station and onto a dirty street that was chock a block with cars huddled up against a red light. 'Bud, it's big and noisy,' Revel whispered.

'And a bit dirty too,' whispered back Balga.

Pastor Doug was charging ahead of them and they had to trot to keep closely behind him. It wouldn't do to lose him in the crowd. The little bloke reached the head of a street, hesitated then leapt across to the middle where a tram waited. The two Noongars came after him. They jumped aboard as the tram rattled off.

"Bit bigger than our Perth ones,' whispered Revel.

'And a real rattler too,' agreed Balga.

The tram trundled along and began wheeling through the centre of the city filled with tall buildings and shops and bustling with well-dressed people. Real city people, thought Balga in awe.

The vehicle stopped all along the street to let people off and take them on in a steady stream. The two Noongars eyeballed everything and hardly felt Paster Doug digging them in the ribs. They saw him hopping off at a street labeled Exhibition. Clutching their suit cases they hopped down and had to wait for the light to change before crossing over Collins Street and going down towards the sound of trains rushing along. Pastor Doug stopped, checked that they were behind him then ducked through a door into a weary looking building. They went down a short darkish corridor and entered a small office. A white man sat behind a desk facing the door and at a side desk sat a taller dark-haired woman.

'I'm Stan Davies,' the man said jumping to his feet. He was as speedy as Pastor Doug and just as short. Balga supposed that they bred them small in the city as there were so many people crammed up together; but when the woman got to her feet and he saw that she was just a shade shorter than Revel all of six feet. They shook hands all around and exchanged names. With this out of the way Revel was taken off by Pastor Doug to be settled in some hostel or other, while Balga had to wait and have a cup of tea as he was the one with the education and thus could be found a job. He asked for a mechanic's work, but Stan Davies, another Christian minister, shrugged and got onto the phone. Balga listened in. Yes, he was in good shape and not at all rough. He had passed the Junior Certificate with distinction and there was no doubt that because he had spent much of his life in a home he had fallen into trouble when he found himself adrift in the wider world. Yes, he could come in tomorrow and fill in the forms… The lad shrugged and sipped on his tea and chewed on a biscuit, the woman (the rev's wife) gave him. Now his accommodation was firmed up in a suburb called Hawthorn.

'Yes,' Stan Davies (call me "Stan" so Balga nicknamed him Stand the Man) said: 'you'll, be staying in Hawthorn. It's a nice quiet suburb with a tram route straight to the city along Victoria Street. I have a car and I'll take you there in a while. Tomorrow, you are to go to the Public Service employment section in the Treasury Building at the top of Collins Street. I'll show you that on the way. Now as to clothing -- what have you in the way of work gear?'

Balga thought a moment and replied: 'It depends on the work, I guess.' 'It'll be an office job in the Public Service and you'll be expected to dress neatly, that means a suit and tie. Have you got these?'

Balga grinned: 'I have the tie, but I lost the suit as it had a habit of picking up everything.'

'Oh,' he exclaimed not getting the lad's meaning that it had been a prison suit made out of shoddy material. 'Well, you can have your pick of what's here. Clothing is donated to us and there's a few suits, shirts and ties and just about everything else. When folks pass on, often there is a problem of what to do with the clothes of the dear departed and some of the grieving people think of us. We'll look through them and see what will fit you.'

The Noongar felt a bit queasy about wearing dead man's clothing; but he followed Stan (as he wished to be called, though he was another pastor of the Baptist heresy) into another room with any number of cardboard cartons as well as racks with suits hanging on them. Balga checked the gear over. Square; but he could get the trousers pegged when he found a tailor. He selected a couple of the larger suits that were less ancient and then looked about for shoes. He found a pair of brogues which seemed "hep" in an odd way and they fitted nicely enough for him to keep. There were any number of socks, none of them clocked, but he took about six pairs. He selected half a dozen white shirts on Stan's suggestion, one for each work day, and then a cardigan which Stan assured him public servants wore. After that, the Rev decided that Balga was well equipped for an office job and they were packed into his suitcase which now bulged as though it had eaten a good meal.

'Now we have to get you to your digs,' Stand the Man said. Balga looked blank and he explained the word meant board and lodging, though why a room was called "digs" he never elaborated on. Balga didn't ask and followed him out to a car and got in. He drove down to Flinders Street where Balga added the sight of railway lines to the sounds he had heard. The car turned left and then made another which took them along the side of a park. Next to it loomed the gray bulk of a building which Stand the Man told him was where he had to present his self the next day. 'You should find the office easily,' he informed Balga. 'Just ask anyone for the Public Service Commission. You are to see a Mr. Rogers there. He'll help you with the paper work. Just ask anyone there,' he reiterated, anxious to see that Balga had taken in the inform-ation.

'I will, I will, sure I will,' the Noongar replied with a bit of iteration of his own to put the Rev at his ease. Indeed, the man had nervous man-nerisms that jerked him this way and that and telegraphed to his driving. Stand the Man proceeded in fits and starts and almost missed making a right into a broad avenue which he identified as Victoria Parade. It was a strange double street with hedges separating a space in the middle along which the trams ran.

Now the Rev took his hands off the steering wheel to wave them about as he began to acquire a stutter: 'This this g-g-goes straight to Hawthorn where your lodgings are so it'll be easy for you to get on a tram and run straight into the city.' As he said this, his hands fell onto the wheel and he managed to stop at a traffic light.

Balga had become a little nervous at the driving, but Stan settled down as they left the double avenue to enter an ordinary street lined with shops. The man began repeating his instructions on what Balga should do on the morrow and the Noongar kept nodding his head while wondering if Revel had settled in and then of how he might find him. Stand the Man went on repeating his instructions and Balga looked out of the window. They were crossing a narrow stream.

'The Yarra,' Stand The Man said curtly.

'Oh,' Balga exclaimed. A conversation he had had with a con came into his mind, 'the river that flows upside down,' he added.

'It has that reputation,' Davies agreed as he went wide and did a right into Hawthorn.

He ensconced Balga in his "digs" and left his phone number in case there were any problems. Now Balga had a room and with it came breakfast and dinner with lunch on the week end if he wanted it. An ordinary house in an ordinary suburb with an ordinary elderly woman in charge and he was the only boarder. The quietness chilled him, but he knew he had to doss there for at least a while.

THIRTY THREE

WORKING STIFF BLUES

Got to get up each and every morning
Got to rush to catch my bus or tram
Get up every morning rush to catch my tram
I'm just a working stiff with the working stiff blues
Yeah, just a working stiff with the working stiff blues
Needing a place to rest my bones
Needing a place to hide my sins
Got a pay cheque week by week
Just for the working stiff blues
Oh yeah hear me cry these working stiff blues.

The very next morning, after a breakfast of tea, toast and a boiled egg, Balga set out for the centre of the city following Stand the Man's advice and reiterated information. He strolled to the main road and didn't have long to wait until the tram rattled up, Kew 69. Balga hopped aboard, paid the fare to the conductor and soon was moving along Victoria road through Richmond towards the city. The tram reached the top of Collins Street and a fellow passenger got up and pressed a button. A bell sounded and he hopped off as the tram stopped. Balga followed him off making a mental note on how to stop the vehicle. He dodged cars as he ran across Collins Street then crossed another to go down the lane alongside of the government building. This was blocked to regular traffic by a thick chain stretched between two iron posts. He came to the side entrance which Stand the Man had indicated yesterday as being the way in for him. He walked through into a foyer and stopped to get his bearings. It was a very brown place with the walls being in different shades from almost cream to deep chocolate and there were corridors that went north, south and west without any signs to give him his direction. Balga sighed and stared at himself in the inner glass doors through which he had come. He almost saw a stranger. There were the familiar spikes of his hair; but he wore the brogues which he now decided were as square as square could be although they did go with the suit so square. He sighed again just as a bloke that had hopped off the tram before him and also wearing a similar suit came out of a passageway. Balga suppressed a sigh and tentatively smiled. The bloke was an ordinary looking man without distinguishing marks and he was carrying a large canvas bag. Balga asked him where the employment office was.

'You wanting to join us navvies,' the bloke replied and jerked a thumb for the Noongar to follow him.

He stopped at a door, said: 'that's it,' and then went on in.

Balga followed him and saw a counter and behind it a large room with about half dozen desks at which men sat studying papers. There were more of them behind a glass partition. He took all this in as he waited at the counter until one of the blokes looked up, saw him there and came to him. Balga asked him for Mr. Rogers and he exclaimed: 'You must be the Western Australian boy. I'm Rogers and, well, we'll set the wheels in motion, shall we?'

The Noongar nodded noting that Mr. Rodgers was another of these nondescript men neither short or tall, neither handsome nor ugly, that populated this building. Just a working stiff, he thought and hoped that he wouldn't end up like them. He almost shuddered as he stared down at a mousy brown head of hair bending down to bring forth a form from beneath the counter. Balga ran a hand over his own distinct spikes as the man looked up, moved his lips in a slight smile and said: 'Now we'll just get your details, shall we?'

With Mr. Rodgers' help, the form was quickly filled in and the man then took it behind the glass partition where Balga watched him pass it over to similar type of man. They discussed it for about ten minutes, then he returned to thrust out his hand; 'Welcome aboard. You start tomorrow at the Motor Registration Branch in Exhibition Street in the Exhibition Buildings. Just go west along Exhibition Street to the gardens, continue through them and you can't miss it. Report to the staff officer here and he'll set you to rights. You'll be a Temporary Clerical Assistant Grade Two, but you can sit for an examination to become permanent and work yourself up. These are held fairly regularly and are not all that difficult. Well best of luck.'

Balga thanked him and shook hands. He found himself without difficulty outside the building where now he had the time to dig the scene. The Noongar saw a wide garden across the lane and went walking there to get a grip on his emotions. He was more than a little dazed that everything had gone so smoothly. He wasn't used to such breaks in his so far wretched life. Only his second day in Melbourne and already he had a job. Well, things certainly were different here and with this the slight traces of trepidation that still lurked within him fled out and away. How nice the day had become. Sunny, but not the harsh glare of Perth and the gardens were filled with English trees, neat lawns and pretty white girls.

Balga gazed about him at a Melbourne which was glowing with a subdued light that made everything soft and gentle. He relaxed even more and felt happy as he left the park and crossed over into what he later learnt was called the Paris end of Collins Street. All the shops strove to look posh and just about all of them were selling women's things, conservatively fashionable, and expensive he supposed. Not a thing that his mum had ever worn and certainly not even a scarf she could afford. He sighed and went down past and then crossed Russell Street to regular shops a bit like Hay Street in Perth with stores bulging with goods. The shops were on a bigger scale as was the theatre, the Regent which he came to as were the ornately carved tall buildings after Swanston Street. Balga stared about him open mouthed like a yokel, though he didn't feel overwhelmed by the city's size. Indeed it felt good to be adrift in such a neutral sprawl that was neither friendly nor unfriendly and he even felt just one of these folk rushing along anxious to do whatever they had to do. Quickly, he withdrew from such absurd identification. He wasn't one of them. He lacked their purposeful striding and their set stern faces.. Not a smile to be seen and all of the faces were white and pinched unlike his brown dial which reflected the brown of his West Aussie heritage. Now he reached the corner where they had boarded a tram yesterday. He wondered how Revel was faring and turned back to go and see Stand the Man at the League to tell him the good news and also get news of his Noongar mate.

The building in which the Aboriginal Advancement league had its office under the sunlight looked scruffier than the front of a police station. Balga hesitated to enter as if he might never come out again; but shrugging aside the make-believe he went inside to the office, poked his head through the open door and brushed his bristles as if they were untidy before asking if he might come in.

Stand the Man was sitting at his desk which faced the door. He looked up with a sincere smile and replied: 'Of course, of course, we were expecting you. Of course, it went well; of course it did, didn't it?'

Balga heard the query in his voice and walked into the office. He glanced at the Rev's wife sitting at the side desk smiling as if she knew that he had succeeded.

'And I see you did take my advice and go there properly attired,' Stand the Man exclaimed. 'Public servants must wear a suit and this was just what was needed. Mr. Rogers has rang me already with the good news. Now it is up to you to make a go of it, it is isn't it?'

Again Balga heard the query.

'Congratulations,' his wife, whose name Balga never learnt, said.

Balga nodded and looked at her carefully for the first time and saw a horse. He could see her galloping around a paddock or ripping up grass with those big teeth and masticating it.

'Thank you, both of you,' the Noongar intoned sincerely and then waited for what might come next. Stand the Man was a Minister of religion and surely there would be a Christian come on; but to his surprise there wasn't any and so he asked him about Pastor Doug.

'Oh, he's out and about somewhere,' Stan replied, 'he's our field officer and is always contacting people.'

'And where's Revel?' Balga asked about the only person he knew in town.

'Oh at the art school getting signed in and hasn't got back yet.'

'We're putting him up for a while,' the Rev's wife replied.

'Yes,' added Stand the Man, 'he's settled in. Your accommodation okay? Best we could do, but it's close to a tram route into the city and all that, it is isn't it? You like it, don't you?'

Again the query and Balga smiled and said: 'Yeah, it's fine,' and couldn't help adding, 'for the time being.'

'So everything else is as fit as can be, is it? You have enough cash to keep you buoyant until your first pay day,' Stand the Man asked ignoring the lad's last words.

'I have a few pounds and if that doesn't last I'll cruise by and pull over to see ya,' Balga said attempting a joke.

'That's what we're here for,' the Rev said convincingly.

Yes, he certainly was a good man, Balga thought and couldn't help retorting: 'That's mighty Christian of you.'

'We are here to help,' Stand the man replied sincerely.

'Building your mansion in heaven...'

'You may put it that way. Yes, you may if you wish, but it is the Christian thing to do.'

'Yes it is, isn't it,' Balga the Bodgie sneered.

Mrs Davies, the Rev's wife suddenly jumped in and said with a laugh: 'Everyone for tea.' She set to work to make it.

Stand the Man smiled in acknowledgment then bent his head over his desk saying that he had letter to read and it wouldn't take a minute. Balga stared at his head noticing that his black hair was graying at the roots, though he seemed only in his late thirties or early forties. Well, it didn't concern him and he looked around for something to occupy his mind. There was a newspaper in the side desk and he picked it up. It was a broadsheet, The Age, and thicker than any newspaper he had seen before. This reminded him that except for these people and Revel he was alone in a city much larger than Perth and really needed them. Gee, he had to see Revel too and compare notes.

Stand the Man's wife handed him a cup of tea with two bickies in the saucer and he left off the paper to sip and bite after a "thank you".

Stan Davies left his letter to do what the lad was doing and engaged in conversation about their office and the street. 'It may look a little down in the mouth,' he said.

'Seen worse.'

'The rents are cheap and the locality convenient. We have another place in Northcote, but that is a bit far from the centre of the city.'

'And what is this "Aboriginal advancement" you advocate,' Balga asked.

'Full citizenship rights of course,' was the prompt reply.

'Oh,' Balga replied, wondering what that meant. He was after all just a kid in his teens and didn't know much.

'How long has the League been going?' he asked, making conversation and hoping that soon Revel would put in an appearance.

'Well,' he began, 'Victoria, I have to admit, has the same awful history in regard to the Aborigines as the rest of Australia, but things since the end of the war have started to change for the better here. Yes, it has. We may have a Liberal government but the premier Henry Bolte is a rather astute politician who has made Victoria the most progressive of all the Australian states. For example Aborigines have the same rights here as any other Australians to enter hotels as well as to vote in the state elections unlike Western Australia...'

'Yeah, but that doesn't matter if you don't drink all that much,' Balga stated, then continued: 'Still, yeah, in W.A. if you're an Aborigine, a Noongar or considered to be one you are not allowed into a pub unless you can show a special exemption certificate, what we Noongars call a "dog license" Anyway, I've never bothered about one of those, but perhaps Revel has. You can ask him, he's more cluey about things than me.'

'Well, there is nothing like that here now. Our government does give its support to the Federal policy of assimilating Aboriginal people into the general population as quickly as possible; but any harsh laws segregating them are of the past. I don't think that you know that Pastor Doug and his family are not locals, but are originally of New South Wales where the laws were and still are quite strict in comparison to ours. They and others rebelled against the restrictions placed on them at the end of the Second World War staged what has come to be known as the Cumeragunga Walkout. Cumeragunga was an Aboriginal government mission just across the border and the folk there got fed up with the treatment they were receiving from the New South Wales government which more or less kept them confined to their mission as if they were prisoners. They had to take permission from the superintendent if they wanted to leave the station and he could refuse this for any purpose. The people there got to know about the better conditions here, the more enlightened attitudes and laws, so one day the entire population got up and walked across the border into Victoria, just like that, you know. They refused to return and it is from this act of defiance that the Aboriginal Advancement League sprung when we mobilized help for what can only be termed our internal refugees. Pastor Doug, he was quite a well known sportsman in his youth, was a natural leader and after everything became settled he came in as our main field worker and has done a sterling job. We have other Aborigines working in our Northcote centre. You'll meet them when you come to our functions. This is only our city office, as I've already told you, and our main establishment is in Northcote where we have a hall and put on all sorts of functions. Come and attend them; at least until you find your feet in Melbourne. I know that you'll enjoy them and get to know the local community. A big city can be a pretty lonely place and Melbourne, I know, is a much larger place than you are familiar with. Yes, it is. So, don't feel that you'll impose on us if you need help or even company. You are very much welcome to participate in our activities too. Workers are always needed, you know, especially Aboriginal ones to show a public face. We have a function a dance on at Northcote on Saturday. Come along and meet the local Koories.'

'Koories?'

'The name for the local Aboriginal people.'

'Will Revel be there?'

'Yes, he'll accompany us.'

'I'll come, but I sure would like to see Revel before then.'

'You might check the art school.'

'Where is it?' Balga asked Stand the Man.

'At the Art Gallery, there's a side door leading in.'

'Maybe, yeah, I'll go there and see if I can find him.'

'He is a bit late,' Mrs Davies put in.

'Yeah, and after that I'll get home and familiarize myself with it.

Revel wasn't at the art school so Balga went and walked around the pictures in the gallery paying special attention to those featuring nude women. After this he went home and read a book. It was all that he could do until he found his way around.

THIRTY FOUR

THE PUBLIC SERVANT BLUES

Mundane, mundane and all to a plan
For life, for life oh heck, the public servant blues
Oh no, oh yes, you've got the public servant blues
File some cards, type out those forms (send them out)
Drink your lunch down at the bar, the beer so cool (oh yes)
But don't be late or it'll go down on your slate
Hold that class, he's failed to make the grade (late)
Oh it's the public, public servant blues
Oh heck, I've got the public servant blues.
You have a girl, you face the marriage blues
You make a life, a couple of kids and a mortgage
To the end of your days, the public servant blues
Oh no, oh yes, the public servant blues.

Balga had found his home state of Western Australia intolerant. Melbourne in contrast seemed to offer a richness of life which he had to experience, but first of all he needed to have some cash and he didn't want to go along the way he had been heading or for that matter did he really want to be an office jockey. He would have liked to be a mechanic with the opportunity to drive fast cars; but he left any idea of work change to the future when he knew the city.

After his interview with Mr. Rogers of the Public Service employment section and happy to be employed, the very next morning clad in his square suit and tie, he hopped off the tram at the stop at the top of Collins Street and walked down to Exhibition Street, turned right and went along the rather dowdy street which had none of the flash of Collins Street to the corner of Bourke Street. Collin's Book Store was on the diagonal away from him and across the street was Thomson's Record Shop. He slowed to glance at the covers of the records on display: classical and jazz records, no rock'n'roll at all. Walking on he crossed Lonsdale then Latrobe and after Victoria Street entered the green expanse of a park laid out nicely with trees, paths, flower beds and he came across a big fountain beyond which lay a long low building with ornate doorways and cupolas. He guessed this was his goal; but where was the Motor Registration Branch? He went to the left and around the flank of the main building to find a wing which extended away from him. Here the park gave way to the tar and cement of a vast parking space and close to the building was a caged enclosure in which was a vehicle weighting machine. Balga checked the watch which Stand the Man had insisted on giving him. It was quarter to nine. He reached a wide doorway to find the doors locked. Still too early for business and he continued along to come to a small and open door through which men (and women) that were obviously public servants were entering. He followed them. They s topped at a rack and pulled out a card which they inserted into a machine which went clunk then put the card in another rack before going on. Balga stood and watched them doing this until a bloke returned his glance and commented "just clocking on," before pushing through double glass doors. Balga looked after him and into what must be the public area. It was empty of people except for the man who had spoken to me. The bloke disappeared through a single door. Balga went to it and pushed through into a large hall filled with filing cabinets and people meandering among them to reach alcoves and rooms filled with desks. He followed a small dark woman who for some reason seemed familiar and when she happened to glance back, he asked her where the staff office might be.

'You're going to be one of us,' she replied with mock amazement and an almost welcoming smile. 'I'm Nancy, welcome aboard; you go through that door over there and follow the passageway to the end. It's there and you can't miss it. I'll see you around.'

Balga thanked her and easily found the office. A sandy-haired bloke checked his watch as he entered, nodded and asked him to be seated in front of his desk. He asked him his name and picked up the file to begin to check the lad's details. Mr. Rogers had done a good job and there wasn't much he had to say or do except to eventually provide him with a copy of his birth certificate.

'I'm from West Aussie,' Balga said, 'how do I go about that?'

'Write to the registrar of births and deaths in Perth,' he was told. 'Now come with me and we'll get you settled. I'll introduce you to Tom Jones the in-charge of your section. He's a fairly reasonable chap,' and with that he got up.

They went into that large hall filled with filing cabinets about which in alcoves and nooks and crannies were desks at which people sat. Among them were a few typists who looked up and then bent back over their machines to rattle the keys with a clickety clack. Through a wide doorway he saw another room filled with half a dozen rows of desks at which women and girls sat typing with a massed clickety clack. One of these was the woman who had introduced herself as "Nancy". She glanced up towards him, pulled a face, ripped a form out of her machine, screwed it up and flung it into an overfilled waste paper basket. There were more desks alongside the partition beyond which lay the public space now sounding with voices. At one end of the partition were a few offices with glass walls towards which the man was walking. Balga hurried to catch up with him..

Tom Jones was a large dark haired man with a round bald patch to go with his round face with round blood shot eyes to go with a rosebud pink mouth. His heavy body was covered by a double breasted navy blue suit which was not unlike the one Balga had been given when being released from prison and which he had ditched after a single wearing. This was colour coordinated with a blue on blue striped tie, a white shirt and brown shoes. All in all, the man was the office type, though his cheeks were pinkish as if he had been exercising as was his nose and those blood shot eyes were sleepy looking when he stared up at the Noongar and then glanced at the staff officer who nodded and left.

Mr. Jones got up and said: 'Come, we'll get you started. You do much office work before?'

'No, I'm a mechanic really,' Balga answered.

'No hot rods here, but you get your pay once a fortnight. The job is easy enough, but when you get too bored with it take the p.s. exam, get permanent and you'll start to rise. So stick at it and one day you'll have my job.' He grimaced as if in pain and Balga nodded.

The sad bloke took Balga through the maze of filing cabinets to a niche holding four desks, one of which was unoccupied. He gestured at it and said: 'that'll be yours.' He then turned his attention to one of the men, a light-haired bloke with a huge round red face. 'This is Mr. Bogaars. He'll give you a quick rundown on what to do. Simple filing, but any problems that might crop up he'll set you straight.' And with that Mr. Jones lurched off.

Mr. Bogaars stopped peering down at his work, scratched his pink scalp lightly covered by sandy hair, then stared up at Balga with faded blue eyes. He put a smile on his face and grunted: 'Call me Malcolm, sit down a moment and I'll get you a bundle of renewal certificates. I'll start you on those and once you get the hang of it, I'll put you on the vehicle transfers. It's more of the same thing, but the sequence has to be checked.'

Balga squeezed through to his indicated desk, sat and checked out the drawers. There were only a few paper clips and a pad on which someone had been playing hang man. The Noongar scowled then smiled as Malcolm tossed over a couple of bundles of renewal certificates. 'Sort that lot out into car registration number sequence, from the old single numbers up through the alphabet and to the doubles and triples.' Balga went blank as the man added: 'It's what you see on vehicles. The certificates have to be sorted out so that you can file them without wandering about the whole room and taking all day. Okay!'

'Sure,' Balga replied, taking the rubber bands off one of the piles and spreading them out on the desk. It wasn't at all difficult and when he had finished with that lot, he did the other and inter-sorted it with the first. By then it was 10-30 by the wall clock and there was a general slackening off. A young bloke in the desk behind him said: 'Tea break!'

The Noongar wondered how to go about getting a cup of tea, but didn't have to wonder long because the young bloke got up, stopped beside his desk and said: 'There's a caravan at the front where you can get a cup of coffee or tea and snacks and things like that. I usually go out for a bit of fresh air, want to come along?'

Balga nodded. They went out a side door and crossed the parking lot towards the road where a caravan was parked. 'He'll give you credit when you're broke too,' his fellow worker informed him, 'it helps towards the end of the fortnight.'

'Is it a long way to that,' Balga queried.

'Next week it so happens so be stingy with your cash or you might have to walk to work.'

'I'll remember that, so I have to hang on to next Thursday?'

'Yeah, but you started in time to get most of your money.'

The two ordered cups of tea and sipped on them as they watched the traffic zipping past.

'I could do with one of them,' Balga nodded at the cars.

'Start saving,' his companion grunted as the man behind the counter began talking cricket to which Balga half listened and learnt that there was a test about to begin which Australia naturally would win. The Noongar recalled that Melbourne was famous for its cricket ground and decided that he might go along to see it.

'Do you think it'll be a good game,' he asked the caravan man.

'It might be,' he replied, 'though maybe you should take along some snacks and drinks as the Pommies are said to have a strong batting lineup and we have weak bowlers.'

'Yeah, I'll remember that,' Balga answered and turned his attention back to his companion. Strangely, like the woman, there was something familiar about the young bloke and then it struck him that he was almost a dead ringer for Tommy Cooper, his dear old mate who had been lost along the way. The memory made him sad and then he remembered his old mother and was sadder. He should have sought her out before he left Perth, but then everything had happened so fast. 'Maybe this bloke might be a replacement for Tommy,' he thought and putting action to the idea, stuck out a hand out and introduced himself. The young bloke thrust out a hand and Balga clutched a rough red-skinned mitt which was exactly as he remembered Tommy's hand to have been just as he stared into a face which was as freckled as that of his old mate.

'Ray Drew,' the lad as young as Balga said and with that they became at least work mates.

They finished their tea and went back to their desks. Now he was to learn the next step in sorting. Malcolm took him into the maze of filing cabinets and showed him where they began with the plain numbers and extended into the HHHs. He slid open a drawer and pulled out an envelope holding the registration paper and told him to put the new renewal one on top after checking that everything was in order as to name and address. This was all there was to it, or almost as some of the envelopes had been taken away for summons to be sent out for parking offences or even to be held if the car had been stolen. Balga smiled at this; but Malcolm took him wandering about the branch looking for a missing envelope to put the registration slip in and then passed him over to Ray or the third member of their group, George a Greek from Egypt with the usual Popadopalous type of surname. He was typical Greek with a black moustache and olive skin. Balga got on well with him, though he was older with a wife and kids.

Balga had no problems with the blokes he worked with and even Bogaars proved to be friendly. When lunchtime came Call Me Malcolm (as the Noongar nicknamed him) jerked his watermelon shaped head and grunted: 'How about a counter lunch?'

Balga was hungry by then and replied: 'Yeah, lead on.'

They walked across a busy thoroughfare which Call Me Malcolm told him was Rathdowne Street, went down Pelham to come out on the shopping street of Lygon. There was a pub on the corner, the Albion. Balga hung back, but Malcolm merely said: 'This is it,' and they went into the saloon bar and studied the blackboard displaying the counter lunches.

The barman came to them without a hard glance at Balga asked: 'What will it be gentlemen?'

Malcolm looked at Balga and the Noongar boldly said: 'Two beers.'

When the barman came and put them down they were ready to order. Balga had the rissoles at 2/6 and Malcolm had Beef stew at 3.6. These were the cheapest dishes on the menu; but they were substantial and apart from the main dish came with chips, mashed potatoes and peas. Balga's trepidation fled as he filled his stomach. He finished and sipped his beer as Malcolm asked how were the rissoles and then ordered a plate. Malcolm had a big appetite as he declared. Balga had another beer to keep him company.

On the way back Malcolm told him that he came from Ceylon and was a European, a Dutch Burger, and thus qualified for entry into Australia. He didn't say much about Ceylon except once or twice he mentioned odd things such as how peddlers boiled oranges to increase their size and how hot the curries were. He sneered at the curry flavoured stews of Australia and said that they were not in the comparison with the tasty ones from his island home.

Balga agreed with everything he said. The beer had put him in a mellow mood and he was pleased and happy that he had been treated at the hotel as just another customer.

Seeking out purloined files sent him roaming and he got on first name terms with quite a few people including two typists that struck his fancy though in different ways. One was Nancy, the woman he had spoken to on his first day. She was a thin neat woman in her late twenties or early thirties who modeled herself on Audrey Hepburn, not the female of Roman Holiday but the one his first girl had copied in Perth, the Audrey of Sabrina (1954 and onwards) in which the unsophisticated princess was replaced by the professional actress wearing garments fashioned by Hubert de Givenchy as Nancy informed me with a deprecating smile as she added: 'I may look and be as slim as Audrey, but I'll never be able to afford her clothes and thus must do with these facsimiles.' She got up to show him her high necked costume as well as the slimness of her figure. She w as skinny and seemed to be sickly with it, but this didn't stop Balga from digging her. He told her in a few terse sentences about his lost "Audrey" and she replied with a giggle that now he had found a replacement. He replied with a laugh and then went on with his work. She was a bit too old for his nineteen; but then he needed a bit after those months in prison.

He would have tried to get his wick in there as with her short hair she did look a bit like a Widgie; but Malcolm found him talking to her and gave him a bit of office gossip. It seemed that she was getting it off with their boss, Tom Jones who was an alcoholic with a vicious temper and held a grudge against those he didn't like.

So passed the first day for Balga at the Motor Registration Branch. The people were relaxed and the work simple enough that he decided to hang on in there.

THIRTY FIVE

BLACK FELLOW PARTY BLUES

Hey, youse black fellow party boys (oh, get ready)
Hey, all youse black fellows come together
All together for the Black fellow party (oh yeah).
Under the tree, squatting on the lawn
Passing the bottle, marking the time
Getting the spark, don't sit this one out
Have a drink, pass the bottle (sparking, sparking now)
Hey, hey for this black fellow party
Hey, hey for this Black fellow party (oh yeah)
A guitar plays, strummed by one of our kin
No one's dancing, all waiting for the other to shine
Oh the black fellow party blues (oh yeah)
The glad old black fellow party blues (oh yeah).
Now we's up and now's we's grooving
Sweat sweet mellow country music moving
Dancing cheek to cheek without a care
But she's taken and you'll be decked, oh yeah
For dancing cheek to cheek, for dancing cheek to cheek
'Cause it's the mean old black fellow blues (oh sad)
Hey, it's those mean old black fellow blues (be glad)
While you're dancing cheek to cheek,
Yeah, dancing the Black Fellow party blues away.

Under a spreading tree of some European name that kept the men safely in the shadows Balga carefully not to crease his gear squatted beside an old bloke with a shock of white hair and a black face lost in the darkness so that he could only now and again see the gleam of what he imagined were false teeth. The oldie had gestured him down beside him as he came up and then introduced himself as Laurie Moffat, the last Koorie full blood of Victoria. Balga accepted him at his word just as he accepted the sweet bottle of port that was doing the rounds of a circle of men that were waiting for the dance to begin. He heard Revel talking, but didn't get to him as the old bloke began yarning to him in a soft voice that hesitated and rambled on like a soft Victoria brook. 'Plenty of water in Victoria,' Balga thought as he listened.

'Yes, William Berak, Baruk, long gone now, yeah, long gone, he wrote a book, naw told a book, all our culture to that white bloke, anthropologist William Howitt everything he knew. It was his book.'

He stopped, took a slug of the wine and passed the bottle to Balga. He felt the warm glow of the liquor hit the right spot and he smiled and said: 'Willam Baruk.'

'Yeah, you look in the library for those books. They all about us Koorie people and spot on 'cause that old black fellow, he passed on our history and ways to him,' Laurie told the lad and went on to say that there was a statue of him in a town called Healesville where there had been an Aboriginal settlement, Corenderrk, or some name like that. Old Laurie didn't have many teeth left or his falsies were loose. He slurred his words so that Balga missed out on a lot of what he said.

'Healesville?' he queried, to get at least the name of the town right and then took a swig on the bottle and passed it on to the old fellow.

'William Baruk, the artist,' a voice cut in and Revel plonked himself down between them. He took the bottle and finished it off.

'You know, him, you know him,' the oldie slurred.

'Artist, just like me, Bud, checked out some of his work. Good with the figures, likes a lot of movement, doesn't do the bush much at all.'

'Naw, yes, what you mean, he sketched everything he want to. Us blokes dancing and things like that. He was a culture man and did what he could.'

'Yeah,' Revel grunted and turned to me: 'Didn't catch up with you this last week, Bud. We have to keep together, only Noongars in this city. Yeah, get out and do yourself a turn. There's a pub where the artists go, called Tatts just down from the Museum art school. I'm there most times in the late afternoon until 6 o'clock closing. Come and we'll sink a few jugs, eh, just kidding, but you gotta come. Hey, miss you, bud and we Noongars have to stick together,' Revel stuck out his hand and they solemnly clasped wrists and then shook hands.

'Gotta keep together,' Balga intoned, 'sure do miss the old state, but too busy to notice except at night when the loneliness comes creeping like, like well, like a black cat.'

And with his simile Balga felt the urge to get into this city that flowed all about him rich with promise. 'Yeah, yeah, and now the dance beckons him to his feet. Do you think they'll have a rocking band?' the lad asked.

Old Laurie Moffat came to with a start and exclaimed: 'Music, the dance is starting. We have to get in there and join the ladies.'

He began to push himself up to his feet and Balga extended down a hand to help him to his feet.

'Yeah.but it doesn't sound like rock,' he said somewhat sadly.

'A kin of mine is playing country, sweet sweet country, can't stand that noise,' the Oldie exclaimed

'I'll join you later,' Revel said, 'it's nice here and well it'll take awhile for the folks to get moving.'

'And maybe never grooving,' Balga said, feeling the Bodgie flaring up in him. 'Catch you later,' and he escorted the Oldie to the hall.

The function was a fund raising event for the funeral fund the League had started for Koori people. A group Harry Williams and the Country Outcasts were laying down a country groove to unresponsive men and women. Only a few couples were up shuffling about the floor. When the number came to an end Harry spat into the microphone and declared a talent quest. A few men and women were summoned up with much urging from Harry who knew everyone to sing their way through sentimental old country songs until Balga had had enough. He decided to give them a song. He got to his feet and went to the foot of the low stage and waited for the last singer to strum to an end.

Harry looked at Balga and said; 'Don't know you, cuz, but are you ready to give it a go.'

'Yeah, but I can't strum that thing to save my soul.'

'Well, just hold it so you don't get nervous. What's your name and where you from?'

'Balga Jackson and I guess I'm from Perth, West Aussie.

'Hey, brothers and sisters, we have Balga Jackson a Sandgroper who's about to finish off our contest with... with ...?'

'Well, I'd like to sing,' (and with a rush) 'My West Aussie Home.'

'Never heard it, how does it go, what key is it in?'

'Oh man, make it low, make it sad, find the tune and I'll be on top of it.'

Harry Williams winked around the hall, grinned and hit a low note, the drums came in and a slow low tune began.

Balga shrugged, took a stance, cleared this throat and let the words come out. He sang:

I come from the plains of my home
Where no fences keep me bound
I'm a Noongar without surrounds
No fences can keep me bound
No fences can keep me bound.
Now I'm lost in the streets of the city
Faces grey and white make me cry
Oh ain't it a pity, oh ain't it a pity
I miss the sunny plains of my home
Oh the plains of my Noongar home.
I came to have a look around
I come to make some sort of stand

Now I feel that I lack a plan
Man, oh yeah, I have no plan
To make it back to my Noongar home
Oh yeah, sadness for my West Aussie home.

Someone loudly clapped as Balga finished. Revel. 'Sing it again, Bud,' he called, 'sing it again.'

And Balga did as best he could and after he finished, Harry Williams shook his hand and presented him with a footie sweater. 'Fitzroy, the Lions,' he held it up and everyone cheered.

After this everyone loosened up and the floor was filled by couples dancing and enjoying themselves. Balga managed a few sedate dances and then went to get a cup of tea with his last partner.

This was Margaret Briggs a largish woman, with deep brown eyes, a light olive skin and a brusque manner. Balga sat with her over a cuppa and listened as she got to talking about her family. They belonged to the Melbourne area thus had a claim on the League. She even told him that the Briggs' family were descended from Trugerninni and thus belonged to the Aborigines of Tasmania as well as the Koories of Victoria. Trugerninni had been styled the last of her people, but the Briggs (the name came from a sailor that frequented Bass Strait between the mainland and Tasmania in the 19th century) were directly descended from Trugerninni's daughter who came to the mainland from her island home with her mother in the 1830s. Balga nodded to this as he wondered why no one had really worked out his own pedigree.

As they were talking Revel came up to him and said: 'Hey Bud, you made your mark. I paint and you sing. Too much, right,' and he wandered off. He was not to be found when the function finished and Balga went looking for him.

Instead he met, Alec one of those short bustling men that seemed to populate Melbourne. He took him to a house close by for some tucker and tea. It was the inner circle of Koories that kept the league going. They all sat in a circle in the lounge room and took turns dancing. This wasn't a part of traditional Koorie culture Margaret informed him. She said that during the second war the government had evacuated the people of Thursday Island from up north in Torres Strait between New Guinea and Australia to Melbourne where they mixed with the city Kooris who learnt some of their culture. This included a canoe dance which she decided to demonstrate with him. Balga felt awkward in his Bodgie threads, but got up with the rest. They formed a line of paddlers and began singing a song.

Balga began enjoying himself, but it was time for the last bus. He hurried to catch it with 'goodbyes' ringing in his ears.

THIRTY SIX

ST KILDA ROUGH TRADE BLUES

Got the rough trade, rough trade,
Rough trade Saint Kilda blues
Got the rough trade, rough trade
Rough trade Saint Kilda blues
You look at me, I look at you
We come together holding hands
We walk and lie upon the sand
We make love, call it what you will
'Cause I'm rough trade, rough trade
Yeah watch out I'm rough trade
No bluffing, a rough rider, don't argue
I'll give you the rough trade, rough trade
Rough trade, Saint Kilda Blues, oh yeah.

Squares or do-gooders usually picked the quietest accommodations in their efforts to reform blokes like Balga. So Stand the Man had settled him in the suburb of Hawthorn which was similar to North Perth where they had once put him and right next to the zoo too, but not this Melbourne suburb with its empty streets and with the recent introduction of television into Victoria, the front windows of the houses fluttering with the blue glow of screens. Not much to experience there, so on the weekend. Balga used the two days to wander through the inner city suburbs, Richmond,

South Melbourne, Fitzroy and Carlton, looking for odd bods and with his antenna up to catch the vibes of any place that might switch him on. He had sought out the pub Revel had mentioned, Tatts, but pubs were closed on Sundays and he made do with a coffee lounge and listened in on blokes talking about nothing much except cricket, football, or how dull it was compared to the war years. As the day ended Balga sought out a street through which one of the infrequent Sunday trams rattled him back to Hawthorn to the house which could never be a home.

The lad revolted against such dullness. He wanted to move to a livelier area and listened to some blokes engaging in man talk and how St. Kilda was the place to let it all hang out. Ah, St. Kilda and Fast Eddy, remembered Balga and the following Saturday afternoon he getting off the tram at the Flinders Street railway station stop, he glanced to one side and saw on the front of another tram just pulling up, St. Kilda Beach. He jumped aboard, sat on one of the wooden slatted benches and stared out as they rattled across Flinders Street, past the station, across the bridge over the Yarra River, then along a tree lined avenue to reach a junction marked by a football oval which proudly declared: Home of the Saints. Balga felt that it was a welcome to him as he still considered himself a member of the Saints' juvenile gang. He jumped off the tram to admire the sign then walked through the scrap of park in front of the oval to come out at the head of a busy street. He crossed over to find that he was in Fitzroy Street which Fast Eddy had mentioned to him so long ago. Remembering Fast Eddy and his flair for smart threads made the lad glance into a mirror to check out his threads. Very neat in the Bodgie fashion and his hair was flat top and unlike any style the blokes sported. Satisfied that he was with it Balga sauntered along feeling his antenna quiver, his nose twitching and his eyes flickering here there and everywhere for a sight of the fabled gang.

Balga went past a big pub sign, The Prince of Wales and got into an area of coffee lounges and cafes filled with people that seemed not to have a thing to do except to direct quick glances to check him out. None of the eyes were really challenging and Balga, well, felt at home. This was what he had expected of Melbourne. He smiled a tight smile his mind filled with memories of Fast Eddy and his two molls that might have become his if the cops hadn't arrested him. Tough luck and Balga wondered if Fast Eddy might still be in the same trade. This excited him. His eyes went this way and that way sliding into coffee lounges with smiling jukeboxes sending out rocking songs to boys and girls looking city tough, walking razors rather than the bunched fists of louts. Ah, yes, this was his scene! His steps slowed and he found himself standing in front of the The Prince of Wales hotel, a large ornate fronted hotel with its importance spilling out over onto the pavement. He smiled and was about to enter when a voice suddenly shouted: 'Hey, hey Bodgie!' Balga gave a start and his eyes darted towards the owner of the voice and held: it was, it really was, his old mate of Boys' Town and Fremantle Prison, Tommy Cooper. God, he was happy, at last someone from his home town and in the right place too.

Yes, there was the freckled face still as blotched as he remembered it from his Clontarf days, though his hair had changed and now he sported a style similar to the duck's tail that Balga with his nappy hair could never master. 'Lo Tommy,' he drawled across the space between them which his old mate quickly crossed to thrust out a speckled hand. Balga gave him the less complicated Saint's shake, as he wasn't one of the gang. As their hands brushed away, Balga drawled: 'And how's the world treating ya?'

'Like sugar and spice,' Tommy replied with a grin.

Balga looked him over and saw that he was dressed like a movie waiter with an auburn bow tie, a white shirt, a wine coloured velvet waist coat, dark pants and shoes. 'How's the waitressing,' he leered though with a grin to take the edge off, 'get many tips or only pinches?'

'Ah, come on Bodge, I'm a receptioner in this grouse big pub towering right over you. I sit at a desk and check guests in and out. Come to the bar and I'll get you a free beer. Just one though, 'cause the boss is stingy.'

He was as good as his word and in an instant they were sitting at a table with beers in front of them. 'Good drop,' he exclaimed. 'See. I've made it East,' he said with a laugh, 'and just need to find where the action is.'

'It's here, Buddy, it's here if you can find it,' Tommy sneered with a hip smile that showed that he had the edge over his mate.

'Well, yeah and I'm looking,' Balga retorted.

'And you'll find it too. I've been here a few months, but I'm about ready to split to Sydney. King's Cross is the next place to be they tell me.'

'Yeah, yeah, cutting out as soon as you catch a glimpse of me, eh?'

'Naw, Bodge, gee it's grouse seeing you. Real grouse, first Clonny boy I've seen in donkey's ages.'

'What about blokes from the other place?'

'One or two have come through. St. Kilda is the place for them, but they never remember someone who was a juvenile in the can.'

'Yeah, and St. Kilda seems like my place too,' Balga said with a laugh. 'It looks as if it could rock as well as roll, you know what I mean.'

'Yeah, but be cool about it,' Tommy replied seriously. 'It can be rough and not like Perth at all. There you only had the Abos to contend with, here you got, just about everybody, sometimes you just look at a bloke and he wants to do you one way or the other, you get what I mean?'

His reference to "Abos" made Balga go on guard. He remembered that he had always hid that side of his identity from even mates like Tommy and in Perth had been passing himself off as a Yank with a father from New Orleans. Since reaching Melbourne it hadn't been necessary, but maybe, he thought, maybe it was.

'Yeah,' Balga said, easing away from that forbidden subject, 'but I'm as tough as they come or if it comes to that I can run a mile as fast as John Landy so St. Kilda will suit me fine. Now I just need a place to flop and then we can make the scene together. How do you like this cardigan thing? I got it just the other day. New and nothing in the city can touch it. Green, red and blue stripes and hanging halfway to my knees, gas, eh?'

'Yeah, bit bright though; doesn't look too warm for this weather and that Ivy League style is in now. You know the pants are tighter and the coat is without padding and loafers, man, they're cool. I never liked that loose draped Bodgie style anyway.'

'It's still with me, man and I can stroll well as rock, you know. Just new in town and been taking it easy, just feeling my way in this big city and now,' Balga almost shouted with glee and indeed raised his voice so that the barmaid all frizzy blonde hair and big blue eyes stared over at them. The lad winked at her as he said: 'Yeah, and now I'm ready to see what this town is made of and listen to some good rock'n'roll and then there's the Saints, the Bodgie gang to hang out. Man, it'll be the most, like (and he laughed) New Orleans.'

'Yeah, yeah, the best of luck, but now I have to leave you. Duty calls in five minutes. Sorry to split, but I have to. Anyway you know where to find me. Gee, it's great meeting you, Bodgie. Yeah, find a room, there are lots in Dalgety Street and we'll jive together. Grouse, huh,' and he got up, made to rush off, then stopped and said: 'Hey, I'm off at ten. Hang around the street until then and you can doss with me in my room. The boss won't mind if it's just for one night. Besides he has a floozie and is just settling down for another round by then.'

'Uhuh,' Balga replied staring down at his beer then lifting and draining the glass. He got up and followed his mate to his desk at the side of the foyer not wanting to leave, but also to see if he was on the up and up. One never knew, but when Tommy sat down as if he owned it, he knew he was genuine and said: 'You sure it will be okay to come back?'

'For sure, the front doors will be locked by then, but see that side passage there. It ends at a door which opens onto the street. Check it out now so you'll know where to meet me after ten.'

'Right, see you then,' and Balga grinned as he went down that passageway happy as Larry. Tommy was as right as rain and he wouldn't have to rush back to Hawthorn that night.

Time didn't hang around in bars, it put on wings and flew so when Balga came out on the street evening was reaching out its fingers and even a few lights were winking at the setting sun. It wasn't that late as the bar had to close at six, but it was getting towards that and as it was early spring the cold darkness was rushing in. He hoped that it wouldn't get too chilly. His cardigan may have looked like the dog's balls, but as Tommy had said it wouldn't keep much of the cold out. He needed a warm coat, but didn't feel like going for an overcoat. As Balga thought this he came to a shop, The Gents and in the window was featured a garment he fell for. It was called a car coat and was like one of the long draped sports jackets he still fancied. Balga studied it and if the shop had been open, he would have entered to try it on. Well, it was closed, but he could see himself in it; but for now it would be best to seek out a nice warm coffee lounge with a jukebox of great tunes for him to spin. No, he wanted to check out the whole of this street first while there was still some heat left in the day.

Balga sauntered on still smiling at his luck in meeting an old friend as soon as he had hit St. Kilda. Maybe he would meet Fast Eddy tonight as well. He came to a coffee lounge and ducked in for a coffee. He checked out the god and rang a coin for a new singer, Eddie Cochran and his song, Summertime Blues. It was grouse and he bought the reverse side, Come on Everybody. It really rocked his soul and finishing his coffee he bopped out of that place ignoring the sneer of the square shop keeper and suddenly came to a halt as the smell of roast pork hit him from a shop with a window filled with lots of good things to eat. A side of pork brown and juicy made him drool. It drew him inside and he got the bloke behind the counter to cram a long roll with the meat with a few pieces of crackling to keep out the cold. He got a bottle of coke to drink and then went on looking for a place to sit and eat. The street ended at a cross road and beyond lay the rippling water of Port Phillip Bay with lights twinkling on it. He crossed over to sit on the sea wall. He scoffed down his roll, crunched on the crackling and slurped up the coke. The chill was beginning to reach for his bones, but he shrugged it off as just part of the feeling that it was good to be alive. Yes, he was thinking that the world was his oyster when a bloke sauntered up to ask if he had a cigarette. Balga replied that he didn't smoke.

'I do,' the bloke replied, then added: 'Nice spring night tonight.'

Balga looked at him. He seemed harmless enough and so the lad answered: 'Getting on to being a bit chilly.'

Balga jumped down onto the beach from the sea wall which was about four or five feet above the sand. He stumbled and came down with a thump on his behind. The sand was warm and he stayed there. The bloke followed and sat down beside me. 'We're out of the wind here. Lights look nice on the water, don't they?' he commented.

'They do,' Balga replied glad of the company. 'You know it's been a while since I came to Melbourne, but it's the first time that I've seen the sea. Lazy, I guess,' and he gave a laugh still feeling at ease with the world.

The bloke was looking around, this way and that way. Balga's eyes went this way and that way too but there wasn't anyone else on the beach. He was staring at the sea when he felt a hand on his thigh. He left it there and on a whim asked: 'You got any dough on you?'

'A couple of bob, maybe a quid,' the bloke replied.

'You won't get much for that,' Balga retorted, shifting away from him and his paw. It came back on his thigh. He left it there. It was kind of exciting and he was getting hard too.

'A quid,' the bloke replied, his fingers touching the lad.

'Two and right in this hand now,' Balga snarled, dropping his hand onto the bloke's lap palm upwards.

The deal was settled and Balga had two crisp notes in his hand. His fingers closed on them as he jumped up. 'Thanks buddy,' he shouted, 'that'll do me just fine. Not hard enough for anything,' and he ran to some steps he had glimpsed leading up from the beach and was across the road and in Fitzroy Street in a flash. He sauntered along flushed from his adventure and wondering what else the night might hold.

He ducked into a coffee lounge for the warmth and a coffee. It had a juke box, all rounded glass and with those new 45s in it. He thought of the big god in the The Royale Cafe bar in Perth and this got him thinking of Fast Eddy again. Balga thought about him as he sipped on his expresso while staring at a heavy girl with super breasts, curly dark hair and a slash of red lipstick on her white face which flashed at him as she caught his eyes. The girl got up and went to the juke box. She bent over so that her big behind stretched tight the cloth of her tight skirt. Balga ambled over to the god and bent his face next to hers. 'You like a good rocker, try Summertime Blues. Naw, you don't have to buy it, I'll get it for you,' he said dropping a coin into the slot and out came the number really loud, hot and pulsating.

'Grouse,' she replied without much enthusiasm in her voice, though her foot tapped to the beat, 'but I prefer something softer and sweet, like Sugar in the Evening.'

'Don't know that one as I only like it hard,' Balga answered, his hand coming up to rub his short spiked hair.

The lad bopped back to toss off his coolish coffee. She was still at the god, so he went back to her and she said, 'I like that one too.' She had a finger on E14, some tune called; Please, Help Me I'm Falling. 'It's yours,' Balga drawled and dropped his coin into the slot. Out came a song that wasn't rock, some sort of hillbilly number, but the lyrics were okay, perhaps for her. 'You want a coffee,' he asked her.

'No,' she replied, 'I'm waiting for someone and he won't have me drinking with strangers; but if you're still hard, I can let you have it for a fiver.'

'Huh,' Balga exclaimed, not believing his ears.

'Yeah, you should get off in a short time as you're ready for it,' she said touching him.

'Make it three and I'm in,' Balga grinned.

'What are you grinning about, loose change,' she said and Balga said that he was a stranger in the big city and she was the first doll that had offered him anything.

'Well, you're in luck, if you add another quid,' she replied sardonically. 'Then you'll have a real born and bred Melbourne doll.'

'Well, I suppose that you'd be better than a pull,' Balga answered cynically.

'Four quid and you'll find out.'

Balga found another note and sneered as he asked her where the ground might shake.

'Just follow me, flat top, or will I call you Brownie.'

'Naw just Blackie, you know my dad was from New Orleans.'

'Yeah, yeah, I know you're not from around here.'

Balga followed her out of the coffee lounge down a lane which ended at a brick wall. She stood with her back against the wall and opened her legs, one forward and the other slightly back.

'Get it out and put it in,' she urged. 'There's a cold breeze and I don't want my fanny all frozen.'

Balga was a bit put off, but quipped as he got ready: 'Don't I even get a kiss.'

'Christ, hurry up,' she replied, her hand grabbing him and squeezing hard. She pushed it in and Balga wobbled once, twice and then emptied into her. 'Call me Flash Gordon,' he commented.

'Lucky for you, I might have charged you a tenner if you had gone on any longer.'

'Yeah, well, see you' Balga shrugged, doing up his fly. He started to say something else, but she wasn't looking at him and so he made his way back to the coffee lounge to order a coffee and ponder the ways of "love" - and soon had Jerry Lee Lewis the wanker singing Whole Lotta Shaking. Such a great rocker put him back into a good mood and he sipped on his piping hot coffee and thought that he should have asked the moll if she knew Fast Eddy. It was then that the door opened and in came a well-dressed bloke. Balga stared and grinned. It was Fast Eddy though his Bodgie gear was subdued enough to seem square. He wore a striped blazer, thin dark pants and sharp toed shoes, though he still had kept his D.A. hairstyle. Balga's hand went to his own spiked hair as he envied that Tony Curtis style.

Fast Eddy's light blue eyes flickered here there and everywhere about the room. They hesitated on everyone, lingered on Balga, went away and came back for a longer stare. Recognition for sure and the Noongar got to his feet and strolled over to him. 'Hey, man, give me some skin,' he accosted him with.'

'Some skin,' he asked coldly, but held out his hand so that Balga might commence the ritual.

After it was over, he demanded, 'and who might you be?'

'Remember West Oz not all that long ago, Audrey and Leslie and the Royale as well as the big house in FreO.'

Fast Eddy still looked puzzled and Balga had to say: 'I'm "Bodgie" and you told me to look you up if I ever got to Melbourne. Well, I've gotten to Melbourne and I'm looking you up.'

'Yeah, and now you have, what's the deal,' Eddy sneered then lightened up enough to add 'How are things going with you in the big smoke,' in a dead pan voice that indicated that he didn't care two hoots how the lad was getting on.

'Fine, fine, how else could it be' Balga sneered in reply and was turning to go back to his coffee when Eddy said: 'sit!'

'Why not,' Balga shrugged then slumped in a chair with his back to the wall so that he could keep an eye on the door.

'You took my seat,' Eddy commented, then said, 'yeah, FreO and that awful Western Australia! God, I'll never go back there, not even if my life depends on it.' He broke off then and this was because the girl that Balga had shagged was coming through the door with another one just as heavily built.

Balga stared at them. They might have been sisters with those 36 24 36 bodies that blokes liked.

'Lo, Jane and Rita,' Fast Eddy intoned as they reached the table. 'If you like I'll introduce you to one or the other or both,' he said to Balga.

'Naw not really, I still like the Audrey type,' Balga answered, then suddenly tensing as to what Fast Eddy might do when he learnt that he had already shagged his Jane moll.

Fast Eddy asserted his authority by sneering: 'Can't you get the girls a coffee.' Balga was tempted to say "No," but what the heck? He got up, went to the counter and got himself a fresh brew at the same time. He even got Eddy one just for old time's sake though he was being a real arsehole.

When he returned to the table, Eddie was in deep conversation with Jane, snarling and sneering at her: 'You don't go with anyone unless I give you the say so,' he grated. 'So what if you got paid for it and it was just a quickie. I didn't get you the customer, did I? Yeah, so you want a little stick do you? I'll give you stick all right. Ah coffee,' he said and drained the cup Balga placed before him. 'Now you Rita, you would never do that, would you, so I trust you to stay and entertain, no keep my friend here company while I just fix this moll up. Sorry, sorry she shouldn't of done you,' he directed at the lad. 'She just wanted a bit of stick; I'll give her one all right. Stay here and buy Rita a tune, not Please Help Me I'm Falling, I hate that one.'

He went off dragging the offending girl by one wrist. Balga stared after them and then went to the juke box and put on the number he didn't go for too; but then what Eddy hated he decided he liked. Still he followed it up with Eddie Cochrane to get the sound out of his ears. Rita smiled at him as he came back and then defended her pimp. She said: 'No worries, his stick is better than his bite. He just likes to come down on us especially in front of blokes. He thinks it impresses them. You know him long?'

'Haven't seen him for a year or so, but he was different then, cooler, not so strung out.'

'Yeah, I suppose we all were back then; but now we're as we are, for better or worse.'

'As the song goes, right; but I like Summertime Blues, better.'

'Kiddie song.'

'Yeah, but it bops.'

'Maybe.'

'So your name's Rita, right,' Balga said, hoping to change the subject or something, perhaps even elicit a smile from the sour puss.

'Naw, it's really Mary, but Eddy thinks I look like the film star, Rita Hayworth.'

'Yeah,' Balga broke in, 'and the other's Jane Russell, right?'

'How did you know?'

''Cause it's my business to know such things,' the Noongar said, laughing and even getting to his feet and bopping about a little to the music. After all it had been over a year since he'd been in such company

'Yeah,' she answered, staring up at the lad as he scrubbed at his spiky hair with his left hand.

Balga looked down at her thinking that she was really top heavy. He winked and went back to the juke box, bent in prayer over the titles and the singers and his eye fell on a number called I'm a Wild One sang by someone called Johnny O'Keeffe. He got that and it rocked out. 'Hey, that's good,' he called to Rita from the jukebox. 'Yeah, he's a real Wild One,' she replied. Balga got the other side and the words boomed out as he strode back to the girl and the table. 'When I left school, they said I was bad, the very worst they ever had ...That's a gas,' he yelped, his feet moving to the beats and then Eddy appeared with a scowl on his face and no Jane. 'Got her a customer, for an half an hour,' he gloated. 'Hey you got Johnny on the box. He's Bodgie, though not a Saint. I've met him and he lives just as he sings: wild, huh!'

'Uhuh,' Balga agreed. 'If it rocks roll it and the world's not that bad when you've got a rocking tune on the box.'

'Yeah, yeah, but you get old and the music starts fading away into eternity,' Eddie said sadly.

'Maybe, maybe, man, but you got Jane Russell and Rita Hayworth working for you, that's something that is.'

'Something like nothing; something like work, these lazy sluts,' he sneered, 'Something like nothing much, that's them. All they can do is lie on their backs or stand still while some bloke prods them. As for me, I'm something, I have to be if I'm to protect their fannies and collect the dough. Leave it to them and they'd give it away for five bob. Not a thought in their scones. No gratitude either for how hard I work for them to make sure that they don't get done for nothing. I select their customers and try to keep them a class act. I don't like cheap molls or hot chicks for that matter. Both no good for business, man, no good for the profits, though sometimes I get so fed up that I feel like giving the whole game away and get a worthwhile job like driving a truck. It'd be easier, wouldn't it babe,' he flung at Rita.

'Oh Eddy,' was all that she could muster.

'There you see,' he said, 'that's what she and Jane are like. I try to get out from under and all I get from them is "Oh, Eddy," and they big eye me and make me stay on to protect their business. You know what might happen if wasn't around, huh,' he said smiling a deadly smile at Rita.

'Oh Eddy,' she replied again and it was then that Balga began to feel a sarcastic smile tugging at his mouth. Balga had been ready to shag Rita, but Eddy had put paid to that desire at least for the time being. Sitting with him was pretty wearing and he knew he couldn't stay there much longer without cracking up with harsh mirth. God knew what Eddy would or wouldn't do then, for surely he was a walking razor quick to take offence and cut off his pound of flesh. Balga glanced down at his watch and saw that it was ten. Now he had an excuse to split the scene.

'Hey, Eddy, I've got to cut out,' Balga told him. 'Nice meeting up with you and all that, but there's a mate waiting for me and he won't wait much longer. One question though before I split, your duds are all changed. Once the threads were like the heppest, now, well, they're cool, but what happened to the drape shape?'

'I grew outa that old set of rags,' he retorted. 'Man, we're at the Sixties and everything has tightened up and look, the foot ware has gone all pointy. I'm a sharpie, if you want to put a name to me. Cool, huh?'

'Yeah, you've always been a sharp dresser so you might as well put your name to it,' Balga grinned, then added: 'How's the Saints these days? You told me that you were all together like a fist, but that was awhile ago and things change.'

'Yeah, when you're a kid you hang around in a gang, but once you get past eighteen, there's other things besides your mates, so they're around, but not into having parties and things like that anymore, too grown up and one by one they're dropping away and even getting married.'

'So I'm too late,' Balga remarked with a scowl.

'You were always too late,' Fast Eddy sneered.

'Maybe, well, at least I got my wick into Jane Russell and I'll be back to try Rita Hayworth,' Balga wanted to say, but held his peace.

'Yeah, see you around.'

'Yeah, I'll see you.'

'Yeah, I'll be around here and so no sweat, eh Buddy? Fast Eddy signed off and began heckling Rita as if Balga wasn't there. 'What do you think,' he began. 'You want to do him? You like these tall, black types don't you. You'd do him for nothing, wouldn't you; but you won't, will you?'

THIRTY SEVEN

ROOMING HOUSE BLUES

A space for a bed to lay my body down
A space for a bed to let my body down
Easily, slowly, the silence is deafening
The light low enough to let the gloom
Peer into my mind, don't feel gladly
Or sadly just got the Rooming House Blues
Yeah, the rooming house blues (oh no).
The bloke next door he groans no lullaby at all
The corridor it sounds like a couple having a ball
Clinking bottles and a smell of piss flows through
The door, land lady singing a dirge, nothing but
The rooming house blues from her to you
Oh yeah the rooming house blues from you to me.

Balga hurried towards The Prince of Wales noticing that even though it was after ten some shops were still open and blokes were hanging out, strolling real slow as if they had the whole night to plod through. Yeah he could understand this even though the cold was giving him the shivers. Ah yes, that sweet feeling of padding through the darkness, black cat on the prowl hit him as he reached the dead front of the pub. A figure separated his shadow from the side door which he had been told to use. ''Lo man,' that still familiar voice called to which Balga replied. 'Well, it must be that Tommy Cooper that once I knew so well that we even ended up in prison together and now we've met up again in this Melbourne town, to wit the suburb of St. Kilda.'

'Yeah, yeah who else could it be, man,' Tommy replied somewhat tiredly.

The lad guessed that his turn of duty had wearied him, but this still didn't make Balga stop the gab. 'Well, it could be the famous Bill Haley of the Comets,' he said mockingly.

'Yeah, yeah, bet you didn't know that I went to his concert when he came to Melbourne.'

'You really saw and heard the man live,' Balga said seriously knocked over by the news. 'He may be a bit old, but he started the whole rocking thing. Yeah, if he ain't hep, who is?'

'Old and wise and going hard at it. He and his band were a gas, a real gas,' Tommy told his friend using the "gas" word so casually that Balga was jealous having only heard it from a couple of kids in the street. Fast Eddy had been right he really was stuck in the past. Balga became all ears as Tommy went on. 'We were sitting there and the band came on stage, but no Haley. Where was the boss man? We waited a minute, then two. We were getting restless almost ready to tear up the seats, when the band began the opening bars of that ever famous song Rock Around the Clock, Still no Haley! Then suddenly behind us the doors were flung open and in he came jogging with his kiss curl like glued to his forehead. He got to the stage and without even waiting to catch his breath took up the words. Man, that night he did all the old numbers, flung in a few good new ones like Skinny Minnie and really rocked the joint.'

'Gee, I wish that I had of been there,' Balga whispered in awe. 'I ain't seen any of them singers, not one rocker. Gee maybe one day Elvis will come to Australia and then it'll all happen.'

'That would be too much, man, too much,' Tommy replied as he lead his mate through the door and along a corridor and up stairs. All was quiet as the den of a mouse. Compared to this empty cavern the street was a hive of activity.

Tommy stopped in front of a door right at the head of the stairs and inserted a key. Balga followed him into a small room holding two beds, a small table between them and a landscape reproduction of an Albert Namatjira painting on one of the cream walls. There wasn't a window and this made him wonder how his mate could stand being cooped up there.

'This certainly is no place much like home,' he commented.

'Yeah, just like a cell in boob, isn't it,' Tommy grinned as if it was a great joke.'

'More like solitary, except there was a window,' Balga replied.

'Yeah, but there is one,' Tommy answered, pointing to the transom over the door.

'Okay, okay that'll do, but don't you even have a radio to listen to some tunes?'

'Naw, besides why doll it up if it's only short term? Not worth the bother. I intend to cut out to Sydney soon as it gets warmer or maybe next winter, for it won't be as cold up there, then on to Brisbane. Work my way right around Australia.'

'Yeah, gotta keep on moving' Balga replied, not knowing what else to say. This was a different Tommy Cooper from the old one, though he had always been a self assured little bastard, but square as they come. Now not only had he seen Haley, but he was sporting a hair style that he envied.

Balga watched Tommy fish out a bottle of beer from the big jug that sat on the table along with a basin. He clenched his teeth about the top and wrenched it off. He took a swig and passed him the bottle. Balga took a long pull then shoved the bottle back. They leaned back against the wall and the bottle went back and forth.

'So do you miss West Oz,' Balga asked Tommy.

'What do you mean, Castledare and Clontarf not to mention Fremantle Prison?'

'Yeah, not much to miss there, I grant you unless you're into woe and no go. Still I do miss the place a bit, even Clonny where I grew up, though not the country town that came before. Anyway, what was the best place for you?'

'I suppose Clontarf was. You know they flogged us, but it wasn't just that, we could elbow a space for ourselves there. I was too young to feel much about Castledare.'

'Yeah, hey, you know I can still copy Dicky's signature. You got a piece of paper and I'll show you.'

Tommy found a pencil and a bit of paper and Balga looped PLOD on it. 'There Patrick Lawrence O'Doherty, can you remember that? Just like the real thing, perhaps I should've kept a Shadow comic with a suggestion of a cleavage in it and thus one which he would not have signed. Compare them and you wouldn't know the difference.'

'Yeah, maybe you should have if that's all you have to remember them by. At least they taught you to write as well as to read those comics.'

'Yeah, with a leather strap. First Crowley, then O'Doherty and lastly Doyle who used his boots as well. All that's past, though I can feel the bruises sometimes when I'm in a rotten mood. You know that Dicky taught me religion, perhaps that's the reason I don't go to church now.'

'Naw, you don't go to Mass 'cause you too lazy to get up on a Sunday, besides you haven't even been able to find a church here yet. Why you only made it to St. Kilda today and after, what did you say, weeks?'

'You so bright and right that you shine like a traffic light,' Balga answered, then added, 'but you don't know that it was the Proddy dogs that got me over here and they mightn't like it if I became a Mick again, though nothing would stop me if I wanted to.'

'Ah, it's all the same heaven and hell especially when you die,' Tommy retorted. The bottle went back and forth a few times while they contemplated their shitty lives. Finally Balga broke the silence to say, 'Do you remember that short blonde Bodgie type in our division in FreeO.'

'You mean Eddy Steady Ready, something like that -- you two were pretty thick in there, weren't you? I was a bit jealous us being old mates and all.'

'Ah, he was just a Johnny come lately that I found I had to dig. He got me into this Bodgie thing, you know and also into what I thought was his sister, Audrey, a sweet little Widgie who helped me celebrate my seventeenth birthday just before they picked me up, which reminds me my birthday falls down soon and I hope we can celebrate it together. Gee, I hope I get a room near here soon and a doll like that Audrey, man. She really dug me rock steady.'

'I bet she did and you did the Stroll together, uh, rocking and a rolling the night away.'

'Yeah and you'd never guess almost the same thing happened tonight. I done Eddy's moll up against a wall though she was big and slack whereas Audrey was small and tight. He doesn't know it yet, but who cares if he does. He's no mate of mine, and so maybe I'll try for his other moll. You know, I met up with him tonight and he came out like a big lump of hard turd. Yeah, a constipated shit! When he was in W.A. he was happy to call me mate, but over here he doesn't even want to pass the time of the night with me. Gee and once I thought him to be so cool, but tonight he came over like a big tabby tom whining out his blues to an audience who just don't dig his kind of rough gruff too sad to be glad stuff. I know that you aren't like that, you know, a sad sack who can't have a good time.'

'Naw, I'm not like that. I do my work and life takes care of itself, though as I told you I'm off to Sydney soon and then straight up the coast and beyond to that new place they have up there called Surfers' Paradise. I want to see more than a bit of the world before I get too old to dream if you know the song.'

'Yeah and a bit square it is too.'

'Be that as it may, but as I said before you find a place to doss in St. Kilda and we'll have a ball together to celebrate your birthday, right?'

'Right,' Balga agreed.

'Yeah, cast an eye over Dalgety Street, it's the next one up and lined with rooming houses. You can get a nice big room for a couple of quid a week.'

'I'll check it out tomorrow,' Balga replied, 'but what gets me is that you could do the same, so why are you living in this little cupboard, why not get into something better say in Dalgety Street.'

Balga said this in the hopes that they might share a place together; but only received the answer: 'Why, there's only Tommy Cooper and not only doesn't he have to pay for this room, but can get free grub from the kitchen. It's a good lurk and I'm not complaining or changing.'

'Well, if you like it here, stay; but I'm ready to cut from my place. It's in Hawthorn which is dead, dead, dead, man and suddenly tonight I just came back to life seeing you and all. Yeah, but then I thought I had to make compromises because they sent me to Melbourne and I felt I had to pay back some of their kindness so I've been as cool as ice. Well, I've served my time and this cat is ready to stroll.'

'Yeah, you sound like you are, but as for me, I've got to get some sleep. I get up at eight and start work at nine.'

'Okay, I'll just stretch out on this bed and drift into slumber land.'

Tommy put the light out and Balga lay on the bed feeling a little woozy from the beer. He floated away into this St. Kilda where he not only had made a couple of quid, but had gotten a shag later. He went to sleep dreaming of that Rita and awoke as Tommy got up. He showed him a communal bathroom along the hall and after he pissed and flung water at his face took him along to the kitchen where a hung over cook filled two plates and slid them in front of them. Balga was hungry from last night and got stuck into eggs, sausages, bacon and chips. When he had finished gulping it down, hot tea was waiting for him. Now he could appreciate Tommy wanting to stay in the hotel.

'Well,' Balga said, 'now I'm ready to check out Dalgety Street to see what, what "digs" I can find.'

'Digs?' Tommy queried.

'Just a term, I picked up,' Balga smiled, 'see you Gator real soon.'

'A while Croc, a while,' came the old now dated reply.

Balga left the hotel happy and with a full belly. It was a little blowy outside and the sun at nine o'clock hadn't any warmth in it. He shivered just a little as he went along Fitzroy Street which at this time in the morning was pretty dismal with the pavement wet from being washed by a slow moving water tanker. He wanted to get that coat, but the shop was still closed, so he retraced his steps and turned up Grey Street and yes the next street was Dalgety just as Tommy had said.

The lad wandered from one end to the other, past terrace houses with every third or fourth one having signs in their left or right front windows advertising rooms for rent. It was hard for him to pick one. Some radiated weariness as if having experienced too many solitary blokes with long gone sour dreams tossing and turning the nights or days away. These sad ones, Balga guessed most likely had old men living their lives away in the smell of piss. His Mum had lived in one of them and he still could remember the awfulness of it. He stopped right in the middle of the street daring a square to run him down in his old Holden. His eyes swept the street. First one side then he turned and his eyes fell onto number 28. The front door was wide open to show a length of faded carpet leading to stairs down which descended a blowsy brunette on the wrong side of thirty, but behind her came rocking the sound of Roll Over Beethoven, by the one and old brown eyed handsome man, Chuck Berry. The woman was carrying a broom and she did a dance step with it as she began sweeping the passageway.

Chuck drew the Bodgie over to read the sign in the window next to the door which read in misshapen letters: BUNGALO AVALABLE. That decided him, not the misspelling, but the word bungalo. He didn't know what one was and so he went through the wrought iron gate which separated a narrow length of concrete from the narrow length of pavement. The woman stared at him without saying a word. Balga saw a bell button, pushed it and she decided to come to the open door. She leant on her broom and stared down the street before turning her eyes on him. Big brown eyes like a cow. He smiled into them and said, 'The bungalow?'

'The bungalow,' she repeated and scratched between her breasts. She seemed to be thinking as her eyes went for a stroll down the street again before returning to examine his well dressed figure that is if one liked the Bodgie garb. Balga thought something was up, but repeated 'The bungalow.'

'Ah, yes, the bungalow,' the woman said. There was a pause before she continued: 'It's out the back, but I warn you it's a bit small. We got four. The others are better, but they taken. The best one, the biggest one is occupied by some sort of dago, but he pays his rent on time and never causes any trouble. The other two, both together are all but vacant. A couple come in to do their business in one and as the in between wall is so thin, they took both so that leaves the last one. It is small, but is by itself so you won't be disturbed by anyone next door. It's nothing special, but only thirty bob a week and you can't get anything cheaper than that unless you go to the St. Vinny's. You can afford that, can't you,' she asked suspiciously.

'I haven't even seen it yet,' Balga snapped, 'so don't mention rent until I decide, okay.'

'Yes, but I have to ask, don't I, so don't get niggardly. I only manage the house and I have to lay all the rents on the line every week and so do the tenants.'

'I'm a public servant and can afford it,' Balga told her, 'so let's see it!'

She took him down the passageway and around the stairway to a back door which opened onto a concrete covered yard around which were the "bungalows". These Balga saw were small huts made out of plywood or masonite. The one the door of which she now unlocked was just large enough to hold a single bed, a table and chair. A corner was curtained off to serve as a wardrobe. It certainly wasn't much and was close to being downright awful; but he decided that it could do for starters. He really wanted to escape Hawthorn and well nothing was permanent and one day he would get himself a flat.

'There's a kitchen at the back of the house where you can do her cooking and the bath room's next to it. You don't have to come inside at all except to go out. You can see there's no back gate,' she informed me.'

The lad stared about the big greasy room with a large table and a couple of old gas stoves in it. 'This is sadness,' he mumbled; but Bonny, as she introduced herself, took his words to mean that he wanted the place and before he knew it he was in her flat upstairs drinking a cup of tea while she wrote out a receipt for his first week's rent. When it was over Balga stumbled out feeling hardly able to face up to anything even Fitzroy Street which had sparked up by now. He thought about the coat, but didn't have enough money to try for it. 'What the heck, I had to move,' he muttered to himself. A tram came trundling along and he ran to a stop, leapt aboard and let it rattle him into his future. 'Twenty one today,' he sang mirthlessly as it went along. 'I've got the key of the door and I hate the place all bloody ready.'

THIRTY EIGHT

FAST LIFE BLUES

Oh sometimes I go so fast
Like a rocket rushing to the sun
Evading the moon
And burning out too soon
Oh this is the fast life, fast life
Fast life, fast life blues
Let the missiles rain on down
And the wars increase too soon
No fuss, this is the fast life, fast life
Oh yeah the fast life, fast life blues.

Balga's new place may have been small and bleak; but he could spruce it up later. He had moved out immediately from Hawthorn lugging his case and now he pushed it under the bed then rushed off to Fitzroy Street to check out the coat, but it was Sunday and the shop was closed. At least, the hot food shop wasn't and he got a couple of long rolls to fill his belly as well as a bottle of coke. He didn't take these back to the bungalow but went to the patch of park outside the Home of the Saints and sat on a bench staring at the sign and wondering how Fast Eddy could have been so mean to him.

Balga couldn't stay in the park for ever and a night and it was getting chilly. He really needed that coat and with that thought he got up and went to The Prince of Wales to see how Tommy Cooper was. He was busy at his desk and Balga told him that he had a room in Dalgety then left as the bar was closed. He came through the front door of the rooming house and from Bonny's flat at the top of the stairs rock music came pulsing out. He stopped trying to identify the tune and the woman opened the door of her flat, and invited him in for a drink. She and her husband were there with a half dozen bottles of beer and the television blaring. He had seen television before in shop windows but never in a private house. He stared at the small screen and didn't find the bluish black and white appealing. 'Maybe, it'll be in colour one day,' he remarked.

'What's that,' Bonny asked.

Balga repeated his words and her husband a nondescript sort of bloke who obviously didn't wear the pants in that flat smiled and said: 'It is, in the States.'

The lad stared at the screen watching jiving couples that were replaced by a short fair bloke who seemed cool. 'Who's that?' he asked.

'Johnny O'Keefe,' the husband replied.

'Why haven't you seen Six O'Clock Rock before? I thought you were a rocker and everything,' Bonny said, thrusting a full glass into his hand.

'I am and you know my dad was from New Orleans and was friends with Fats Domino,' he almost bragged and then tensing as the one and only Jerry Lee Lewis appeared on the screen thumping his piano with everything including his fists and boots and giving such a great rocking version of Whole Lotta Shaking Goin' On that it made him almost fart.

'Noisy isn't it,' the husband whose name was William Tell or something like that commented and clicked channels only to arrive back at the same one with Johnny singing his new song, She's My Baby.

The evening continued on and Bonny gave him a plate of stew almost as bad as that of Clontarf. He was hungry and polished it off as on the telly flickered The Jack Davy Show. Balga had heard him on the radio when he compered a quiz show, but this was the first time he had seen him. He was a ruddy white haired old gentleman who didn't turn him on. 'I expect that Bob Dyer will be on next,' he commented. Bob Dyer was the friendly competition to Jack Davy and Balga used to listen to him in prison as the convict in charge of the radio system preferred him to Davy.

'Naw,' he's on Friday night and on Seven,' Bonny commented just as there came a knock at the door and a red haired woman pranced in.

'Hey, hey,' she exclaimed, 'hubby's on the night shift and Jeannie's on the town.'

She poured herself a beer, gulped it and refilled her glass. 'Ah, that's hit the spot,' she commented with a vivid lipstick smile.

'Hey go easy,' Bonny said, 'there's only another bottle after that.'

'No problema, hey, we'll have a whip around and I'll ring for some, but only when we're opened that last bottle.'

'But the pubs are closed on Sunday,' Balga commented.

'So what, Darkie' she answered, 'and who are you anyway? Haven't seen you here before or even after a few beers, so what's your moniker?'

Balga explained himself a little and by the time he had finished, she had that last bottle open and half finished.

'Got any cash on you,' she asked.

'I think I've got a bit in my bungalow,' Balga answered reluctant to squander any of his coat money.

'Right let's go and see how much you're got,' she exclaimed, jumping to her feet.

Perforce he had to follow.

They carried their glasses with them. Balga opened the door to his dismal pad. But Jeannie didn't comment. She sat on the bed and said: 'Let's see if it's green, orange or blue, the notes I mean.'

'What,' he said, not quite getting it.

'The colour of your dough,' she replied with a low laugh.

'I have to find it first,' he replied.

'Well, finish your beer and then get it out.'

Balga sat beside the woman and feeling a bit uneasy with her drained his glass. He put it down on the floor and turned to watch her finish her glass then place it beside his. 'Yes, let's see what you've got.' Jeannie said. He thought she meant the money, but before he could move, she flung herself down on the bed and dragged him up on top. She thrust up and he thrust down and he came just as she flung him off. 'Now we'll just get the note,' she said coolly pulling down her skirt.

Balga pulled out his suitcase. 'It must be in a pocket,' he lied as he pawed through his messy clothes.

'It may be in your pant's pocket, Sweetie,' Jeannie giggled she pressed herself against him so that he could feel that she had on a hard corset just as women did in the movies. Her green eyes held his as she went through his pockets. He saw that there were a few lines about those eyes.

'Nope,' she said tugging at him so that he had to turn to the business in hand. She held him as her other hand went into his other pocket, She gave a grunt as it emerged clutching his fold of notes.

'Ah, here it is,' she said following her comment with a giggle.

'It's all that I have,' Balga protested not wanting to lose all his dough. He really wanted that coat and he had to eat too!

'I'll just take a fiver and with what I get from Bonny, we'll be good for a dozen,' she exclaimed, flinging the rest of his dough back on the bed. She scooped up the glasses and went.

When Balga got back upstairs Jeannie was on the phone to the sly groggers as they were called. She urged them to drop off a dozen in a flat ten minutes. 'They're just up the way in Middle Park,' she told him, 'and they'll be here in ten for sure. They know their business.'

'While they were waiting Balga told her that he was from Perth and asked her if she was a born and bred Melbournian.

For some reason, this flustered her and she gave a nervous giggle before explaining her origins: 'Yes, well, as good as any, I expect. Been here, well, just about all my life. My Grandmum she came from Whitechapel, London and it was there that that Jack the Ripper got cutting up the girls so no one could earn a few bob. Grandmum got scared and decided to get as far away as she could when he cut up a woman she knew, and that far away was Australia, Sydney to be exact. She stayed there then came down to Melbourne where the money was flowing from all the gold they were dredging up. She went to Bendigo, moved on to Ballarat where she had Mum and Mum came to Melbourne during the Great Depression where she had me. So that's my story and I know yours, well as much as I want to. You're a West Aussie and just got here and haven't got a girl friend or anything,' and she gave that giggle again just as a knock came at the door and a bloke came in carrying a carton of beer. He set it down on the table, declined a drink, hugged Jeannie and then went off.

It was getting towards eleven when Jeannie gave a giggle then explained that her hubby would be home by twelve and she had better get back. 'Hey, how would you like to escort a gal home,' she said looking at Balga.

'As long as it isn't too far,' he replied feeling the need to go to his bungalow for a sleep as he had to go to work in the morning..

'You'll never get a gal if you won't even go a little way to sit on her porch,' Jeannie retorted. It sounded so rural that he doubted that she was as city bred as she claimed. "Still, what did it matter," he thought as he got up having let her goad him into accompanying her.

They left the house and in the street she placed her hand on his upper arm which she explained was the proper way for ladies to walk with their beaus. Balga nodded to this as they reached Grey Street and turned left. A car slowed to check them out and Jeannie giggled and called: 'Hey, can't you see I'm with a fella. Maybe tomorrow, huh!'

In answer the car sped up and away. Jeannie told the lad: 'A lot of those pavement crawlers are such scaredy cats, though they are good for a couple of quid when a gal needs it,' and she gave that giggle again as she went on to order: 'Now wrap your arm about me and keep me warm, sweetie pie. That's nice. Make believe we are a couple.'

She snuggled against Balga and he looked down at her red hair She only came up to his shoulder and he had thought her much taller. 'You're only a little thing,' the lad exclaimed.

'And you're got a big thing, like Harry Belafonte' she retorted, flashing her face up at the lad so that he had to kiss it, his lips hitting her nose before they found her mouth. 'Clumsy, clumsy,' she said as he wondered if his breath smelt as much of beer as hers did.

'Bonny's a good friend,' the woman told him, 'and I meet up with her whenever I get the chance to have a drink and a laugh together, but never along with hubby though. He's stingy, not a good sport at all. I've just about had enough of him and his ways. Anyway, when he's on late shift I duck down this way and then back again. Now after Grey we do a right into Barkly here and down we go to that big picture palace on the corner. Oh, From Here to Eternity is on, but hubby never takes me anywhere. Maybe you will,' and she flashed her face up at him again. They stopped for a kiss outside the quiescent cinema which meant that it still was a little early with the people inside getting an eyeful of Deborah Kerr.

'When I got the time and when hubby's not around,' Balga replied carefully.

'You're not much for giving a gal a good time are you?' she retorted sharply.

Balga might have replied that he had to go to work in the morning as well as that she had a husband and was a little too old for him. Instead, he merely kissed her again.

'Oh you must be a Mick,' she exclaimed.
'Why,' he asked.
'I know what you're thinking.'
'Naw, I'm nothing like that. Indeed we are two of a kind.'

'Don't even joke like that,' she said. 'Now we go along Carlisle and here we are.'

It was a duplex block of flats and she fumbled in her bag, got out her key and opened the door. 'We've still got a little while so come in and have a cup of tea.'

Balga followed her inside into the kitchen where she put the kettle on the gas then excused herself. He supposed that she had gone to the bath room to get rid of the beer smell and was thinking of following after when she returned having exchanged the costume she had been wearing for a dressing gown. She made the tea then said that they would be more comfortable in the lounge room. They were.

Seated next to each other on the couch, they sipped their tea and suddenly she jumped up and said that she would put on the radio. She did and some middle of the road station droned out the Jim Reeves song, He'll Have to Go.

'And you have to go,' she said brightly, finishing her tea and standing ready to take his cup.

Balga left and as he reached the picture palace a bloke plodded past. Balga turned and watched as he went on to go into Jeannie's flat. He must be the husband; and the lad pitied him, then yawned and hurried home.

THIRTY NINE

WHEN THE SAINTS...

Oh when the saints come marching in
Oh when the saints come marching in
Oh, we'll all be in that number
When we all come marching in.
Oh when I show my tat to you
Oh when I show my skin to you
You flash your thighs without a smile
Then you show your tats to me.
Oh when we saints, we all come together
Oh when we saints we trust each other
'Cause there ain't no other, no bloody other
When the saints come marching in (give me some skin)
Oh yeah, when we all come marching in (give me some skin).

Balga awoke at eight to stare at the wall a few feet from his face. It was just about time to go to work. He lay there. The bungalow felt nice and snug smelling of the perfume Jeannie had been wearing last night. At last he got up and got ready for work by putting on his drab business suit. He hurried off without taking into account that St. Kilda was much closer to the centre of the city than Hawthorn and arrived early. Balga took this to be a good omen. Life in the boarding house, he found out was quiet enough during the week and even Saturday (when he expected Jeannie, but she didn't put in an appearance) was also quiet. Bored he went to hunt up Tommy and found him busy with the accounts of the hotel. He left him to his work and. actually went to see that film, From Here to Eternity which he didn't like much. After that, well, he put on his dark clothes and went on the prowl. He passed a parked Ford car, drifted by, turned and came back. He tried the door handle. It turned and he was in. Only seconds to reach under the dashboard, tug lose the ignition wires and join them. With a whoop, he pulled away from the kerb and went flying down the street. He turned into Fitzroy Street and burnt to the end not caring that he was way over whatever the speed limit was. Not a cop in sight. He was prepared to race any cop car that might come after him. Not one did and deciding it was foolish, he slowed down and turned at the end of the street onto the esplanade road and kept on going. Every now and then he put down his foot to feel the power of the engine. It was towards midnight when he reached an outer suburb called Dandenong and did a u-turn and without regard for any other vehicle, slipped into high gear and kept his foot flat to the floor and made St. Kilda in minutes. He left the vehicle parked in front of the big face of an entertainment park and exhilarated with his evening went to check out the coffee lounge where Eddy hung out.

A car slowed and he stopped to stare insolently at the bloke behind the wheel then strolled off down the street to the clothes shop where he examined what he thought of as his coat. It looked bulky but maybe he could get it re-cut by a tailor so that it became a drape coat. He smiled at this and retraced his steps and turned into the coffee lounge for a coffee. He was biting into a sandwich when Rita came in by herself. He expected Fast Eddy to follow, but she was alone. She sat at a table. He finished his sandwich and got two fresh coffees and went to her.

'Have a coffee, kid,' he said, sitting down across from her. He examined her boldly taking in her Rita Hayworth styled curly red hair reaching almost to her shoulders, the slash of her red broad mouth, the two prominent bumps of her chest. She was regarding him coldly from cold blue eyes so he winked at her Bogart style.

'Hey, hey,' Balga exclaimed, 'you remember me, the West Ozzie bloke from a few nights ago. I was just looking at a grouse coat in the window of that store a few doors down and came past, saw you and decided to say "hello", where's Eddy?'

'He'll be here in a quarter of an hour,' she replied staring past his right shoulder.

'Hey that's just enough time for us to get together,' he said with a grin.

'Huh,' she exclaimed taken aback.

'Well, don't you remember what Eddy said when we were talking altogether last time?'

'No, what did he say that would make me do you?'

'Think and then come through,' he grinned. 'If I had known you would be here I would have kept my car, but I had to give it back.'

'If you had a car, it was a hot one,' she flung at him. 'Anyway how close were you to Eddy in Perth?'

'As close as this,' Balga pushed up the sleeve of his black shirt to show the tattoo of the saint Eddy had pricked there. 'He did that so that we would remember our times together. We are like this.' And he held up two fingers, then stuck his thumb through them and closed his fist. 'He said to give it to me for a three,' he lied.

'It's always a fiver, but are you sure he didn't say for free seeing you were as close as this,' she flicked up her skirt to show a thigh on which through the stocking he could see the tattoo of a saint.

'You know Eddy,' Balga groaned, 'his favours have got to be paid for.'

'Yeah, you're so right so give me a fiver right now,' she demanded flicking her eyes at him and then away as she thrust out her hand. 'Come on give me the dough!'

Balga produced his last fiver which was meant to see him through to payday. Well, what the heck, if he needed a couple of quid he could borrow them from Tommy or someone at work.

She took it then hung back to say: 'We have to wait for Eddy. You know he doesn't like me going off with guys by myself.'

'I'm his mate and if I wasn't on the up and up wouldn't I want it on credit?'

'Maybe, yeah, sure, blokes are like that.'

'So are we making that short walk to the head of the alley?'

'Sure, why not, nothing doing here anyway, and who knows when he'll be coming.'

Balga grinned as Rita swayed her ample hips in front of him to the spot where he had done Jane just a few nights ago.. She adopted the same pose with her skirt hitched up so that she could spread her legs with one slightly behind the other. As she got into this position she actually giggled as she informed him that the tar was all pocked from their high heels. She added: 'If you can count, you can figure out the quickies that we've given here by adding up the marks and dividing the number by two.'

'Dividing it by two,' Balga queried.

'Well, we've got two legs haven't we? Now hurry up or it'll be a tenner which you most surely haven't got.'

'Right,' Balga grunted, thrusting against her. He wanted to get the deed done before Eddy arrived on the scene to spoil his fun. She guided him in and he went at it for a full minute thinking of the car and how he had gunned it from Dandenong to St. Kilda. 'Ah the saints are right the way in,' he whispered, sinking and withdrawing from her soft flesh, feeling her bra hard against his chest making him think of Jeannie as he began to spurt.

'Grouse,' he said again thinking of how he had handled that car. It had been so long since he had been behind a wheel and he sighed.

'Finished,' she stated without any interest, dropped her skirt and walking in front of him went back and into the coffee lounge.

Balga watched as she entered the door and was about to follow when he decided against it and walked off grinning at how he had had both of Eddy's molls without his say so. 'Serves him right,' Balga said to himself, 'he deserves it from not giving it to me as a welcome gift. Hot dog, buddy, buddy, hot dog, a hot dog just down the line -'

FORTY

TRUST A TART TO GIVE YOU THE BLUES

Trust a tart to give you the blues
Trust a tart to make you her fool
Trust a tart to take you apart
Oh brother take care, they'll break your heart
Strip you bare and leave you a broken cart.
Trust a tart to give you the blues
Trust a tart to make you fail
Love and discard you without bail
Oh brother, take care, watch out
Leave you alone without a sail.
Oh yeah, trust a tart to give you the blues
Trust a tart to make you her fool
Trust a tart to build you up, break you down
Leave you sighing for her again (yes again)
Oh yeah, only a tart can give you the blues.

It was on payday that Balga got back to his bungalow and had just opened the door when there was a flash of gold as Jeannie appeared to push him inside.

'Hubby's on the night shift and I'm all on my lonesome so I came to see my good friend Bonny and you of course stuck down here in your little shelter with not much to do and no girl friend to spend your dough on.'

She stood pressing herself against him and with her face tilted up so that he automatically kissed her on the lips. She sucked at his bottom lip for a long moment, then detached her mouth to whisper, 'what do you say, Sweetie, that we get a few bottles in to celebrate my release. Come on be a sport and do me for a few, huh,' and she kissed him again, felt his response and gave a giggle as the lad stepped back. She looked down saying. 'Have to let it rest while we get the bottles. How much have you got: a tenner?'

Balga was so flustered that he gave her two fives before realizing that then he mightn't have enough left for his coat. 'Eh, maybe you should give me back a five,' he almost pleaded, but she was already at the back door. The lad followed her knowing that his dough was gone.

The evening went as the other had and when it was getting towards eleven, Jeannie suggested that Balga walk her home. By then he had been thinking of getting her alone for even a few minutes and eagerly followed her. They were walking along Grey Street when she began swinging her hips and even humming a song. The lad recognized Smoke gets in your Eyes, the Platters' version as she detached her arm from his to whisper: 'Eh, there's a bloke following us. How 'bout I get me a fellow. I feel like doing a strange one tonight. Just keep with me, okay!'

Before Balga could say a word, she had dropped behind. He heard the tap of her high heels and then the shuffle of heavier shoes sounding along with them. He didn't know how to handle the situation, but just kept on walking until the woman Jeannie appeared next to him. She put a hand on his arm bringing him to a halt. She pressed the lad around so that he could see the bloke who stood there nervously shuffling from foot to foot.

'This is John,' she said brightly, 'and he'll be coming along with us.'

The three walked along with Jeannie directing bright comments at each of them. Balga felt angry and it must have showed, for she squeezed his arm, saying: 'It's still early and we have lots of time.'

'Uhuh,' the lad replied.

The three reached the woman's flat and entered. Jeannie and the man went into the bedroom while Balga hung in the kitchen. It was just after eleven and hubby wouldn't be reaching home until twelve. 'Hey Sweetie,' she said coming into the kitchen, 'be a dear and put on the kettle for a cuppa. Hold this for me, will you, and she handed him twenty pounds. 'He's hot for it,' she whispered, before disappearing back into the bedroom.

After another fifteen minutes the front door opened then closed on John. Jeannie came into the kitchen wearing her dressing gown. 'He was so hard for it' she laughed her giggle, 'that he shot off thrice. Hey, hey, don't look so glum. It's just a little business I turn to every now and then to get some dough. It doesn't mean much, nothing at all.'

She came up to him and smoothed his lips with her ring finger on which was her wedding band before planting a kiss on them. She pressed herself against him. Nothing under her dressing gown, at least nothing hard and as she moved against the lad he felt himself responding. She murmured a soft, 'Oh' as he spurted. Balga excused himself and rushed to the bathroom to clean up a bit. When he came back to the kitchen, the woman was drinking a cup of tea. She hadn't poured him one and when he looked at the clock he saw why. It was ten to twelve. She showed him to the door and planted a kiss on his lips. Balga clutched her breasts and was about to rush off when she said: 'Hey, come tomorrow after six when the pubs have closed. I need someone like you to look after my little business. Keep the twenty, you earned it.'

'Huh,' the lad could only say as she closed the door behind him. Balga reached the picture palace and stood and looked at a still of a couple embracing. He heard footsteps coming towards him. They stopped behind and then went on. After they were some way along, Balga turned and saw that it was the husband. Now he really pitied him.

That was how the lad became Jeannie's pimp. She picked up a bloke for a fiver or tenner and gave him what she was always promising Balga. He got little except a few caresses and some of the dough he collected for her, though sometimes if she liked the bloke and fancied him he got it for free. On the prowl they usually walked along Grey Street where the gutter crawlers and lone blokes prowled. Jeannie never went with men in cars. No, she preferred wriggling her arse in front of one of the stalkers she fancied and then getting to know him while Balga hung back or strolled ahead knowing he looked tough enough in his Bodgie gear to protect her fanny. Now, he began to understand Fast Eddy and his problems with this job, although he supposed that Eddy didn't fancy his tarts or had got over it by the time he put them on the street.

Jeannie never worked beyond twelve so Balga could manage his day job. Being young he didn't need all that amount of sleep and then his public service position was still easy though Jonesy now had him on the counter where he couldn't slack off. His main problem with being a pimp was that he fancied the merchandise and couldn't get over it because she kept playing with him, hardening him up and slacking off. This made him edgy and he scowled like the pimp he had become. He even wanted one of the johns to make trouble so that he could clock him, but none of them ever had the guts to tangle with the young tough looking black guy.

After too much of this teasing Balga decided that he should get in touch with Fast Eddy for advice. His mind also flashed onto Eddy's molls and he fancied getting it off with one or both of them. Just in case the opportunity arose he put two five pound notes in his back pocket, sighing as he did so for he hadn't as yet managed to get that car coat. He checked to see if it was still in the window before going on to the coffee lounge and looking inside. There sat a lonely Fast Eddy with not a tart in sight.

'Lo Eddy, you want a coffee,' Balga said coming to him carefully as he might be holding a grudge against him for doing Rita without his okay.

'So it's the Western Bodgie,' Eddy sneered.

'Yeah, so do you want an expresso or not?'

'Aren't you going to ask me for some skin?'

'Yeah!' And they did the complicated ritual that was the Bodgie hand-shake which Eddy had taught him quite a while ago now.

'Get me my coffee,' Eddy ordered.

While the bloke behind the counter fiddled with his machine, Balga went to the god and picked out I'm a Wild One, by the one and only Johnny O'Keeffe. He picked up the coffees and took them to the table. 'Where are the girls,' he asked.

'They seem to be taking a little holiday and so I'm having a little holiday from them. I'm thinking of a Kim Novak, I've met the chick already and she's a natural blonde, and another one, a Vivien Leigh, what do you think?'

'Cool, if you can track them down, but maybe they're a bit old. '

'Chicks can look any age. Remember Leslie and Audrey, they were only sixteen. Lamb is always much more tender than mutton.'

'Yeah, I take your point, but how do you get the chickens onto the game?'

'Well, there are tricks of the trade. Love breaks all boundaries.'

'Well, how do you get them to love you?'

'They just do and that's the funny thing. I don't lift a fist to them; I give them a little stick and stop it if they protest and it works.'

'For chicks, what about older women?'

'Who knows, who cares, the young ones bring in the most dough. Old blokes dig what they think is fresh meat and are willing to pay double for it. As for blokes like you, all you want to do is get it off, fling some spunk out and it doesn't matter what sort of hole it's in.'

'Okay, so if I wanted to be a bludger, a pimp, and had a chick already lined up and willing, how would I keep her under control?'

'One, never ever let her choose a customer, you pick the bloke for her; two, never let her give it away for free; three, never let her handle the money and definitely never let her keep it. When it's in your hand then and then only the business begins. In this game there are no freebes even for mates. The fifth thing is keep her without any ready cash, if she wants dough to buy something she has to ask you.'

What happens if she gets out of hand?'

'Well, tease her with a little stick that works wonders.'

'Huh,' Balga exclaimed. Jeannie was the one who was teasing him and he was doing everything all wrong about how to bring her around? She wasn't any spring chicken and wouldn't take kindly to a kid trying to change the way she did things.

'If it doesn't work throw her out and get another one. Don't try and hold onto her for any reason. She's spoilt goods. My tarts stay as long as I want them to and if they start pissing me off, I piss them off. Dolls, you know, love their faces and a razor shining in the dark is more than enough for them to see the light and split.'

'Yeah,' Balga said unable to think of anything else. Eddy's advice wouldn't help him at all. Flashing a razor in front of Jeannie might have the opposite effect and as for money, well he had a good job and didn't need to pry every penny from his tart's tight little fists.

'Thanks for the tips,' the lad said with a grin, 'but I don't think the horse is good enough to pay a dividend. Maybe one day I'll write a book and put in your advice for any would be bludgers to read.'

'Sure,' Fast Eddy answered and actually a smile changed his habitual sneer. He got up and Balga watched as he went to order coffees, then while they were being readied, he went to the juke box and lo and behold the song he had said he hated smooched out. "Please help me, I'm falling: Please help me, I'm falling, and that would be sin." He was grinning as he came back and smirked: 'This is the type of stuff they like, the molls.'

'Yeah, like Smoke Gets In Your eyes,' Balga replied.

'Ah, the Platters, slow rock for a stroll,' and he laughed, then said seriously: 'If you get around to doing that book write me in as Steady Eddy, I prefer that to "Fast" as I'm really a steady bloke,' and so he began holding forth and Balga had to listen to this man of many parts most of them rotten narrate to him selected parts of his life. At last he stopped and the lad quickly said: 'Yeah and another yeah for luck, perhaps you should be the one writing the book, you've got such a lot to say. Anyway I have to split now, but I'll be back in a day or two to test out your new molls. Only joking, only joking and now I'll be on my way as I've got to get to work early in the morning and hey, morning has arrived already.'

And a third yeah to you for luck,' Eddy said quietly. 'You know, I could envy you for having a square job. It beats hanging about nights entertaining my molls and any customer that wants one. It takes something out of your - , but, well, a fourth yeah,' he sighed, 'I like the soft darkness and the bright lights and sitting here letting the world take care of itself or coming up just for a sniff at what I'm offering.'

'A fifth yeah to your fourth, I dig you, you're a real, real hep cat,' Balga replied enviously. He grabbed Eddy's hand and exchanged a simple Saints' shake with the pimp before rushing off.

FORTY ONE

I WANT YOU, I NEED YOU, LOVE ME BLUES

Singing along in a quavering falsetto voice
I won't say, I need you, I want you, yes I do
The blues have got me down on the street
No girl next door, just a feckless whore to meet
I know that I feel sore, no girl next door
I want you, I need you, I love you, oh those blues
Oh yes, I have this street moll, need her special loving
How can I call her, how can I crawl, sprawling yes
Cold drink in my hand, a ciggie between my lips
I sigh, I pine, I'm collapsing not doing fine
'Cause I got the I want you, I need you, do me (please)
I love you, I love you (oh I love you) blues.

Balga's head continued to be in a swirl from Jeannie's treatment. He felt like the Elvis song: I want you, I need you, I love you. The lad had to see Jeannie even in the daytime when business usually wasn't conducted and so the next afternoon as he came towards her flat, he looked at his watch. It was already after two. The day was overcast with a cold breeze from the south. It looked like rain and already smelt damp. He really wanted his warm coat and vowed again that he would get it on pay day. He reached the picture palace. "There's No Business Like Show Business" with Marilyn Monroe was playing. There was a matinee that day, and Jeannie might want to go, though as always it depended on what time hubby came off shift.

The lad reached her flat and knocked. There was a stirring inside, but no one came to open the door. He thought the husband may have stayed home taking a sickie, but that didn't deter him. He knocked again and finally Jeannie poked her head out of her bedroom window to see who it was and yelled: 'Hey, Sweetie, glad to see you. Hang on a sec until I get decent. Been entertaining a fella and she made a circle with her mouth and her head disappeared. 'I hope you got paid for it,' Balga whispered. He sat down on the door step and waited for what seemed ages. Finally, the door opened and he had to jump to his feet as a heavy set bloke came out, brushed past him and went on his way. Balga stared after him. He saw cop!

'He's a good bloke to know,' Jeannie said about the man.

'He didn't pay,' Balga stated in his best Fast Eddy manner.

'No, he didn't. I went to the pub for a drink and met him there. It wasn't business, it was a social call. Now you want a cuppa or not?'

'Yeah and a bite to eat while you're at it, so please please me for just this once.'

'Say "pretty please" and you can have a couple of snags.'

'Well a double whatever as long as you throw in a couple of slices of bread and a kiss or two.' Balga said with a rueful smile.

Jeannie bustled about fixing the food and Balga looked her over. She was a bit bedraggled and he knew why. The woman glanced up at him and smiled and it hit him that what draw him to her were her grey-green eyes. She kept them wide open as if she was an innocent like one of the characters played by Marilyn Monroe. This reminded him and he said: 'Eh there's a good flick playing in that picture palace. There's No Business Like Show Business with the one and only Marilyn in it as well as the one and only Johnny Ray, you must remember his song Cry it mightn't have been rock, but it was good as was his The Little White Cloud That Cried. We can make the matinee show if we hurry.'

'I don't know about that, there's hubby to consider, he's on the afternoon shift and gets off at six.'

'The show finishes about half past five so you'll be back cooking dinner for him by the time he arrives.'

'We'll see,' was her only comment as she turned the snaggers and then herself onto her favourite topic, though this time her planning had gone further. 'I've just about, no I've had it with hubby up to here,' she said pushing a hand right over her head. 'I'm ready to move out and that bloke I was with told that there is a house going in Middle Park, the next suburb along and it's not all that much, though' (and here she gave her giggle) 'I can't manage it on my own yet. I know that bungalow of yours is downright awful and so move in with me, huh, Sweetie?'

The way she said this made him agree and he might have mortgaged his very next pay to her without a thought except he wanted that coat and so he cheated a bit and said that she would have to wait a fortnight unless they made the money from the night trade.

'That'll be fine. It'll give me time to get out from under,' she agreed, coming to him and brushing her body against his. 'Now you must promise, double promise so that you won't go back on your word. This is final you know, goodbye to hubby forever and a day,' and she did a little jig.

'Yeah, it's fine, I promise,' the lad said without hesitation and this made her happy enough to hum some square song as she dished up the sausages and then poured out the tea. By the time he had finished eating it was too late to catch the matinee and by the time she had finished dawdling over the dishes and a few drinks there was no time for anything else except to skedaddle before hubby arrived.

'We never have time to ourselves, do we love,' she said giving him a kiss before ushering him out.

As he turned into the street Balga was confronted by a short dark bloke. The husband! The lad raised his fists ready to defend himself. No need! The wronged husband merely stood there trembling with what Balga took to be fury. Whatever it was, it didn't drive the bloke into a fight and so the lad stepped around him and went on his way.

Balga shrugged any thoughts aside and grinned as the image of the coat came into his mind. Man, he wanted that coat! Tomorrow was pay day and he would get it, even take an hour off from work so that he could get there before the shop closed and after that go and have a yarn with Tommy Cooper. His birthday was next week and he wanted to celebrate it with someone who had known him for many birthdays.

Next day when the lad received his pay envelope, he went to Jonesy and requested that he be allowed to go an hour earlier to see the doctor. Mr. Jones passed him the requisite form. He filled it out, signed it and passed it in and was free. He rushed off to Fitzroy Street and dashed to the shop and hesitated at the window. His coat was no longer on display. He went inside and the man who he supposed was the owner looked at him and then stared. My God, Balga recognised the bloke he had diddled on the beach. What to do, but brazen it out.

'Eh,' he said, 'remember me? Sorry about that, I was skint, you know, and hungry. Now I'm fixed up and ready to return the loan.'

Balga pulled out his pay packet and took out three one pound notes and put them on the counter. The man looked down at them then up at the lad with a quizzical expression on his face. Balga relaxed and smiled nicely as he said: 'No hard feelings mate. I've also come to put a bit of business your way. That car coat you had in the window for the last few weeks, you still got it?'

The bloke was also smiling and he replied 'Yes, I took it out as it is not exactly your summer wear and new stock is coming in.

'May I look at it?'

'Of course, of course,' and the man went to a rack and took off the coat. He held it up and Balga slipped into it. The material felt nice and soft, but it hung on him like a tent.

'It's a bit big,' he cried in dismay.

'It's meant to be, it's a car coat after all,' the bloke replied snidely.

'I know that, but I want a tighter fit.'

'We all would, dearie, we all would; but then you do want a car coat, don't you?'

'Not exactly, it's the length I like. It is just the length for a great drape coat.'

'Perhaps, perhaps and it is your dough – now there's a tailor next door, perhaps we'll go and ask him. It's just about closing time after all.'

'Yeah, we'll just do that.'

Balga watched as the bloke took whatever cash he had out of the till then switched on a burglar alarm before closing the front door. 'It's activated by the key turning in the lock,' he warned him.

Keep the crooks out,' Balga grinned knowing that if he wanted too he could go for the bloke and relieve him of his dough. He was big and tough after all, though the bloke didn't seem to be in awe of him.

The tailor was on the first floor. He looked at the coat, pulled it this way and that, tugged at the lapels, the sleeves and buttoned up the front, then pronounced: 'Rubbish!'

'You mean it's no good,' Balga exclaimed.

'No the tailoring, that's rubbish, but I can redo, make it what you want?'

'A drape coat, like Bodgies wear.'

'Ah, yes, like that Fast Eddy used to wear before he went Italian and stylish.'

'Not Italian,' Balga snapped, 'Ivy League.'

'Whatever, it does not matter. The style it is Italian, but you don't want that, you want outdated American style, yes?'

'You know it; you do it,' snapped Balga unable to accept that he was outdated.

'Know it, this is Home of the Saints after all,' the tailor said immediately cheering him up.

'Yeah, and I'm here,' Balga sneered in his best Bodgie style lifting up the corner of his mouth just like Elvis Presley.

'Yes. Put on please.'

Balga did so and the tailor began pulling and pinning. 'There,' he said, 'I do like that if you give me the nod as they say. You just look in mirror please. Is this what you call Bodgie style?'

'Yeah, it is, right there.'

'It is what you want?'

'Yeah, man, what else?'

'It must be right for you. I can only cut it once. Look again and tell me please.'

'Man, it's the works so do your cutting and sewing,' Balga said then had to ask 'How much will it cost?'

'For you, for Eddy's friend, I do it all for five.'

'That's a lot!'

'That's it, yes, or take it away.'

Reluctantly Balga forked over the fiver and as he did so felt the store keeper touch him on his arm. He left his hand there as he said coyly, 'My, aren't we forgetting something?'

'Oh' and Balga repeated 'Oh' again as it hit me that he still had to pay for the coat. 'What did you say the price was?'

'I said "sixty" but as it is off season I'll bring it down to "twenty five", below that I won't go, unless of course, we can come to some amicable arrangement.'

Balga looked at the leering face and thought it over. 'No way is that piece of shit worth fifty. Who's going to buy a shapeless bit of sack cloth for that -- make it twenty.'

'But the tailor vouched for the quality of the material,' the shop keeper retorted.

'Ah, he needs the work, give you twenty one,' Balga sneered, looking tough though a bit limp wristed at the same time. With a smirk he counted out the money. Not much was left in his pay pack, but he wanted that coat. He needed it!

The shop keeper touched his palm suggestively as he took the money. 'Enough,' Balga smiled at him and then turned his attention to the tailor: 'When will it be ready?'

'The day after tomorrow...'

'It's a Saturday.'

'So what I still open.'

Balga turned and left. The store keeper came closely after him. 'You ready for a beer before it hits six,' he asked at the bottom of the stairs.

'You mean you're going to shout me,' Balga asked coarsely.

'Of course, I'd like to get to know you. I like rough trade, but I'm meeting a friend there and want to make him jealous.'

'Well, okay, but only one mind,' Balga agreed, knowing that he had made a conquest, a bloke with a shop on the street with some good gear he might get cheaply.

Balga was into his second free beer when the friend cut in, a younger man, and friendly too, but he excused himself to go and look for Tommy. He was at his desk and wouldn't get off until after nine. The lad arranged for his mate to make time to celebrate his birthday and then went home to feel sad about using most of his pay on a single coat though he loved it. This perked him up and he went to pay his rent with the rest of his money. He would have to rely on night trade earnings to keep him solvent through the next fortnight; but the rent came first. Balga always paid special attention to keeping up to date with his rent. He always regarded his room as a hidey hole and the bungalow certainly was a hole. This made him think of Jeannie's offer and her place would be a regular house. He paid Bonny, accepted a drink, then some stew as he watched television then went back to his hole to lie there thinking of his birthday and the gift he had got himself: a nice warm coat with finger length drape.

FORTY TWO

JUST LIKE THE OLD DAYS'
BLUES

Just like the old days, how blue (how true)
Now I'm playing them again, how weary
Now I'm just living those old day blues (again)
They sent me to the clink, caged me like a rat (raging)
Doing simple things just like stealing a car
Doing the simple that got me doing time
And gave me just like the old day blues
A cop comes up, I know the score (his score)
Click go the handcuffs, clickety, clickety clink
The days slip around my wrist, old day blues
Got to change my ways, got to keep so clean
Give up the road and the smile of my whore
Oh yeah, no more old day blues for me, oh no more, no more.

Tommy was as good as his word even though it was a work day. Balga met him as soon as he reached St. Kilda and took him to his bungalow. Tommy took a loan of his long striped cardigan while the lad flashed his modified car coat at him. The tailor had done a good job and it was such a well fitting garment that Balga had even spent some of his small cash stash on getting a new pair of strides at a discount of course from his new friend. These were the new thin straight legged ones and he had to admit they went well with the coat making him look like the Frankenstein monster but sharp and even better than Fast Eddy. Indeed, he was tempted to go and show off to him later and maybe score one of his girls to celebrate his birthday.

'Where will we go to celebrate? What about a feed first,' Balga suggested.

'Good, I'm starving. Hey, you know there's a grouse fish and chip shop in Barkly Street. We can have a great feed there for less than a couple of beers.'

'Okay, I'm with you. I haven't had a good feed of fish and chips since I left Perth.'

'Let's go, it's not far,' Tommy said and they sashayed out to reach the shop. It was run not by the usual Greek but by a friendly Aussie who they found out was second generation Greek.

'Well, what will you Sharpies be having, cod or whiting?' he asked cheerily.

'Flake because we're a couple of sharks,' Balga replied, 'with two bobs worth of chips and a happy birthday thrown in for nix.'

'Same I suppose,' Tommy added, 'but hold the happy birthday.' After they got their tucker with a happy birthday free for Balga, they walked along a bit and came to a tram stop bench where they quickly demolished their fish and chips. As they were wiping their greasy mouths and thinking of getting a drink, a city tram trundled up.

'Hey, how about the pictures,' Balga exclaimed.

'I wanted a drink,' protested Tommy.

'We'll have time for a couple at that pub just opposite the station. What's it called?'

'The Melbourne I think, that's the pub with the Cloe painting in the public bar.'

'Yeah, I think that's the one, but I thought it was The George.'

'Well, whatever,' and the two mates went on arguing about the pub's name and thus forgetting that public bars in Victoria closed promptly at six and so when they got off at the station and crossed to the pub, which they found was called Young & Jacksons, it was completely dead so not only didn't Balga and Tommy get to see the famous nude painting over the bar but had to cross over to the station for a coke with which Tommy ironically toasted his mate.

'Let's see what flic's on at the Regent,' Balga suggested.

'Yeah,' Tommy answered not very enthusiastically.

Balga felt his birthday was turning out a bit of a dud and all the enjoyment he had had so far was when Nancy at work had given him a kiss not on the cheek, but on the mouth. They reached the Regent. The show was Blackboard Jungle which must be a gas as it was about juvenile delinquents. 'Remember those days when we were rebels without a cause,' Balga grinned at Tommy.

'Yeah, I remember them well as I was locked up for far too long.'

'Yeah, but look they're made a picture about us. We're famous.'

'Maybe, but I can give that sort of fame a miss.'

'I can't and maybe one day someone'll get around to Aussie Delinks and do a whole picture on us and when that happens will you still be saying: "Oh, it's a bit late, ain't it?" Well, it's the time to say a last goodbye to my kiddy life so let's get in and see this flick,' Balga retorted with a shrug of his padded shoulders before checking his pockets for money to find that he had forgotten his wallet which held all his notes. He tried to borrow from Tommy.

'Hey, you still owe me a couple quid and I've just got enough cash for my ticket,' his mate retorted.

'Okay, but I'm going to see this movie even if I have to steal for it. Come on let's walk along a bit,' Balga said suddenly angry.

Just a short way up from the theatre was an alley passing through to Flinders Lane. Balga turned with his mate and began walking down it. In front of them was a bloke an office worker from the looks of him. 'There's my ticket money,' Balga said with a grin to his mate. He hurried and caught up with the bloke. 'Hey, Bodgie, it ain't worth it,' Tommy began; but Balga wasn't listening. He felt big and tough in his coat and dangerous so he called: 'Hey, Bud, hold on a minute. Yeah, just a minute! You know me and me mate here are a bit short of cash. Can you spare a quid?'

The square stood still. His eyes flickered from Balga to Tommy and back again. What would these louts do if he didn't come through, he must have thought? Balga looked mean and nasty. He grinned like a wolf as he stared at the mark's right hand coming up to sneak inside his jacket to his pocket. He made out the bulge of the wallet and watched the man fumbling to get out the note. He felt like taking the lot, but Tommy had his hand on his shoulder. The bloke brought out a note. Balga gave a giggle. A nice blue blue fiver. Balga snatched it and said softly 'That'll do nicely, thank you.'

The man hurried off. Balga watched him and then with Tommy hurried back to Collins Street.

'Bodgie that was stupid, what if he goes to the cops,' Tommy protested.

'How can he, all we did was ask him for some dough and he gave us a fiver. Let's get into the theatre anyway and hide out. A joke, but we'll be off the street.' He laughed harshly.

God Save the Queen came on but they stayed sitting while everyone else stood. A Tom and Gerry cartoon flickered out its old story of cat chasing mouse and they laughed loudly. This was followed by a newsreel. Some war was going on in an Asian place called Vietnam and then there was Eisenhower swinging a golf club as he said that it was a communist plot. Balga yawned and suddenly out belted the opening bars of Rock Around the Clock. Their feet banged on the floor to the beat. Balga's birthday was being celebrated. The Delink gave it to the squares playing as hard as Balga had with his life and future. Of course, he ended up in prison; but this was what happened to those who rebelled against what society flung at them.

'Eh,' Balga overcome by the film whispered to Tommy when it was over, 'that was the grousest flick I've seen since ever, Let's go and pinch a car and get some kicks. Who wants to ride in a bloody tram when there's lots of cars just sitting idle.'

'What,' Tommy asked.

'That one! I worked on the same model as a mechanic. I can get into it easily.'

He did. Tommy hesitated and then got in. They blasted up Collins Street and Balga gunned it through Richmond to Hawthorn. 'This was the square place they put me in,' he shouted and roared through the deserted streets, zoomed back across the Yarra and charged up Punt Road.

He ditched the car at the big face of the Amusement Park and as he got out shouted to Tommy: 'Yeah, that was a great beginning wasn't it, the theatre silent then Rock Around the Clock slamming in. Nothing like a driving beat, man, such a buzz, hey, hey!'

'But...' Tommy began.

Balga was speeding in his mind, still hyped up from the film: 'Hey,' he said, 'let's go and see Fast Eddy. We can do his chicks.'

'Not tonight, I have to go on duty early tomorrow.'

'Ah, come on, it's on the way home.'

Tommy was about to protest then went quiet. A car slowed to move along with them. 'Bloody pavement crawlers,' Balga said angrily; but it wasn't. The bloke sitting in the passenger seat released the catch on the back door and gestured at them. He was just a blur of a white face in the darkness; but they knew that cop voice that brooked no denial. 'Get in!'

They got in. Balga flashed a look at Tommy. His face had gone pale. He was shaking so Balga had to put some spirit in him. 'Come on,' we haven't done nothing,' he said to the big bloke beside him!

'Shut the fuck up,' the driver growled.

'Yeah, shut the fuck up,' his mate backed him up with a similar growl.

The car pulled up in front of what appeared to be a block of flats and the two lads were ordered out. One of the demons went before them and the other behind. In between like the meat in thick crusts of bread they were carried up stairs and into what turned out to be a police station.

'What the heck,' Balga began.

'Welcome to the station, kids,' the first D. growled. 'My God don't these two look right nongs. Ey, you come and sit with me at that desk,' he ordered Tommy.

'And I'm to go with the other bloke,' Balga exclaimed suddenly aware that there was something familiar about the detective.

'Keep your gob shut,' the demon spat out. He winked and then blam his fist came out in a short jab into Balga's belly.

It was then he learnt the uses a thick coat had. He fell back in surprise or double surprise for the heavy fist sunk into the cloth and he wasn't even winded. The bloke shoved him into a chair and he recognised the detective as the man that had been with Jeannie. He hoped that this might be to his advantage as questions came: name, date of birth, address and work.

'How come they got you working there,' the detective queried.

'I have to work somewhere if I don't want to be a crim,' Balga retorted.

'We'll see about that crim bit,' he said and picked up a phone and got onto records. He got Tommy's name as well from the other demon and gave it in.

The two lads waited in silence, well, almost silence as Tommy suddenly began to snivel as if he was a little kid. Gee, what was wrong with him, Balga thought. He would never give those bastards the satisfaction of crying in front of them. Not on your Nelly and then the phone rang.

'Christ, they both got records as long as your arm,' the phone bloke exclaimed, 'and this bloke's an Abo.'

'I'm not, my father was an American from New Orleans and I've only got a juvenile record,' Balga protested refusing to be intimidated. 'It's supposed to be destroyed when you reach eighteen too.'

'Tell that to the judge when he reads it,' the demon sneered, 'and as for you, you ain't no juvenile delinquent are you? And I've seen you around St. Kilda. Trying to get a racket going and without my sayso.'

'Not me, I just want to remain straight. We were only out celebrating my birthday,' Balga whined.

'By stealing a car -?'

'No sir, not me, I can't even drive. I ain't got no license.'

'And this one is working at the Wales. God knows what he's up to there,' broke in Tommy's cop.

The only answer from Tommy was a sob that made Balga feel sorry for him. No wonder he wasn't a Saint. Well, not everyone could make the grade.

'So, you two better stay clean and now that we've been so to speak formally introduced, I'll see you around,' said Balga's cop. 'Go on, get out of here. Scat and consider yourselves lucky that we don't book you for being you and not us.'

Sardonic laughter followed them downstairs and outside where Balga told Tommy: 'You know they were just bluffing, just trying to make us scared of them. Notice, they didn't even bother to search us. Just cops doing something to fill in a boring night.'

'Yeah, but what if they get onto my boss, he doesn't know that I've been inside.'

'Arrh, they won't do anything, besides I know one of them.'

'You do?'

'Well, almost.'

'Yeah almost and you nicked that bloody car. I'm off to Sydney tomorrow. I've been here too long already. This is what happens if you stay in one place for too long.'

'Arrh, don't take on so.'

'I'm off, happy birthday, Bodgie,' said his friend quietly and walked off leaving Balga alone and scared about what might happen to him.

FORTY THREE

TRUST A TART TO GIVE YOU
THE BLUES (REPRISE)

Trust a tart to give you the blues
Trust a tart to make you her fool
Trust a tart to take you apart, make you smart
Oh brother, use you for a horse and cart.
Trust a tart to give you the blues
Trust a tart to strip you all bare
Yeah, make you sing the careless blues
Your love is but a midnight ramble
Your love is but a money scramble
Take you up and do you in (blues)
Oh trust a tart to give you the lovesick blues
Trust a tart to give you the lovesick blues. (yeah).

Balga lay on his bed in the bungalow feeling glum. Tommy was gone and he felt so alone, so alone it hurt. Yeah, and then Jeannie bustled in not looking for dough, but to invite him up for a drink and he perked up. He grabbed her for a kiss then followed watching her behind moving this way and that way. With a glass of cold Vic. Bitter in his hand and some going down his throat, he thrust the blues away. After all he had been on his own since Clonny and even during Clonny for that matter and so he was used to solitude. He smiled at Jeannie wondering when he would get to shag her again. This seemed to be the last thing on her mind. It was filled by her new home plans. Next week, to be exact on the Friday, she would move to her new house, minus hubby. 'He's history,' she said with a giggle lifting her glass and saluting the past.

'And what about me,' Balga couldn't help asking.

'You sweetie will be with me of course.'

'How far away is the house from Fitzroy Street,' Balga enquired.

'You'll see it next Friday and all we need to do is get together fifty quid for rent. Your pay day's on Thursday, isn't it?'

'Yeah, but I have to eat and all that.'

'I'll be there to cook for you and so no hunger. Hey, Bonny how about that, the kid's moving in with me. I'm a land lady like you. Let's drink to that, shall we?'

They all tossed down their drink and had a refill.

So on Friday afternoon, which he took off from work, Jeannie watched as he loaded his stuff into the taxi he had ordered. 'Bye bye, Bonny,' she called and they were off. Across Fitzroy Street and after a few streets there it was an ordinary house in an ordinary suburb that felt like Hawthorn or North Perth. He was frowning as he paid the taxi driver.

'Well, nice and quiet which is what we want,' Jeannie said brightly. 'I had all of my stuff moved today and so there's only arranging to do. There's a nice little annex which will suit you fine.'

'Yeah,' Balga replied glumly.

'Hey, you're with me now, perk up. Let's have a beer and get you ready for moving and shiftin,' she said to him with that giggle of hers.

Balga followed her into the lounge room first which had all the furniture from her flat in it, as did the kitchen. She poured a beer for him and put on the radio. It was then that a small nuggety bloke looking the typical Melbournian appeared. 'Hey, this is Pete, he's taking care of the house,' Jeannie told Balga.

'How you going, mate,' the short bloke said sticking out his hand.

'As well as I can be,' Balga replied wondering what other surprises were in store. Peter or Pete had been a shearers' cook and now while they were guzzling beer he went to prepare a spread for them. While the tucker was cooking, Balga went to his annex. This was almost like the bungalow he had vacated except the walls were brick and it was half the size again. There was a single bed, a chest of drawers and that was it.

'Tucker,' Pete called and he went back to the kitchen for a feed of steak, chips and eggs. This cheered him up a little, but the next surprise didn't.

There was a scraping at the back door and who walked in but the detective that had winked at him then hit him in the stomach. Balga scowled at him, not being able to change his expression to the blankness of Pete's face.

'This is my detective,' Jeannie said with almost a squeal as she rushed to give him a hug. 'Come in, come on to the lounge and have a drink.'

'I'll follow you in a minute,' the demon growled staring at the lad. 'Well, how did you like my introduction? Hope you got the message.'

Balga dropped his eyes and mumbled: 'Yeah, I got the message.'

'Well, me boy be my boy and we'll get on,' the detective snorted with what passed for a laugh.

'What's with this shit,' Balga snapped at Pete.

'Nothing, mate, he comes with the house. Just keep your gob shut around that geezer.'

'That bastard whacked me in the guts the other night. Arsehole! First time I've met one of them without being arrested,' Balga snarled hating the setup he had walked into.

'Yeah, yeah, that's what I mean about blabbin',' Peter retorted cleaning up the dishes as Jeanne called Balga to her. The lad went in slowly. The demon was ensconced on the sofa.

'I'm Detective Phil Kingston as in Jamaica,' the demon shot at Balga in what perhaps was an attempt at humour, or simply referring to his colour in an oblique manner.

'Yeah,' the lad replied.

'Yeah, but we blokes well we're in the same line of business so as to speak.'

'For sure,' Balga mumbled.

'Doesn't say much, just like Pete here,' Kingston added as the man came into the lounge.

Jeannie poured them beers from a bottle she took from a full box.

'No phone here,' Balga said gesturing at the beer.

'We don't need one as its special delivery,' she replied, smiling at the big detective who actually looked sheepish. Balga pulled himself together. He stared at the bloke's drawn white face, his graying hair, his hard hands and his gray crumpled suit. Not much there except cop, he decided. He would ask Fast Eddy about him.

'I have to meet a friend,' he said. 'I won't be long,' and with that he all but ran from the room. In his annex, he fixed himself up a bit, put on his new coat and rushed off. Friday night was a good night and Fitzroy Street was buzzing. Balga relaxed among the crowd and was in a better mood as he came to Eddy's hangout.

He was in there too -- with two new tarts: a hard faced little blonde and a dark counterpart, both of them could have been anything from sixteen to twenty. They aimed for the teens. Each wore bobby socks with flat heels, matador pants and long men's shirts. Eddy was talking quickly to two blokes who after every second word or so darted glances at the girls. Balga went to the counter, ordered coffee and turned to watch the negotiations. Money was passed and Eddy escorted the men and his molls out. Balga strolled to the table he had vacated and sat down. There was a smell of perfume lingering and he wondered which chick would be the best, the dark or the light. While he was thinking this, perhaps with a smile plastered on his dial, he became aware that Eddy was staring down at him.

'You look like a museum,' the pimp declared.

'Why,' Balga asked huffily.

'The coat, I wore one like that back in '55.'

'Well, I'm wearing one now in '61.'

'Yeah,' he replied, closing the subject as he went to the counter and perhaps because he had scored more than the usual from the two marks, he got him a coffee.

'So now you have Kim Novak, but who is the other one?' Balga joked when he came back.

'Jane Wyman.'

'Can't remember her in a flic.'

'Nor can I, but I like the name and she was a small brunette.'

'Well, which one is the best?'

'Depends on what you want?'

'The usual.'

'One or the other, they are about the same.'

'Uhuh, but I didn't come about that. You see the other week I got picked up and one of the demons answered to the name of Phil Kingston. You know him?'

'Listen, man, in this business you better know that, that bozo and watch out or you'll be in deep shit. He's vice and thus has a personal interest in me and my girls and any others in the same line of work. He's competition he is and has stocked a couple of houses by grabbing up the best stuff off the street. The threat of arrest and then an offer of protection does wonders for the sluts who actually feel they are getting a good deal.'

'A couple of houses, which reminds me, where do your girls go with their clients? It can't be the wall for each and every one.'

'Why do you want to know, you becoming one of Phil the Prick's boys are you? Well, he already knows. I rent a couple of bungalows with a handy back gate and a bloke to keep an eye on things.'

'And where do you live?'

'That's a state secret that is,' he replied. 'I don't want anyone bugging me in my home. My private life is private, see!'

'Okay, okay, just asking. You want to hide away, you can. Now back to that D. and his houses, I thought, well, brothels are illegal here and were just tolerated in Perth.'

'Well, yeah whoring is illegal and the vice squad manages it as a business. They keep the trade quiet and they like their few quid and a free shag. Blokes like me keep them glad and with them happy so are we.'

'And the houses,' Balga prompted.

'Well Phil Kingston moved from just getting a few quid from us into the business in a big way. You know there is a way to rub the law and keep it legal. As long as the molls only massage their Johns no law is broken and everything is fine and dandy - ain't it? No! The vice squadies come down on your house and entrap you by getting one of your girls to give a hand job. A massage parlour is really a wanking shop. When you think of it the molls have it easy and don't even have to open their legs.'

'Uhuh,' the lad grunted. This explained quite a lot of things, though Kingston seemed to fancy Jeannie as well. He supposed that this was why Jeannie had rid herself of hubby and his money. 'Gee,' Balga said, 'you live and learn.'

'Yeah,' Eddy replied, looking at his wrist watch, 'but time's up and I have to go and pick them up. If you want one, it's still a fiver for a wall job.'

'Not tonight,' Balga replied grinning as he drained his coffee. 'I have to get back to my place. I'm in Middle Park now.'

'Well, take care and watch out for that Kingston prick unless you want to be on his pay roll minding one of his houses. Not so bad, if you like having it steady, but he is a right bastard and can do you if you get on the wrong side or just because he needs an arrest.'

'Yeah, Steady Eddy, but I just lost a mate and I'm getting his feeling that it's time to cut out from this scene. I don't want to work for a cop, no way!'

'Yeah, whatever,' and Fast Eddy was gone without a goodbye.

FORTY FOUR

BLUES FOR REVEL COOPER

Another friend done gone
Another friend done gone
Another friend done gone
That long black train it took him away,
Took him away, took him away from me
I watched him go, I watched him go
I watched him go and shed a tear
Blues for Revel Cooper
Blues for Revel Cooper
Blues for Revel Cooper
Gone away, far away too far from me
Will I ever see him again, never again, (oh no)
Oh blues for Revel Cooper
Oh blues for, a friend done gone,
Oh Revel you took the sunshine of your smile
The flashing of your grin, the light (oh yeah)
From my eyes, oh blues for Revel Cooper
Blues for Revel, oh for Revel Cooper.

Balga in losing his mate Tommy had lost a part of his past and now he was about to lose another friend. He walked with him towards Spencer Street station feeling that his life was emptying out. He had to refil it with better than what he had in St. Kilda or else scram home too just as Revel Cooper, the Noongar artist was doing. He could sympathize with Revel's happiness at leaving Melbourne, and even felt like getting on the train with him. Balga scurried along lugging a big old suitcase which was obviously a cousin to his and could have been his; but it wasn't. It was Revel's, his mate and he glanced across at him to find him not at his side. He looked around and back and there he was standing in the middle of the pavement with a big grin plastered over his mug.

'Ya know, cuz,' he said with a chortle, 'I got into trouble over this woman, this old sheila, you wouldn't believe me if I told you her name, but I don't kiss and tell. When it came out the shit hit the fan and I got me marching orders, scholarship cancelled and a free ticket home. No worries, eh, bub? 'Bout time I got back, see my family and that warm brown land with its black boys and...'

'Harsh laws that'll land you in boob again,' Balga cut in. He knew how bad it was for Noongars so he added a "Good luck" as they entered the station. He didn't think it was a good idea for Revel to go home, but he didn't say this. Only the opposite: 'Maybe it is a good idea to get out of here while the going is for the getting. Anyway, cuz, whatever, let's go and I'll buy you a few of your last legal drinks.' Balga steered him into the station bar where they toasted one another enjoying what they couldn't do in West Aussie.

'Won't be able to do this in the West without an exemption certificate, your dog license,' Balga scowled as he ordered two schooners.

'It depends on what pub it is,' Revel replied with is grin, 'there's a few places that if you're not jet black will serve ya.'

'Yeah, but there's no pub like that artists' one you introduced me too. Yeah, I like it, yeah and better than St. Kilda. I'm getting out of that place. I have to.'

'Whatever bub, whatever, it's all history to me so drink up, I've got a train to catch and a long journey to make.'

'Yeah, but home is where the heart is,' Balga couldn't help saying as he thought of Jeanne and the lack of a heart.

They walked along the length of train until they came to Revel's carriage. He found his seat just as the engine whistled that long lonesome cry.

'Catch ya, bud; catch ya, mate,' Balga called as the train gave a lunge and began to pull out.

'Wait, hey have a real catch. Maybe ya can use it; maybe ya can keep it for me, maybe it'll remind you of home. Have a good one on me, bud. Get outa St. Kilda, that place can do ya in.'

He threw a parcel that rushed at Balga as the train gathered speed. He caught it like a football and held it up high like a triumphant mark; then his hands dropped. His friend was gone and the train was gone and his heart had gone along too. He missed his land and was so alone. 'Give my love to West Aussie,' he whispered to himself and people stared at him and didn't share his grief.

The lad clutched the parcel like a hand as he got into a train that took him to Flinders Street station where he changed to the St. Kilda one. He got off at Middle Park and sighed as he walked slowly back to a place that wasn't much of a home. He crept to his annex and tossed the parcel on his bed. He thought that perhaps he should have gone on to the artist's pub, but it would have been too lonely without Revel. After a time he went to the kitchen where Pete had cooked up a meal. He ate listlessly then went into the lounge room where Jeannie sat. This time without Phil in attendance!

'Hello, Sweetie, just in time for a beer. How's life with you?' she said giving a giggle as she spoke.

'Just saw a friend off,' he told her.

'Hey, you've got me and life is looking up for both of us as well as Pete,' she replied slurping on her beer, then called: 'Pete come and bring another bottle,' before turning her attention back to the lad and saying, 'you remember, Sweetie, how we talked about going into business…'

'Yeah, you talked and I listened.'

'It's my, our, chance to get ahead of the game. A "doll" can do only so much on her own, she always needs a minder. Well, I have you and with Phil we'll have protection and we can even fix this place up into a … well,' and she giggled and poured herself another beer.'

'Yeah, and what will Phil get from this,' Balga sneered.

'He knows the ropes and he'll get a cut; but it won't be his business, but ours, you, me and Pete.'

'You know that dick, you know his reputation,' Balga blurted out.

'He's my detective and likes me so I've got an edge.'

'Don't you know he practically runs the game in St. Kilda. Cross him and you get crossed out.'

'My, we are in a bad mood aren't we! All you'll have to do is hang around and keep an eye on the customers. Nothing to it as Pete will be there to lend a hand when needed. We'll be ready soon as Phil gets me some massage tables. He'll even direct the girls to us. No problems, but you'll have to give up your day job as this'll be full time.'

'Yeah, yeah and a triple yeah,' Balga sneered. It was the last thing he wanted to do. He liked his public service job and indeed next week was even sitting for his permanency exam.

'I'll think about it,' Balga replied and drained his beer and went off to his annex. It was all but over as far as he was concerned. Who wanted to work for a demon after all?

Balga sat on his bed and stared at Revel's parcel. He reached out and pulled it to him. He ripped it open and spread the contents out on the bed. All the painting stuff Revel had used in Melbourne as well as lots of his art works, stuff that he had been studying such as nudes and flower pots. There were a couple of sketch pads and when he opened them he saw the familiar landscape pictures complete with kangaroos, black boys and black fellows of his West Aussie land. Now he was sad and gloomy as well as homesick. He toyed with a charcoal stick then began sketching out a landscape in Revel's Noongar style. When he realized what he was doing he stopped.

Not so good and the lad checked out a couple of art books even trying to do a copy of a face and figure according to their instructions. Not very good, hard in fact and he went back to working on his landscape imaging the bush around Serpentine Falls in the Darling Ranges.

FORTY FIVE

CHANGE OF LIFE BLUES

Oh I'm changing my style
My walk, my talk, even my shirt
Leaving the streets where I used to strut
Biding my time and losing my mind, a nut
I can't keep sane, I can't go loving the way I do
Change of life blues hitting me where I sleep
Yeah, changing my life hiding away from you
Welcoming the new, even my hair style too
Well, my friends not a one like you
Changing my life blues, so long honey
Chasing away the blues while I count my money
Oh, singing goodbye to a love lost, goodbye, goodbye
On the – make it - my change of life blues.

The lad heaved his suit case aboard a tram that went up Swanston to eventually cross Lygon Street in Carlton. He didn't go that far and when he reached the Melbourne University stop got off as there was a lot of life with young people crossing to and from the University campus. He dug the scene. Lygon Street was only a couple of blocks away anyway and Balga shifted his suitcase handle from hand to hand as he went down Faraday Street passing lots of students dressed and behaving differently from the people of St. Kilda. They acted as if they owned the place and not one of the males was dressed in Bodgie threads. Instead they wore tweed jackets or duffle coats with toggles down the front which he liked. Some wore jeans, but most were in corduroy trousers. These came in two basic styles with thick or thin pipes in colours from black to a bottle green which didn't belong to Squaresville. He decided on this new look which might disguise him so that Jeannie or that dick Kingston would have to look twice to recognise him.

Balga reached Lygon Street filled with shops, coffee lounges and restaurants just like Fitzroy Street but without that touch of tension, of eyes sliding over you and judging so that you tensed up into an act. He went into a coffee lounge for an expresso coffee and sat drinking and thinking of where to look for a room. He remembered coming from work along Drummond Street and how it was similar to Dalgety in having big terrace houses with rooms to let.

Drummond ran parallel to Lygon and the lad walked there and turned towards the city checking out the houses for room to rent signs. The street was more respectable looking than Dalgety and he guessed that the lodgers were of a different type with steady jobs or were students with piles of books. Well, he would fit in wouldn't he with his public service job? Balga was almost at the Victoria Street crossing when he saw a sign in a terrace house that looked nice but a little grubby. He inspected the peeling face of the building and then knocked on the door. A woman similar to Bonny opened it. She wasn't a Bonny though and without much in the way of negotiations he rented a large room at the top of the stairs. It was nice and airy. He put down his suitcase and as he had not slept the night before stretched out on the bed and went off into dreams of being free of Jeannie and that whole scene. He saw her clearly in a dream and awoke feeling lonely.

He shrugged off the mood and checked out the lodging house. It had a communal kitchen and bathroom. He used the bathroom and then poked his head into the kitchen. Not a soul and so he rushed out to see what Lygon Street had to offer on a Sunday evening. He expected just about everything to be closed as it would be in Fitzroy Street, but there were quite a few coffee shops open. All of them seemed to hold a table of aging Italians sipping coffee and talking among themselves. The lad went further up past Grattan Street and between it and Elgin turned into a coffee shop that seemed to be a restaurant as well. It was and he ordered, what else, but spaghetti. When it came, he faced a dilemma in that he didn't know how to eat the real thing. Any spaghetti Balga had eaten before had been from a can. This lot was not soft and squelchy, but long strands that were like serpents. They refused to be mashed by his fork. The lad stared at the darn things and the man that had served him took pity though he grinned as he showed him how to twirl the strands about a fork before shoving them into his mouth. Balga spent about an hour getting it right concentrating so much that he didn't notice how the stuff tasted or how cold it became. When he had finished he paid the bloke and didn't add a sneer. He walked on to Elgin Street to be suddenly hit by déjà vu. A scene flashed into his mind of the time he had burglarized that Italian furniture shop in Perth. "None of that anymore,' he told himself. 'I've got a job and money in my pocket. And no more bodgie,' he suddenly shouted.

Balga took Monday off from work and walked down to the city and to the Lonsdale Street entrance of the Myer Department Store. He went to the office where he applied for the credit card. They did a phone call to check his credentials then gave him one with one hundred and fifty pounds' credit which he could pay off a couple of pounds every fortnight. Immediately he went to their optometrist section to select a pair of dark glasses. Many persons had been wearing these in the artists' pub where he had met Revel a few times. After this the lad went to the gentlemen's clothing section to select a pair of thick ribbed black corduroy trousers which would go with his black desert boots. He still had credit enough for a black duffle coat with wooden toggles and white rope fastenings. Now with these threads and dark glasses he felt that no one in St. Kilda could recognise him and that he was ready to hit the streets of Carlton looking just like a student. Reluctantly he decided that his flat top hair style had to go too.

Balga walked back and along Lygon to come to a barber shop which he entered to find there an Italian who reminded him of the barber he had frequented in Perth at least in those short periods when he was free. 'Hey,' he said, 'are you Marcello? I used to go to your brother in Perth and he laid the basis for this.'

'He did, did he,' Marcello replied, motioning him to sit in the chair: 'Now, what can I do you for. You keeping this or...?'

'I want it rounded out, short and nice and neat.'

'You mean short, back and sides with a razor part,' Marcello said as if he knew how to deal with any sort of hair.

'Yeah, whatever will blend in.'

'Good for you,' the barber replied setting to work and when he had finished so had the Bodgie. Balga could have cried when he surveyed his altered appearance in the mirror. He felt almost as sad as when he had watched the train wheeling Revel out of his life. 'It had to be done,' the lad muttered then rushed to his rooming house to get into his new clothes and check out his altered look.

'My God, my God,' he cried staring at the new Balga in the mirror. He couldn't call it hep or even gear, let alone cool. He eased out of the door and went to the nearby Albion Hotel for a beer, decided against it and went to another hotel filled with students. There just one of the mob he sat over a beer and decided that he should get some provisions that he could eat in the lodging house. He had been given cupboard and refrigerator space and so he walked around until he found an Italian grocery store. He got to talking with the bloke serving him and ended up with crusty bread, salami and cheese.

'Am I going Italian,' Balga said to him with a grin.

'Am I going Aussie,' the bloke flung back with a flourish.

Balga left the store feeling a bit at ease with his new world and reached Elgin Street to turn down it to go to Drummond when he came to a second hand store which reminded him that he needed things like a mug for drinking tea as well as a plate and cutlery. Inside he wandered about in the chaos and found what he needed and more. There was even an old guitar there. He picked it up, but saw that the fret board was cracked and dropped it back. At the counter the things only toted up to 5 bob so he went back and got an old tea pot that he fancied. Now loaded up Balga went home.

He took the food and things to the kitchen and made a salami sandwich which he didn't like much as the meat tasted a bit raw. After finishing it without any one coming into the kitchen the lad went to his room and decided that it was too nondescript and devoid of personality. He tried to make it his by putting up some of Revel's sketches and studies. As the lad looked through them, he noticed that they weren't signed. It seemed that they needed an owner, an artist. Well, he could be one, couldn't he? Balga opened a pad on nude sketches of an older woman's body which reminded him of Jeannie even though he hadn't seen much of hers. Suddenly he gave a start. He knew that woman. No, it couldn't be, he decided and selected three of the nudes to put up because it reminded him of his old flame. Then he lay back on the bed and thought of what he had missed by leaving St. Kilda. He could have been a pimp in a massage parlour where he might have had the pick of the girls. He cursed the Demon for being there and forcing him to flee, then left his room to wander the streets and sit in a pub until closing time at 6, but no one approached him. He was truly alone.

No one commented on his changed appearance at work. Of course the lad had never worn his full Bodgie regalia there and had kept to the square suits he had selected at the Aboriginal Advancement League when he first arrived. Only Nancy commented on his new hair style remarking that since sitting for his permanency he was becoming just like the other men. The lad shrugged at this. 'I'm even becoming an artist now,' he smiled at her and she replied seriously that when he was ready she would pose for him.

His assumption of artist status caused him to begin to do Revel-like sketches of kangaroos and black boys using the blank pages of the pads. After a few of these he tried faces, the best of these being an Aboriginal face. After this he checked out the art books and began doing ears and eyes and so on. Balga even began to think of joining an art class, but put it off until he had sketched a little more. On weekends as it was getting into summer and there was hardly any rain, he went to one of the many parks of Melbourne to draw plants and trees. One Saturday afternoon he was in the Treasury Gardens sketching a big old foreign tree, there weren't any eucalypts, when he was approached by a bloke of about his own age. He went on sketching, not wanting to be disturbed.

'Oh the Bohemian beat blues,' the bloke murmured.

FORTY SIX

BOHEMIAN BEAT BLUES

Oh those Bohemian beat blues
A little different
A little bitty tune
In a minor key
Outwardly controlled
Inwardly, well, make my scene
Moving to a slow, slow, jazz-me beat
Strolling down the street
Evading the people I meet
Oh the Bohemian beat up blues
Oh, the knowing of it
Oh, a skiffle beat
To a folksy tune
Oh the Bohemian beat blues
Oh yeah, somewhat different
Play it, skiffle it, folk it
The Bohemian beat blues,
Join me in the Bohemian beat blues.

Balga sketching in the gardens became annoyed with the bloke watching him. He stopped and was about to say: 'What do you want?' when the bloke, a little older than he was, got the first word in, 'hi'. The lad nodded not wanting to be disturbed and went on with his sketch. 'Ah, I see that you are an artist and are drawing out the life of that tree,' the guy said in a strong voice in which all the words were equally stressed as if he had rehearsed or used such sentences often in his approach to strangers.

'The shape of that tree,' Balga corrected him.

'Perhaps you should try for the inner shape of the tree,' the man suggested, looking down at Balga's sketch, 'it should help to strengthen the outer form and imbue it with the dignity of the spirituality it possesses.'

'Why don't you buzz off and let me get on with doing my tree as I see it,' the lad protested.

'Without Blakean ecstasy,' the silly bloke queried with a smile.

Balga knew the name Blake from school, from reading "Tiger, tiger burning bright" so he grinned back and replied: 'You see a tiger there, bud?

'No, but what else do you have there,' and he took away Balga's sketch pad and looked through it, stopping the longest at Revel's Western Australian bush scenes. 'These are nice and the best of the lot,' he commented.

'That's because I'm from West Aus and when I get homesick I do one of these,' Balga lied. 'Are they good,' he added.

'Well, they are if you are into bush scenes. There are some people who are …'

'I can give you one,' Balga broke in suddenly deciding to be generous with Revel's work.

'Keep them,' the bloke said, waving a plump white hand before handing back the pad. 'I said "some people" and I'm not one of them, I dig Abstract Expressionism and artists such as De Kooning and Jackson Pollock.'

'Oh, yeah' Balga exclaimed, not having heard of them and then not to be outdone, he declared that he liked Revel Cooper himself and his landscapes which were much better than any he could do,' which was really a confession that the lad was no artist.

The man nodded at this and Balga noticed that his chin sported a small goatee and that there was a scar on one cheek as if he had been in a bad accident or been bashed with a broken bottle.

Now the ice having been broken or the guy having succeeded in distracting the lad from his sketching, he extended his hand into a shaking position. Balga took it and it was then that the young bloke introduced himself as Adrian Rawlins the poet and public lavatory cleaner. He said that he lived not far away at the back of a building and then asked: 'Do you like Jazz?'

'Maybe if it's got a backbeat you can't lose,' Balga answered, cribbing the line from a Chuck Berry song.

'Well, you must like traditional jazz. You must have heard the Yarra Yarra Jazz band they are the best of the Melbourne lot.'

'Yeah, but I really dig the blues,' Balga declared.

'If you have time you can come and listen to some sounds and see if you dig what I've got. You know Bessie Smith?'

'Why, yes,' Balga replied, having met guys like this Adrian before and knowing how to follow along with the talk.

'The Empress of the Blues so come and hear her great voice singing great songs as well as top musicians playing great jazz behind her.'

'Yeah, why not! You know I don't even have a radio, let alone a gramophone.'

'Yeah, and I've got all the essentials,' Adrian bragged.

'Yeah, I ain't got much at all,' Balga added.

'So hip,' Adrian almost sneered.

'Yeah, I know I'm hep.'

'Hip, so you like jazz?' the young bloke corrected.

'I got no kick against modern jazz as long as it doesn't start sounding like a symphony,' Balga replied going along with the conversation and quoting the same Chuck Berry song, Rock and Roll Music and as for the Blues, hadn't Fats Domino sang a couple, Trouble in Mind for example, so

Balga knew he was hep (or hip) even though he was now in disguise and looking squarer than the bloke before him. His dark curly hair was long and his baggy suit was closer to the Bodgie threads he had discarded for the cords he now wore. Suddenly he rued the change. He couldn't strut his stuff in such gear.

'What,' Adrian asked and Balga realized he had been muttering to himself.

'Just agreeing with myself, so let's go and listen to those sounds,' he said closing his sketch pad or rather Revel's. Indeed, he was tired of sketching trees and things.

He walked with Adrian across Spring Street and then into a yard at the back of a building and into what he called his "pad". This was an old garage that had been made over into a room or small flat. It was less than the size of Balga's boarding house place, but there was enough space to swing a kitchen in so it was big enough. A wall was lined with books; against another was pushed a table on which rested a portable gramophone and beside it a shelf on which stood long player records all on edge. There was a cupboard and a bed and that was it. Balga finished his examination and said: 'It's not as big as my place.'

'It may be small, but it's cheap and right in town.'

'Yeah and mine's in China,' he sneered and sat on the bed. The lad saw a journal and picked it up and looked at the cover. It was called the Evergreen Review and was a couple of years old, 1957 to be exact and featured something called The San Francisco Scene. He looked at the back and found out what that was:

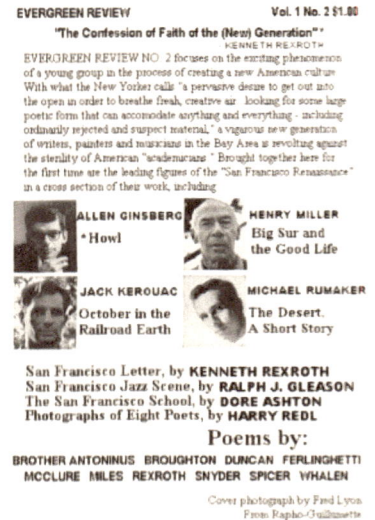

EVERGREEN REVIEW   Vol. 1 No. 2 $1.00

"The Confession of Faith of the (New) Generation" *
KENNETH REXROTH

EVERGREEN REVIEW NO. 2 focuses on the exciting phenomenon of a young group in the process of creating a new American culture. With what the New Yorker calls "a pervasive desire to get out into the open in order to breathe fresh, creative air looking for some large poetic form that can accomodate anything and everything - including ordinarily rejected and suspect material," a vigorous new generation of writers, painters and musicians in the Bay Area is revolting against the sterility of American "academicians." Brought together here for the first time are the leading figures of the "San Francisco Renaissance" in a cross section of their work, including

ALLEN GINSBERG
*Howl

HENRY MILLER
Big Sur and
the Good Life

JACK KEROUAC
October in the
Railroad Earth

MICHAEL RUMAKER
The Desert.
A Short Story

San Francisco Letter, by **KENNETH REXROTH**
San Francisco Jazz Scene, by **RALPH J. GLEASON**
The San Francisco School, by **DORE ASHTON**
Photographs of Eight Poets, by **HARRY REDL**

Poems by:
BROTHER ANTONINUS BROUGHTON DUNCAN FERLINGHETTI
MCCLURE MILES REXROTH SNYDER SPICER WHALEN

Cover photograph by Fred Lyon
From Rapho-Guillumette

'Check out Allen Ginsberg's Howl,' Adrian told him. 'If you don't dig it you can forget about poetry.'

Balga did and read: "I saw the best minds of my generation starving hysterical and naked dragging themselves through the negro streets at dawn looking for an angry fix. Angel-headed hipsters – "Yeah,' he said stopping and watching Adrian fiddling with his gramophone.

'Keep on with the reading and now here is Bessie Smith, the Empress herself,' he said.

It certainly wasn't rock'n'roll. The sound was thin and without a back beat. He listened and heard "Give me a pig foot and a bottle of gin and lay me for I'm in my sin," Other tracks followed to which Adrian exclaimed either "Great" or "Dig this, Satchmo's on trumpet."

Balga had never heard this type of music before. He thought about it and listened as Adrian told him that Bessie Smith began life as dirt poor but she had a tremendous voice and was given a break by another singer, Gertrude "Ma" Rainey, one of the first of the great blues singers. After this, she traveled through the South singing in tent shows and bars and theatres in small towns and in such cities as Birmingham, Alabama;

Memphis, Tennessee; and Atlanta and Savannah, Georgia. After 1920 she made her home in Philadelphia, and it was there that she was first heard by Clarence Williams, a representative of Columbia Records. In February 1923 she made her first recordings, including the classic "Down Hearted Blues," which became an enormous success, selling more than two million copies. She made 160 recordings in all, in many of which she was accompanied by some of the great jazz musicians of the time, including Fletcher Henderson, Benny Goodman, and Louis Armstrong.

'My God, it's older than I am,' Balga thought and then Adrian switched to Louis Armstrong. 'Hey, he's the cat with the gruff voice with the white handkerchief and the trumpet,' he said. 'What was that film he was in with Bing Crosby?'

'Who knows and who cares,' the Hipster replied with a shrug. 'Whatever it was it was far from his prime. This is his Hot Fives from the Twenties.'

'It doesn't sound like swing,' Balga retorted.

'It does swing,' he replied, 'you have to listen carefully. Some say that traditional jazz doesn't swing, but we, if you listen to our Yarra Yarra Jazz Band you know they can.'

'Uhuh,' the lad answered, not wanting to admit that all he had heard was Gene Krupa, Henry James and the famous Glen Miller that cons from the war years really dug and which he didn't, except for Gene Krupa and Buddy Rich bashing away on the drums.

Balga became thoroughly bored until Adrian eventually put on Leadbelly, to him a really, really authentic black singer who had done time for murdering a bloke. This was more to Balga's liking and he even found he knew one of his songs, "Goodnight Irene". At last he had found something he liked and Adrian added to his knowledge about such old singers. A white bloke called Alan Lomax had recorded Huddy Ledbetter in an awesome collection that had been released in a boxed collection by Folkways Records. Balga decided that eventually would he would begin his own collection with that one.

FORTY SEVEN

JAZZ CENTRE 44 BLUES

A face staring through the windows
A laugh crackling at a score
Hitting us as we walk through the door
And we call, fluttering our notes
Wailing out the sax, flickering to the beat
Oh, sing those Jazz Centre 44 blues
Sung to an old time band bluesy
Oh yeah, let the trumpet blah
Let the clarinet go la-laaaah
An old tune and an old sound refound
Blue it boys as around and around we go
Dancing, twisting, hold your girl and go
Cool, moving, moving, moving just so
Boys and girls and boys and boys
Move to the tune of the blues
The jazz centre 44 blues (play it).

Evening came creeping through the door. It was summer time in Melbourne and nice and warm. Adrian suggested that Balga come with him to a Jazz place in St. Kilda.

'I hope that it isn't on Fitzroy Street,' Balga replied, hesitating to accept as he didn't want to collide with Phil or Jeannie. They were sure to see through his disguise. He found his dark glasses and put them on. Every-thing was changed now. He was, well, anonymous in a sort of Bohemian way that stood out.

'No, it's opposite Luna Park and on a different tram line so that you don't even have to go down Fitzroy Street,' Adrian replied wising him up.

'Yeah man, let's go and dig the jazz and get some tucker before that or there,' Balga declared putting on his duffle coat even though it was warm.. He left his sketch pad behind and went with the guy to a coffee place in a building in upper Collins Street called "The Proscenium" for coffee and a sandwich. It was run by two young snotty women and was, as Adrian informed him, frequented by theatre people after their shows. It may have been, but apart from the young women they were the only customers. He had a coffee and a sandwich and put up with the yacking from Adrian until he mentioned Johnny O'Keefe. The woman serving them heard this and immediately declared that he was a little Bodgie. Balga was about to retort that he was one too, but kept his gob shut. He was now an artist after all and with it wearing his dark glasses in the evening.

After they had their snacks the two young blokes went down to Swan-ston Street where they caught a Luna Park tram to St. Kilda. It reached the junction and turned away from Fitzroy Street. Balga breathed a sigh, not of relief but of sorrow in that he might have gone and seen Fast Eddy and his molls, but surely the pimp would have sneered at the new Balga. He had to avoid him now just as he had to avoid everyone he had once known in St. Kilda. It was then that he thought that clothes did indeed make the man and by altering his appearance he had said goodbye to his past life. He sighed again and Adrian asked what was wrong. 'Everything,' Balga replied. 'Yeah, just about everything. I miss a lot of things, but I had to grow out and away.'

'Perhaps,' Adrian replied, laying a hand on his shoulder. 'Anyway tonight you're with me and will hear some cool sounds and I have a sur-prise for you too.'

'You have; you do?'

'Yes, and all shall be revealed in time,' the hipster replied with a laugh.

They got off in front of the giant face through the mouth of which one went into the Luna Park amusement Park. Canned laughter echoed from it. Balga stared at the face and shrugged. There had been such a park in Scarborough Western Australia and it wasn't that exciting, but this one looked much better with the track of a roller coaster rising and falling all around the outer fence. He watched a line of wagons rush down, then climb up a high rise from which there must be a great view of the city and bay. Screams of terror real or fake came as the roller coaster rushed down.

'My God,' Balga couldn't help exclaiming as the wagons plunged down.

'It looks better than it rides,' Adrian said as he turned away from what Balga desired and wanted to sample.

They crossed the road to an eating place with hamburgers and such things as coke on the ground floor, but didn't enter. They took the stairs on the left up to the first floor. At the top there was a door with a bloke sitting behind a table. Adrian nodded at him, smiled as he indicated Balga and went through into a big round hall with windows almost all around the walls under which were tables and chairs. The middle was left bare and at the end without windows was a stage or platform.

'Well, welcome to the Roundhouse, Jazz Centre 44,' Adrian declaimed and then added: 'It pays to be an entertainer as well as to know one – me!'

'Sure,' the lad replied as they sat at a front table. The club was all but empty and the band hadn't arrived as yet, but this gave Balga the chance to get used to the place. Indeed it had been a long time since he had even been in a dance hall. He remembered The Snakepit in Perth and smiled then scowled. He had only made it once before being locked up and away from all temptation. It had been a kid's place and didn't have the atmosphere of this jazz joint, though this didn't feel or look like night clubs he had seen in films. There wasn't any bar for r example and only table and chairs and that platform at the end away from the windows. Now some men had appeared to test out their instruments, a trombone, a trumpet, a clarinet, a banjo, bass and drums.

Friday nights at the Roundhouse was for traditional jazz. 'The Yarra Yarra Jazz Band,' Adrian told him. They play the real stuff unlike Frank Traynor and his Jazz Preachers a good time raunchy band without soul. They also can't "swing"' and this settled the matter for the hipster.

People started drifting in. They looked a bit like students but were older and inclined to full beards, corduroys and gruff manners that Balga found a bit uncool. The Yarra Yarra Jazz Band was similar to their fans and Adrian greeted them as mates and stood talking with them while they readied their instruments.

The band played that good time music that early jazz had descended into, but they "swung" as they were serious exponents of the art, but Balga was a bit bored and began checking out the crowd. At the next table there were two girls sitting and talking above the music. One was tall and brunette and she was commiserating with the other, a short blonde, about the way her boy friend had dumped her. She went on and on eliciting each and every detail so that by the time the band put down their instruments for a break the lad had all the facts necessary to make a spontaneous entrance. He sat at their table and declared that he was a palm reader and asked the blonde if she wanted her hand read. Balga smiled into her hesitant smile, stared into her blue eyes and saw that she was indeed suffering. She wanted comfort and reassurance so he took up her left hand, traced the palm lines with a delicate index finger and declared that someone was coming back into her life. He left her smiling and her friend for some reason scowling. He went to the back windows that looked over the giant face and found a table and sat there, close to two blokes who were talking earnestly. He heard one saying to the other: 'I'm bi, you know and tonight I'm feeling camp.' 'Yes,' his mate replied, 'and so am I,' and with that the music began and he lost the conversation.

Adrian came towards him and sat down as the band hesitated between numbers. It was then that Balga lied to him that he was a singer and that was what the band needed. 'You know,' he declared, 'my dad was friends with the rhythm and blues singer Fats Domino and he could lay down a tune himself.'

'Oh, they have a girl singer most Fridays,' Adrian said and then, 'Why don't you give us a number. Let's see if you have the licks.'

And before he knew it, Balga found himself talking to the Yarra Yarra Jazz Band leader the horn player who asked him if he could sing.

'Of course, man, of course,' he declared. 'Yeah, I've sang one or two songs in my time.'

'Sure,' the horn player said somewhat sardonically, 'but with a trad jazz band?'

'No big deal. A band's a band.'

'Okay, if you think you're up to it. What do you want to give us?'

Balga got cold feet. He cleared his throat and coughed ready to beg off.

'Hurry up, you do the first number. What key do you sing in?'

'Whatever man!'

'Yeah, but you know we have to know the key and what song is it?'

'Never said a mumbling word and in the key that Leadbelly sings it in,' declared Balga remembering the name from the session at Adrian's place.

Luckily, he had a good mind for remembering or improvising on lyrics and was a natural in holding a tune. The band leader introduced him as Balga Boy Jackson, a folk singer and the lad listened to the intro and took it away mimicking Leadbelly.

> *Oh my Lord oh they crucified my Lord,*
> *And he never said a mumblin' word.*
> *When they crucified my Lord,*
> *And he never said a mumblin' word.*
> *Not a word, not a word, to me,*
> *They nailed him to a tree*

Oh they nailed him to a tree
Oh they nailed him to a tree
And he never said a mumblin' word to me..
They nailed him to a tree
And he never said a mumblin' word.
Not a word, not a word,
They pierced him in the side,
And he never said a mumblin' word.
They pierced him in the side,
And he never said a mumblin' word.
Not a word, not a word to me..
He bowed his head and died
He bowed his head and died
He bowed his head and died
And he said a word, yes a word to me.
'I'm coming back again;
I'm coming back again.
He's coming back again, my Lord.
One day when I was lost,
They hung him on a cross
And he never said a mumbling word to me.
Not a word , not a word, not a word, my Lord
And he never said a mumblin' word, my Lord,
My Lord, my Lord, never a mumbling word to me.!

FORTY EIGHT

PUB HANGING JUST SITTING DOWN BLUES

Pub hanging just sitting down blues
Drinking a beer, got a feeling for a wine
Yeah, got the pub hanging, sitting down blues
Oh yeah, there's a perky chick, making time
Just sitting, waiting for a dime to dine
Sooner, no later, a sandwich or a pie
Sigh, just sitting on, but I'm not alone
I'm with you, but I'm still feeling those blues
Right to my bones, right to my thighs, the blues
Oh the blues, Oh God got to escape this scene
Hit the door make the street, blues after me
Falling like the Melbourne rain, oh no,
Yes, just got these pub hanging, sitting down blues
Yeah, oh yeah, no matter, I'm with you, yeah oh yeah
So make me lose these blues, these pub hanging blues.

Revel Cooper had taken Balga to the Swanston Family Hotel where the art students and their models hung out. Revel was at home there and popular. He sat at a table crowded with young folk as he regaled them with stories from his homeland. Sometimes these were mysterious; at times erotic, and at other times homesick stories of when he had been a small kid. Balga listened to these campfire yarns and sipped on his beer.

He wasn't an artist and felt out of it. Indeed, he clung closely to Revel and so missed what was happening in the rest of the pub. He didn't even go off to any of the parties as he always had to get to work in the morning or to St. Kilda for a different scene. Thus he missed a lot, but now he felt that he was an artist and readily agreed to accompany one Saturday afternoon Adrian to the Swanston Family Hotel which was where the Bohemians of Melbourne hung out. It was in Russell Street almost opposite the Victorian Art Gallery which had the arts school that Revel had attended.

Students and models were there, but Revel was a felt lack. Balga felt sad at not hearing the sound of his cheery beery voice. Adrian soon got lost in a conversation and the lad wandered about the pub listening to snatches of talk about things he knew and more about things he didn't know. With Revel he had felt a connection, but now, apart from his dark skin, he might have been one of the younger blokes and no one even stared at him. He stopped near a folksinger with a round freckled face and an old guitar on which he strummed chords as he said that he had written a hundred songs all in the key of C just to see if it could be done. He then began to sing the Rock Island Line which Balga knew wasn't one of them. He had heard it at Adrian's from the Huddy Leadbetter recordings.

The joint was crowded and as he was standing there watching the chord changes, someone bumped him. He looked down onto the dark hair and then the fair face of a girl smiling up at him. The song ended and the bloke put down his guitar to swallow his beer. Balga asked the girl if she wanted a drink. She agreed to a red wine and followed him to the bar as he went to get it. As he passed her the glass, Balga introduced his self and said that he was an artist.

'Hey, the way you were watching the fingers of that guy I would have sworn that you were a folksinger,' she exclaimed after sipping at her wine. 'So an artist, well, I'm a model.'

'You must know Revel Cooper,' Balga replied while wondering if her form was among the ones Revel had left behind.

'Naw just got in from Sydney, that's where I'm from. My name's Ross short for Roslyn,' the small, round dumpy girl said with a smile as if there was some joke attached to it. 'As I've said I'm just down from Sydney and staying with a friend until my next move which will be, I think back to Sydney.'

'Never been there,' Balga smiled back because she radiated a warmth and friendliness that made him like her.

'You have to dig it,' she replied. 'I'll show you some of the hip places, like the King George just like this pub, but the Cross is where the action is.'

'Oh, I don't know when I can get away. You know I have a job.'

'I thought you were an artist.'

'Painting doesn't pay the rent.'

'Modeling does though. Maybe you could model. You've got the body for it.'

'Better a folksinger. People seem to like that stuff and I've been practicing a bit. A bloke I know showed me some simple chords too, but I want to go beyond that and into the blues.'

'Well, youth is the time for experimenting, for finding out what you're capable of and then doing it. Yeah, man, just do it and be damned with what it does or doesn't bring!'

'I think I've lost the urge for change,' Balga said with a shrug.
'Oh come on, when you are old is the time to be steady, get married and have kids and all that when you've beyond thirty.'

'Well, just on nineteen, just a few months ago though it seems years ago now,' Balga said scowling as he remembered his brush with the law.

'Gee, you're really old aren't you,' she replied with a mischievous grin. 'Well, what about me, can you guess my age?'

She looked about eighteen and so the lad added two years and said "twenty." He had guessed right or she agreed with him to be agreeable or to be older, whatever. Balga bought her another glass of wine and talked to her about art and in the fashion of the pub complained that the artist was the true outsider.

'Aren't we all,' she queried.

'Not all,' Balga replied, thinking of the people at work, but then Nancy and Jonesy came into his mind and he amended it to most people. 'Maybe we are all suffering outsiders,' he went on, considered what he had said and had to add, 'but some of us are more outer than others who are more inner.'

'So we are all different?'

'Well, yes, but there are degrees of difference.'

'And sameness,' she replied and their conversation went on like this until six o'clock came and they were turfed out into the street. Balga looked for Adrian, but he had gone off. He thought about The Roundhouse, but that place didn't really start until after eight and as St. Kilda wasn't safe for him to hang in, at least he thought so, he suggested that they go to Carlton for a plate of Spaghetti and a glass of red wine at an Italian club that he had discovered one night when ignoring the sign saying "members only" he walked in hungry and was served with no problems at all.

'Sure, sure,' she agreed and they walked up Russell Street past police headquarters and into Lygon Street. After their spaghetti it was still early and he asked her if she want to listen to some sounds at his place.

She replied: 'Only if you can get us a bottle of this fine red red wine here.'

Balga hadn't tried to before, but well, there was always the first time and he went to the counter and asked the bloke there who said "yes" as long as it didn't come from the club.

'Never been here in me life,' Balga said with a grin, pocketing the unlabelled bottle in his deep duffle coat pocket.

'Got one,' he told Ross as they went out into the evening. It was about seven thirty and they could have gone on to the Roundhouse and with wine too. He suggested it to her and she immediately agreed. As they walked to the tram stop, the girl took his hand and it felt like the most natural thing in the world. They scrabbled aboard the tram and sat hand in hand. "So corny," Balga thought, but he was glad and at peace with the world as the tram took them along St. Kilda Road and pushed them out beneath the giant face laughing at the guys and chicks of this world. It was then as they hesitated before crossing over to the jazz club that a car slowed to give them the eye over. Balga froze up inside. His hand fell from the girl's.

'Beatnik scum,' a familiar voice muttered distinctly and the car moved off.

Balga breathed again. It had been the Kingston demon and, and he gave a nervous grin, he had not recognized him, or had he?

Ross looked up into his face and asked what was wrong? I felt, well, a dingo crossing my path and stopping to sniff at my scent', he replied feeling that his disguise had been sprung.

'You kidding or just mystical,' the girl retorted.

'Let's go and dig that jazz,' Balga said and skipped across the street. She came after him and they went up the stairs.

It was a trad jazz night with a singer, Judy Jacques wailing the blues. The couple sat in a dark corner at the back and finished the bottle as the night passed until eleven when the snugness came to an end.

Outside, the night was cool, but the sky was clear. The big face went off and they walked along towards – oh my God, Balga thought Fitzroy Street and who might he meet there? The lad thrust on his dark glasses and picked his way along like a blind man so that Ross laughed and led him along.

A few coffee shops were still open along the street and one of them was where Steady Eddy hung out. It must have been the wine because suddenly Balga decided to go and meet his old mate.

'Let's go in there for a coffee. We have enough time before the last tram goes to the city and then it's an easy walk to my pad.'

'Sure, that wine was the best,' the girl giggled.

Balga flung the door open a bit too dramatically and marched in. He was feeling like one of the locals though he didn't look like one. The lad stopped in the middle of the floor and spun around. No Steady Eddy and he felt like a stranger as he went to the counter and ordered two expressos and while waiting he asked the bloke what had happened to his star customer.

'That one,' the counterman sneered. 'Haven't you heard or read about it in the papers. They want to clean up St. Kilda, make it fit for, well, blokes like you. That Detective Kingston took him and his girls away last night.'

'But he's as bent as any cop can be. He's the vice in the vice rep St. Kilda has.'

'Maybe, but he doesn't deal it on the street, does he?'

'He's a cop,' Balga replied and took the coffees back to the table where Ross had sat.

'I dunno,' he said to himself, 'I dunno.'

During the sipping, Balga could feel the counter bloke's eyes on him as if he was trying to place him. It made the lad uneasy he was glad to get out of the place and its memories.

'Poor Eddy,' he thought as they got the last tram out of St. Kilda. 'Steady, Eddy, he done gone away, stretching out the time, another day the same old cell, oh yeah,' he sang quietly to himself.

'You feeling okay,' Ross asked him.

'No,' he said, 'no, I dunno,' and he shrugged. The world wasn't grand, but a blues tune sung by a lonely black fellow in a lonely hotel room waiting, waiting, oh no, for the police to come and handcuff him away. Oh no, not again,' he sang softly to himself.

FORTY NINE

PARTY TIME TIRED OUT BLUES

Party time, oh those tired out blues
Party time, oh those bored out blues
Been up all night now feeling the strain
Just picking out a chord, bending it like Cain
Not being Able enough oh to hang this song
Just the blues, oh those tired out blues (play)
Oh those weary blues, uneasy blues swinging
Winging it, oh tired out party time blues (tired out)
Oh those party time, tired out blues.

Balga thought that his pad didn't look like the studio of an artist. It was too small for any large size painting and he really needed a loft. Revel's sketches he had pinned on the walls roughly. A nice touch as it might seem that he had put them there to study and amend. The lad had bought a few art books and what was more had started two paintings using oils although he had no knowledge on how to mix or apply them. One painting, a dark portrait of an old Aboriginal man whose features he had dragged up from some forgotten Perth scene was not all that bad; but the other another portrait was hideous, an out and out failure that he should have scraped it off. It floated there in all its loathsomeness. He hated it.

Hiding his chagrin he found a half bottle of red, and filled two cups. Ross was looking through one of Revel's pads. She stopped to take the cup and gave a start as she saw the painting. 'What, how did you manage to do that?' she asked.

'I was experimenting and it came out all wrong,' he stuttered.

'Maybe, but you should see what some of the students do, how they attack my body,' she said with a laugh, arching her back so that her breasts jutted out.

'Yeah,' he replied, knowing that he was nowhere proficient enough to attempt to sketch them.

Balga filled her cup again and tried to see his "art" through her eyes. Revel's sketches were fine, but not his. Should he change styles? The lad had checked out abstract expressionism which was the art of the present and not the square stuff he was attempting to do. Maybe he should follow the examples of Jackson Pollock, Willem De Kooning, Franz Kline and forget kangaroos, old black fellows and trees. Yes, just splashing paint on canvases or boards but they had to be big. He needed a studio with floor space the size of a warehouse or at least a large loft. Yes, he must ask Adrian if he knew an empty loft he could rent.

Ross was a very nice girl and what was more was used to shucking off her clothing without a thought. Balga soon had her naked and then really had to lean back to admire her body. She really was a fine artist's model and unconsciously posed her body so that one looked at her breasts or the curve of a hip as objects to be admired that is until one started touching that resilient flesh and then falling in it to be engulfed in warmth that made him forget all about art.

They aroused themselves as dawn was cracking the sky and went out to one of the all day and night Italian coffee shops for a coffee. They sat sipping and smiling at each other as the sun arose. At about six, she suggested that he come along to where she was dossing at a friend's pad.

'Isn't it a bit early,' Balga replied.

'No, they are having a weekend party so it will still be swinging. We can walk it as it not all that far away, Richmond, Swan Street.'

'The other side of town, but I used to live in Hawthorn. I rambled along that street more than once looking for kicks.'

Melbourne was dead as a Sunday morning in Perth. Richmond which was a little lively with a few people walking on the streets and hand in hand they wandered along Swan Street. Ross checked out numbers and stopped when they reached 350 on the corner of a thin side street.

'This it,' the lad asked.

'No,' she replied, 'it's the sixth house down this street.'

They reached a shabby house from which guitar music was sounding from the open front door. They walked in. Balga peered into a room which had the floor completely covered with mattresses on which a number of people were talking, drinking wine or sleeping.

A bearded face with red-rimmed eyes looked up and called: 'Ross.'

The girl went and hugged him. Balga dropped onto the mattresses feeling the night catching up on him. There was a bottle of red wine standing against the wall. It smelt okay and he swallowed a mouthful. The folk singer, the one that had been at the pub, finished and passed the guitar to a long haired girl who tuned it then sang a mournful ditty in a high voice about the low life. Balga got up and went to look for the toilet. The back of the house was one big room, an artist's studio with work similar to what he had seen in books. The paintings were a mixture of styles, none featuring kangaroos, but everything else from nudes to pots and pans. Staring at them, Balga sighed a great sigh. After his piss he decided that he wanted to go home; but when he returned to the front room he found Ross there holding a guitar.

'Hi,' she said, 'ready for your act?'

Balga shrugged.

'I told them that you can play the guitar as well as sing,' Ross said brightly.

'No,' Balga declared.

'Just one song,' she implored him.

'I'm not a folk singer.'

'But … well?'

'Woman, I know a few blues,' Balga retorted.

'You just sing, and I'll back you,' replied the folksinger coming to them.

Balga felt trapped and thought about Fats Domino and how he had sang a blues, Trouble in Mind. He remembered the words and how it went and said, 'just one, okay, Trouble in mind.'

Trouble in mind, babe, I'm blue,

but I won't be blue always

> *Trouble in mind, babe, I'm blue,*
> *but I won't be blue always*
> *Yes, the sun gonna shine,*
> *in my back door someday*
> *I'm goin' down, down to the river,*
> *I'm gonna take my rockin' chair*
> *Lord, if the blues overtake me,*
> *I'm gonna rock on away from here*
> *'Cause I've trouble in mind, you know that I'm blue,*
> *but I won't be blue always*
> *Yes, the sun gonna shine,*
> *in my back door someday*
> *I'm gonna lay, lay my head,*
> *on some sad, old railroad iron*
> *I'm gonna let that 2:19,*
> *pacify my mind*
> *I'm trouble in mind, baby you know that I'm blue,*
> *but I won't be blue always*
> *Yes, the sun gonna shine,*
> *in my back door someday*

(Richard M. Jones, 1924)

He stopped singing and the guitarist, the folkies name was Wyndham Martin Reid bent a note or few. A couple clapped and Balga said thanks to the guitarist and went to sit on the bed with Ross.

After a while she hugged him and said: 'I'm thinking of going back to Sydney.'

'Never been there,' Balga rested on one elbow too tired to let her words penetrate.

'Pay for the petrol and you can come with me,' she replied. 'I'll show you some of the places like the King George pub where we all hang out and then there's the Cross. It's a wow scene for folks like us.'

Balga was about to beg off when he thought of the long drive and how he could get his hands on a wheel again so he asked: 'You got a car, what sort?'

'Something I borrowed from hubby. Just a regular old Holden, but it's steady as she goes. It can do the distance. Come fly with me.'

And Balga said to heck with it and took off.

FIFTY

STRAIGHT AHEAD BLUES

Don't be bent, don't be bad, take it slow
Oh, this straight ahead blues, straight ahead
The sun is shining and my eyes are bleeding (light)
Oh, yeah this highway got the straight ahead blues
No bends, no curves, no corners, straight, yeah
Don't be bent, don't be crooked, hold the wheel (straight)
Oh yeah, the goal lies straight ahead, no crookedness now
For this is the right time, the right time, straight (ahead)
Yeah, straight, oh straight ahead (no curve) blues.

Ross's car was one of those newish FB Holdens but seeing it had made the distance from Sydney most likely it would make it back without breaking down.

'Take it straight north along any old road and that should get us to the Hume highway,' Balga said not sure of how to get out of the city.

'Yeah, Coburg and Sydney road,' Ross replied sure of the route. She swung around in a smart v and drove off keeping to the speed limit. She obviously didn't want to hang around Melbourne.

Balga fiddled with the radio and found a station playing, oh, the blues. He smiled and listened until the news cut into the music. Australian soldiers were in a country called Vietnam, but he wanted some sounds and got top forty as the city suddenly gave way. The country opened up through which the Hume Highway extended north.

Ross swung into a petrol station to fill the tank and Balga dutifully forked over the cash. He felt good to be on the road; great to be moving after long months in Melbourne. Now he had the country around him; but, and it hurt a little, no Grass Trees, just, well, farms and roadside trees and whizzing cars and trucks and soon he was one of them. He was behind the wheel, coaching out what power was in the engine. He managed to sit on seventy.

'Australia's own car isn't a Ford,' he commented dryly as the speed dropped below seventy.

'Well, my husband's a bit like that. No get up and go,' commented Ross as she fiddled with the radio to tune in on some strange music.

'Pablo Casals playing Bach,' Ross observed.

'Nice, sounds a bit Churchy like they had in the orphanage,' Balga replied. 'I actually was in the choir and sung some of that stuff slow and steady just like the car eh?'

The motor hummed, the wheels rolled and the wonderful cello played the wonderful music that Balga had never really dug. It fitted in well with the movement through the open countryside. He slowed, saw a side road and swerved into it.

'Where are you going,' Ross asked a little anxiously, Balga thought, as if he was about to kidnap her or dump her and steal the car.

'Just want to dig the bush. That music is sending me into peace,' Balga assured her as he pulled up under a tall spreading gum tree.

He got out and Ross joined him. The music from the car stopped. Cicadas sounded and a Kookaburra laughed. Balga whooped back and even did a little stamping dance. It sure felt good to be part of the land again; but, no, it wasn't West Aussie and he got back into the car in the passenger seat. Ross drove them along and along until at long last they reached a river, a wide river which could only be the Murray.

'Hey, a swim,' Ross screeched and turned along a road that went along the river bank.

They came to a nice indented spot surrounded on three sides by trees and Ross jumped out of the car, pulled off her jeans and shirt and leaped into the water. Balga watched the current suddenly take her. He panicked. He wasn't much of a swimmer and she could drown.

Ross angled to the bank some yards downstream. 'Come on, come on,' she urged the lad.

'No, that current looks too strong,' Balga answered afraid to trust his self to the river.

'Come on, jump in. I've done life saving. Just reach out when you are swept to me and I'll grab you. We can have a hug,' she urged him'

Balga took off his clothes slowly then quickly jumped into the Murray River before he could draw back. The current swept him out and along. He tried to paddle closer to the shore. The current clutched him and then so did arms which held him and guided him along. They went on and on until about a hundred yards along Ross had angled them successfully to the bank.

'There,' she said, 'that's all there is to it.'

'Ah yes,' Balga said still unsure of his self and holding on to an apprehensive mood.

They walked back to their car and dressed. The sun was going down and both were hungry. They crossed the border over into Albury in New South Wales and Balga's mood persisted. He suddenly realized as his identity returned with a rush that he was an Aborigine. He didn't know what laws might confine him in that state. Why, he might even end up on a reservation. He hadn't even thought of this.

'Cheer up, the water wasn't all that bad,' Ross said easing the car into a service station and parking in front of a restaurant. 'Come on, let's eat,' she said and Balga reluctantly followed her. Were Aborigines allowed to eat in a restaurant? He didn't know; but it couldn't be as bad as Perth where they were only banned from hotels. So he forced a smile as he accompanied the white girl into the place. A few men glanced at them and one hard faced bloke examined him carefully. Balga guessed he was a copper; and so he straightened up. He hid his weaknesses and put a Bodgie swagger in his walk as he went to the toilet. When he finished pissing, he turned to find the bloke there. 'You passing through,' he stated.

'Yeah, just passing through, boss,' Balga replied his head hanging.

'Yeah, see that you do,' the bloke said and left.

Ross was tucking into a hamburger and chips. Balga glanced at his and ate a few chips.

'You want that,' Ross said gesturing at his burger.

She scoffed it down and then they had coffee. Finished they went to the counter to pay and Balga saw a poster advertising a movie he had heard about, but never seen. It was Rebel without a Cause. 'Hey,' he said, 'I want to see that. James Dean's in it.' 'Yeah, the James Dean,' the woman that was ringing up their bill spoke. 'It's showing at the Drive In and the show starts as soon as it's dark enough.'

'Well, if we drove all night we would be in Sydney early in the morning,' Ross said.

'No hurry, let's see the movie and then go along a bit and sleep in the car. I haven't been ever in a Drive In and I want to dig it.'

'Why not, yes, I'm a bit tired at that.'

The Drive In was a new experience for both of them. They drove through a gateway in a metal sheet fence to stop at a building containing the ticket office, toilets and a snack bar. It was only a pound and after they got ice creams they continued and parked right in front of a large screen. There was a small speaker hooked on a post and they brought that inside the car and then got out and settled in the back seat.

The movie was in Cinemascope and began slowly. Balga decided that it wasn't The Wild One, but Ross liked it enough to take his hand. The lad decided that she looked a bit like Nathalie Wood and whispered to her: 'You know I had this friend. He used to name his girls after film actresses.'

'Girls?'

'Well, he would have called you Nathalie, uhuh,' replied Balga edging away from her question. 'Hey look,' he called and their attention returned to the film which was a bit slow.

It was about high school students to which Balga couldn't relate. He watched them go on a trip to the Griffith Park Observatory. The subject was "The End of Man" and the lecturer described the sun growing larger until it exploded and wiped out all trace of mankind. "The Earth will not be missed," the lecturer informed the students. "Through the infinite reaches of space, the problems of man seem trivial and naive indeed, and man existing alone seems himself an episode of little consequence." This was not the note of optimism Balga wanted when he was with a girl in a car and on the road.

And the film reached the scene of a deadly game of chicken in which the hip guy, Buzz challenged the main character, Jim to a chicken run. A really dumb charge at a cliff edge at which he went over and that was enough Balga fell asleep to be followed by Ross.

The lad woke up to the sounds of cars starting and revving. 'Okay movie,' Balga commented, 'but not enough action. Well, now that we've had a sleep we can drive to Sydney tonight. You drive us out of town and then I'll take the wheel.'

Before they left they stopped at the toilets and when Balga came out, he found a bloke talking to his girl. He came up and the young bloke glanced at him and sneered, 'Don't worry, but you have to wash before...' It was then that Balga hit him. Down the man went and he stayed down.

'We better get away before we get the Aussie fair,' he grinned clenching his fists and feeling his knuckles.'

'What do you mean?'

'He goes and gets his mates and they beat me all to hell and who knows what they'll do to you. Let's cut out right now, hurry!'

No one came after them as they escaped the town. Balga was at the wheel and it was with the night closed about them and the headlamps thrusting the darkness away that he finally felt he was a James Dean with a Nathalie Wood sleeping beside him. Life sure was great what with the vehicle burning away the night and with a chick breathing easily at his side. Yes, Sydney would be an adventure, he knew it, he knew it. Life was there for the living and the taking. He knew it; he knew it.

FIFTY ONE

KINGS CROSS WITCHERY BLUES

King's Cross, oh the vibes, the witchy blues
Hanging loose with a chick knowing the scene
Oh, yeah, the strange vibes of, oh another Roz
With the witchy blues, ripe and black
Asking for more making me sore
Oh no, the witchy blues is not for me
No, a brother with a guitar singing
Away those witchy blues, yewah oh yeah
Lay it down, boy lay it down (play, play).

Sydney! Balga gawked as only a yokel can at the Sydney Harbour Bridge .Well, he had never seen the thing before and it was an icon of modern Australia after all. Next, it was Bondi Beach, and Balga left off all thoughts as he plunged into the surf and kissed his girl on that fabulous beach. Exhausted after the long drive of the night, the couple slept a couple of hours lying on the sand. And after it was just roaming about digging the streets, even the big central railway station and China Town and as the day descended into the evening Ross parked her Holden on a street called Wylde which she told him was part of the fabled Kings Cross.

She shrugged as only a true Sydney-sider could leading him along to the intersection of Victoria and Darlinghurst roads. 'The Cross,' she said with a dramatic gesture.

And there it was, just like Fitzroy Street in St. Kilda. Yeah, and with the same sort of street vibes that he knew. He rued wearing only a pair of simple working men's jeans and rough checked shirt. The Bodgie still within him wanted to revert back to his street crawling gear. Yeah, he needed to be bouncing along on high crepe soles, feeling his tapered pants clinging to his ankles; shrugging at the weight of his padded finger tip length draped coat with patch pockets and hearing the clink of the long key chain dangling from his hip to his pocket that could serve as a weapon and swaying, yeah swaying and sounding out a tiny message of watch out, watch out here comes a walking dagger seeking out a fleshy sheaf to be plunged into. Balga shook his self to rid his mind of his old image. He was acting out the part and had even moved a few feet away from Ross so that everyone could get a good look at him as a solitary object 'Hey, what's wrong with you?' Ross demanded and he wrapped an arm about her waist and entered into his Bohemian self. He wished that he was carrying a guitar to show that he was into the folk scene.

'Nothing,' he said. 'Just reliving old times, old spaces and -- this place brought back memories that's all.'

He smiled at her frown and then to avoid any further conversation about old lives and old memories, he exclaimed. 'Hey, the fabulous Cross; the fabulous Cross and look at this fabulous place. Let's go in and get a coffee and cool it for a bit.

'Yeah, I know that place, old memories, eh? It's the Devil's Lair, one of the hangouts of my friendly witch, Roseleen Norton, model and artist. Maybe you'll get to meet her. She gets off on your type.'

Balga hesitated to enter the coffee shop as he had decided it wasn't so fabulous at all. Indeed it looked dark and, well, sinister. There wouldn't even be a juke box there. He wanted a brighter place with rock sounds, but Ross had already entered.

He followed her into flickering candle lit darkness with a brooding atmosphere as if the whole place was waiting for something to happen or it had happened and it was getting over it. Whatever, it wasn't a fighting feeling or even dangerous. He perked up and began to check out the place. It wasn't all that dark either, just reddish. Perhaps too red as small flood lights illuminated murals that he saw, and recoiled from as only a lad that had been raised as Catholic could. The pictures were all about ugly devils and half naked women and one which his eyes hesitated to examine. There was an almost caricature of a black man engaged in caressing a white woman with horns. "The occasion of sin, avoid the occasion of sin," he thought he heard a voice intone. He shrugged as these days he never went near a church and this was the first place in ages that made him think of one and of his old Christian Brothers' school.

Ross was already sitting at a table with the yellow flame of a black wax candle casting shadows on her face. He found it downright spooky, very churchy and suddenly there was a shout from a familiar voice "Bodgie." Oh my God, it was his old mate and he whooped back "Tommy Cooper". And they were exchanging a bodgie handshake even though Tommy really had never been one of the Saints; but what did that matter. He was an old mate that he had missed.

'Hey, Tommy I'm with a chick, just call me by my real name, Balga, I'm a bit of a blues singer now and no longer the Bodgie rocker you once knew,' he warned him.

'Yeah okay Bodg-, I mean Balga what are you doing in Sydney?'

'And I might ask what are you doing in a place like this? Not even a juke box. Hey, man, you've come down or what? Oh put on the lights and let's rock.'

'I manage this joint, man and let me tell you it takes in a fair bit of money over the weekends from the visitors, naw squares that want to catch a glimpse of real life, or what they think is real life in the Cross.'

'But what's with the devils, not very Catholic eh? What would the Brothers think of you?'

'Well, let me tell you man, you not being from Sydney and all it's like this. The squares or at least some of them have a thing for witches and such like creatures that go bump in the night. The newspaper did a story on this woman, not your sort by the way, and they dubbed her The Witch of the Cross. Now cats (and chicks of course) come looking for her and where can they find her on most nights? In The Devil's Lair of course, sitting at that back table nicely lit by the flood on that mural, it's not the devil by the way, but something she calls the god, Pan. So how are things down south?'

'Same old job in Melbourne. That chick there, Ross was coming to Sydney in a car and so I came with her to get the wheel in my hands again. Did the trip in a day and a night in a Holden, underpowered, that's good going, mate.'

'You haven't been knocking any off anymore, have you?'

' Me, no, never again, not after that D Kingston put the fear of, well, of that hairy devil there into me. Hey, he most likely would like this place. That demon would be right at home and with that woman of his, Jeannie. Christ, the people I got mixed up with in St. Kilda. This Kings Cross brings it all back. Yeah it does.'

'Hey it's where the action is and even this Coffee Shop isn't all that bad. Man, we have live music, or should have,' Tommy replied, then frowned 'That bloke should be right here now singing for his supper, but no show. Oh he showed then and went. You know in keeping, well, with the black theme, I have this Abo folk singer. And black is slack. There is his guitar. Say, did you say that you are now a blues singer?'

And with that Tommy Cooper went behind the counter and switched on a spot light which fell on the stool with a guitar on it.

'No, no, no,' Balga protested, but he had been caught by his own bragging or rather had said that he had been a blues singer to explain away his square clothes when he saw that his old mate was dressed in a neat dark suit and looked, well, a part of Kings Cross which the bastard was of course.

'Just a couple of numbers until he turns up - know any witchy songs?'

So Balga found himself going to the stool and picking up the guitar. Well, he knew a few chords and could strum them and whine a note every now and again. He struck the strings, pretended to tune them and then well launched into 'Dark was the Night, Cold was the Ground' and found he didn't know the words. No problems he began playing with rhymes, hoping that the few people in the joint didn't know the song. 'Night so cold, no light, the blighted ground, rising from the grave, they give him a rave, how brave, the devil struts and takes their souls, On no, witchy woman.' Balga whined a few blues notes and left that fragmented song to shift into 'Goodnight Irene' which he knew. A few claps and this got him going. He did a better job on another song by Huddy Leadbetter. As he was repeating the hook verse with his mind searching for another song, a voice startled him: 'My guitar and my gig, cuz. What the heck, trying to take my place and my bread.'

'Hey, hey,' Balga protested, 'the boss just got me to fill in for you I'm out of songs anyway so take over and do your job.'

'You did Irene, okay, but you need more feeling,' the singer said as he took the guitar, tuned it up and began a lively song:

Hey Black Fella what sort of blues you got for me to day play,
Singing and a crying, like the morning rain what a pain same
No way to make my guitar sigh my-my-my way play
No sway to let it slay swinging sounds so glad, so gay say
Like Liberace and his piano, laughing all so high oh my oh my
Old Blackfella Blues why you got me singing this tune
Oh yeah, yeah, yeah, why when I should be shouting the blues.

Balga stood just out of the spot and listened. The bloke had a rough tough voice and he actually sounded like a real old time blues singer. Balga felt humbled and crept back away to Ross who had shifted to a back table lit by the only white light that reflected down from a mural where a black man (what white people called a "negro") was snarling at a thin white woman – similar to the dark haired woman to whom Ross was chatting to and thus ignoring the music. The woman looked attractive but when the lad reached the table he found the white face with carmine lips and arched eyebrows had extremely ugly teeth that made him look away. When Balga sat down the woman stared so intently at him that he felt a short of shiver pass over his body. He glanced at her as she took a long draw from a cigarette in a long holder and then stated: 'You're a negro, aren't you?'

Ross began explaining him and Balga every now and again flashed a glance at the face of the woman, caught sight of the ugly teeth and flashed away to where the folk singer was pounding on his guitar. He was extremely uncomfortable and too aware of the woman that Ross had introduced and with a laugh added: The Witch of Kings Cross.

'Bewitching too,' Roie (her nickname) murmured leaning forward until her face was only inches from the face of the lad. She sought to catch the lad's eyes, but he pretended he was interested in the folk singer. Her hand came out and cool fingers clasped his right hand and the grazed knuckles he had gotten when he had hit the country lout. 'Does it hurt,' she asked. 'Would you like me to suck them well,' she said and Balga actually shuddered. His eyes were on the mural on the wall.

'Her art is really spectacular,' Ross said.

'And daring, darling,' Roie added.

Balga's eyes darted away.

'Roie wants to use you as a model. She says that she needs a negro to give an added strength to her, well, her artwork. In fact she's invited us to her flat tonight. She's having a get together. It is always interesting and people actually vie for an invitation.'

'I need you; you must come and I must paint you. We can even start tonight. I shall unveil my inner self and reveal to your true strength of panic fury,' exclaimed Roseleen. The lad darted a glance at her and then at Ross. He wanted to be saved. The last thing he wanted was to be with this evil witch.

Balga was thinking desperately about how to escape the invitation especially as his eyes kept reaching out to the 'negro" a figure which he found more and more frightening. Indeed he could imagine himself being the subject of such a scene in real life. He shuddered and turned his attention to where the Aboriginal singer sat on the high stool under the spotlight. He watched him press and pulled at the e-string whining out a note, then strike a chord to end his song, and set. He got off his stool. Balga watched him go to a table where he began chatting to a girl. 'Hey, I want to catch the singer,' the lad exclaimed and rushed off to the Koori singer who lifted his head and exclaimed: "Hey, man, you catch my sounds. I was blowing mellow for you. I even did one of those black American songs that have a different guitar tuning. Hey, you heard this one. New one, and he began singing to a thumping beat on the body of his guitar:

You get a fine for walking

And a fine for talking,

But the best damn fine is that fine for walking

So walk on Alabama, sure you're a friend of mine.

'Never heard anything like that before, is it a Sydney song?'

'Cuz you got a lot to learn, and play too. Civil rights, man, civil rights! You mean you don't know 'bout civil rights?'

Balga shrugged to hide his ignorance.

''Bout voting rights, equal rights for Blackfellas in America, we are just like them here, no rights at all.'

'How is it for us in Sydney,' Balga asked. 'Seems okay, you here ain't you!'

'This is Sydney, cuz, big city and unless you hang out in Redfern, the cops they turn a blind eye. Can't see you in the dark anyway, too black for them,' and he gave a great whooping laugh that made the coffee house go silent. 'Ah, come on,' he exclaimed and gave them a song about a Cinerama mamma that bounced her way to stardom.

'Hey, that's darn good,' the lad exclaimed. 'I'm Balga and I'm a Noongar from the West.'

'Yeah and I'm Allan from New Sucking Wales. Anyway I'm cutting out of here now, did my singing and when I get my dough, I'm off. Come with me to Redfern, lots of cats there that can sing and play. Good place, cuz, guitar there too. I'll teach you a few licks as well as a song or two. Not hillbilly eh, but the real blues, man. I'll teach you how to sing and play the real Koorie blues.

'Hey be here tomorrow on time, or I give Bodgie, I mean Balga your spot. He's just as good. He'll get half the money tonight,' Tommy Cooper said coming to them.

'Naw let him have it all, eh Tommy. He needs it more than I do and he's a professional singer.'

'Whatever you say, but tomorrow night, I want you on with him. A fiver more okay? That witch at the back table digs you, see, and what she likes she gets.'

Balga shuddered, but agreed: 'Yeah, I'll be here, but Alan wants me to listen to another singer, I'll be back later, maybe. Hey handle that chick for me will you. Tell her, she can link up with me tomorrow night, eh?'

Balga thus managed to escape the witch and even Ross by going off with Alan. He spent a few days with him in a house in Redfern so unlike the Cross and spent his time just trying out all sorts of music with a lot of Blackfellows, Koories that wandered in and out. Playing with Alan he began to think of himself as a Folk Singer or rather a Blues man. A week passed and he knew that it was time to go back to Melbourne or he wouldn't have a job. He thought of hitching but his experience in Albury put him off. A problem was that he didn't have enough money for the bus fare; but Alan got him a job singing in a folk club introducing him as a Blues Man from New Orleans and gave him the name of Balga Boy Jackson. With Alan as backup he got through a whole set and had the money to split from Sydney. As he sat on the bus going south he felt sad about not seeing Tommy again or Ross' but that witch had really scared him. Throughout the long journey he practiced to get down some songs that Alan had taught him. His favourite was A Refugee of the Road. 'The road is long, so long, so narrow, but don't get off the track, brother. Oh no. don't get off the track. We is refugees of the road in our own country.'

FIFTY TWO

THE HOUSE WITH THE YELLOW DOOR BLUES

There's a house with a yellow door
In Melbourne, in Melbourne town
Where the blues are sung
The blues are strummed
And rocked and strained through an old man
With a face of stone and a tone so mild
When he says, he says he writes the blues
Making poetry out of a God forsaken
For the blues, sighing as he sits alone like stone
Until he finds the tune and writes the melody true
For the House with the yellow door (oh yeah)
And don't forget the buttons lying on the floor
And the faded rose upstairs, the kitchen hazy
With the smoke of the blues, bending the notes
Flowing the words from the broken down woman
Singing the house with the yellow door blues
Oh singing the house with the yellow door blues.

Balga sat in Adrian's pad and listened to the famed gospel singer Mahalia Jackson singing a song about God. He didn't say anything. He didn't like hymns overmuch, having had his fill of them in the orphanage;

but his friend loved the black woman's voice. So he waited until the poet stopped his listening and got up to carefully put away the record.

'Yeah, I dig her, yeah, but I've been thinking. You know I'm stuck in that rooming house and I want something, well, with more space, a loft! Man, I need a loft.'

'Yeah so would we all, but look at this place. It's small but contains all I need.'

'Sure, but I would like to do some practicing without anyone getting annoyed.'

'Yeah, we all need space to explore. Well, most of us. Now let me think.'

Adrian had hundreds of contacts and Balga watched him stroking his goatee. He got up put on a Louis Armstrong Hot something or other, jiggled until the track finished and then said: 'We could try the house with the yellow door. Behind it is a big loft which hasn't been used, well, hasn't been used since the horse and buggy era. I guess Leo would rent it out to you, with my recommendation of course.

'Good for you, Adrian, you always come up with something. Let's go and get it; but wait is it close to the city and I can play my music there?'

'The house with the yellow door is just about on the corner of Lygon and Victoria streets where the Trades' Hall is and across from it is the 48 hour a week work monument, so it'll be perfect for you. Now as for your future landlord - Leo Cash is one of nature's gentlemen and though old is hip. A poet he digs new and ancient things.'

'Yes,' Balga breathed ecstatically. 'It is for me; I know it.'

'So let's go and get it' Adrian said taking off Louis Armstrong and carefully putting him away.

'Lead on McDuff,' Balga exclaimed.

It was a simple matter to get a tram down Collins, alight and jump onto a Swanston Street one that took them up to Victoria where they got off at the City Baths. They went up the side of the buildings towards the column of the 48 hour week monument. Across the street Balga saw a row of terrace houses ending with a pub on the corner of Lygon. His eyes traveled back from it to stop at one of the two storey buildings which had a bright yellow door.

'That must be it,' he said pointing across.

'Indeed it is, now how shall I introduce you as an artist or….?'

'Well, I am thinking of getting deeper into folk singing. Man, I want to sing the blues.'

'Okay, an artist it is. Leo used to be with the New Theatre and digs all things theatrical.'

'Yeah and you said he writes poetry. What does he write? He old and wouldn't be doing Beat like you do?'

'Well, do you know Thompson's Hound of Heaven,' Adrian almost sneered as if he knew Balga had neither read or even heard of him..

'Who,' the lad asked niggled because the only poets he knew were the ones he had been forced to learn at school and the Beatniks Adrian had insisted on reading to him.

'Him,' Adrian retorted then declaimed:

> *I fled Him down the nights and down the days;*
> *I fled Him, down the arches of the years;*
> *I fled Him, down the labyrinthine ways*
> *Of my own mind; and in the mist of tears*
> *I hid from Him, and under running laughter.*
> *'Well, it has rhythm,' Balga commented dryly.*

'It certainly has and Leo is reworking this into a satire called, Smith's Hound. Maybe, he'll read you a bit if he digs you enough. It's just as good as the original.'

'I'll wait for it,' the lad said not all that interested.

By then they were at the yellow door and Adrian lifted up the knocker and gave three raps. The two waited. Beside the door was a dirty window through which the lad could see an office.

'What does he do for a crust,' Balga asked.

'Buttons' came the reply uttered in a low, level gruff voice as the door opened and there stood a small gray haired man with a round dead pan white face in which grayish-blue eyes glowered. Balga thought he looked a bit like a leprechaun because of the rigidity of his features. His general rigidity, the lad later found out was due to his contacting Parkinson's disease from chickens he asserted, though Balga didn't know if you could get the disease from chooks. The disease caused the old man to suffer from muscle atrophy and when he walked he tottered. Balga guessed this was what it was like being old; but behind the expressionless face was a sharp mind.

This rigid little man gravely regarded the Noongar his face unable to give expression to his thoughts. Adrian introduced him and the old bloke said: 'Walk right in,' and shuffled in front of them down a short corridor lined with boxes of buttons each identified as to type by a sample card fastened to the front. At the end of the passageway the three entered a small kitchen where the old man began boiling water. He made a pot of what wasn't tea.

'Red Bush from South Africa, healthy,' he observed.

'Healthy,' Balga repeated.

'For the stomach,' he added.

'For the stomach,' Adrian repeated.

'Ordinary tea has tannin and this harms the stomach lining.'

'Harms the stomach lining,' Balga repeated.

'It also keeps the mind alert. Adrian has mentioned that you are an artist. Exhibited, yet?'

'No, I'm thinking of giving it away, taking up the blues and writing and singing songs of my own devising. Need to work on my guitar though so I need some space about me.'

'So you have performed?'

'He had a gig or two in Sydney,' Adrian butted in to build his friend up.

'The Blues, jazz?'

'Sort of…'

'My daughter, Deidre used to sing for Swing Bands when she was young and well … now she's taken up writing and has just had a novel called The Delinquents accepted for publication by a London publishing house. You should talk to her, compare musical notes if you have a mind to, she sings a good Stormy Weather.'

'Stormy weather,' Balga replied politely.

'She's unwell these days, but her voice is still there. A well trained voice too. You should listen to it. Her pitch is perfect. You know, I too was in the performing arts, the theatre until I became a sort of lame duck.'

"Or a robot," Balga couldn't help thinking somewhat cruelly.

'The theatre, art for the people or so I thought then. Do you think it still is?'

'No. music is,' Balga couldn't help exclaiming.

'Part of theatre it is, so why not become a song and dance man? Get into theatre, vaudeville. I was active in the New Theatre, a communist, no a left wing theatrical movement of social realism. We sought to create and put on valid proletariat pieces taken directly from life. An example of this was Waiting for Lefty about a taxi drivers' strike. It had songs too. You might have seen it….'

'Yes,' Adrian said hurriedly. 'Theatre must be valid and authentic, but styles change. The Union Theatre at Melbourne University is extremely progressive under John Sumner. He is producing a season of the best of recent British drama. John Osborne's Look Back in Anger is on now. I'll take you to see this contemporary expression of proletariat drama.'

'Perhaps I should, perhaps I may, let us fix the date,' Leo intoned like a theatrical character and with a dismissive gesture.

'Tonight then, I can have two tickets waiting for me at the box office.'

'Take our budding song and dance man here. He might learn how to project some of his ideas or gain some ideals, who knows what he may beg, borrow or steal,' the old man said in his toneless voice. He may have been joking. It was hard to tell with his expressionless face.

'No, I want you beside me,' Adrian exclaimed. 'Give me some of your expertise so that I may write a decent review. Yes, so it is fixed, now how is your long poem progressing?'

'Smith's Hound?'

'What else, I have already introduced Balga to Thompson's Hound.'

The conversation went on like this and the lad wondered if he would ever find out if the loft was available or not.'

At long last Leo fixed his eyes on Balga's and asked him where he was from and in which school he had been educated. Balga spoke the truth. He was from Western Australia and had been educated by the Christian Brothers at Clontarf Boys' Town.

The old man managed a smile though his eyes continued to read him as he replied: 'The Irish Brothers, and of course you are now a lapsed Catholic?'

'Well, I don't go to church or even think about it all that much.'

'That's the best way to be, lapsed, and if you are of course you'll be a socialist, one of those reds you're always reading about in the papers.'

'Well, I ...'

'Exactly and now you have entered this, this den of lapsed Catholics and Communist fellow travelers seeking out a refuge from the Bourgeoisie.'

'Yes,' Adrian spoke up. 'Balga's come to the House with the Yellow Door in quest of that space behind it. He has his heart set on a loft.' Adrian finished off quaintly.

'Yes, it does need to be filled' Leo replied his eyes moving slowly to Adrian then coming back to Balga's face.'

'And the answer is?' Adrian asked abruptly.

'Well, let's see,' Leo replied, his face deadpan and his tone flat . 'Deidre has the room just up those back stairs there. That's a nice large room. She's out at the hospital now but will be back soon. We Cashs aren't in the best of health, as you can see by staring at me. Now there's the front stairs. There is a short corridor or passageway across which are two doors opposite each other. One opens onto my room which faces the street and the other opens onto a room with the window facing onto the back yard and beyond is the loft quite isolated. There' a bit of a space at the end of a yard beyond which is the dunny and next to it the back gate too opening onto a lane. Yes, your loft now. It needs to be cleaned and you are must pay the nominal rent of two pounds ten per week, cheap because there are few amenities, no furniture, but the company here is priceless.'

Balga grinned he had a new pad and a loft at that. Things were going his way.

FIFTY THREE

OLD WOMAN SWINGS
THE BLUES

Old woman swings the blues
Oh Deidre swings the Bodgie blues
Crying, sighing for the days gone by
Oh yeah, crying sighing for the Bodgie boy (he's gone)
Oh Deidre swings the blues, crying
Oh Deidre swings the blues while dying
Oh, yet her voice is gutsy, flying
Oh, oh the old woman swings the blues.
Her face is lined, but her voice is fine
Her body is frail, but she can sing up a gale
Oh no, now she whispers faint like a breeze
Oh yeah, whispering with a slight wheeze.
Old woman swings the blues (swing it)
Oh Deidre sings for her Bodgie lover
Crying, sighing, seeking for feelings gone
Times dry as a bone, oh Brownie I'm alone.

In Melbourne in those days a lot of houses and buildings had a stable with a loft above at the back of their yards. These harked back to the old horse and cart days and with these gone, artists had moved into some of them. The space was large and one could spread a canvas on the floor and do an action painting; but Balga had left painting forever, though he still had a few of Revel's sketches to put on the walls after he had dusted and washed, scrubbed and cleaned away the grime of years. He left his old room and after dumping his clothes and checking that there was an electric outlet for his record player, he went to a Carlton second hand shop and got a double mattress and blankets. A bright coverlet caught his eye. It would give his mattress a sofa look. Next he found an old table that with the legs sawn off would be perfect for the style he wanted. There were lots of cushions and he got a dozen of these. The shop man arranged for a truck to pick up the stuff and Balga went back to the loft. The load came after an hour. The loft had a high door and the driver flung things up to him and pushed the mattress up so that he could grab it and then the table. It would take some days to get the space just right for him, but at least he had a bed, He left the mess to go down and into the kitchen to see what he could scrounge to eat or if there was convivial company there.

The lad found a faded but absolutely interesting woman boiling a kettle. She instantly reminded him of those faded roses in the pulp fiction he used to read, the older sheilas with a lot of dough and a lot of mouth to go along with it.

This was Deidre Cash, he decided as he saw that although she was past her prime she still clung to a certain modishness. She wore makeup with a red vivid lipstick smeared over her lips. Her head was the shape of a lozenge, but she had a full head of black hair laced with white that swept to her shoulders. From her face stared green eyes that challenged him, though he was merely a boy to her womanhood. He was so taken by her face that he barely noticed that she was wearing a green dressing gown over a cream nightdress.

'Hey there,' Balga greeted her sort of testing the waters before diving in and perhaps making an ass of his self as he sometimes did when he was under the gaze of a female.

'Well hey there back,' the woman replied. 'The penniless artist in his loft eh! Ready for my portrait yet?'

'No, I'm a blues singer and I take it that you are Deidre, Leo's daughter.'

'You can't take me, but I confess that the word is apt. I am indeed her. I'm staying here with my father until my husband Otto reaches town. He's a seaman but only on the coastal ships so he's never away for long.'

'Oh,' the lad replied not knowing what to do with this information.

'Have a cuppa and you can make it too. Real tea! My father likes that South African concoction, even though it comes from the land of Apartheid but I prefer the good old Bushels. Make it strong and black,' she said examining him with her green eyes that suddenly flickered with what Balga thought was pain. 'Yes,' she gasped clutching her stomach, I would play the mother and pour except that I'm not at all well and get these spells.' She broke off, gave a sigh and the light of her eyes faded. She suddenly looked as gloomy as a nun and even her shoulder length hair appeared to Balga a veil.

'You were educated by the nuns,' the lad said.

'Of course and you by the Brothers, that explains our predicament. Boy, they mess you up, don't they?'

'Oh,' Balga replied not wanting to go into Catholic details. Instead he had the urge to ask her to sing Stormy Weather, but seeing how drawn her face was and how frail she looked, it seemed cruel so he found the tea pot, emptied out the remains of an earlier pot, washed it out put in three heaped teaspoons, one for each person and one for the pot. After waiting about three minutes he poured out two steaming mugs, added a heaped teaspoon of sugar to each and was about to hand her one when she requested.

'Please bring it up to my room and stay with me, give me some company,' Deidre asked him. She slowly made her way up the stairs.

Balga somewhat reluctantly followed after her and into the back room where she got into a big double bed where she rested a minute before propping herself up on pillows and reaching for her tea as she explained: 'I'm not as weak as all this. I have good days as well as bad days, but let's put that out of mind shall we?'

'I heard that you had written a book about us,' Balga said reverting to his recent past and identity.

'About us,' she queried, 'but I thought, well, that you were from W.A. and that's a backwater if there ever was one. I actually suffered Perth once. Spent too much of my time there in hospital to have fond memories of that city. It was hot as hell too and the streets lacked the social grace of a decent "good morning" if you get my meaning.'

'Yeah, I think I understand. Perth can be a bit off putting,' Balga replied.

'You should know; but I didn't realise that they actually had Bodgies there. I thought it was an East Coast thing where we have some kind of night life. In Perth, I mean they actually put the street lights out at eleven when the pictures come out. Only the Seaman's Club in Fremantle broke the early to bed rule and stayed open for ever and a day; but then ports are as different as sailors, aren't they?'

'I suppose so,' the lad replied, 'all I know is that Fremantle has a prison smack dab in the middle of it.'

Balga was trying to be tough but Deidre may have been a faded Rose, but she had a past perhaps every bit as tough as his. She began talking about World War II when Australia was filled with American soldiers and it was great to be a singer. 'I was only eighteen then, but I wasn't going to sit at home when I had this voice and could get a job as the singer for one of the local swing bands in which American soldiers always sat in to give them an edge. Christ, if I couldn't swing, I would have been hooted off the stage, attractive doll or not. Ah, those were the days...'

Balga forgot about her book. He was in the presence in fact alone with a nightclub singer, something he had only come across in one or two stories he had read or movies he had seen. He couldn't help thinking that Adrian might have recordings of Bessie Smith or Lady Day, but here he had a real living breathing singer with a past as hard or as loose as his own.

'So what was your favorite song,' he asked her and for some reason he felt sad as she told him with a laugh which showed that she had recovered her strength, Mad about the Boy.

'Not Stormy Weather,' he couldn't help exclaiming.

'That was their favourite, but not mine,' she replied tartly as if it brought up some bitter-sweet memory and then she began singing it.

Don't know why there's no sun up in the sky
Stormy weather
Since my man and I ain't together,
Keeps rainin' all the time
Life is bare, gloom and mis'ry everywhere
Stormy weather
Just can't get my poor self together,
I'm weary all the time
So weary all the time
When he went away the blues walked in and met me.
If he stays away old rockin' chair will get me.
All I do is pray the Lord above will let me walk in the sun once more.
Can't go on, ev'ry thing I had is gone
Stormy weather
Since my man and I ain't together,
Keeps rainin' all the time.

'Hey it's a blues,' Balga exclaimed happily and with a trace of awe

Deidre positively beamed at his words. 'So you want to be a blues singer,' she said, and then added 'and what do you know about the blues?'

Balga was ready to retort saying what did she know about the blues, but he kept his peace and replied somewhat coldly: 'Well, not much.'

'Well,' Deidre began. 'World War II was a special time in Australia. The city was flooded with American soldiers all ready for a good time and among them were quite a few jazz musicians. Of course Australia tried to keep the whole scene under control. The pubs and night clubs had to shut early but after the doors closed the space became private. We had some great jam sessions and the musicians, especially the Black ones, took time out to explain the music. They thought that if you didn't understand jazz, how could you sing it? So I learnt to swing the blues, well, like Lady Day.

Now there are quite a few types of blues, but the one the bands favoured was 12 bars blues. You know what the pattern is?'

'No,' Balga admitted, 'jazz musicians talked it, but no one explained it.'

'Well, do you know music?'

'No.'

'Okay, okay, thanks you've got me going strong enough to enlighten you boy. Singing the blues, when you don't even know what the blues is. You heard Glen Miller's In the Mood. You even heard Glen Miller?'

'Yeah, old guys used to listen to that stuff in…'

'And the pattern of In the Mood?'

'I've heard it."

'Well, it is 12 bar blues?'

'Are you sure?'

'Do pigs lay eggs?'

'Well…'

'Well, listen you kid and learn. A bar is a musical phrase, a way of measuring the music against the rhythm, and the blues are usually structured about a 12-bar format. Clear?'

'As mud!'

'Yeah, I thought so. Go and get me another cup of tea while, well while I think this out.'

Balga obeyed and while he did this, he could hear Deidre singing, well, what else, but a blues song.'

He returned for the next lesson.

'Now you know what rhythm is — no, not the tempo or relative speed of the music. It is the time signature.' She began tapping out a beat. 'This is what rhythm is: the time signature, and what is the beat I am tapping?'

'Easy,' Balga grinned, '4/4 time -- one two three four; one two three four.'

'Gee you've got something,' Deidre smiled. 'Ninety-nine percent of all blues music is played to a 4/4 time signature. Now onto a bit about music. You should learn to read music. It helps you know. The term bar is derived from each of the vertical lines that are drawn through a musical staff. (The staff is the set of horizontal lines on which musical notes are written.)

The bar lines mark off metered units of a piece of music, which are called measures. The terms bar and measure are interchangeable. Got that?'

Balga nodded though frowning.

'To hear where the backbeat falls, just stress the 2nd and 4th of a four-beat count (1-2-3-4, 1-2-3-4) and you've got your basic rhythm down, but you must know that. Yeah, I can see you do. Now take that rhythm, speed it up or slow it down according to the tempo you want, and you've got the blues beat. Of course you know this since you've played and sung what you thought were the blues. Well, listen on big fellow and I'll clue you in on how to swing the blues.

'Old guitar style blues progressions generally consisted of three chords that were usually, but not always, played in a major rather than a minor key. In a 12-bar progression, each of those chords was assigned four bars of the progression (although that number may change depending on the song's structure). This is how it was and most likely how you play the blues; but in jazz, in swing well we swung the blues and put in all sorts of chords and stuff.' Deidre scatted and swung a version of In the Mood that made Balga realize that this woman had known and still did her business He had a lot to learn and that it was like painting. You had to learn the technique and get it right or you were nowhere.

The lesson stopped there, but Deidre wanted company and so did Balga. They came together often in the evenings. He sat beside her on the big bed and she taught him the Blues.

'In basic, bare-bones blues, the main musical theme is expressed in the first four-bar line, and then repeated again in bars five through eight. The closing four bars usually cap the original theme line by putting a twist on it or summing up the original statement. And that adds up to 12 bars (or measures). Understand,' she asked watching him scratch his head.

'A musical theme is simply the melody that distinguishes one tune from another. The lyrical theme is the story line. Get it?'

'I think,' Balga replied wrinkling his brow and then running his hand through the brush of his hair.

Well, let's try this Bodgie type song. I think about it when I think about my book and my Brownie. It's a typical jazz blues sung by Lady Day with the typical bar count for a standard 12-bar blues verse. (This 12-bar "chunk" is a stanza of the song lyric.) Listen, boy, and count out the rhythm for me. To hear the rhythm, count each number out loud. The lyrics state a basic theme that's repeated in the second line, and then wrapped up in the third.

1-2-3-4, 2-2-3-4, 3-2-3-4, 4-2-3-4

My man don't love me treats me awful mean . . .

5-2-3-4, 6-2-3-4, 7-2-3-4, 8-2-3-4

My man don't love me treats me awful mean. . .

9-2-3-4, 10-2-3-4, 11-2-3-4, 12-2-3-4

He's the lowest man that I've ever seen.

Now that's the blues,' Deidre exclaimed and then sang another stanza.

> *He wears high draped pants stripes are really yellow*
> *He wears high draped pants stripes are really yellow*
> *But when he starts in to love me he's so fine and mellow.*

That was the last lesson, Balga had from the faded rose. The next morning she went to the hospital and didn't return. It was then that her husband arrived and Balga went looking for a guitar.

FIFTY FOUR

ROCKING THE BLUES

Hell, We're Rocking the Blues.
Hey, hey, hey lay down that rocking beat
Find a riff hit it all down the street (blow)
Hey, hey, hey, what the hell we're rocking the blues
Oh yeah, grab her, grab that moll (that doll)
Rock her, rock her, hell we're rocking the blues
Hey, hey, hey what are we doing, oh yeah
We're rocking, hell, we're rocking the blues
Grab your frail, watch her wag her tail (yeah)
Oh yeah, rock that moll, let's rock that doll.

Balga stopped entranced by the beautiful guitar in the Window of John Clements Music Shop. It was a six string but with a metal pie plate in the middle of the body. He needed a guitar, but had never seen one like this. The lad pushed open the door and picked up the instrument. He struck a chord and was mesmerized by the sizzling crisp ring. It was a real blues guitar he needed and he wanted it.

'It's a resonator guitar,' John Clements, a tall man with sandy hair and sort of yellow eyes and a rat trap mouth that only loosened when he saw a good musical instrument, commented. He took the instrument from the lad's hands and played a blues riff and explained: 'Resonator guitars are the bright shiny objects of the six-string world. Once you've heard and seen one, you want it don't you? It's hard not to be mesmerized by the sizzling, crisp ring of its tone. Look, see that metal pie plate in the middle of the body that's where all the sound comes from.'

'A what?,' Balga asked.

John Clements knew his musical instruments and replied: 'A resonator guitar. The distinctive sound of a resonator guitar, sometimes called a resophonic guitar, is derived from the spun metal cone or cones under the instruments' round faceplate, which serve both a protective and decorative function. The wooden or all-metal body of the guitar itself certainly plays a role in generating that tone and in sustaining notes, but not anywhere near as significantly as in conventional acoustic guitars, where the top of the body is the instrument's essential tone-generating component.'

'Oh, it's nice,' Balga replied taking the instrument back and striking and listening to a chord progression. 'Yeah, it almost plays the blues by itself.'

'That's what it was invented for. No pickups in the old days for the guitar and so it was drowned out in noisy juke joints or house parties. This was well before plugging in was an option, in the mid-1920s and it was the National Company in The States that first began making these singing beauties. They take particularly well to the slide playing of such Delta Blues greats as Son House and Bukka White.'

'Hey, yeah, I want it, no I need it. Yeah, but how much is it?'

'It's an original Gibson Hound Dog Deluxe wood bodied and necked, to produce a warmer tone. They also make an all steel one except for the neck which cuts through rooms with the authority of a switchblade. You play them just like conventional acoustic guitars too; and as for the blues, this is your instrument; but cheap, no!'

After some dickering Clements knocked off twenty and sold it to Balga for a down payment of fifty and a fiver a week for any number of years. To clinch the deal he threw in a book on how to play the blues, by the authentic and superlative guitar player, Josh White.

Learn to play like him. Get a few songs together, play one for me, and if you're any good I'll put you on upstairs,' he told Balga.

Clements used the large room above the shop as a folk club and Balga knew he wasn't kidding. He immediately rushed home to practice on his instrument. He played blues riffs until his new mate came bounding into his loft with his big booming but cheaper rocker guitar.

Bodgies were aging dead meat left behind in the fifties, if they hadn't changed as Balga had; but well there still were Rockers, kids that were sent by the rock'n'roll of Eddie Cochran and other white boys that had taken over what Balga now called rhythm and blues. Rock and roll music wouldn't die. And there was his young mate, Andy Campbell who had thrust his friendship upon him and even invaded his space. He was a slight kid of seventeen or so with yellow straw hair, pale blue eyes and a skin that verged on the albino. Indeed he looked a bit like the one in the film, God's Little Acre; but he was city through and through and no hick. Andy admired the shininess of the resounder guitar, but he liked to use a plectrum for a heavy rocking beat. He decided that the metal plate would interfere with his playing and left it alone. Balga watched him assume a rocker stance over his own axe pressed against his groin. He bent over it, struck an E-major chord with a plectrum and was away into Twenty Flight Rock. Balga may have forsaken the rock for the blues; but it was still within him. He began riffing with his fancy guitar rocking the blues.

He felt that he was getting somewhere as he whined notes about the four-four time with a back beat that couldn't be lost.

The duo pounded through Carl Perkins' "Blue Suede Shoes" and "Honey Don't"; the great Gene Vincent's, "Be-Bop-A-Lula", "Woman Love"; Jerry Lee Lewis's, "Whole Lotta Shakin' Goin' On" or better yet, "High School Confidential"; Buddy Holly and The Crickets, "That'll Be the Day" and "Peggy Sue". They really enjoyed themselves and did Buddy Knox with the Rhythm Orchids' so very corny "Party Doll. Andy Campbell's idol was Eddie Cochran and he began singing his great Summertime Blues. It may have been a rock classic; but there was little space for any fancy lead guitar sound playing so Balga just went with the beat which wasn't really a blues eat at all, but who cared, it rocked.

As they finished off there was a banging down at the back gate and a harsh woman's voice screamed: 'Andrew!'

Andy's mother was a domineering woman that Balga liked to avoid. 'Better go or she'll be up here,' he told the kid.

Andy didn't reply, but taking his guitar he went down the stairs. Balga opened half of the loft door looking out over the lane and glared at the large back of Mrs. Campbell who was leading her son back to their house the third one along the block.

The lad watched her disappear through her back gate. She was a dark heavy woman in her forties and once had been attractive, but she had aged into a termagant with a vicious temper and a dictatorial nature akin to Joe Stalin's for she was a dedicated communist not a so-called fellow traveler as Leo was. There was a Mr. Campbell whom she absolutely dominated so that he was a pale figure silent without a voice of his own. Leo had known her for a long time and they had been in the New Theatre movement together and perhaps even had been lovers, for no one in that movement accepted such a thing as conventional bourgeois couple arrangements. Free love was the aspiration and the practice when it could be practised, though Leo had been married and she had been for a long long time. The result of her union was the son, Andrew, the small thin albino neurotic completely dominated by his mother and resenting her as much as he could without starting a quarrel.

Balga felt he had his reasons to dislike her. A while ago the Communist Party organization had put on a fair in the North Melbourne Town Hall and Andy and he went there to see what they could find and maybe buy. To Andy's delight though not Balga's there were quite a few volumes of The Left Book Club of Britain as well as bound volumes of the American New Republic journal. Andy didn't have any money and as the bound journals were only a few shilling each Balga lent him the money to buy the lot. Andy left the journals in his loft and then his mother came up for some reason, saw the bound copies of The New Republic and wanted them. She looked at Balga, but he only shrugged and looked away.

'Can I borrow them,' she asked the lad.

Balga shrugged again.

'I want them,' she demanded.

'Oh mom,' protested her son. 'They are mine! I was going to bring them home.'

So she took them and Balga felt pity for the boy and let him come up whenever he wanted to and even pound out the rock whenever he wanted to even in the middle of the night. Indeed he began to welcome the sessions now that he had his own guitar. It was a little later that Andy suggested that they hold a party. Balga leapt at the idea.

FIFTY FIVE

STOMPING THE SUPER BLUES

Wave your hands, stomp your feet
Hey, stomp stomp where the surfers meet.
Yeah, yeah stomp stomp stomp those blues.
Sand is flying, dust is blowing, music flailing
So stomp, stomp, stomp those God darn blues
This way, that way, balance on the ocean waves
'Cause we are stomping, stomp stomping what
The surfer blues, oh oh, stomping the surfer blues.

'Yeah we're having a party, but no loud roll'n'roll,' Balga said to provoke Andy.

'Don't knock the rock,' a painter, a long blonde haired and bearded bloke named Ian retorted into the conversation.

'Give me folk and blues any day,' the lad insisted.

'Yeah, you really get that on the radio, don't you? Go with what you can hear. When I work, I have 3UZ, the pop station on for energy,' he sneered.

.

Balga shrugged and smiled a superior smile, though he was a bit jealous of the man. Ian unlike the failed Balga was a real painter and not only that he was accepted by critics such as Adrian as a talented one. The lad had tried to get an invitation to his studio to check them out for himself;

360

but had failed. No matter, he consoled himself with the fact that he had given up art forever. Ian was one of the artists that popped in every now and again to see Leo and sometimes cooked up a meal for whoever was there quickly and efficiently. He said that if a meal took longer to cook than to eat it was time wasted. He had been a soldier and taken part in the occupation of Japan about which he had interesting stories mainly of the brothels there. Returning from the occupation, he had turned to teaching in a girl's school and had interesting tales about teaching a class of girls. Balga like hanging in the kitchen and listening to whoever turned up to learn what was going down as Leo and his house were popular to Melbourne's Bohemians. Another artist who came in often was the painter, Max, a Serbian who lived behind them in rooms above a shop fronting on Lygon Street. In order to earn some dough he made jewelry out of copper wire twirling the stuff in spiral designs which looked mystical and witchy. He even had painted Balga's portrait and the lad sat through the sittings as petrified as a model. After, he had wondered if he should offer to buy it, but now it wasn't in the bloke's studio and he guessed he had lost the opportunity to get it.

The party was held on a Friday evening and the first to arrive were a couple of sisters, Darlene and Francis Koops of Moonee Ponds. Balga had met them in some folk club or other. They were public servants, but Commonwealth working in the green Immigration building on Spring Street. Darlene was a true find with dark hair about a pointed face in which large eyes peered through moon shaped glasses. She had a jumpy sort of personality which she disguised by speaking in a lecturing way intensely stressing words, though most of the time she really didn't have anything to be intense about except perhaps being intense. Her much quieter sister faded away next to her leaving no memories behind. What made Balga dig them was that they actually lived in the suburb of Moonee Ponds which the standup comedian Barry Humphries recently had made known by inventing a female character supposedly living there, a cliché in cliché land. All the Bohemians dug Barry Humphries and Adrian had taken the Noongar to one of his shows where the comedian came out dressed as a woman a skit which made Balga smile. It was this that had made him befriend the sisters.

'So what is this celebration about,' Darlene asked staring at the lad through her dark framed spectacles with a similar butterfly shape to those worn by the Barry Humphrey character, Edna Everidge.

'It may not be a celebration,' Balga replied.

'Yet you said it was,' she replied.

'It depends on whether you like Mao Tse Tung or not.'

'The Chinese leader?'

'The one and only.'

'Why, what has he done now?'

'Only broken the Australian communist movement into two,' Balga replied trying to locate some feelings about whether he felt sad or happy or even indifferent about this.'

'Oh, why and why is it something to celebrate?'

'That's what I'm not at all sure about. Are we are celebrating it or merely having a few drinks to fixate our minds on that question or to forget it. I don't know,' Balga ended morosely.

'Well, at least I'll celebrate. It must be a good thing, who wants to be communist anyway and they're already in South East Asia and may soon be threatening us if we let them.'

'Well, well, well, Edna,' Balga retorted, 'it may be a bad thing for Moonee Ponds, the Toorak of the eastern suburbs, but some of us would welcome a change of system.'

'And most of us wouldn't,' she replied stressing each word.

Balga wasn't about to fall into an argument with her as they were poles about in just about everything including politics so he went off to Andy who was trying to get the record player on. The switch was broken and it had to be turned on and off at the wall socket. Now Andy put on a record either his own or borrowed if not stolen as there was a second hand record shop, Norman's which lent itself to pilfering. It certainly wasn't something that Balga or even Andy might buy, for out came of all things Surf Music which was popular then. Andy loved music loud. He turned the volume up as high as it could go. Everyone found the skiffle like rhythm infectious and great for dancing. They began stomping away doing the Surfer dance and having a ball. And then Leo made it up the stairs. He shuffled his feet to the beat before withdrawing from the sound.

The evening continued on loudly without the sound of folk. Balga fueled the party by passing around some once apple cider he and Andy had found at a liquor shop. The proprietor let them have it cheap. It was old and sour and gave a strange sort of intoxication. No matter how much you drank, you never fell down drunk. Balga and Andy had bought up the last of the stuff about a dozen bottles which after some red wine the partygoers got down without comment.

The party was winding down and Darlene and her sister had left thinking that it was the end or Balga guessed the folks in Monee Ponds really did go to bed at an indecent time. But the party wasn't about to end just yet. Balga opened another bottle of once cider while Andy hunted in his pockets for a plectrum. Soon the loft would be rocking; but then there was a loud banging at the bottom door. Balga went down to fling it open and receive hugs from Ross and a whoop then a handshake from the Koorie singer, Alan. They were fresh from Sydney. Ross still had the car which was parked just outside the back gate.

'Missed you bub,' she said and kissed him again.

'Yeah the blues man, the blues,' Alan grinned.

'Come up Ross, come up Alan and have some almost cider, it's a bit old but still, well, I don't know,' Balga trailed off as he had had a cup too much of the brew which was affecting his vocal chords as well as his mind of course. He wanted to get onto his guitar and play and sing some blues. 'Come on come on, nothing to eat, but maybe later. Yeah, for sure, there's a woman Mrs Campbell who's always checking up on her son. We are about ready to receive a visit and she'll bring some snacks to hide the real reason. She's a pretty good cook anyway, so we'll bear her presence until she finds everything's okay.'

Andy was thumping on his guitar preparatory to launching into a rock number. 'Hey man,' Alan drawled, 'hang on a moment until we moisten our throats and then we'll do some blues. Hey, what is that there I spy. That guitar, that's a blues guitar for sure. Got a bottle neck, nay, make you one later, now let me do some picking.'

Alan handed Balga his own guitar and took up the Resounder, hit a few notes and became one with the instrument and the blues came tumbling out. Andy never had a chance after that. He gave up the rock and began laying down chord patterns under the blue notes. The kid forgot his Eddie Cochrane and went over the top and met Sun House rocking him by muffling the treble strings of the guitar and using only the bass strings. After a break in the session, Balga got back his own guitar and sometimes played rhythm sometimes lead or exchanged roles with Alan who was really smoking. Ross clapped them on and the party went through into the dawn and beyond. They had found their groove and by broad daylight were playing as a trio.

FIFTY SIX

TWO BLACKS AND A WHITE BUSY WITH THE BLUES

Yeah two blacks and a white busy with the blues
We know how to rock you, send you to the moon
Oh those sad blues, oh those jive too slow blues
They really got to go, go down with old Hannah
Oh don't you worry me now more, no more yeah
Two blacks and a white, busy with the blues
Strumming and shouting busy with the blues
Singing the blues, the black and white blues, oh yeah.

In the old days Balga had to dress and look the street hooligan to get attention. How things had changed! Here he was dressed in a checked shirt and jeans, rough working men's clothing, in front of a crowd that all but filled John Clement's folk club. They all were there to hear him and his two mates sing and play. They wanted this. Life certainly had changed. He plucked out a chord with his fingers and Andy laid down a bass line, Alan came in and they were away.

Balga flashed his eyes over the crowd some of whom were from his work place. He had resigned from the Motor Registration Branch and this was his going away party. He was amazed at how many had actually come; but Balga had been a cheerful sort of lad who didn't shirk his work and now he realized that he had made quite a few friends there.

There was Nancy with a tipsy Tom Jones; Malcolm Bogaars looking very much like the cartoon character, Fred Flintstone in the new T.V. series and a serious Ray Drew with his face bent over a book. He did look like Tommy Cooper who was either still in Sydney or already in Queensland. Thinking of him made the lad sad and thinking of him made him remember his other mate, Revel Cooper. This caused him to begin his slow blues, Blues for Revel which they had been practicing for the show.

After this the trio broke for a rest and Balga glanced at some people just entering the club. He gave a start and wanted to hide. Two men and a woman from his old St. Kilda days had entered. Fast Eddy winked at him. He was neatly dressed in a dark Italian suit and with his hair brushed back in a sort of flat 20s style that made him, well look like the walking razor he was. Beside him in a rumpled suit scowling was no one but the tough dick, Phil Kingston and, the woman, oh no. Oh yes, it was Jeanne holding onto the detective's arm. She was tarted up in an Upper Collins Street expensive suit and her hair was brown and waved and tinted away from the harsh red she once had favoured.

Balga was scared of these people. They could reclaim him and take him back into the petty crime of St. Kilda. He wanted nothing to do with them and scurried off to talk to his old work mates. He began a nervous conversation with his eyes every now and again jerking towards the deadly trio. Unable to keep still he went to where the guest of honour Leo Cash sat together with his daughter Deidre in a wheel chair. She had taken leave from the hospital and with a laugh she commented: 'I taught you to swing the blues' then her eyes clung to someone standing behind him and her face went blank.

Balga became too conscious of a man standing closely at his side. He tried to smile at Deidre then flinched as a heavy hand descended on his shoulder. Had he had been nicked for a past offence? The gruff voice of Kingston stated low and menacing, through long use it was his only tone and meant to scare any perp. 'Boy, we just had to come to see you and hear you sing. I'm like your God Father ain't I? Yes, and I've been following your, shall we say new career and catching sight of you every now and again.. Been keeping out of trouble, haven't we; been keeping to the straight and narrow it seems and he has become a singer. Good job too,' and he gave a harsh laugh which caused Balga to feel a quivering up his spine.

'Yes, his voice sometimes flows as sweet and sticky as port wine,' added Jeanie kissing him directly on the mouth and then saying. 'We caught the end of your last number. I hope it pays enough to keep you going. Perhaps you should have stuck with us. We have a dozen houses now and guess, you'd never believe who our manager is.'

'Fast Eddy has steadied. He has seen the problems inherent in being an independent operator and has come in with us to oversee the whole shebang,' grated the Kingston demon.

'So no more Jane or Betty or Audrey and who ever film star his molls might look like,' Balga couldn't help saying about his once mate.

'Them old days are gone and with them private enterprise,' replied Eddy clasping his hand, but there was no old Bodgie handshake just a quick exchange of sticky palms. The singer felt sorry for him being in that mob; but that was how the cards fell and it might even be for the better, though he was sure that it was not a winning hand.

'Yep, fashions come and go,' Eddy added sadly, then grimaced and said: 'But a singer, good job, but not much future in this stuff, go pop and electric.'

'What replacing Elvis still going strong and into making movies now.'

'You ain't Elvis, but you could be, well, wasn't Fats Domino your friend?'

'No my, I don't know, I sing the blues but don't rock them.'

'Yeah, well try it and keep to the old story about how your dad knew Fats Domino and sang the blues with him.'

'He did know Fats Domino,' began Balga hotly.

'There you are, you have the real blues tradition. It's in your blood,' a female voice cut in and Ross rushed up with Alan and Andy in tow. The deadly trio smiled and winked in a travesty of good will and excused themselves after Phil Kingston had examined each of the new arrivals with his hard cop eyes.

'This is Marcus Herman of Crest Records. He wants to record you,' Ross began hotly introducing a quiet rather nondescript man in a causal sports jacket and slacks.

'He does,' Balga exclaimed, 'but we're just started.'

'Yeah, he'll press some 45s which we can sell at our gigs,' the girl stated.

'We can sign the contact tomorrow; do the records in our studio the day after, and press the 45s after that,' the record producer said.

'Things move fast eh,' Balga observed.

'In this business they do,' Marcus stated, 'in today or gone tomorrow.'

'But we musicians,' began Alan.

'Have to eat and to eat they have to sell records,' Marcus Herman stated with a shrug that underlined his assertion.'

'Well, yeah,' Andy said, 'but I get to eat already.'

'He does too,' his mother said coming up and staring at the record producer. 'And I want to read that contract before he signs it. I know your sort from my theatre days.'

'Oh mum,' began Andy.

'For your benefit! You think your mom doesn't know about contracts well she does.'

'Well,' Herman said with a grimace, 'It seems that it is settled and we'll see you all in my office tomorrow at 2 o'clock or thereabouts – and without your mother,' he added to Andy.

Adrian had joined the group and had been listening. Of course he knew the record producer and complimented him on his choice. 'This trio is not only fabulous but groovy,' he declared, 'and I've just opened a new club, The Stray Cat, in Prahran and I am putting them on from next Friday. It's a paying gig too.'

'It better be,' flung back Mrs Campbell as she went off towards Leo Cash.

Suddenly another lot of people came through the door. It was a crowd from the Aboriginal Advancement League. There was Pastor Doug somewhat quiet with his wife; Stand the Man with Kooris from Northcote including Harry and his band members. 'Hey, bud,' he called, 'you near finished. We got an event going at the league and I promised to bring you there for a couple of songs. They still remember you from that time you sang there.'

'Just about finished, a couple of more songs, and we can be with you,' Balga quickly agreed.

Things had happened quickly and were continuing to rush along. Balga was slightly dazed as he went back to the raised platform that served as a stage to continue the gig singing some songs that he had written. The trio finished off with a remodeled folk standard.

> *The Noongars are behind us*
> *We shall not be moved*
> *The Koories are behind us*
> *We shall not be moved*
> *The Murris are behind us*
> *We shall not be moved*
> *Even the Gubbas are with us*
> *Yeah, we shall not be moved.*
> *Just like rocks standing in the flood*
> *We shall not be moved, citizenship now!*

The trio bowed and Balga clasped his hands over his hand then dropped them as he said: 'Thank you for coming to hear us. I'm Balga Boy Jackson; that lad there is Alan Wardell and Andy Campbell on bass guitar. We'll be playing at the Stray Cat next Friday so come along and hear us. Thank you, thank you and good night!'

And so the evening ended and the career of Two Blacks and a White began to rise towards the full moon high in the night sky.

THE END